Also by Kathleen Shoop

Historical Fiction:
The Donora Story Collection
After the Fog—Book One
The Strongman and the Mermaid—Book Two

The Letter Series
The Last Letter—Book One
The Road Home—Book Two
The Kitchen Mistress—Book Three
The Thief's Heart—Book Four
The River Jewel—A Letter Series Novella

Tiny Historical Stories
Melonhead—One
Johnstown—Two

Romance:
Endless Love Series:
Home Again—Book One
Return to Love—Book Two
Tending Her Heart—Book Three

Women's Fiction:
Love and Other Subjects

Bridal Shop Series
Puff of Silk—Book One

The Thief's Heart

The Letter Series
Book Four

KATHLEEN SHOOP

shoop@kshoop.com

Kshoop.com

Cover Design: Jenny Toney Quinlan --Historical Editorial
http://historicalfictionbookcovers.com

ISBN-13: 9781519582003

To the readers who wait eagerly, yet patiently.

This is for all of you.

Chapter 1

June 1892
Des Moines, Iowa

Fifteen-year-old Tommy Arthur manned the doors of the Savery Hotel, anticipating each guest's needs.

Mind occupied, heart empty.

Couples, families, and business associates moved in and out of the hotel, leaving a sense of loneliness for Tommy in their wake. Alone, unimportant, unmoored. Now that Mama, Katherine, and Yale were back in Des Moines, now that they'd found a place to board next door to the illustrious Miss Violet Pendergrass, he should have felt *found*, part of something big, like his dreams, the opposite of the despair that swept through him.

True. Mrs. Mellet's promised inheritance and all the potential it should have brought the Arthurs had fallen through. But Tommy was with family. Finally. That should have solved everything money couldn't. He blew out a breath. He knew why the darkness persisted. His brother was dead, and his father was off somewhere unable to get back to them, trying to finish grieving for the loss of James.

Tommy pushed the desolate sensation away and stretched to his full six-foot-one height, projecting professionalism and maturity, traits that being a bellboy demanded. His position would lead to greater things; he was sure of it. He repeated that silently, salving his soul, keeping alert for the next set of arriving guests.

Down the street a ways, Mr. Alcorn, a savvy businessman, breezed along, his scarred stovepipe hat floating above the other pedestrians. His smart shave, glossy wingtips, dandy pinstriped pants and coat mesmerized Tommy. The man's clothing draped his limbs as he took long strides, making each expensive stitch obvious. The man lifted his gaze to Tommy, smacked his paper against the palm of his hand, and gave him a three-by-nine grin.

"Afternoon, Arthur," Mr. Alcorn said.

Tommy couldn't help but smile back, nodding as he opened the hotel door. "Lunch, Mr. Alcorn?"

"Big one." Mr. Alcorn handed his paper to Tommy. "Check the finance sheets, Tom. This Violet Pendergrass is taking the town by storm. Could learn a few things from her, I suspect."

Tommy stuffed the paper into the waist of his pants and started to tell Mr. Alcorn that he knew the woman, that he lived in the tiny house next door to her, but the debonair man was already halfway through the door.

"Well, good luck," Tommy said.

"Thank you," Mr. Alcorn said over his shoulder. "I'll take all the luck I can get."

"Leave some for me." Tommy closed the door behind the loping man and hoped Mr. Alcorn's good fortune rubbed off on him. Tommy shined the brass handle with his sleeve, then took his place where he could see every which way, hands latched behind his back. Across the muddy road, a newsboy called for takers, his raspy voice belying his baby face. Patrons rushed past, pressing coins into his hand, taking the *Des Moines Register* without breaking stride.

"Scandal breaks the bank yet again!" the newsboy yelled. "Scorned wife stabs second husband!" Another yelled from down the way, "Interest slips like girls on icy sidewalk!"

A lady's maid bought a paper and collided into a man because she'd already started reading.

"Teenage murderess haunts East Des Moines! Teen boy lifting cash right out of women's pocketbooks! Get your next installment of Phantasia Clark's *Upper Crust Harlot* fiction series! Or is it real life? Chapter sixteen's called 'Second Inheritance Shrivels Up Like Tumbleweed'!"

The news and entertainment churned and milled and rolled off the presses two times a day at least, chronicling all that was important and much that was just plain gossip.

Tommy knew Mama liked to be informed and her life used to hinge on writing the *Quintessential Housewife* column right there in Des Moines. Because of that, he sometimes used his extra change to buy her the freshest news of the day.

Usually he fished old papers out of garbage cans, and the head hotel maid, Harley, would give Tommy papers left behind in rooms. His friend Pearl would do the same at the post office. Mama happily accepted the old news. She just needed to read what was happening beyond her door, whether locally in Des Moines or throughout the country. Tommy rearranged the paper stuffed in his pants but couldn't get it to lay flat, so he took it out and refolded it. The *Upper Crust Harlot* headline the newsboy had been yelling about, continued in print. "Second Inheritance Shrivels Up Like Tumbleweed in Deadwood."

Tommy suspected the author with the pseudonym, Phantasia Clark, was writing veiled stories about the Arthur family, as people often did when they had a grudge to nurse against an enemy or even a neighbor.

Tommy read a few lines. "To catch intermittent readers up . . . Recall that our former society lady had a new inheritance in hand . . . dangling there for the taking, but then it was snapped away like a hand rising from the grave of 'Mrs. Mullen' just as our anti-heroine was closing her dirty fingers around it. Oh. Lost again, poor, used-to-be-rich woman with nothing but an empty purse and backward children to tend . . ." The author must have known his family—the story was just too similar not to be the case.

He seethed at the last line, thinking of the way his family had lost Mrs. Mellet's inheritance. He tried not to let the bitter poison that filled his mouth stay there too long before spitting it out. *He* wasn't backward. Neither was Katherine. Most days Tommy pretended no one knew anything of the scandal—that his grandfather had rooked the townspeople out of their life savings way back in 1887. The Arthurs had paid dearly for it with their

3

grandfather's life, their brother's life, their father's absence, a ruined reputation and the loss of all their money.

After their year on the prairie and the deadly blizzard, Tommy's mother and Yale went one way, his twin sister, Katherine, went another, and Tommy went his. That is, until just one year back, when the Arthurs returned to Des Moines to collect a promised inheritance, a financial apology from Mrs. Mellet to the family—the one Phantasia Clark delighted in fictionalizing.

The loss of the money that Mrs. Mellet had pledged to the Arthurs stung, but Tommy was determined to earn enough to support his mother and sisters and pay his father's debts and bring him home.

The wheezing came from across the street. Tommy raised his gaze slowly to confirm what he knew. Hank and Bayard. They sauntered toward the newsboys. Tommy considered the two to be friends, but often the sight of them meant they wanted something that might or might not be completely legal. Tommy avoided eye contact, busying himself by rubbing at the glass on the door. Whatever fun or trouble they wanted to have, Tommy couldn't put his job in jeopardy.

They stepped into the street. Tommy knew they were coming for him. He shook his head, locking his jaw, quietly warning them away.

"Arthur!" A rumbling voice came from the Simmons' carriage as it pulled in front of the Savery.

Tommy rushed toward their footman, relieved the arrival of guests stopped his friends in their tracks.

Mr. Simmons hopped down, grimacing, hiking up his trousers. He reached for his wife's hand. "If you're still looking for that recommendation for the desk clerk position, you best stay awake. I don't wait for anyone. Especially not someone with so little to offer me. Your high school years won't pay for themselves."

"Yes, sir. I apologize." Tommy hauled three suitcases from the carriage and set them near the door. Returning for another load of luggage, he noticed Mrs. Simmons's hem was covered in dust. He brushed at the skirt.

She looked down at Tommy, blue eyes squinting into her grin, soft and kind. "Thank you, Tommy."

He stood.

"Don't mind the mister. Surly since we left." She took his arm and pulled him close, whispering, "Digestive issues. When things stop up on him, he's a bear. I nearly suggested he stay home."

Tommy nodded, wanting to comfort her. "I may be able to help. My sister's wonderful with cures. Once Katherine made me a morning water with crushed berries and honey. Followed by some type of bark thing that—"

She held up her hand to stop him from saying more. "Yes, please. Get the exact recipe. I'll pour stones, hay, and whiskey down his throat if it means easing his mood and his . . . well, you know."

Tommy led Mrs. Simmons to the concierge. "Mr. Duke'll escort you to the ladies' lounge to rest until your room's ready."

Mr. Simmons met them at the concierge desk. Mrs. Simmons extended her hand to shake Tommy's, and when she turned her attention to her small train bag, Tommy saw that she had transferred a dollar bill into his palm. His heart soared. Paying extra attention nearly always paid off. He told himself to remember to ask Katherine to write down her belly cure.

He started to thank Mrs. Simmons, but she gave him a shake of the head, letting Tommy know she hadn't discussed the large tip with her husband beforehand.

Tommy avoided the elevator since he tended to panic in small spaces. At first one of the hotel managers, Mr. Diamond, doubted Tommy could do his job if he couldn't get the luggage upstairs fast enough. But Tommy proved he could move even quicker, balancing large, unwieldy luggage, strong enough to carry as big a load as the carts most of the bellboys used when working.

Up the stairs Tommy went, carrying the Simmons's suitcases as though made of paper, happy to do his job. When he reached the last room on the fourth floor, way at the end of the hall where the light sometimes dimmed, he dug the key from his pocket. A squeaking sound made him turn. He hated when a guest appeared before he had a chance to organize their things, but no one was there.

He was about to slip the key into the lock when heavy wheezing came from down the hall, growing louder. No. Please no. He turned. Hank and Bayard strolled toward him, scowling.

"Well, well, well," Hank said. "We'll take the dollar that woman just gave you."

Tommy's breath caught. This was not how he planned for his day to go.

Chapter 2

He had to get rid of them.

Tommy's mind flew as fast as his heartbeat. What were Hank and Bayard doing there? Tommy had met the boys when he returned to Des Moines about two years back. They'd offered Tommy some opportunity for work, money, and friendship, but their path snaked through a particular Reverend Shaw's garden of good and evil, leading Tommy to toe the line of legal and moral trouble. Trouble he tried to avoid as much as possible. Since they did the reverend's odd jobs, they had access to homes, to people hurting in broken times, and with that privilege came the opportunity to earn money and steal it. But none of that had anything to do with Tommy's job at the Savery Hotel, and he didn't appreciate Hank and Bayard showing up.

Hank put his forearm across Tommy's chest, pushing him against the door to Mrs. and Mr. Simmons's room. Tommy struggled to breathe and glanced down the hallway, looking for Penelope, the maid assigned to the Simmonses when they stayed at the Savery. No sign of her. Nothing but Bayard's raspy breath and Hank's incessant throat clearing, his breath sour as it hit Tommy's cheek.

Hank dug his arm into Tommy's chest, sliding it up to his throat, cutting off more of his air. If Tommy hadn't been hemmed in by his manners in the hotel and worried about losing his job, he would've wrenched Hank's arm behind his back, booted him in the ass, and done the same to fat Bayard. But the two "friends" knew that, and that's why they approached Tommy when he would be unwilling to fight back.

Bayard leaned against the wall. "Rev's catching on to your game."

"What game?"

Bayard spit, his filth disappearing into the red Oriental rug. Tommy struggled against Hank, wanting to protect the hotel that had provided him with the chance to contribute to family finances and meet important men who might take him on as a business apprentice once he finished high school.

"Don't play with us, Arthur. We saw you selling wares at McCrady's the other day. None of that loot came from the day we sold prayers and Bayard lifted those coins. Rev said he hasn't seen you in ten days, and he's suspicious and tired of giving you leeway."

"I found an old bag by the river with some things in it. Sold them at McCrady's. I wouldn't steal from the people we sell prayers to." Tommy's shoulders relaxed. For a moment, he was afraid they might know he gave away an extra prayer or two when someone needed it. Once he even scribbled an extra scripture down for a particularly desperate soul. Tommy's years of Bible reading—before he stopped believing in religion—paid off, and the woman had given him a few extra pennies. Nothing compared to what else they'd turned into the reverend later that day.

Tommy strained to speak past the pressure on his throat. "I pay Shaw what he requires. And when I'm not with you two, I'm busy working here or helping my mother and sisters."

Tommy was careful not to give too much information. Since his family lucked into boarding in a house let to them by Miss Violet Pendergrass, he was attempting to lead an exemplary life. He didn't want Hank or Bayard skulking around, offering information to his mother that would worry or anger her.

Tommy enjoyed the fellas' company from time to time, like when they would go swimming in the river. But their easy acceptance of their wayward lives and lack of goals unsettled Tommy. He knew many of the games the boys and the reverend were running, but he was still unsure about the extent and depth of what they did. He understood the need to support boys who were lost, orphaned, or abused, but he worried the law wouldn't see it the same way if they were caught skirting it.

The elevator doors opened, startling them.

Hank pulled away, and Tommy rubbed his collarbone, glancing down the hall. "Not doing anything wrong, boys. Just pulling as many shifts here as I can."

Tommy glanced down the hall again. Penelope was coming toward them, gliding gracefully, her skirts whisking as she moved.

Hank coughed into his fist. "Sure 'bout that, Arthur?"

"Tommy?" Penelope's gait slowed, and a worried expression spread over her face.

Hank signaled Bayard with a jerk of the head, and the two walked away, tipping their dust-covered caps at her. She slid aside to give them enough room to pass shoulder to shoulder, pressing her back against the wall.

Her raised eyebrows demanded an answer for what she saw happening.

"They were lost," Tommy said. "Wrong room is all."

She watched Hank and Bayard disappear into the stairwell, but didn't ask more. Tommy exhaled and quickly covered his relief by unlocking the door and letting Penelope inside. He hauled Mrs. Simmons's luggage into the dressing area so Penelope could hang everything and press as needed.

Tommy got busy with Mr. Simmons's things, opening the first case and removing a stack of trousers. Penelope startled him, inching closer, her arm and hip brushing against him, watching him work. Tommy stiffened. He puffed out a breath.

Concentrate.

He removed a shirt and shook it, hanging it in the small closet. Penelope ran her fingers up and down his back, sending chills through his body. "Better check the irons to make sure they're getting hot," he said. When she didn't respond, he turned. She caught his hand in hers. Her fingers were rough, but her palm was soft and pillowy.

They stared at one another, both knowing she had barely unpacked a single thing. He loved Penelope's attention and he wanted to return it, wanted to kiss her and envelop her in his arms. But no. He wouldn't risk his job just to snuggle up with a pretty girl.

He took her shoulders and eased her back toward the dressing room.

She touched her lips with dainty fingertips.

He turned back to the open suitcase.

She returned with a sigh and collapsed onto one of the cases. She rubbed her temples then gave him a half smile with sultry, half-shut eyes. "You're no fun, Tommy Arthur. All this I heard about you being loads of fun, a real carnival."

Tommy chuckled. "More like a steel mill. That's about how much fun I am these days."

"You think Mr. Simmons is gonna reward you with a fancy job because you don't take me to dinner or dancing at the riverside soiree?"

That's exactly what Tommy thought. He brushed the back of his hand against her leg. "Up, you beautiful girl. I've got work to do."

She stood and took his hand, brushing the back of it, sending chills through him again.

"*You* have work to do, too," Tommy said. "Won't do any good if the two of us are out on our hind ends, jobless, will it? Consider my declining your offer a favor."

She gave him that sensual, lips parted glance again and made him think this was how she might look waking up in the morning. His body hardened at the thought of it.

"You have to eat sometime." She yanked him closer, his forehead against hers.

She tilted her head, went up on her toes, and pressed her lips against his, her tongue tracing along the seam.

He wrapped his arms around her.

No.

He gently pushed her away just as voices came from the other side of the door and knew he'd soon hear the slip of a key in the lock.

"Get moving."

She giggled. Stretching her arms over her head, she sashayed away. "Oh, Tommy Arthur. What you do to me."

He wiped his brow and worked the latches on the next suitcase, his clumsy fingers still wanting to be against her skin. "Didn't do a thing to you."

"How I wish you would," she said with a final glance over her shoulder before disappearing into Mrs. Simmons's dressing area.

Chapter 3

Tommy finished his shift with one eye on the hotel guests and one eye out for the return of Hank and Bayard or even the reverend. Out of his uniform and back in his comfortable, worn shirt and pants, he scratched along the dirt road that led to the post office, where he was expecting to collect at least one letter from his father.

Satisfied with most of his day's work at the Savery, but disappointed that his dollar tip from Mrs. Simmons was now in Hank's pocket, he settled on being pleased there were no more signs of his pals.

Tommy was whistling past McCrady's Trade and Buy when a large gilt-framed painting caught his eye. The gold surround flashed and winked as sunrays slipped through the clear parts of the sooty glass. He looked twice before he believed what he was seeing, then stopped. People ran up his heels, jostling him until he shuffled out of the way, feeling for the porch step with his foot, adjusting his hat, slack-jawed.

The rendering filled nearly half the window. He glanced around to see if anyone else noticed the artwork or understood what it meant. He pulled his hat down tight. The painting was of none other than his very family, circa 1886. Tommy's heart thumped, unable to match the image of who the Arthurs had been when they sat for John Singer Sargent with whom they were now.

In the portrait, James, Tommy, and their father were clad in fine woolen summer suits, his father's hair perfectly slicked back. James stood off to one side of Mama as though watching over her. Tommy laid on the floor, fingers poised to shoot a marble. Mama and Katherine wore white dresses so delicate the ruffles around the neck and down the front seemed to flutter right off the canvas. Their sister, Yale, hadn't yet been born.

It shocked him to see it there in a shop window with a note that read "Make me an offer" next to it. Humiliation gathered bitter on his tongue as he tried to remember all that had happened the day all their household goods were sold off to repay their grandfather's failed investment scheme. How quickly things went from wealthy comfort to prairie squalor, dead crops, fire, his brother's death, and then the family's split, the awful years alone as the Arthurs tried to put themselves back together. A lifetime ago.

Tommy tried to remember who took this painting the day of the raid. He could see two men lifting it off its wall hook, but he couldn't remember their names—if he ever knew them.

He'd been too busy protecting Mama, keeping her from shooting people streaming into their home, shoving trinkets into pockets and purses, lugging furniture—marauding, but legally so, according to the courts.

Tommy had tried to help Mama keep some of their things, and with all the folks pushing and taking and fighting over items of value, he hadn't remembered until that moment that people had taken their family portraits. It was one of the few times Mama had seen Tommy as her protector instead of James.

Now, five years later, standing at McCrady's window for what felt like hours, Tommy tried to make himself believe that the wealthy people conjured with thick, moody, oil-painted brushstrokes were his family members. Tommy breathed deep and looked around to see if anyone matched him to the boy in the painting, anger growing.

He stomped inside, prepared to negotiate with McCrady to trade for the painting, to stop the insult of it being cast off, just barely more than trash. A shopgirl slid back and forth behind a counter arranging things, marking in a ledger.

"Painting in the window. Bottom line it."

She leaned past Tommy to get a look. "Big daddy there? That one?"

Tommy nodded.

She paged through the ledger, licking her finger with every turn. She shrugged and tossed the notebook aside. "Must be a new acquisition."

Tommy felt out of his body, disoriented by the concrete reminder of what they'd lost, the weight of it thumping in his chest. He removed his hat and leaned on the counter.

"Take it out of the window. Save it for me in the back room."

"No how," she said. "McCrady's strict on the window display and what everything costs and such. *Make me an offer* means pay me a boatload."

"But that's not an ordinary painting."

"I gathered."

Tommy sighed. "Not like you're thinking."

"You're barking at a knot with this. I can't change window items out willy-nilly." She dragged her gaze up and down his body. "No way you can afford that anyhow."

He pulled up. "Says who, I can't? I've a good offer."

"No how."

"Yes how." He had no idea how much to offer for such a thing. Tommy shook his head. Having it made had been a fancy affair, an appointment years in the making costing a massive amount of money. Pride kept him from explaining that the painting was rightfully his, that whatever McCrady might take for it, his parents had already paid a huge sum in the first place.

He pushed away from the counter. "I'm coming for the painting. Don't sell it except to me."

"Sure, sure." She put her back to him, fussing with cups and saucers on the shelves behind the counter. "Same sad tale all day long."

He wiped his mouth. He was different. He'd return for it. He wove through the crooked path around tables and cabinets, trying to decide if the money he'd saved to help bring his father back to town would be better spent on something that would outlive them all—the painting that was evidence of what they used to be: a successful, complete family. He imagined bursting into the tiny home where they were boarding and leaning the painting against the wall between the two windows in the front room, surprising Mama and Katherine with a piece of who they used to be.

He dragged his fingers across items strewn on tabletops—boxes of marbles, buttons, yo-yos, tops, spatulas, mixing spoons, and bowls—and was nearly to the door when the blue-and-gold spine of a book caught his eye. He slid it out from under some others. An English translation of *D'Aulnoy's Les Contes des Fées—Tales of Fairies*. The mushrooms and whimsical fairies embossed on the cover took him back, remembering the joy the stories brought his family in their early years.

He paged through the book, looking for an inscription from Mama, hoping it wasn't there. He couldn't bear to see another Arthur belonging orphaned in a shop, mocking him. The tattered cover nearly fell away. He exhaled, not realizing he'd been holding his breath. The page where it would have been inscribed was missing. Relieved, he ran his finger down the contents, noting the story titles. *The Blue Bird, Prince Sprite, Finnette Cendron . . .*

This made him think of Pearl, who often called him a prince despite his desperate finances. She saw beyond his tattered clothing to the riches he carried in his mind, as his mother always put it. He chuckled. If there was a girl who needed fairy-tale rescuing less, it was Pearl.

He envisioned her gutting the deer that he could not, how she'd been surgical and matter-of-fact with the pearl-handled knife, the way she seemed to keep herself decidedly independent. But oh, how she dreamed of someday being what amounted to a princess with proper English and fancy manners. Pearl was rough, her beauty hidden, encrusted by the grime that splotched her clothing and skin. Though Penelope was far from a wealthy, educated girl, she was nowhere near as hardscrabble as Pearl. Yet it was Pearl who sparked his imagination, who he thought of when he ran into something interesting like this book.

Pearl's face came to mind, the way an expression often folded her features in puzzled concentration as she read letters she shouldn't have been reading when working at the post office.

Perhaps she just needed a book to keep her occupied. "How much for this?" he asked the shopgirl.

She sighed as though she'd been asked to lift heavy furniture. She stared at Tommy for a moment, then pulled another ledger from behind the counter. She blew dust off the cover and paged through it. "Where is it, where is it?"

Tommy gave a little shake of his head, knowing he wouldn't have enough for it anyway, not for something so unneeded.

"Here!" She ran her finger along the page. "Says right here, this book . . ." She brushed dust away and pulled it closer.

"What?" Tommy asked.

She turned the book toward him. "Says it should go *economy priced* due to its condition and 'cause every happy home needs a book of fairy stories."

Tommy thought that sounded odd, but he was excited by the notion. "What's economy priced in this instance?"

She licked her finger and turned the page. "Says here *price to be determined by the buyer and . . .*"

He leaned closer, but her finger was blocking the words. "And what?"

She rolled her eyes. "His circumstances."

She looked over the top of the notebook and took in the sight of Tommy again. "Determined by his circumstances."

Now pleased his appearance would make a claim of poverty more believable than wealth, he looked down and opened his arms. "I'd say my circumstances are bleak."

She narrowed her eyes on him before rolling them. "Suddenly bleak, Mister I Want the Painting in the Window?"

He shrugged his shoulders.

"I have to agree. Bleak as the dickens. But I don't think . . ." She pulled the book away, shaking her head.

Tommy pointed at the book. "Says it's for the person who inquires of it. Fork it over."

She flipped a ledger page and reread. "Sure does say that."

He smiled.

"Fine. It's yours." She gestured toward the book.

He drew a deep breath. "Thank you. I can't believe my luck."

"Suppose I should pay better attention to inventory from now on." She shrugged, turning away. Tommy jammed his hand into his pocket and rubbed the Indian Head penny and fingered the dime he had there as well. Perhaps this was a new beginning in more ways than one. He asked the shopgirl if he could borrow her pen and ink to inscribe the book. She scowled and grimaced but allowed it.

Tommy turned to the title page. He almost wrote a simple *To Pearl, From Tommy*, but then decided that would be offensive. This book of literature and wonder was a worthy gift for Pearl, and she deserved a worthy thought dedicating it to her. He dipped the nib into the black liquid and was as precise with his lettering as he could be.

**

Money. The thought of it popped into Tommy's mind like a minute hand ticked around a clock face. He told himself to enjoy this moment, the gift he'd found for Pearl. He drew a deep, satisfied breath, staving off the endless list of needs that filtered through his mind all day long. The book of fairy tales would be the perfect way to thank Pearl for that day in the woods one year back when she stumbled upon him and the deer he'd shot, for her tact and friendship when she had to dress it without any help from him. A year was a long time to make an overt thank-you, but Pearl would think it was worth the wait.

Pluck, pluck, pluck. Hollow-sounding raindrops splattered off the brim of his hat, keeping rhythm with his steps as he strode in the direction of the post office. He tucked the book inside his coat and pulled it tighter around him.

Acquiring the fairy-tale book took the sting out of seeing his family portrait in the window, made him think as though it was meant to be that he was there at that moment and saw the book peeking out below the others. He reassured himself it wasn't as though anyone would recognize him from the painting that had been made seven years before. Growing to six-foot-one and changing from a boy to a man did wonders for disguising his appearance.

Mama was another story. She'd enough burden to carry; she didn't need to see that painting in the window. This discovery solidified his plan to pull all the pieces of his broken family together. He'd get that back. Someday. For now, he'd focus on how happy the book would make Pearl.

Rain continued to peck at the dirt road, releasing a distinct harmony of odor—manure, clay, sand—aromas rising as the moisture unleashed each layer.

He smiled into the sky, alternating between a run and a shuffle, slowing enough to kick a rock into the air. The broken-down section of town gave way to the newer, busier section of Des Moines. His feet fueled by his good mood, he passed stocked storefronts, dodging distracted businessmen and women laden with shopping bags.

"Hey!" a man's gruff voice came from inside the grocery. The scolding tone caused Tommy to break into a full run. He looked behind him to see the grocer shaking his finger at two delivery boys.

Tommy blew out his breath. It'd been a while since he'd been in trouble, but the fear that came with the memory stuck with him, rising up when he least expected it. He could not go back to jail, not ever. He wasn't a criminal. He was a kid. Except for the times he felt like a man, which was most of the time these days. But jail? Nothing shrank his sense of manhood like jailtime. Having Mama and his sisters back in Des Moines reminded him that only in the most dire situations should he do anything untoward.

He assuaged his guilt with what defined his present circumstances. He'd done well despite the downturn his family suffered. Hell, any boy whose father left, who buried his brother and was separated from his mother and sisters for years and managed to survive was not a criminal. He was a victor. If he took an apple or lifted one out of the fifty-two silver spoons from a wealthy family so he could eat that day, it was evidence he was capable and smart, everything a mother wanted a son to be.

It wasn't as if Tommy stole upon the rising of each and every sun. The job at the Savery made use of all his early breeding and education and provided opportunity to earn a better position. And his schooling—just another year or so and he'd collect a diploma like his mother wanted for him so badly. He wanted that too but wasn't so sure it would be as easy to fit it in as she thought. Not when she needed him to make enough money to contribute to savings for a cottage. This summer Tommy wanted to squirrel away as much money as possible before schoolwork intruded on his time.

Tommy rubbed the back of his sore neck, his fingers grazing the thin scars, reminding him of the policeman's fingernails as they'd scraped his skin when the brute grabbed his collar and hauled him away like a dog who got too close to a steaming bowl of stew. He'd just been helping a child and his mother. He shivered. Tommy hadn't planned for a life of crime and punishment, justified or otherwise, but in order to move forward with his plan to help his father and bring him back, he needed resources. Trouble was, the way things had gone since the blizzard of 1888, well, he'd learned resources were hard to come by for anyone other than folks who already had them.

Chapter 4

Tommy headed into the crowd moving along the sidewalk. "'Scuse me," he said, tipping his hat as he shouldered a woman beside him.

He made eye contact with her. "Katherine!"

She pressed her hand to her chest. "Tommy. My God, you snuck up on me."

They slid out of the crowd toward Lace and Notable Notions Boutique. Several men looked twice at her, even three times, making Tommy study her, still in awe of how much she'd changed in the past few years, noticing it most when he ran into her unexpectedly like just then. Though she was his twin and they resembled each other in many ways, he could objectively see how beautiful she was, how she never seemed to notice passersby staring at her. This made him worry how fragile she seemed despite her beauty, despite the strength he knew she carried within.

"Where you off to?" he asked.

"Errands for Miss Violet." She waved a list.

"She's always got a list, doesn't she?"

"Sure does, but boy do I like her." Katherine's face brightened. She squeezed Tommy's arm. "Don't you adore her? Smart and worldly and so *bold*. A combination of how Mama used to be with this independent streak that I couldn't have imagined until I met her. I mean, that big home and employees and her business. I'm hoping she might take me into her schooling with the other girls."

Tommy agreed she was an impressive woman, but was less swept away by her. "'Course I like her. She's letting out a whole house with gardens and a shed in the back to us, and . . . I like her all right. Lots of chores and errands and such. Lots of opportunity for us to make money—Mama could use it. I really want to

contribute to that cottage she's dreaming about. And our father . . .
If I could help him get back here, then Mama could spend more
time with her old friends and the women's club and such. I want
her to have what she used to, Katherine. I wish we could all
just . . ."

"I know, I know." Katherine looked at the book in Tommy's
hands. "What's that?"

Tommy thought of the painting in the window. He wouldn't
tell Katherine about it; he didn't want to hurt her. "Remember
ours? Found this one at McCrady's. *Free*, of all things."

"For Yale?"

"No. Pearl."

Katherine nodded, and a slow smile spread over her face.

"No, no. It's just a thank-you."

"You like her." Katherine straightened, her pride in making
this assertion clear.

"She's a nice girl. Yes."

"You like her. I know it."

Tommy looked away, shy about the unexpected grin covering
his face. "Move along, Katherine. Scratch off a few of the things
on that list. Let's keep Miss Violet happy with that baking and
cooking of yours."

Katherine stuffed the paper back into her pinafore. "Lots of
cooking and baking. Yes."

Tommy put his hand to his forehead. "That reminds me. A
guest at the hotel is suffering with blocked belly something awful.
I mentioned you might have a cure. Remember that awful thing
you had me drink?"

She nodded. "Did the trick, though, didn't it?"

"Did that, and more."

"I'll write the recipe down when I get back to Miss Violet's.
It's in my book."

The two of them ambled toward the next intersection where
Tommy turned toward the post office and Katherine toward the
grocer's. In those sweet moments his loneliness slipped away,
feeling normal again, much like he had before . . . He watched

Katherine for a moment thinking how lucky it was they were in the same town once again. And he hoped with all his being, it was the end of all that had gone wrong.

Chapter 5

Tommy approached the post office, the book stiff against his chest. One hand in his pocket, he flipped the lucky Indian Head penny back and forth. He couldn't wait to surprise Pearl and hoped no one else was collecting mail so he could give it to her alone. He opened the door, lifting it slightly to ease the squeak that usually announced a patron's arrival. He entered and sneaked forward, breath held tight in his lungs.

There she was.

Pearl sat on the stool behind the counter, back to him, slight and straight as a flagpole. Her head was cocked to the side, her hair tied half-up in a knot, errant crimson strands swirling down her back, bouncing as she shifted. Something about the sight of her made him hesitate. He felt a tickle in his belly, and a happy shiver danced up his spine. He edged closer. From this angle, he saw she was doing it again—reading letters that weren't hers.

He jogged the rest of the way to the counter and pulled himself onto it, stomach flat on the wood, book off to the side.

"Gotcha, Slim!"

Pearl's bottle-green eyes widened as she startled and fell off the stool with a screech.

Tommy swung his legs over the counter, sitting on it, amused at her reaction. Flat on her bottom, skirts up around her knees, worn black stockings barely hanging on to their garters, pages of the letter she was reading fanned around her, Pearl caught his gaze on her legs and hopped to standing, pushing her skirts back into place.

"Whose letter?" Tommy said.

She looked away.

"Yours?"

Pearl pursed her lips. "Tommy Arthur, git off that counter right quick. I'll sock ya one." Chin in the air, she was confident and bristly. He grinned.

She pegged her fists on her hips. "Don't call me Slim no more. Tired of that. Name's Pearl."

He squinted and shook his fist, mocking her outrage before setting the book aside and sliding off the counter, wanting to help her pick up the scattered pages of the letter. He squatted and rubbed his chin. "Whose letter's that? Best not be mine you're pushing your tiny . . ."

She froze, meeting his gaze, sending thrills throughout him. He hesitated, taking in her pretty, heart-shaped face. "Your little button nose . . ."

She pressed the end of her nose.

"Pushing it into . . . not my . . ."

A smile crept onto her face. "Button nose?"

"Well, you know." Tommy's cheeks flooded hot, liking her response to his clumsy wording, overcome with something he'd never felt before. To prune back the sensations he couldn't control, he focused on gathering the scattered pages. "So whose letter?"

Pearl scooted from one corner of the space to the other, rushing to put the papers into a neat pile. Tommy glimpsed the fine cursive writing and inhaled deeply as a rose scent lifted from the correspondence and filled his nose.

"Mine. It's mine." She stopped and looked over her shoulder at him. "You ain't the only one in Des Moines to get mail."

Tommy grimaced. Were those tears threatening to spill? Aww, no. That wasn't what he needed. The flash of sadness in her eyes stabbed at his chest. He pressed his hand to the spot and felt the strangest pulse of pain at seeing her turn delicate, mixed with a rushing thrill at being near her.

The intense sweep of feelings and sensations confused him. She was nothing like the girl he imagined someday making a home with. Yet her serrated edges grabbed at him, kept his gaze longer, held him in her universe in a way he couldn't resist. Perhaps it was that sense of admiration in her eyes when she looked at him. Yes, that was it. The very something Tommy normally associated with the way people had looked at important men. And he saw a specialness in Pearl, something beyond the obvious, something lovely, hidden from the eyes of all others.

Tommy knew the letter wasn't hers. Anyone sending perfumed pages with schoolmarm-type writing wasn't corresponding with his orphaned friend Pearl. She loved working at the post office because she could see the world through the comings and goings of other people's correspondence.

She kept a list of places she would one day visit from the postmarks of the letters that came in. She kept a second list of words she stole from mail she wasn't supposed to be reading. When she told Tommy that she made such lists, her little treasures she called them, she had meant to imply she drew only from postmarks and stamps, but he knew she was doing more than eyeballing addresses.

"Hop back to the other side," Pearl said. "I'll lose my position if Postmaster Brandt returns and catches you back here."

Tommy absorbed the silence of the space. No one was there but them. He sat back against the counter and sighed. "In a second."

He squared off a set of pages. Pearl sniffled. Based on her ease with her pearl-handled knife and deer blood, he wouldn't have thought she was the crying type.

"You ain't gonna report on me?" she asked. "For you know . . ."

Tommy shook his head and pointed just beyond where she was kneeling. "Under the cubbies. Another page."

She reached under the cabinet and retrieved it. "So you won't?"

"'Course not. Never. You know that."

She sat beside him and held out her hand. "Pinkie promise."

They'd shared plenty of pinkie promises since meeting, keeping both of their failings secret, even though the routine was silly. He offered his finger and shook hers.

Her finger wrapped in his made him think of the fairy tales he'd bought. He reached up and pulled the book from the countertop above them and held it out. "For you."

She stared, frozen.

"Got it today. A little broken-down. But the words are clear. The stories are complete."

She leaned closer and ran a finger over the mushroom on the cover, then over the frolicking fairies and the embossed letters of the author's name, awe lighting her face.

"Go on." Tommy pushed the book closer to her.

She held it tight against her chest.

"It's a thank-you," he said.

She tilted her head, staring at him with wonderment, and again he thought she might burst into tears. He drew back, hoping she didn't.

"I inscribed it."

Her mouth fell open. When she didn't move to look at the inscription, he took the book and opened it, setting it in her lap.

> *To Pearl,*
> *Read these stories and imagine all*
> *that might be yours—words, places,*
> *princes. Your discretion is*
> *admirable. And I thank you for it.*
> *Safe travels to you.*
> *T.A.*

She read aloud, choppy, like a much younger student. She attempted the word *discretion* several ways.

"Discretion with a soft *e* not a hard vowel," Tommy said. "Not like secretion."

"Discretion, discretion, discretion," Pearl said.

"Know what it means?" he asked.

She drew her hand over Tommy's writing and nodded. He wasn't sure she did, but he knew she'd find out. She would understand him being grateful at how she banked his secret failings as though they might earn her interest someday. He couldn't have felt more princely in that moment, giving something to Pearl she so clearly loved like he'd hoped she would.

"Helloooo? Anyone?" A voice came from near the door. Tommy and Pearl stiffened, staring at each other.

"Anyone?" The voice grew closer.

Pearl set the book aside and jumped up. Tommy started to stand, but Pearl gripped the top of his head and pushed him down, her fingers digging into his skull so hard the force slammed his eyes shut.

"Mrs. Calder," Pearl said.

Tommy batted Pearl's hand away, then stuffed the pages into the envelope.

He pulled his long legs to his chest, making his length as small as possible. Sweat gathered under his hat as he studied the address on the letter. It was hers, Mrs. Jeremy Calder's letter. He knew the name well. Just one year ago, Tommy had been in Judge Calder's courtroom, sent to jail for doing nothing wrong except saving the life of a child being tormented by a fat, cruel baker.

Luckily the judge hadn't recognized him as Tommy Arthur, son of a former family friend of his wife's, and he believed the phony name Tommy had given him. Still, Tommy couldn't gamble on Mrs. Calder not recognizing him. He'd spent plenty of time in her company as a young boy. Since the scandal broke, Elizabeth Calder had been punishing to Mama, one of the people who had dug through the Arthur home, not only taking things that were owed them, but marauding, abandoning the orderly line and list of items assigned to specific people. Elizabeth had taken Mama's sapphire necklace and waltzed around town in it to this day, torturing her with its daily wearing.

Tommy's pals, Hank and Bayard, were willing participants in Judge Calder and Reverend Shaw's system of cash for children. The scam provided two payoffs. One came when boys were farmed out to workhouses and private correction farms for fees paid to Judge Calder upon delivery. The other remuneration was paid in the form of bolstering the judge's and reverend's reputations. Children were provided for the judge to hold up as examples of cleaning up the streets. Then he'd send them out to get in more trouble to show off his iron-fisted justice all over again. They were faceless souls to those who happened to notice them tossed in jail at all. And the process worked well for Judge Calder, phony keeper of civility and fairness.

Pearl shifted from one foot to the other, dragging her shoe up one calf, scratching it. "Your mail, right. Will that be all today?" Her voice cracked.

Pearl and Mrs. Calder discussed an order of calico coming in later that week. Tommy studied Pearl from his crouched position. The toes of her black nicked boots curled up.

He'd seen that type of shoe before, the ugly, utilitarian, too-big boots that a woman wore only when desperate, when she was dirt-floor poor. It was then he noticed the odor, the scent of Pearl, a young woman who didn't get regular bathing. The odor took him back to the prairie, the way his family had smelled, the contrast to before they lost it all, the least being the ability to bathe on a regular basis.

Pearl dropped to the floor beside Tommy, startling him. She whispered, "Give me that one." Her eyes were wide and panicked.

"It's not sealed!" Tommy said.

"I ain't stupid." She snatched the letter.

Tommy pressed his chest, his heart pounding. Elizabeth Calder was not the kind of woman who would embrace molested mail.

"Something happened," Pearl said, clearing her throat, speaking louder. "Feller threw the mailbag from the train topsy-turvy like, and it sailed onto the tracks and got run smack over. Yours was one of the only letters to survive the bag being sliced right in half. Like a fat ham, they said, sliced right through."

Tommy heard the letter crinkle as it exchanged hands. He held his breath and squeezed his eyes shut, hoping Pearl could get the woman out without the kind of ruckus that would land them in front of a judge—Judge Jeremy Calder, to be specific.

Pearl put her hand to her side, dangling it just beside Tommy's head. Each oval nail bed was blackened, the edges ragged, like her shoes. She grabbed her skirt and bunched it in her small fist, her knuckles whitening as she held tight. Tommy felt as though she were doing the same thing to his heart. He wanted to rescue her, to leap up and tell Mrs. Calder to move along and tend to her flock of maids and butlers and cooks. But Pearl would lose her job, so he didn't do anything except squeeze his eyes shut again.

"Well," Mrs. Calder said. The envelope crinkled louder as he imagined the woman removing the pages to examine the condition. "The railroad ought to be more careful with precious cargo. It's protected by the U.S. government, you know."

"Yes."

"This is *serious*. I'll be filing a complaint when Postmaster Brandt returns."

"Yes, ma'am." Pearl did a little curtsy, lifting her skirt and knocking Tommy in the nose.

Elizabeth Calder's heels clicked away. When the door squeaked shut, Tommy shot to his feet. Not wanting to take more chances he'd get Pearl in trouble, he hopped back over the counter.

He straightened his hat. Pearl's expression was indignant, as though *her* mail had been violated. This girl! He couldn't stop the smile from lifting his lips at the sight of her. His tongue tied into a knot, and he couldn't speak.

"What?" she said.

He cleared his throat and collected his senses, unwilling to reveal that she often turned him inside out with her every emotion and reaction. "My mail. I'm expecting letters."

She stomped to the cubbies behind her, pumping her arms the way she did when set on something important. She ran her fingers along one wooden row of cubbies, then the next. She pulled out a stack of envelopes and slapped them on the counter.

"Thank you, Tommy Arthur. For keeping quiet when Mrs. Calder was here."

He stuffed the letters into his pocket. "You're welcome."

She lifted the book of fairy tales from the floor and patted it. "And for this." Her words came in a whisper. She traced the title again. "It's really . . ." She cleared her throat, glancing at him, eyes glistening. Before she finished her thought, she'd swung around, busying herself at the cubbies, book under one arm. "Thank you is all."

Suddenly he wished they were back on the floor, gathering the scattered mail, his pinkie finger hooked around hers. "You're welcome."

She riffled through the envelopes. "Go on. I'm busy."

"Pearl?"

Keeping her back to him, moving from one cubby to the next, straightening the envelopes, she spoke. "Hmm?"

"You don't read mine, do you?" He couldn't bear the thought of Pearl seeing that his current circumstances put him even further from a prince than he wanted to admit.

She turned and flicked her hand at him. "Skedaddle 'fore you get me in trouble for fraternizing."

Tommy drew back. "Fraternizing? That's a mighty big word. A five-ton, heavy-lifting word, I'd say." He didn't want her to know that his father had financial limitations at the moment.

"Out." She pointed at the door. "You lily-livered beast!"

Tommy walked away. "Where'd you get that word, fraternizing?" he asked over his shoulder.

"Old Lady Mitchell drops a good one at least once a letter."

He turned back and opened his arms. "Pearl. Stop. I'll give you words. Heck, you have a whole book of them now, all to yourself. Stay out of people's envelopes."

She grinned and patted the fairy tales again. "Oh, here." She pulled a newspaper from under the counter. "Day old. For your ma. Sorry it's not fresh."

Tommy strolled back to her, unwilling to tell her Mr. Alcorn had already given him the same issue. He knew she liked to help him help Mama, and Pearl didn't mind that sometimes day-old news was all a man could afford. Their gazes locked. He reached for the paper, fingers sweeping past hers as he took it. She pulled a sack of mail onto the counter and yanked envelopes out. "Go on, pull foot," she said, sorting.

He drew back, the stirring deep inside him.

"Out." She lifted her chin in the direction of the exit.

He couldn't make himself move. A smile came to him as he watched her hands fly, categorizing the envelopes. She pointed toward the exit again. "Scat."

There she was. That was the Pearl Tommy was accustomed to seeing in the post office, and that was the way he liked it—strong, assertive. Unusual to catch a glimpse of vulnerability in her, it nearly made him fold up and die. He simply didn't know how to be someone else's strength.

Chapter 6

Tommy left Pearl to her sorting and exited the post office. The rain had stopped and waves of scent—fresh earth, trees, and flowers—expanded in the humid air. Proud that he'd been able to gift Pearl with the book of fairy tales, excited to read his father's letters, Tommy sprang down the stairs. He looked into the sky, a ray of sun washing over his face, warming it. He was certain the letters would bring good news. This released a swell of optimism inside him, like when winter thaw bloated the Des Moines River nearly above the banks. When the thought of the painting in McCrady's came roaring back, he stomped it out. He'd worry about that later.

He tore into the first letter. Pearl was correct about the way she saw letters—they held mystery, adventure, secrets, hopes, joys, love of fathers to sons. Opening the ones from his father, Tommy felt like it was Christmas morning. He slid a thin piece of paper from its envelope. Before he read a word, an iron grip locked on his arm, squeezing so tight it numbed him down to his fingertips.

"Where's your two buddies?" the man with the vice grip said. Tommy squinted into his suntanned mug. Who was he?

"Wipe that stupid look off your face." The man clamped harder.

Tommy shook his head, struggling to pull away.

"Train station. You, that big lout, and the wiry, devilish one. One of you relieved me of my cash."

Tommy tried to remember what the man was talking about. Hank and Bayard would pickpocket their own mothers, but Tommy didn't do that type of stealing. He looked down.

Alligator shoes.

In an instant, he remembered the night as if he were back at the depot, hoping to help someone carry their luggage for a penny or a meal. Tommy hadn't known that Hank and Bayard had planned to take anything from anyone. He had simply been near them at the time of the crime.

"I didn't do anything." Tommy's mind ran through that evening. He looked at the man's fine clothing and neat mustache and knew that it wouldn't matter that Tommy hadn't been the one who stole from him. Men like this had influence in Des Moines, and they lumped everyone "else" in the same leaky canoe.

Tommy's throat closed and fear rose up. He tried to wrench free again, and when it was clear the man was holding tight, Tommy hauled back with his free hand and socked him in the belly. The man buckled, letting up on his grasp, giving Tommy the opportunity to wiggle away.

He leapt into the road and ran. One foot hit the muddy street, sinking in, while the other hit the top of a wagon rut, his ankle twisting as his body jerked upright. He glanced over his shoulder and saw that the brick-like man in the dandy shoes had given chase. He should have been no match for Tommy's speed, but the man's girth seemed to make him faster, bearing down as he pumped his arms, cheeks full of forced air.

Tommy's breath came short as he leapt onto the sidewalk. He rose up on his toes and turned sideways to make it through the space between two women out for fresh air.

"Sorry, ladies," he said, doffing his cap as he kept moving. His feet pounded over the wood sidewalks, his thighs tightening as he picked up speed, moving straight ahead again.

"Vagrant! Stop!"

The wind rose up, stinging Tommy's eyes. He pressed on, faster than he thought possible, images of jail tumbling through his mind, driving him forward. Not now. Not when things were going his way. He glanced back once more and saw that the man had tripped over a grocer's apple cart, belly-down in the mud, spitting out a mouthful of dirt road.

Tommy broke east down the alley that ran between Carson's Jewelry and Dillon's Haberdashery then stopped. He peeked around the corner. Deliverymen unloading butter churns, wooden bread bowls, and stacks of fabric from a wagon into Martin's Variety Store blocked Tommy's view. He heaved for breath. No sign of alligator shoes. Tommy was satisfied he'd gotten away clean—for the moment anyway. He left the alley, heading down a lane that would lead home, practically abandoned compared to the street he'd just been on.

Moving slowly, sucking in as much air as his body would take, he looked at the letters he'd crumpled in his hand.

He removed his hat and wiped his brow with his forearm before unfolding the letter, hands quivering. His father wrote that he was impressed with Tommy's plan to help pay off the debt Frank owed in Oklahoma, but that it wasn't necessary, that he would pay that debt just as soon as he got some extra. His debt in Texas was really what he needed Tommy's help with.

He appealed to Tommy to keep saving for himself as well, that one never knew when luck might turn for the worse. He also indicated he planned to arrive in Des Moines by midsummer. Reading this made Tommy stop right there. He glanced over his shoulder.

Still no alligator shoes.

He pushed his hand through his hair, relief and joy at his father's pending arrival coursing through him. He reread that part again, then looked at the wording near a drawing at the bottom— an orb, shaded gray and black.

Black Pearl—the treasure a fella gave me in exchange for my assistance on a personal matter. He harvested it in the deep South Pacific, and I think it's good luck. Tahiti. Remember when I mentioned it? This pearl sits deep in my pocket, like the penny I gave you that sits in yours. I think it might be the source of riches and good lives for all of us someday. If only I had a faster way to get to the oyster beds. Will fill you in when I arrive this summer. We'll be knee-deep in clover as well as fine jewels sooner than I can say. Maybe you and I will combine finances, forces, and intellect and head to harvest black pearls together. Always looking forward, Tommy. Both of us. Dreaming of better times.

A grin spread across Tommy's face at the thought of it—his father returning to Des Moines and the two of them heading off to harvest pearls. He'd seen plenty of creamy-white pearls from the Orient. The Des Moines River had its share of mussels that produced pink and blue and creamy pearls. So did the Raccoon River. But black? Tommy didn't quite believe there *were* black pearls, and he'd never thought much about reaping pearls of any type. He finished reading:

If you'd like me to keep a hold of your earnings, save them for when I arrive and I can invest them for you.

Tommy found himself nodding at the last sentence, but then something crept into his mind.

No.

Thinking the word shook him.

No.

Oklahoma, Texas, heading out to harvest black pearls? What would make this Frank G. Arthur venture any different? Hell, could his father even *get* to Tahiti? Bitter disappointment turned his stomach. He would help his father with debt, but Tommy would invest his own funds, alone. Alone. There it was again. The word, the feeling, the promise?

He no longer trusted his father completely, but until he'd had that thought, until that *no* crept into his mind, he hadn't fully realized it. And that broke his heart.

Mama. Katherine. Yale.

No.

He couldn't believe how clear his opposition to his father's plans hit him all of a sudden.

He didn't trust his father to provide for the female Arthurs. The feeling was so strong he wondered if the sense had been growing for some time and he'd just ignored it. Tahiti? Black pearls? It all sounded wonderful and ridiculous at once, like the fairy tales he'd just given Pearl.

Midsummer.

He scoffed then scolded himself. It was disrespectful to lose faith in family.

Tommy walked on. He folded the letter and reassured himself with the excuses he'd provided his father for years by then. One more chance? Why did the sense that his father deserved it return to him again and again? He supposed it was meant to be, to keep believing. So, he'd save money for the both of them. He'd raise enough to help relieve his father's debts, and he'd save enough to buy Mama the little cottage with the lush garden she'd been yearning for.

He tucked the letter into its envelope. No return address. Marked Katy, Texas. Tommy imagined his father on the move, headed to Des Moines, wondering where exactly he must be. He wondered if he should give the Indian Head penny back to his father when he arrived. It sounded like he might need it more than Tommy did.

He wiped his mouth with the sleeve of his coat and sighed, ignoring the realization he'd just had that his father was not the man he wanted him to be.

He envisioned his parents seeing each other for the first time in years, feeling the joy that would erupt, that would shock them to find it readily there, between them, making everything forgiven and forgotten.

Tommy knew how that felt when he'd seen his mother and sisters after years apart, how being together filled a large part of his emptiness, how it soothed a particular aching he'd not even noticed until they were all hugging again, creating a life all over.

He didn't trust his father anymore, but he still wanted him with them, *needed* him close.

Surely his parents would recall the reasons they fell in love when they were young. Together they were better. Their lives were strung together by their children, connecting them over time and place. They just needed to remember that.

Tommy hit Main Street and zigzagged into the lunchtime crowd, hoping that perhaps just the fact that he had a plan would please his mother enough, that having the foresight and will to put their family back together, Frank Arthur and all, would be enough to make his mother think him as great as his brother, James, had actually been.

Chapter 7

Desperation. Tommy had gotten so used to feeling it over the years that when it descended on him, it actually brought a stench with it, stinking up the air he breathed. The desolation like a trip and fall, something he couldn't control if he didn't catch it soon enough.

But things had started to shift for him, for the Arthurs. The shift had brought them to Miss Violet M. Pendergrass. Moments before luck took them to her, the bitter taste of a lost inheritance, the hope it had promised, and the shame at being turned away from landlady after landlady choked Tommy.

But then, out of nowhere, Miss Violet happened. A tiny advertisement on the last page of offerings, an ad they'd missed until they tried every last one ahead of it drew them right to her. A miracle. At first Tommy thought the enormous pink-and-green home that called through the rainy fog was a mirage.

The family, holding every belonging they owned trudged toward it.

Impossible.

The last overlooked advertisement for boarders couldn't be pointing toward the stunning home. They approached, one bumbling into the next, just as Miss Violet breezed onto the porch, pristine, purple dress, sweeping across the planks as she moved, a beacon in the darkness. They inched closer, looking at the newspaper and back at her.

Her shiny, styled hair, sultry voice, and title as Des Moines's fabulous female financier made it unlikely she'd invite them to board at the former servant quarters to her house, the one next door.

But there she was, Miss Violet, their miracle. She was forthright. To board there, the Arthurs had to make the old servants' house livable and keep away from Miss Violet's clients. Tommy did chores for her when she beckoned and she allowed him to set his tent back near the old shed where none of her clients would see it.

He didn't explain the panic that swept him in small places without enough air circulation. Her eyes narrowed and Tommy read the question in her mind, her gaze burrowing into him, and he'd seen the moment she realized whatever led to his need to sleep in a tent rather than inside with his family was better left alone. He appreciated that, especially in a woman.

Sleeping in a tent allowed Tommy to keep his fear of walls falling in on him at bay. He hated that panic ruled him when he felt cornered, that he couldn't keep his lungs working when fear gripped him, forcing his mind back to when he'd been relegated to a cellar, caged at the Hendersons' house.

He had tried to stay in the servants' house with his family, but in addition to him liking outdoor ventilation, the upstairs bed space was cramped. He needed privacy, a place to feel the fear if it visited, a place to expand his independence.

Happy as he was in the tent, close to his family but in the path of fresh air, Tommy had begun to think the shoddy shed at the back of the property might do well for him when winter came. Barely hinged together with rusty nails and crumbling plaster, he wouldn't feel hemmed in by the structure or by the company, which would be just him. It had a fireplace and just needed a good cleaning and some patchwork.

It was all working well, boarding at Miss Violet's property. Katherine had become the kitchen mistress in the big, fancy pink-and-green house. Mama had been charged with bringing the gardens for both houses back to life. Tommy lit the morning fires and did all manner of errands and odd jobs for Miss Violet when he wasn't working at the Savery or selling prayers.

Tommy convinced Mr. McHenry to pay him an extra few pennies a week if he gave up his room at the Savery. He still ate there before his shift and sometimes after, but being closer to Mama and the girls was important after so much time apart.

And proximity would make it easier for him to soften Mama's heart toward his father's impending return, easier for Tommy to be the bridge between them.

Tommy cut through the hole in the hedge that separated the yard on the Arthurs' side and Miss Violet's side. He wanted to get Katherine's cure for constipation for Mrs. Simmons before he forgot.

He knocked at Miss Violet's kitchen door, expecting Katherine to have returned from her errands, but instead Miss Violet answered. She was pressed into a blueberry-colored gown, buttons dotting the shape of her bust and down her belly, where the fabric pulled in drapes against a backside bustle, accentuating every curve. Her face was creamy, her lips a warm red, and though she wasn't a classical beauty, her confidence and poise drew Tommy's gaze every time she was near.

She swung open the door and allowed him to enter. "I was just thinking of you, Mr. Arthur."

Tommy straightened, knowing she'd issue a list of chores.

"Take rainwater from the catch up to the bath."

Rainwater. Again?

"Don't frown, Thomas. We've been over this. We have indoor plumbing, yes, but the ladies who work and study long and hard require fresh water dumped right from the sky from time to time. That water is better. The stove for the bathroom we'll use to heat the rainwater even arrived the other day."

He shook his head. Had his mother been like this, requesting daytime baths with water hauled from the garden back before they lost everything? He'd been so young that he could not remember what Mama had done all day. He certainly wasn't privy to her toilet habits.

Tommy shrugged. "Next thing I know, Katherine'll be daytime bathing too. Maybe you can pencil *me* into the schedule?"

Miss Violet clenched her jaw and brushed his sleeve, holding his gaze. "That's cute, Thomas. I like a sense of humor. But your sister's duties are confined to the kitchen. Or serving food to guests. She's not the same level as the other girls."

Tommy bristled at Miss Violet saying his twin sister was less than anyone. But he sealed his lips, wanting to keep his job. "Where *is* Katherine?" Tommy asked. "I've a question about a cure for one of the hotel guests."

Miss Violet gestured. "Look it up in that old book of hers. There's something in there, I'm sure, but . . . Well, just get the water, and Katherine'll be back by the time you're finished to find you the cure."

Tommy traipsed back outside and poured water from one catch into an empty tub. He bumped slowly up the stairs, barely breathing as the water sloshed up against the edge with every step. "Move along, Tommy," Miss Olivia said from the other room, her voice unfurling down the hall like a pretty ivy vine. The sound of piano music told him she'd sat down to practice.

"Moving along," he said through clenched teeth. He wondered if they were learning as much about finance as grooming since a good portion of their time was spent preening and floating around smelling as if lilacs and vanilla grew out of their ears.

He kept that thought tucked away as well. The Arthurs were fortunate to have found this chance to make a home next to a prominent, unusual businesswoman—something divorced mothers with children rarely found for themselves.

He reached the third-floor landing and set the tub down to catch his breath. Two ladies, not much older than he, dressed in silken robes, stood before him, teasing smiles on their lips. Miss Helen and Miss Bernice. His gaze flicked from one to the other with a nod, then Miss Bernice lifted her skirt and bent over to scratch her ankle, luring his gaze. Miss Helen stretched her arms up, and her movement allowed her robe to fall open, exposing a creamy-white thigh. "Oh," she said and lowered her arms, the robe closing again.

Oh was right. His breath stopped. His skin tingled with the thrill of what he saw. Every day since he'd started working for Miss Violet, he'd noticed the ladies' smooth, rolled hair that spiraled down their backs as they bent over their books, figured their numbers, and studied equations. And now, here in their private quarters, undressed for bathing . . . Tommy burst into a sweat.

Miss Violet leaned out of the bathroom and shook an empty vial with a stopper. "Helen. Finish your figures and hurry back. Tommy, I'd like you to mix Bernice's medicine. She'll watch this time because she said it didn't sit right with her last time."

Miss Violet went downstairs with Helen. "Be back in a blink," she said.

Tommy hauled the tubful of water from the landing to the bathroom and poured it into the massive porcelain tub. Miss Bernice gestured at the table where all the ingredients for medicine sat. "Miss Violet wants you to be able to do this without supervision, but for now . . ." She shrugged. "There's the recipe."

He added the liquids to the herbs and powders. He put his finger over the opening and shook the vial the exact number of times prescribed. Miss Bernice oversaw his work. She studied him and brushed lint from his shoulder. She stretched across him, her floral perfume dizzying. "Add that one," she said and ran her finger over the lid of the final ingredient.

Her robe gaped open, exposing her creamy collarbone. The sound of Miss Olivia playing piano carried up three flights, making Bernice sway and hum along, her low voice sending vibrations over Tommy's skin, compounding his dazed state.

He corked the vial and shook it again. He handed the mixture to Bernice as the wind kicked up, rushing through the open window. Her silky robe curled away from her legs a little at a time, her hands moving to stop the fabric from revealing her pink thighs above her stockings and garters. But he saw it all. She closed her robe, and the wind whipped her hair across her face, then peeled material away from her collarbone. A flash of dark pink in the center of a creamy breast riveted him. When she finally brushed her hair out of her eyes and their gazes met again, he'd been struck dumb.

A break in Olivia's piano music jarred him, and he ducked out of the bathroom. "I'm so sorry, Miss Bernice. The wind, well, you know." He was halfway to the staircase before he stopped apologizing.

His feet spun down the stairs to the second floor, then to the first, and he folded the sight of Bernice away like a tiny letter. He tucked it into his mind where it might not distract him or cause any trouble. Worried that Bernice might report what he'd seen to Miss Violet and she might throw the Arthurs out of the house next door, he vowed to deliver the water and mix anything that needed to be mixed well before the bather-in-waiting was anywhere near a state of undress.

Still, he knew what would happen with what he'd seen. When he was alone or even in a crowd, when he least expected it, thoughts of the women next door, Bernice's breast, her knee, her thigh would leap to mind. He would try to ignore them, but then he would come to the rationalization that he could at least enjoy thoughts of Olivia's ankles. But giving himself that, would bring the rest of what he'd witnessed with it. The memory of Bernice, the one cocooned away, would unfurl with butterfly wings and waft around, causing him to imagine his fingers spreading her robe open, his hand cupping a breast—now with precise detail, his fingertips brushing past what he imagined were hardened nipples. Even Miss Violet's rose perfume set his skin on fire at times.

That longing, the mix of pain and unrelenting pleasure, perplexed and enthralled him. The women didn't seem to suffer carnal desire set against pressing sexual unfulfillment like he did. At night, he freed his hidden thoughts, the momentary pleasure that came with escalating breath.

Every now and then his mind went to Pearl instead of Bernice, Helen, or Olivia. And when he thought of Pearl that way, it was cloaked in a sadness that lay like a shadow over his heart. As he attempted to imagine what lay beneath her tattered dress, he found he couldn't make his mind, let alone his hands, go there even if he wanted them to. This melancholy told him Pearl was not for thinking about that way.

Chapter 8

Tommy woke the next day to find Katherine had written the cure for slow bowels on a piece of paper for him and left it near the dry sink in the small kitchen of the servants' house. He completed his chores, and readied for work. With some time still left until he was due at the hotel, he found Mama sweeping the porch. Yale sat by the door, playing with a wooden spoon and a homemade dress that made it look like a doll.

"Hey, Mama." He kissed her cheek. Her face was pink with sun and exertion. "Let me do that," Tommy said.

She held the broom away from him. "Finish shoring up the banister. You're almost done."

He nodded and picked up the hammer and pegs he'd left there the day before. He pegged a spindle and slid it into the banister, banging with a mallet. It went in crooked, but a few more slugs and it was straight and secure. Yale giggled and began to thump her spoon-dolly on a bucket sitting beside her.

A door slammed making Tommy and Mama look toward Miss Violet's place.

"Hey!" a man's voice shouted. "Stop that noise."

The man emerged from the shadow thrown by the porch roof. Reverend Shaw.

Tommy's stomach clenched. What was he doing at Miss Violet's? Tommy didn't like the idea of his separate worlds colliding. Mama scooped up Yale, stopping her from banging.

"We didn't mean to interrupt, Reverend. We apologize," Mama said.

Reverend Shaw stepped onto the first stair, puffing on a pipe, sticking his chest out like a turkey looking for a fight. "Tommy

Arthur? Jeanie? That you? Why, yes. I did hear that your family moved in next to Miss Violet Pendergrass."

Tommy cringed. He pressed his chest, hoping the panic would stop. The reverend must be investing church money with Miss Violet. Tommy held tight to the reverend's gaze, willing the man not to disclose that Tommy had been with Hank and Bayard when they stole from caskets and homes where they sold prayers. It wouldn't make sense for Reverend Shaw to reveal such a thing, but still, Tommy's unease caused his mind to churn, to agitate his fear every time he was in the man's presence.

Reverend Shaw yanked the bottom of one coat sleeve, then the other. "I know you'll be fine neighbors to Miss Pendergrass." He rocked on his heels and swept his arm as though performing a sermon.

"Yes, sir," Tommy said. He half expected the man to ask him to sell prayers again, to follow up with what Hank and Bayard had been asking Tommy at the Savery. Mama knew he did some handy work for the reverend and that he occasionally delivered a prayer or two for the man. But she didn't know the extent of his duties, and he wanted to keep it that way. She didn't need another worry.

Please don't say anything…

"When I heard Mrs. Mellet's inheritance fell through for you, Mrs. Arthur, I wondered where you'd end up. This is perfect. Miss Pendergrass has added much to Des Moines in just a short time since her arrival, and she's helping me grow the church's nest egg."

Jeanie nodded. "Glad to hear, Reverend." Her voice wavered.

Seeing her nervous about the noise, drawing a client out to scold them, started Tommy's heart racing.

Reverend Shaw adjusted his pants. "Miss Pendergrass is an astute businesswoman, recognizing the upside of purchasing real estate in this section of town. Before long, this whole ramshackle block'll be reborn. Why, it's biblical."

Mama dusted off her skirts. "Of course." Her voice caught.

Was she only uneasy about the noise? Miss Violet had tasked them with patching up the house and that was all Tommy was doing. Maybe Mama was suspicious of a man of the cloth investing other people's money as though it were his, as though speculations were reliable. Perhaps she was thinking of her own father's financial losses and their impact on everyone they had known.

Please just go away, Reverend. Let us be. Please don't say anything bad about me.

Mama knew nothing of the reverend's illegal and unorthodox methods for raising funds. His unsavory methods fought against the good the man did. He housed and fed boys who would otherwise be sent to workhouses or worse, the asylum, Glenwood, but the rest… distasteful at the least, illegal at worst.

Tommy studied the reverend as he traded small talk with Mama, the way he shifted his relaxed smile with a troubled expression when Mama explained about Mrs. Mellet. Phony. Tommy's skin went goose-pimply at the thought of how easily Reverend Shaw changed from lawbreaker to bastion of God and society. While Tommy had nearly stopped believing in God, he wondered if Reverend Shaw was the embodiment of the devil. He'd long abandoned his belief in the Bible—James's death, his splintered family, the pain inflicted by families he boarded with— all of that had taken care of naïve faith. Working with the reverend reinforced his skepticism.

Until . . . until he saw that the prayers he delivered actually worked for people sometimes. That let a little light back into his heart, even if just for the moment he was delivering one. There were times he really thought he was good at offering solace and comfort. It was the main reason he continued to do that part of his work for the reverend.

Reverend Shaw pushed his hands into his pockets and rocked on the balls of his feet again. "Young Thomas. Why don't you head to the church and fetch Hank and Bayard? They'll help you repair this railing if they're back from their errands."

"I'm due at work, Reverend. But thank you."

Tommy had no intention of inviting Hank and Bayard to help him at home, to put them in Mama's vicinity. Two men walked by the Arthurs' porch and entered Miss Violet's gate. "Gentlemen," Reverend Shaw said. "Miss Pendergrass is waiting."

Looking back at the rickety banister and at Yale playing with her spoon, Tommy was grateful Miss Violet hadn't seemed to have heard the ruckus.

Mama came down the steps with Yale, saying good-bye to the reverend. She removed the little dress from the wooden spoon and handed it to Yale to dig in the dirt near the porch lattice.

Tommy jiggled two more loose spindles. "I should be able to fix these without much noise. A few precise whacks and I'll be ready to paint."

Mama ran her hand over the smooth railing. "You did a fine job of sanding." The contentment on Mama's face made him long for their former life in Des Moines, made him forget that he had begun to see cracks in his father's façade.

Tommy patted his leg as though the letters from his father were still in his pocket. He wanted to believe the words he'd read in them. "I want the place to look perfect for . . ." Tommy lined up a spindle.

"What?"

Tommy whacked the spindle into place. "He wrote again."

Mama drew back, her lips forming a straight line, contentment replaced with tension.

Tommy took a deep breath. He didn't mean to hurt his mother by bringing up his father, but it wasn't as though the man was dead. That should mean something.

Mama crossed her arms.

"Says he'll be here midsummer. Everything should be nice and comfortable by then. And then you two can—"

She shook her head, causing frustration to ball in the pit of Tommy's stomach. He knew he shouldn't get upset at her being upset.

Tommy knew too well how easy it was to unintentionally hurt someone. He also knew his father was fraying the rope that held them all together.

Yet. All the people Tommy sold prayers to seemed to be wracked by just that sort of regret. For years he thought all it would take was his parents breathing the same air again and everything would be good, better than it ever was. When he read his father's letter the day before he'd been ready to let go of that idea. But now, here with his mother, the dream was real as the mallet in his hand. He wiggled another spindle.

"His latest letter was specific this time. Midsummer."

She tilted her head as though doubt made it too heavy to keep straight.

Tommy struck the banister above one spindle, then the last loose one. He dropped the mallet, took his mother's face in his hands, and kissed her forehead the way she'd done to him many times. He wanted to believe his father was coming, but if not, he wanted Mama to feel secure with him as the head of the home. "All's well, Mama. Promise."

She looked startled. He thought of her wanting a small cottage with a small garden, just big enough.

"You'll have the life you deserve all over again." He didn't want to indicate his father needed help with debt. He knew a woman needed a strong man, and though he was sure his father had iron insides, bad luck and grief had pocked his outsides.

Jeanie sighed. Tommy thought she even rolled her eyes.

His heart constricted. Her expression. The disgust that flashed over her face brought the dormant anger right back. Yes, his father left them after James died, but he came back and Mama made him go again. Mama divorced him. That was her doing.

He wouldn't argue, not wanting more regret. He wanted the pain to be gone, so he'd ignore it. "You'll see, Mama. It's going to be great."

She looked as though she was going to say something else, but instead she pulled his hat off, fluffed his hair, and replaced the hat, keeping hold of the brim. "Hurry back after work. Should be enough daylight to paint the banister," she said. She scooped her garden journal off the stairs and held it out to him. "I've got garden plans to get to and arrangements for tilling, or I'd paint myself."

He held her wrists understanding how she could mistrust her husband, but wanting to reassure her. "You can trust *me*."

"I know." She smiled, her eyes glistening with thoughts she didn't share. "I do."

They let each other go. Mama raked debris from the dormant flower beds. Tommy organized the tools against the stairs and trotted away swallowing any defense of his father, both for his sake and Mama's.

It was better to lock his complicated feelings away and move on. He looked over his shoulder. Mama propped Yale on her hip and raised Yale's hand, waving it at Tommy. He saw the doubt in Mama's eyes, but he shrugged it off. She was in a bad place, he knew. Yet he'd made her smile.

He shoved his fist in the air. "You'll see, Mama! Wait and see!"

Chapter 9

Ready for the world, confident he could manipulate his greatest strengths to achieve his goals, Tommy whistled and hummed his way to the Savery. He cut a path through a nearly abandoned stretch of town, past the school where he and Katherine had gone off and on since they'd been back in Des Moines, when they could scrape together the money to attend, telling himself this year he would double up on coursework if he could.

Sweating in the sun, dust blowing up off the dirt road, he stopped at a storefront, wiped his face with his hankie and smoothed his hair in the soot-smudged window. Someone waved on the other side of the glass, startling him. He cupped his hands around his eyes and leaned in.

Hank and Bayard.

Each leaned against the bar; a man tending drinks moved back and forth behind it.

Various game tables were scattered around, and pairs of men were playing billiards near the far wall. A group was perched at a felted round table, cards in hand. Another set of men lined up in front of a dealer, playing faro. The sweet pipe smoke mixed with the grittier, harder scent of cigars and seeped outside, seducing Tommy, reminding him of the times he won big at poker, when whiskey numbed his throat and his soul. But then bitter memories of loss came back, choking him.

You don't have time for this.

Yet he stood there, remembering. He'd had fun carousing with Hank and Bayard and older men who'd seemed friendly at first, teaching him to play, talking about women. Oh, the talk. The male tutorials left Tommy thinking he couldn't wait for the day he lay with a woman, yet petrified of it all the same. It didn't take long for Tommy to realize the friendliness held just as long as Tommy's money.

And, at first Tommy couldn't lose. The thrill of winning, just the possibility of what he might do with the money, had sent his blood coursing, made him feel high against the numbing booze. The sensation returned to him making him think he could win enough to pay his father's debt—and fast.

No.

He stepped back and read the name on the awning. The words announcing the original business that stood there were weathered, and though portions of each letter had been beaten away, he could make out the name: Melanie's Clasps, Crimps, and Ribbon. A favorite stop for his mother and sister way back when, before.

Tommy rubbed away some of the soot on the glass and took another look. Hank waved again; all signs of the menacing threat at the Savery had disappeared.

Tommy didn't trust Hank's mood swing but was glad the bullying had passed.

Just a quick hand.

The dusty saloon windows reminded him of McCrady's and the painting in the window. One good play and he could win enough money to buy back just one piece of his family's past. That would mean something to Mama.

Someone entered the saloon, and when the door opened, sunshine streamed through, lighting on the men sitting inside, giving Tommy a clearer view of who else was there.

Judge Calder.

Tommy froze. When his senses returned, he replaced his hat and started in the direction of the hotel. No way was he going in with Judge Calder there.

"Hey, brother!" Hank's voice rang out behind Tommy. "Have a libation."

Tommy waved him off.

"You act like we ain't pals. Once two fellas do time together, well, they're as good as brothers."

This made Tommy shudder and turn. "Shut up." He couldn't be so casual about jailtime and he wished Hank would stop bringing it up. Beyond the obvious captivity, Tommy had been beaten and humiliated. The heavy fists of fellow prisoners had left his insides feeling as bruised as his cheek and eye had obviously been. And then there was the slow torture, the roaches, the men pissing on everything in sight. It turned his stomach to recall any portion of it. The way the lawmen walked by and let it happen bothered him most.

He looked over his shoulder but kept going. "I've got work."

Hank caught up. "Slow down, cowhand. What's so all-fire 'bout workin' at the Savery, hoppin', skippin', and jumpin' for rich folk like you're dirt under their alligator shoes? Just to get a dollar once in a blue moon?"

This reminded Tommy of the man who'd chased him the day before. He stopped and opened his arms. "Oh, yeah. Alligator shoes. Did you lift that man's wallet at the train station the other day?"

Hank lifted his eyebrows and gave a mischievous smile. "Which man?"

Tommy's gawked. "You don't even know which? You lifted that many?"

Hank gripped Tommy's shoulder and shook it. "When will I stop shockin' you with the basic realities of life, Tom? I swear sometimes you're more ten-year-old girl than fifteen-year-old man."

Tommy let the insult blow past. His uncomplicated good-naturedness wasn't feminine, it was the way everyone should be. "Have to pull foot. Savery frowns on slack employees."

"Come on," Hank said, shoving his thumb over his shoulder toward the saloon.

Tommy lifted his chin. "You're awfully friendly after that routine at the hotel. Next time you need something, ask like a gentleman when I'm off shift. And no to the saloon. I don't do well in them. You know that. I'm better left carrying the reverend's prayers to his faithful folks."

Hank stuffed his hands in his pockets. "I'm sorry about the hotel. You know how the rev is. Sometimes he's hot on us to sell more prayers so we can lift stuff from the rich and sorrowful. Other times he's wantin' us to run the train station like the other day. Come gamble. You had quite the run before you gave up playing with us. What about your father and all that money you plan to save for him?"

Tommy choked. He must have disclosed that while drinking with the boys because he certainly wouldn't confide it while sober.

Hank held his hands up. "Fine. No gambling. But Rev said the other day he needs you on the job with us, and you can be as slack as you want if you just deliver them prayers like you do. 'Parently you have quite the method. All them old ladies tell him so. Come inside. Keep me company while I grab the tiger's tail."

Tommy's ears perked at the mention of people complimenting him. He straightened. "The ladies said I'm good with the prayers?"

Hank gripped Tommy's shoulder and nodded. "And you're right. I should've been gentlemanly at the hotel. My empty belly and Rev's threat got the best of me. Don't like jail any better 'n you, even if I joke 'bout it. You can trust me. Come on."

Tommy scowled and tried to shake Hank's hand off. "No thanks." Tommy didn't want to do anything to mess with his family situation. Still, he knew better than to ostracize Hank completely. "What's Jeremy Calder doing in that saloon?"

"Judge? Relaxin' between cases. Everyone gets a minute to himself, right? Don't look down your nose at him."

Tommy felt the warning in his bones. "The judge is puffing up his feathers by claiming to clean up the very games he's in there playing?"

Hank raised his eyebrows. "Again with the little-girl bit."

Tommy crossed his arms.

"So the prayers. When can you come with and get the rev off my hind end?" Hank lifted his hat so sunlight could illuminate it. He touched his cheek where it was swollen, and Tommy knew the reverend must have hit him. "Please."

Tommy thought of how he'd just seen the man at Miss Violet's. He knew well and sure that the reverend could lie and everyone, including his mother, would believe.

Tommy felt sorry for Hank, but he would prefer pulling out of their partnership. But the prayers. The ladies said he was good at delivering them. Offering comfort for the grieving was no small thing, and it gave him a measure of peace, purpose. More than he originally thought it would.

Tommy thought of the reverend at Miss Violet's again, dealing with investments. "You think if I write some prayers of my own that he'd up my share in the game?"

"No," Hank said.

Tommy walked on. Hank ran to keep up with Tommy's long strides. "But there's plenty of ways to grow your proceeds if you'd just keep a good attitude about it."

Tommy scoffed and picked up speed. Hank doubled his footfalls.

"Why," Hank said, "a gold nugget found its way into my pocket just the other day. Bet your ma and sisters could use a little sparkle in their lives. And I've seen you get an extra dime from time to time."

Tommy's step stuttered with that fact.

"Yeah. That gasbag O'Henry gave you extra when you thought we wasn't lookin'. Saw you slip it into your pocket. Imagine what people might give us if we really worked the business like we meant it."

Tommy stopped, irritated, still unsettled by the idea of them stealing while he was offering prayers, but curious. Maybe someone had been kind like the woman who gave Tommy an extra dime. "Someone gave you gold?"

Hank dug a pitted, gold nub from his pocket.

Tommy moved closer. It was true. His family, including his father, could use funding, but he was fairly certain Hank stole the gold. "You don't think they'll notice gold is missing from their house?"

Hank smirked.

The thought of having gold in the palm of his hand was attractive. Gold could go toward buying the painting of his family from McCrady. Or he could hide the gold away and the savings would move him much closer to purchasing a cottage. So many ways gold would go far.

"Didn't say I stole it, either. About two ounces. That's what Mrs. Terry said when she gave it to me. An-y-how," Hank stretched the word out to a few extra syllables, "a little over or under, it's more treasure than I been given in my life."

"She *gave* you that for a prayer?"

"It was a very inspired set of words."

Tommy drew back, meeting Hank's gaze. "Impressive." An extra dime was wonderful, but gold?

Hank put the gold into Tommy's palm, the weight cool against his skin. Hard to imagine something so little was worth so much. Seeing it there, glistening in the sun, Tommy felt drawn, a yearning for more than what the Savery paid, thinking maybe he'd been shortsighted.

He could work forever at the Savery and not earn a chance to bring home so much so fast. His former position as a wealthy young man had been yanked away with the snap of a judge's fingers; perhaps wealth should return to him just as dramatically, just as quick.

A clap of thunder startled Tommy. He and Hank squinted into the sky. Dark, stirring clouds rushed overhead, tucking the sun away. He still had to change into his uniform before his shift. He looked at the gold again, ran his thumb over its rutted surface and a swell of happiness pulsed at the thought he might earn his own nugget.

A man flew out of the saloon and rolled into the street. Another ran after him, stepping on his midsection, laughing at the fallen man's pain. Tommy was immediately returned to his own bad fortune in a saloon. It all sounded good—fast money, painless, lazy days with like-minded pals. But he knew better. He'd learned his lesson to at least be careful when he had to do something untoward. With his sense of responsibility back in place, Tommy exhaled and pushed the gold nugget back into Hank's hand. "I'm gonna be late."

As he jogged away, Tommy looked back over his shoulder and saw *him*—the man with the extraordinary power to sentence Tommy to hell on earth. Judge Calder's penetrating eyes, full of what Tommy considered to be living death, watched him. He picked up his pace, relieved he'd made the right choice.

Was it possible Hank had comforted a needy woman so fully that she gave him a nugget of gold? Tommy was intrigued, but knew better. Soft prospects like this, chances that weren't fastened to a legitimate workplace, often ended with young men in jail. His skin chilled at the thought, sending him on his way, more content than ever that he had a job waiting for him, a job that would lead somewhere prosperous and respectable.

Chapter 10

About a year back, back when Tommy impressed Mr. McHenry and earned a job at the Savery, he replaced his daily odd jobs for Reverend Shaw for once in a while odd jobs and the glamour of the hotel's crystal chandeliers, Oriental rugs, and guests outfitted in fashionable, high-quality clothing.

Every time he went to work and entered the hotel lobby, a blazing smile lit his lips. Like a performer on stage, he not only turned on charm and solicitousness, he felt it deep inside. He liked being at the service of people who expected the best.

Tommy shook hands with gentlemen coming and going and held the door for ladies as though he owned the whole shebang. He carried more luggage than any other bellboy, and with his polished language and high-class manners, Mr. McHenry appreciated him all the more. Times like that made him grateful for Mama's early, heavy-handed parenting. He saw the value of knowing how to behave like he was wealthy even though he lived in a tent in the back property of a wealthy, independent woman.

Tommy headed for the changing room to get into his uniform but his attention was drawn to a young woman darting across the lobby, arms pumping, expression serious, as though she were on an errand to save the world from itself.

Pearl.

His stomach leapt.

Pearl. He said her name aloud, loving the feel of it on his lips. What was the matter with him? The women he met either excited him, making it difficult to ignore their overtures, or bored him to unconsciousness. But Pearl? Her honest rawness, the beauty underneath her mussed hair, dirt-smudged skin blotched with ink she'd transferred from envelopes to her face, her absolutely accidental beauty, made him feel as though a thousand buzzing insects had gathered in his belly. He walked toward her but then was pulled back.

"You. Arthur, right? Tommy Arthur?" A man angled himself inches from Tommy, staring at him as though he'd tried to walk off with a velvet settee in tow. Tommy drew back as he caught wind of the man's stiff breath. His coat and pants were the same as the other managers like Mr. McHenry always wore.

Tommy glanced one last time at Pearl before he shook the man's hand. "Yes, Tommy Arthur. Bellboy."

"I've been hired to manage the managers."

"Welcome," Tommy said, sweeping his arm across the space.

"You're late." The manager of managers stared at Tommy, working his jaw so hard his teeth would wear to nubs in seconds.

Tommy's cheeks flushed, and he saw Pearl watching him from the mailroom. She waved, smiling.

"This way." The immaculately dressed man with horrid breath spun on his heel.

"I need to change into my uniform, Mister . . . uh, Mister?"

"Wierach."

"Mr. Wierach. Nice to meet you, but I'm going to be later if I don't get changed. Surely Mr. McHenry's told you about my dedication and skill."

The man's shoes clicked in a rhythm that, set against the hum of guests' voices rising and falling, sounded musical.

Mr. Wierach passed his hand down a panel in the wainscoted wall behind the front desk, opened a door, and directed Tommy inside with a jerk of his head.

Tommy held his hat against his belly and rotated it as he cleared his throat. He craned to see if he could catch a glimpse of Mr. McHenry. He was always at work by first light. "Mr. Wierach? I normally check in with Mr. McHenry before my shift. We talk and . . . Well, he must have mentioned . . ."

The man shook his head and waved him in.

Tommy's breath caught. Maybe they were finally restructuring the duties in the "front of house." Yes. He could feel it. He'd be given the desk clerk position. Mr. McHenry had told him twice in the last month he was looking at Tommy for the position. This Mr. Wierach must have been part of the changes. Tommy's heart thudded, thinking of the promotion and the extra money it would bring.

Mr. Wierach stood straight as the seams where the walls met, hands balled at his side, looking as though he were butler to President Harrison as much as some guy running a hotel.

"One." The man unclenched his hands, wiggled his fingers, and balled them back up. "Someone of your position should enter the hotel rear of house. Go down the back alley, through the laundry, into the locker room. You've been here a year and ought to know that."

Tommy felt a jolt in his gut. He began to sweat. Mr. McHenry never told him that. He straightened his posture to show he was listening even if confused.

The manager swallowed hard, closed his eyes, and shook his head as though disgusted. "Who assigned you to bellboy?"

"Mr. McHenry himself."

Mr. Wierach scoffed. "Well, he *himself* has moved on to another job in another state, so it looks like I have a lot more work to do than I anticipated."

Tommy's eyes widened. When was the last time he'd seen Mr. McHenry? He tried to remember but couldn't. Was it a week back? He hadn't heard anything about him leaving. Tommy's throat dried, making it hard to swallow. His heart sped up. Mr. McHenry had been wonderful to Tommy, hiring him after they shared stories about a mutual friend.

"Mr. McHenry gave me glowing reviews. Always."

"*Pfft.* Means nothing in light of his departure. I'm unimpressed with you, so . . ."

Panic sizzled in Tommy's belly, taking him back to harder times.

The man pressed his lips together and took off through another doorway signaling with a wave for Tommy to follow.

Tommy jogged again. He caught a glimpse of Mrs. Simmons heading toward the concierge. He almost yelled to tell her he'd gotten the cure from Katherine, but he bit his tongue and focused on the crisis at hand. "Sir? I'll show you how good I am at my job. I take it seriously and won't come in the front door ever again. You see, Mr. McHenry allowed me to do that because of my manners. He knows my background in Des Moines and—"

He waved Tommy off, silencing him as he strode through back hallways, making sharp turns around corners, causing anyone coming toward them—maid, chef, or waitress—to plaster their backs against the wall until Mr. Wierach was safely past. Tommy thought at first it was due to their respect for the new manager, but down-turned eyes and the quiet "Sir" that came out of everyone's mouth showed fear more than respect.

Mr. Wierach stopped in front of an elevator, and Tommy kept on toward the locker room.

"Stop."

Tommy followed orders.

"You've got a new job."

Tommy's mood surged again. He knew it. Mr. McHenry might have left, but he knew the man wouldn't go without recommending Tommy for the desk clerk position.

Tommy put his hand out. "Thank you, sir. I'll make you proud being desk clerk. You'll see."

Mr. Wierach smirked. "Desk clerk?"

"Yes, I—"

"A judge just sent a boy over. Said to give him the bellboy job. And yes, everyone said you work hard, so I decided to give you a new position."

"Right. Desk clerk," Tommy said.

Mr. Wierach winced. "No, what are you . . . *No.*" He gripped the metal gate that kept people from entering the elevator shaft until the car was in place. "You're going to run this elevator. You must use it two hundred times a day taking luggage upstairs. Lenny got caught giving girls rides back here, and I fired him. Should suit you perfectly. You know the rules. No guests back here. Once you run the back elevator for a time and we trust you won't kill anyone, you'll be trained at the front of the house to run the guest elevator."

A drop of sweat trailed down the side of Tommy's face, curving around his ear, his body reacting to memories of being kept in a dirty, tiny cellar room at the Hendersons'.

He told himself he was perfectly safe and fought the urge to wipe the sweat away and draw attention to it. The odor of greased cables filled his nose. He looked behind him; the dark hallway felt as though it were suddenly closing in. His heart pounded, and he scanned the space for a door to the outside, windows, anything that might open up the space.

Stop it.

Tommy's throat constricted and he cleared it, trying to relax the clinch and breathe easier. Mr. Wierach greeted a man coming from the other direction, the night elevator man. "Mr. Crabtree will train you."

Mr. Crabtree yanked the iron door open. The sound of the metal accordion folds collapsing and scraping the track made Tommy squeeze his eyes shut.

Stop it. It's perfectly safe. It's not punishment. It's not a cellar or closet. It's not a broken-down elevator. Stop.

"Arthur. Don't dawdle."

Tommy nodded and followed Mr. Wierach into the compartment, determined to fight off his panic. He'd boarded in a home where they'd treated him like an animal. They'd installed a metal crosshatched door like this one in the root cellar where he often had to stay. The door created a cage, and the brothers who had suffered at the hand of their father shared a little of that abuse with Tommy, poking at him with broom handles and sticks.

"As elevator man, you'll get room and board and nine dollars a month."

Tommy backed up against the wall, his hands gripping the chair rail that belted the perimeter. He wanted to explain his arrangement with Mr. McHenry: he got paid more than usual bellboy pay because he didn't room at the hotel. He drew heavy breaths. He shouldn't suffer a pay cut for no reason. The elevator jerked to life as the man pulled down on the rope. Tommy gripped the rail harder.

"Arthur!" The manager elbowed him. "Eli's showing you how to work this thing. You'll have lives at stake; you can't afford to play around like some—"

The metal door slammed down, causing the car to go nearly dark. The lurching motion as it shook upward made it feel as though the car would shudder right off its cables and crash to the bottom. His vision grew blurry, and although he was sure he turned his head to meet the manager's gaze, and although he was positive he was seeing the manager's mouth move, the words were garbled and foreign.

The elevator cables ground against each other, causing the occasional spark to fly as the car rose. Tommy would have sworn in court that the wires were unraveling with every inch upward. He moved across the back of the elevator and into the corner. As quickly as the hall light had been squelched when Eli dropped the metal door, the car stopped and light flooded the compartment as he lifted it again.

Tommy grasped the door, fingers through the diamond-shaped openings, and yanked at it like a wild man, making the car swing and the cables jam before it stopped in the proper spot. Leaving Crabtree and Wierach in the elevator, Tommy squeezed through the half-opened door and leapt down onto the hallway floor, rolling into the wall.

He had to get out.

The two men shouted, but their voices faded into dizzying fuzz. He popped up, chest heaving, heat coursing through him. The manager bellowed, shoving through the same opening, but in between Tommy's humiliation and bone-jarring fear, he knew he could not have a conversation.

His legs churned as he bolted down the passage, as he'd done many times before while in the midst of a panic, the movement and pounding of his feet eventually releasing him from his fear. He wove in and out of maids filing down the hallway and pushed into the stairwell that led to the first floor and out the door.

Once outside, Tommy stood against the wall. The humid air added to the streams of sweat dripping into every valley of his body. Voices and the sound of the door slamming open made him take off again, sprinting for Miss Violet's, running for home, attempting to outrun every terrible thing that had ever happened to him, all the awfulness that clung to him like his drenched, sticky clothes.

Chapter 11

Tommy pounded home, thick, humid air burning his cheeks, blood rushing in his ears. He picked up speed, vision blurring, dodging wagons in the nick of time, leaping train tracks, vaulting fences. When he reached the little house where the Arthurs were boarding, he dashed through the front door and stopped at the stairs, bent over, hands on his knees, panting. The space was too tight in that moment making the floor seem to rise up, squashing him into the ceiling.

Outside.

He jogged down the hall, through the kitchen, through the garden, to the shed that stood at the rear of Miss Violet's property. Wheezing and clasping his chest he told himself he was safe, to calm down. When that did nothing, he knew he had to do it.

The knapsack.

He pushed open the shed door, daylight pouring over the rustic, dusty space. Tommy stored his belongings inside even though he slept outside in a tent.

He was beginning to wonder if the panic would ever stop surprising him. His fear that it was a lifelong sentence made its grip on him worse. He pressed his chest, trying to slow his thumping heart. He squeezed his eyes shut and pressed his back hard against the door.

He didn't want to do it, but it wasn't really a choice.

Where is it?

Loft. He climbed the rickety ladder and reached into an old crate. Knapsack in hand he descended, mined through his bag, and yanked out a half-full bottle of whiskey. He dug his thumb into the cork and wiggled it out. He took a swig, the burn familiar, painful, the effects immediate. He warned himself not to drink too much, just enough to settle the fear.

Medicine. A cure. Like anything he might find in Katherine's book.

It was the only thing that calmed him when panic swept in.

His breathing finally evened out. Another swig. Comfort. That's what the whiskey delivered. Like nothing else. And it scared him. Like his father needed laudanum from time to time, Tommy hoped the whiskey cure would stay useful and not overtake him, changing him for the worse, eliminating its curative properties. He set his knapsack down and went back outside onto the tiny porch that fronted the shed. He breathed the open air deeply, ignoring the urge to go back in for one more swig.

He looked up at the vines and ivy woven throughout the rickety trellis suspended over the porch. If he could see inside his mind, his thoughts would appear tangled like the vines when he was having an attack. Each green shoot snarled and strangled by the next with no way to allow ideas to logically move from conception to fruition. He simply responded to his body's need to flee.

The shade under the thick vines cooled him. Every muscle in his body quivered, and he knew if pressed he wouldn't be able to run another bit. The screech of a hawk flying low drew his attention upward, but he only saw splashes of blue sky peeking through the green canopy.

Tommy closed his eyes. The odor of dirt and grass and cow filled his nose. He thought of the crisp blue uniform he'd have worn as elevator man, the one with the gold roping at the shoulder and shiny brass buttons. He squeezed his eyes shut, pain vibrating his chest, mortified at what transpired.

What had happened?

How would he explain this to Mama? She was depending on him, and none of this was fair. He'd done a fine job as bellboy. Who was Mr. Wierach to sweep in and make important changes like it was nothing, without even knowing Tommy's strengths?

He thought again of Mr. and Mrs. Henderson, caging him in that underground pit. He shuddered. The insects crept over him, tiny feet tickling, taunting. He would fall asleep with his fingers wedged in his ears to keep creatures out of them, then bolt awake when tiny legs worked across his cheek or up his pant leg. Buried alive, he was sure that would feel exactly the same.

His eyes burned. He sat down on the step, wishing the hot breeze blew cool. He put his hat in his lap and brushed his hair out of his face with his forearm. Defeated, his plan to raise money quickly averted. *Father.* Tommy laid back. He should return to work, apologize, and accept the job. Could he manage the elevator if he tried harder?

He couldn't get up. Tears gathered and spilled out the corner of his eyes.

Go back. Demand the bellboy position.

He'd been great at it. Mr. Wierach just needed to see that. But with how he'd behaved, entering the front of the building the way he had been accustomed to as a young child, his looney behavior in the elevator—it all added up to a surety that his opportunity to work at the Savery Hotel had dried up and wafted away like cat's ear seed on a late summer day.

He put his hands behind his head. The hawk called again and Tommy squinted, eyes searching between the gaps in the vines for a view of it. The hawk's sorrowful call made desperation take rigid form inside him, and he was sure no one had ever felt despair in that way—as a solid mass instead of fleeting emotion. He had to move forward.

A plan.

Mama always had a plan. At least until she didn't. And it was time for Tommy to act his age and help her, not depend on her. The embarrassment he'd felt at the hotel swept through him again. He rubbed his eyes with his fists, berating himself for letting those unseen fears take control and make him behave like a child. He forced steady, deep breaths in and out, his inhalations finally slowing to normal.

The vines rustled above him.

He got up on his elbows peering into the greens. The movement reminded him of the snakes that used to burrow into the dugouts on the prairie and drop out of the ceiling onto whatever or whomever was underneath. He started to sit up as the vines spread, and a black ball tumbled right into the hat in his lap.

His stomach lurched at the sight. Feathers and beak, lush, ebony feathers pulled close around a body. A crow. Was it dead? Tommy poked at its side and caused it to raise its head and open its mouth as though wanting to talk.

"You're alive," Tommy whispered at the peeping bird, its wings reflected with deep blue when the sunlight shot through gaps above and hit its body. Tommy looked upward, searching for the nest, for a mother bird or siblings. Nothing. The bird had materialized out of thin air.

He waited for it to leap up and fly away or to peck at him. But it just lay there, breathing, probably recovering from bone-deep fear, same as Tommy had just done. In the distance, the hawk's scream came again, then closer and faster and closer, right over the trellis. A chill went through Tommy.

"That hawk had you, didn't he? Dropped you and here you are." Tommy put his hand under the weight of the bird, thinking it was enjoying the feel of the tweed cap.

Tommy examined the bird, pressing its wings here and there, assessing its health. This helpless animal reminded him of the occasion that changed the way he saw animals. He'd never been a big hunter as a small boy. His family had hired people for that type of thing. On the prairie, he'd done his share of trapping prairie chickens and rabbits, but his mother had prepared them for eating. Hunting was not something Tommy enjoyed.

The crow was young, but not a chick. Its beak had darkened from pink to black, and its eyes were dark brown, not blue like a young crow's would be. Its feathers were full and glossy, and it was as big as his foot. Yet it was stunned enough that it didn't even try to escape. It seemed to want Tommy to care for it.

Tommy squatted beside the porch, expecting the bird to fly away even as he dug for a worm. When he saw that the squirmy thing was too large for the crow to eat, he tore it in half and mushed it between his fingers. He knew a crow this age could find his own food, but Tommy wanted to show that he would care for him. "I'm sorry, little worm. I hate to do this, but this fella over here needs his lunch."

Tommy sat on the porch, hat in lap, brushing the corner of the crow's beak to coax it into accepting the food. When the bird had eaten several mouthfuls, it found Tommy's gaze, and he swore at that moment the crow thanked him with a tiny nod before pushing its face into the side of the hat and falling asleep. "My little foundling."

Tommy brushed the soft wings, watching as the tiny body relaxed further into what he deemed must be sweet slumber. Seeing the fragile bird safe and comfortable made Tommy wish he could curl up inside the hat with his new friend, the only thing on earth that actually needed him.

Chapter 12

This bird. Its velvet wings spanned two hands as he stretched them, getting his bearings back. The fella captured Tommy's heart in an instant, its obvious strength tempered by momentary fragility. Tommy stroked its wings, weighing his employment options, considering possible money streams. Voices from the kitchen garden rose and fell over the hedgerow.

The property that stretched behind Miss Violet's big house and the Arthurs' small one was divided into four quarters. One hedge ran down the center, dividing the big house, its social garden, and grazing lands from the small house, kitchen garden, and fruit-bearing bushes near the shed. Another set of hedges cut across, blocking sightlines between the shed area in the back of the property from everything else.

The voices sounded again, a male baritone, weaving through Mama's unusually airy tones. Curiosity pricked him. Even with the heat, he slipped into his coat so he could hide the bird in his pocket. He assumed Mama must have been in the kitchen garden designing and resuscitating the dormant land as she'd planned earlier.

He crossed through the hedge. Mama moved along on her knees, digging. Yale poked a stick at the ground, imitating. No sight of a man anywhere. The elevator situation must have still been playing with his mind.

Tommy drew a deep breath. Time to explain that he'd lost his job.

He stepped on a stick, making a loud cracking sound. Mama looked over her shoulder, the hat brim shading her eyes, cheeks pink from sun and exertion. She'd cleared away a rectangular section of weeds and turned some of the soil along the boxwood.

She wiped her brow with her forearm and stood. "Tommy! Aren't you supposed to be at work?"

He drew closer. Yale lifted her arms. Tommy scooped her up with one arm, angling her leg away from the bird he'd tucked into his pocket. Yale nestled her face into his collar, and he kissed the top of her head and searched for confident, reassuring words.

"What is it?" Mama stood and leaned on her spade.

She knew something was wrong. She always did. Tommy forced his smile to remain.

Mama brushed dirt off her skirt. "Tommy?"

"Lost my job."

Her face fell and she straightened.

He drew up to convey strength. "Mr. McHenry's gone. New manager wanted me on the service elevator instead of bellboy."

She wrinkled her brow at him and shrugged.

He didn't want to confess his attacks, the way he felt, but knew he had to. "It was the rickety one in the back of the house." His lips quivered, and he set Yale on the ground, where she began stabbing at the earth with the stick again. "I tried, Mama, I swear. But as soon as the elevator started up, a few wires split, like the end of a hair, and it was bucking and squealing and . . ." Tommy swallowed hard.

Mama removed his hat, smoothed back his hair and pulled him close, tight. "It's all right."

He hadn't intended to be so soft, but the emotions expanded and grew.

"You're afraid of . . . elevators fall sometimes, but not at a hotel like that."

He shook his head. He couldn't tell her how he'd been treated when he was out on his own, that he hadn't been strong enough to defend himself at times and that he carried the result with him to this very day. Confiding that would set her back some distance. He didn't want her to feel more guilt for having boarded them out.

She took his hand. "Can you convince the new manager to give your bellboy job back?"

He pulled away. "Some bigshot wants someone else to have it." Now he was wondering if he took another fella's job when McHenry gave it to him the year before.

"I know how that all works." She pushed errant hairs back under her hat as anger flicked across her face, then she snapped her gaze back on him. "No use stoking the ire about it. It'll be *all right.* We're together, you can pick up more odd jobs with the reverend, and more for Miss Violet. And when school starts in the fall, you'll need extra time for studies anyway. You had your hands full with both last year."

Tommy nodded. She was right. *Change the subject.* "Garden's coming along."

Mama spread her arms and spun around. "Remember the Pearsons' gardens when they lived here?" She inhaled deeply. "They were perfect, fragrant, architectural. But our gardens . . ." She looked into the sky before meeting his gaze again. "They'll be beautiful but hardworking, important in a different way. And you'll find enough work, Tommy."

"Yes," he said. He loved seeing her like this, her eyes lit from within. She was alive again, as though she'd been dormant, like the shriveled garden, resuscitated along with the grounds. This relieved Tommy, told him he could focus on working as much as possible, that she was going to be all right without him having to watch over her.

She dusted her palms together. "Do the chamber pots, cows, stoves, and hens for us and Miss Violet in the morning, then pick up extra work from there." She sighed. "We need to pool our energy . . ." she put her fingers together as though holding a ball, ". . .keep it close, keep each other close, and build our nest egg for our sweet little cottage."

"Yes," he said. He would keep his eye out for a solid job. It was one thing to do odd jobs if his only ambition was his next meal, but for a man like Tommy, well, this wouldn't do.

Mama straightened her hat. "Every extra penny I can put away for your and Katherine's tuition will make a difference when you graduate and make your way in college."

College? The crow shifted and made a cooing sound that only he seemed to notice.

Mama kept mentioning college as though they were still the Arthurs who lived on Grand Avenue with piles of money for things like schooling. Now? He wasn't so sure sitting in a classroom was the best use of his time, but he didn't want to argue that right then.

He squatted next to Yale and pulled the injured crow from his pocket. "Take a looky. Sweet fella needs a home. You and I can share him. He'll live with you and me and—"

Mama's shadow closed over them. "Its mother's probably frantic. *Wondering...*" Her words faded. "Desperate..." She shook her head and waved her hand through the air. "Put it back. Mother's frantic, surely." Her voice was hollow.

Tommy thought of his mother's pain when they were separated, when James died. Her pain had seemed slow and deep, spreading like molasses dripping from a plate, swallowing her, not frantic, panicked, wild.

"It's a him," Tommy said. "Fell right from the sky." Tommy squinted at Mama. He cocked his head and petted the silky wings. "Figure he's at least a year old. But crows stick together, so something happened. Someone left someone."

"Nature works things out," Mama said, rubbing one arm, folding into herself.

"I'll care for him. *I'm* his someone now."

Mama pulled a face. "Back. In case his mother's looking."

"Sometimes it's too late for looking." Anger laced his words, jolting both of them.

She shook her head just enough that Tommy knew he'd hurt her.

"I didn't—"

"I'm sorry—"

They spoke at the same time, interrupting each other.

He studied his bird to avoid Mama's eyes but then finally met her gaze. "I'm so sorry for sounding mean," Tommy said.

She sighed and sat, Yale in between them. "You're upset about the job. I understand."

"I shouldn't have said that."

She took his chin in her hand. "Keep the bird. But outside."

"Cat'll get it."

"We don't have a cat."

"Any cat. You know what I mean."

Yale crawled into Mama's lap. "You're grown up in many ways, Tommy. Fifteen years old. I'm so proud of how you've helped your sisters and me. But with things like this, I see you're still a boy. I know you feel like I abandoned you, but half of Des Moines has been boarded out at some point in life. It's what parents do to keep everyone alive. You know deep down that's not what I wanted. I wanted you with me the whole time."

Tommy looked at her. "It's just a bird, Mama. I wasn't talking about us." Her fragility was evident in her face, the light happiness he'd seen a few minutes ago extinguished, reminding him of when he'd found her in an attic, emaciated, nursing Yale, sobbing.

"And I know you didn't want to do that. I really know."

It was that very day that he left Yankton and headed back to Des Moines to search for his father. Right then he'd realized Mama wasn't capable of taking care of anyone but Yale, that he'd take care of himself and eventually all of them. Until he'd seen her broken that way, he couldn't have guessed how bad off she was.

He didn't want to be angry at Mama. He understood her pain, he shared it, unable to shake it. He carried it in his skin, hardening his heart, sometimes turning his words angry and mean, leading him to more guilt and sorrow that he was not a better person. And, it led to the whiskey when he wasn't careful.

Her eyes drooped, pulled down with the pain he knew coursed through her.

"I'll keep the bird until he can be on his own, in the tent or shed, never the house—sorry, Yale. And I'm sorry for upsetting you, Mama."

She shifted and put her arm around Tommy's shoulders, pulling him close, Yale between them. "I love you, Tommy. We're going to be all right. I promise."

He nodded and started to stand, but Mama took his face in her hands.

Yale stood and put her little hands over Mama's, holding Tommy's cheeks. Yale tilted her head like Mama, studying Tommy, breaking the tension, making them fall together, laughing.

The three of them dug weeds along the border. Working together felt good. Despite the valley they'd just rolled into, he was optimistic overall. "Yale's growing up, Mama."

"Sure is."

"This feels good, us working together. Losing my job stings bad, but . . . this . . . I see now what you mean about having a small home, property we can live off of, but without servants and any of that stuff I wanted so bad. I see now what you wanted for us."

"I'm glad, Tommy. We have each other."

"That's most important." Tommy would not let his family splinter again. His father may or may not return, but he was confident he could take care of them all either way.

They finished weeding nearly to the back porch when the boxwood branches that divided the Arthur side of the property from Miss Violet's began to quiver and spread. A man poked his face through the greenery then pushed one shoulder through, then his whole body came.

Tall, dark, and lanky. He held up two garden hoes.

"Thought you got lost, Mr. Hayes," Mama said.

The man moseyed toward them, laid the hoes down, and reached toward Mama. She took his hand, and he pulled her to standing. She brushed dirt off her bottom as the man offered to shake Tommy's hand. "Reed Hayes."

Tommy got to his feet without assistance and studied the man his mother obviously knew. Tommy finally accepted the handshake. A firm grip, Mr. Hayes's hand was smooth against Tommy's calluses.

"You must be Tommy. Your mother and I've been making garden plans and arrangements and I must say I feel like I know you. I hear you're a talented scholar."

Tommy pulled a face and petted the bird, an unsettled feeling sweeping over him. "Thank you." Something about the man, his friendliness, his having information about Tommy, complimentary as was, put him off. Silly that it did. He told himself to ignore the sensation.

Mama gestured toward the man. "Mr. Hayes is a doctoral student at Drake and will exchange his skill with a tiller for Katherine's baking and some data from our work together. A fine barter, wouldn't you say, Tommy?"

"Skill?" Mr. Hayes chuckled. "My efforts lean toward energetic and willing rather than skilled."

Mama giggled.

Tommy stared at one then the other, suddenly feeling distant from Mama rather than close and content as he just had.

She covered her mouth and did it again. *Giggled.* Like a little girl. She removed her hand from her mouth and turned her face up to Mr. Hayes, her hat falling off, the ribbons catching around her neck. She shaded her eyes from the sun and grinned in a way Tommy couldn't recall seeing her do. Not ever. Not for anyone.

Reed Hayes, doctoral student, pulled Mama's hat back onto her head, the two of them beaming like clowns. The man looked as though Jeanie Arthur created the very air he breathed, simultaneously sucking away every bit of Tommy's.

Tommy felt protective of Mama, untrusting of anyone other than family. She couldn't change her divorced status, but she didn't have to flirt with strangers, especially a man like this, with a college association, with public standing. Tommy didn't want her to ever suffer public humiliation again. When the financial scandal had broken, he'd felt every bit of her loss and shame. He didn't want her out in the world in a way that could be criticized and further disgraced. Mama and Mr. Hayes continued to yammer on. Tommy drew deep breaths, growing upset. What was wrong with him? They were simply discussing garden plans, how Mr.

Hayes could use the data, and trading labor for Katherine's baked goods. That was it.

He had to get out of there. "I've got to get this bird back to the shed," Tommy said. "He took a tumble."

Mr. Hayes turned his attention on Tommy, bent closer and petted the crow's head. "Fella looks strong. Adventurous soul, isn't he?"

Mr. Hayes's expression indicated genuine interest, dulling Tommy's irritation. He was being silly. This man was simply friendly. "I've got to gather some hay for a pillow and get Frank into the shade."

"Pillow?" Mama said. "It's a bird, not something to name Frank of all—*Frank*?" Shock flooded her face.

Tommy didn't know when he'd named the bird Frank. It was out of his mouth without thinking, but now he appreciated it as a reminder to Mama that her husband was alive even if not there, even not her husband anymore. "It's a him, Mama, not an *it*, and I named him Frank because . . . well, crows are smart. They love people and are loyal. People with wings. That's what they are. Sometimes lost from its people, but . . ."

Explaining was useless. Heck, even he'd been calling Frank an it, earlier. He stalked toward the back hedgerow.

"Tommy," Mama said in her lightest, cheerful voice. "Have some supper with us before Mr. Hayes and I finalize the garden plans." Her voice carried over the vine-clogged hedges.

"No thanks, Mama. Not hungry." Tommy lifted his hand but didn't turn back. He sat on the porch to the shed. Mr. Hayes's presence produced dread in Tommy, a syrupy darkness, something that would stick rather than pass, like his attacks.

He considered Mr. Hayes again and why his presence upset Tommy so. If the man hadn't evoked that girlish reaction in Mama, Tommy would have only been grateful for the tilling trade. Having someone hired to do that work would free him up to make the money the family needed for the cottage and more. He told himself to remove the oxygen that gave his darkness life to appreciate this helpful man.

Tommy could live with his mother's giggling and smiling while Mr. Hayes tilled. The arrangement was short-lived and that was a good thing.

Tommy petted Frank's feathers, and they looked into each other's eyes. "Water," Tommy said. "Let's get you water."

"Water," Frank squawked.

Tommy startled and juggled Frank.

He held him up to eye level, awed. "*You can talk.*"

"I can talk," the crow said.

"Whoa." Tommy couldn't believe it. Like magic, Frank seemed more human than he could have ever thought. Frank wiggled in Tommy's hands, struggling to stand. He set him down, and the bird stretched his black legs, lifting one foot and then the other, stretching his wings and flapping them gently.

"Trying your feet and wings back on, are you?" Tommy teased. "Stay here," he said, getting up and gesturing for Frank the crow to stay as though he were a dog.

But as Tommy picked up the water pail and walked away, glancing over his shoulder . . . *Gone.*

He stopped and turned fully back. Nothing. Frank was gone. Had he imagined it all?

A black blur circled him and then fluttered near his ear before landing on his shoulder.

He looked at the bird, who regarded him right back. "Holy Moses," Tommy whispered.

"I can talk," Frank said.

"Oh, you can."

Tommy walked gingerly to be sure he didn't knock Frank off his shoulder, but when Frank's feet gripped tight, Tommy lengthened his stride.

Back at the shed, he served Frank a bowl of water, which the bird drank from and then bathed in.

"Good thinking, Frank. Who needs separate bath and drinking water?"

"Bath."

Tommy chuckled, thinking he'd move faster on fixing up the shed so he could create a safe spot for Frank when needed.

Mr. Hayes's laugh rang out over the garden. God. What kind of fella did backbreaking work for a divorced woman saddled with children? A bad man, untrustworthy, a con man? No. That was not the kind of man that worried Tommy. It was the exact opposite.

Tommy felt Mr. Hayes's arrival like a clock winding down, making the need to work faster than he'd originally planned to get that cottage clear.

"Money, money, money," Tommy said.

"Gold," Frank said.

Tommy drew back, awed again. Gold. He thought of Bayard and Hank and the prayers they were selling, the stuff they were lifting from homes on the side. The gold nugget. Tommy needed to do a lot of chores and extra work to make up for the loss of his bellboy job.

He could sell prayers with the boys and do some on the side for himself when they got bored and wandered off. Nothing illicit about that.

There, that lifted his mood. That was all Tommy needed.

Chapter 13

With no obligation at the Savery, Tommy completed morning chores and swung by the church to collect the prayers Reverend Shaw would have completed for his members. He arrived to find out Hank and Bayard had been sent on an early errand so Tommy would be on his own delivering the prayers. An easy day and Tommy wouldn't have to worry about the fellas getting caught lifting items while Tommy shared the Lord's word.

Reverend Shaw left a note beside the prayers.

I'll need you to return with fees from each sorrowful soul and the little extra graces we've come to count on . . . Work your magic, Tommy. Everyone is counting on it.

Tommy blew out a puff of air. He'd rather be the distraction for the boys than have to offer solace and return with little extra graces. "Jesus." He reread the note and shook his head.

He paged through the prayers Reverend Shaw left for him. Nothing but the same words each of the members would have had in their Bibles. Repeated in Reverend Shaw's hand . . . what were they paying for? Did they really not notice the small objects that walked out the door when he and the boys left? Not his problem. He had enough of his own.

He shoved the fistful of papers into his pocket and headed out. Seven prayers for seven congregants. He wondered if the prayerful sentiments should just be published and shared by the citizens of Des Moines rather than folded into the palm of some woman's hand or stuffed into the pocket of a man, to be seen by no one else. Except God, perhaps. He was the intended audience in the end, wasn't he?

Tommy's faith started big as a mountain, but had been carved to nothing by life's rushing rivers, weathering, and earth-quaking losses. He now saw it all as a fairy tale like those in the book he gave Pearl. All the Arthurs' suffering . . . How could there be a God who allowed such destruction? The last bit of doubt for formal religion and the men who ruled it was sown into his heart and mind by Reverend Shaw. Though he did provide for wayward boys, that was just the good half of what he did.

Tommy had no right to judge the reverend because Tommy was part of the stealing. But he wasn't the one declaring himself pure and good, out shouting about cleaning up the streets of Des Moines, ridding the city of thieving boys and vagrant men, or warning against an afterlife burning in hell. Tommy's stealing and bad behavior were different. He wasn't pretending to be good when he wasn't. He was *trying* to be good even if he wasn't.

Tommy assuaged some of his guilt with knowing prayers comforted people, at least for the moments he spent with them. They told him often they appreciated that the reverend sat Tommy in front of them, to offer kindness and understanding and prayers when his boss was too busy with big issues to stop by. They felt as though Tommy channeled all the goodness Reverend Shaw embodied. Hearing that turned Tommy sour. Mrs. Brooks even pointed out his pursed lips and stiffened demeanor when she revealed that tidbit last time Tommy was there.

He doubted their contentment lasted much longer than when he was sitting there and hoped they remembered to look at the prayer later to call the peace back up.

As for stolen trinkets, Reverend Shaw usually sent the boys to homes where they could afford it. This time was different. Each of the first five homes he'd gone to had been ramshackle sheds, barely better constructed than the place in the back property at Miss Violet's. He considered taking something, anything from these homes, but just couldn't do it. He would suffer Reverend Shaw's disappointment, but he couldn't take from those who needed it more than him. He would make the reverend understand.

Number six house. This one was different. Massive, soaring, soot covered stone loomed above him as he stood on the sidewalk, the pressure of Reverend Shaw's plea for Tommy not to disappoint making his heart race.

He gave two short whistles, and Frank lifted off his shoulder and perched in the tree along the sidewalk. "Back in a jiff, Frank."

"Chew the fat, Tom."

Tommy startled and looked up, his hat nearly falling off. "Holy cow, Frank. Did you really say that?"

"Chew the fat."

Tommy took the paper he'd been using to write down the words and phrases Frank knew. He was surprising Tommy with something new nearly every day. Frank was clearly older than Tommy had first thought, or he'd lived with someone who'd taught him a lot of words.

"Stay close," Tommy said as he climbed the stairs to the porch. This home on Grand Avenue, near where he lived before the scandal, had bearing in every sense. The twenty-foot-tall door swung open before he even passed the entrance to head around to the kitchen in the back like protocol demanded.

A butler waved Tommy into the foyer and led him to the library. Tommy immediately felt at home, like this family had simply slid his old existence into their space. His gaze fell over a thousand books on deep shelves that covered every bit of wall, top to bottom, east to west. Delicate ceramic frogs and deer and swans sat in front of books along with smatterings of diminutive silver vases and tiny silver beds, dressers, even tables and chairs molded in silver.

Familiar patterns on china vases, Majolica and flow-blue platters littered every tabletop in the way that told Tommy they weren't noticed on a daily basis.

He ran his finger over the back of one of the porcelain dogs with reddish hair, adding up prices in his mind. Sunlight shot through the window and caught a silver tray overflowing with silverware on a Chippendale table. The precious metal intensified the light in the room. Tommy replaced the dog, drawn to the shiny display.

The handle on each utensil was thick with blossoms and leaves. He ran his finger over the design and picked up a large serving fork. Heavy in his hand, he recalled eating every meal with even more ornate silver.

Faint voices came from the hall, making Tommy fumble and drop the fork. The crash as it landed on the rest of the silverware echoed. He held his breath, straightening the forks and knives, and shuffled to the center of the room, holding his hat to his belly as though he hadn't moved once since being led into the library.

Surely this ornate silver would be worth much more than the plain patterns he'd typically seen at McCrady's. He looked over his shoulder at the tray, the sparkling silver teasing him, surprising him how quickly he forgot his guilt at stealing, even if for the boys living at the church. There should be a few minutes between finishing up with the prayers and having the mistress of the house fetch his cash when he could pocket something. The reverend would be pleased.

The way the pieces were scattered around the space would make it easy. A pickle fork or butter knife would slide right up his sleeve.

"Ahem." The butler appeared with a woman in the doorway. "Mrs. Schultz is ready." Her hand was threaded through the butler's arm.

She patted him. "Now, Geoffrey. Don't be short with our guest. I'm sure he . . . Where is he?"

"Right here, ma'am." Tommy squinted at the odd question and lifted his hand. Tommy could see a smile light the butler's eyes as he looked down at Mrs. Schultz. He patted her hand, and she raised her face toward him, smiling back. Her eyes searched lazily to meet Geoffrey's, never finding them.

Blind.

How easy.

Geoffrey guided her to a small wooden chair placed among upholstered settees and needle-pointed chairs with carved wooden arms. He perched her there with sweet, fussing pats.

Tommy glanced over his shoulder at the silver items strewn around the library just waiting. When he turned back, Geoffrey was bothering with the hem of Mrs. Schultz's skirt and moving her hand to show her exactly where he'd placed the Bible. He straightened and bowed. "Your prayers await."

"Thank you, Geoffrey. I've heard wonderful things about this boy." She lifted a gnarled hand somewhere in the direction of where she thought Tommy was standing.

"Thank you," Tommy said.

Her head snapped toward him. "Have a seat, young man. I can't wait to hear what you have." And with that Tommy pulled his prayers from his pocket and shuffled through them, finding the one with her name on it.

"Heavenly Father, thank you for your omnipresence, your strength, your guidance when we cannot see the path in front of us . . ."

Tommy glanced up, embarrassed that his prayer seemed to accidentally note that she was blind. It was the only prayer that contained a preamble like this and he wondered if Reverend Shaw had done that on purpose.

"Luke 15: 6-7 says . . ."

She reached forward, patting her fingers this way and that until she found his hand and gripped tight. "No, no. Tommy, I can hear your investment in this prayer you're selling me, but it's not really for me, is it? I'm blind, but not lost."

Tommy shrugged. "I simply . . ."

She squeezed his hand. "Everyone's lost in some way, I know. But shouldn't you get to know what I need before you—just burst forth with words as though they were meant for me?"

He chuckled. "Well, the reverend prepared everything. Most people like that he does that . . ." He felt awful that she didn't see this as valuable like the others, but also relieved that he no longer had to pretend. He stopped himself from saying it for a moment then leaned forward in his chair. "I once offered a second prayer at the end of a session, but you're right. The prayers are general." He shrugged. *Lazy.* A lure, he wanted to confide.

Don't disappoint.

"Meaningful though," he said lifting his voice to convince them.

"Nonsense. Opposite of meaningful. You questioned it in your voice even as you delivered the first words. I heard it. I hear every lift and fall in a voice telling me who's keeping a secret or frustrated or sad, without having to know another thing about them. The voice, a symphony of information, revealed in every sentence. Tells me more than my sight used to. *Listening* is everything."

"Suppose so." His mouth turned sour. He'd rationalized the stealing but hadn't thought that the prayers were lacking, not any more than prayers in church. And every other recipient had been pleased all this time.

They talked for some time. She expressed her love for her children and grandchildren she never got to see. She cried about the husband who had died a decade before and the butler she was in love with but could never marry. Tommy was less and less inclined to steal anything from her and feeling more ashamed.

When Mrs. Schultz joked that not only didn't she get to see her children, but she wasn't able to see anyone or anything in the world, she won Tommy over completely. He felt a shift inside right then, big and glistening like the silver in the room.

Listening . . . That was it.

A thrill worked up and down his spine. Exhilaration. That's what it was. "Can I use a pen? I'd like to write something for you."

He wrote a new prayer, tucking away the one originally assigned to her.

He drew a deep breath, nervous. "Dear God." He cleared his throat. "Please shine your grace on Mrs. Schultz and allow her family to fully understand her love for them, her sorrow at not seeing them. Provide her peace at the thought they might not visit and offer them the means to find their way back to their birth home to share their lives with her, even if just for a short time."

He paused, wanting to add something to the prayer, but not sure why the idea was coming to him. She leaned toward him, ear cocked.

"God, provide the chance for this kind woman to set her heavy heart to rest. Allow a visit from family so she can set things right, the way her heart has already done, but her lips have not expressed. In Jesus's name, I pray."

When Tommy looked up from his paper, there were tears falling down Mrs. Schultz's cheeks.

"I'm so sorry. I knew I shouldn't have . . . It just came to me, like you said . . . or didn't say, it was all between and inside everything you told me. I didn't mean . . . the idea you might have something to set right. And I didn't mean to—"

She held up her hand. "*That's it*, that's what was hidden between my words, Tommy. Just like I heard your questioning and distance in your delivery of the original words, you heard pleading in mine. My shortcomings. My unsaid apologies. You've a gift for this, young man. I felt it when I entered the room."

Tommy shook his head, face flooding, proud at what she was saying. "That reverend . . ." she stopped herself. He thought of what the reverend was expecting and started to come up with justifications for *not* stealing. He folded the paper and handed it to her. He couldn't speak; his own prayer had moved him in a way that embarrassed him and silently scolded him, conflicting him, making him wonder if every person he sold prayers to just hadn't had the nerve to confide what Mrs. Schultz had—that they weren't actually comforted by the words.

"May I touch your face, Tommy?"

"My face?"

"It's how I'll be able to see you, remember you better." She giggled. "I listen with my hands as well as my ears."

Tommy smiled big, feeling such fullness at being with her. He scooted toward her, kneeling beside her chair. Her fingers were gnarled but soft, and when she pressed her fingertips into the hollows of his cheeks and drew along his jawbone, she smiled. "You're a big man, aren't you?"

He nodded. "Six one or so."

"But gentle."

He froze, not knowing how to respond. He wanted to be strong and protective, not soft.

Mrs. Schultz dragged her hands over his shoulders down to his hands. "I hear your objection to my analysis. I feel it."

"No, I—"

She squeezed. "It's *good* to be big in the body and gentle in the soul. Your prayer, your way with me, they say so much. Don't lose that. Powerful, mean men shred little sections of the world every single day. Each man may be uniquely awful, but their damage is universal. They tell themselves they're protecting people. But really they're just entertaining their black, angry souls. You must keep that softness of yours. Keep it close. Keep your heart open."

It was as though she'd just prayed for him. Maybe he shouldn't accept payment as her words warmed him more than he could have imagined. "Thank you."

She scooted back in her chair and pulled a little sack from her chatelaine, digging her fingers into the neck of it. She pulled out some coins and tucked them into his palm. "Half is yours."

"Oh no. Reverend Shaw—"

She closed his fingers over the silver. "Nonsense. There's extra there. I'd tell you to keep it all, but I know there are other souls, more fragile than you, staying with the reverend. They need the money, too. But you delivered the prayers. You provided me with a personalized one that the reverend would never be able to, never on his best day. He's deaf, that one. Can't hear a single whisper, not even a clanging gong."

Tommy sucked in his breath.

"You know it, too. If I can hear it, you can see it. But I understand the world's complicated. Isn't it?"

"Yes."

"And remember. Sometimes it's the things we do that turn us hard, not the things done to us. Always forgive, especially yourself."

Tommy considered this new way of thinking about how people came to be loving, terrible, wonderful or bitter.

"You get half the money. The good reverend doesn't have to know."

Tommy couldn't speak, overcome by Mrs. Schultz's generosity, floating on it as he left, pockets light, but heart soaring. Outside he whistled twice and Frank swooped in, landing on his shoulder. "You'll never believe what happened in there, Frank. Never believe a word."

Chapter 14

Tommy dropped the money Mrs. Schultz gave him off to Reverend Shaw. The man glowered at Tommy over his half-rimmed glasses, reprimanding him for delivering prayers to seven homes and returning with money from only one and no treasure from any of them.

"Those prayers were worth well more than what we charge to begin with and you let them go for free?"

"Each of the first five had shoeless children who hadn't eaten in days. A bunch had belly problems."

"Sounds like time for the poorhouse, then. Can't keep your children, then shuffle them off to people who can."

Tommy winced, this solution cutting too close. "Those families believed you when you said prayers are always answered, that if they asked for grace they'd receive it. Six out of seven of them were at church for your sermon last Sunday. They believed."

Reverend Shaw balled his fist on the desk. "No one gets things for free in this world. Those imbeciles were naïve to think…" he continued to rail, got up and paced. Tommy tuned him out, unwilling to let the stingy, small sentiments sink into his skin. When the reverend started to indicate he'd punish Tommy for this turn of events, he snapped into an offensive position. "Mrs. Schultz indicated your prayers were central to her soul's cause. She ordered more. She spoke highly of you. I'm sure she'll tell her friends."

Reverend Shaw sank into his seat. "She said that?"

Tommy nodded.

"Perhaps it was just a bad week for us, like any business."

Tommy agreed. "'Course. That's all it was." And he was out the door the very second he could.

Back at the shed, Frank lifted off Tommy's shoulder, circled above the vine-woven trellis, and disappeared. Tommy opened the door. Light and air flowed into the space, helping cleanse and freshen. Time to make the shed livable. He swept the loft a dozen times, dumping dirt and filth on the floor below. He made piles and broomed it out the door. Next he washed and oiled the loft so he could sleep there once cold weather settled in, then did the same with the pine floors downstairs, creating a sense of home and hope that surprised him. Time with Mrs. Schultz had done more for him than he could have imagined.

He still needed to scrub and repair old chairs, a table and trunks that the last family left behind. He pushed the trunks against the far wall. Eventually he'd go through and make use of what was inside. Katherine and Mama were making him a mattress to put in the loft. He inhaled, admiring his simple, hard work.

With clapboards that could use plaster, the shed would be airy enough that he shouldn't feel too confined. The fireplace heat would rise into the loft, and he could bundle up in blankets if needed.

He was finishing a final round of oiling the loft when knocking from below drew his attention. He leaned out the opening where the ladder rose upward. A swish of purple silk hem peeked through the open front door. Miss Violet. He sprang up and descended the ladder as fast as he could, searching his mind for some chore he'd forgotten or an errand he'd been assigned but hadn't completed.

"Miss Violet," he said, wiping his hands on his pantlegs, trying to appear ready for whatever she needed him to do. Warnings from Mama to keep her happy so they could board together had sunk in deep.

She backed away, wafting her hand in front of her face. "That scent. Dead animal?" She covered her mouth and nose.

Tommy followed her onto the porch, thinking that he'd freshened it up better than that. "Still stale? Removed all the trash weeks back, but still lots to do."

She straightened. "Well, yes, I suppose these things take time."

He nodded and replaced his hat. "What can I do for you?"

"Well, the ladies will need rainwater. Thank goodness for this rainy weather. But there's something else. I understand you lost your job at the Savery."

Tommy looked away, embarrassed.

She patted his hand. "No matter. These things happen." She drew her gloves over the palm of one hand then the other. "I have a special job, and I think you're exactly right for it."

Tommy straightened. "Yes. Of course. Whatever you need."

She pulled a handkerchief from her sleeve and patted her neck with it. "I said, I *think* you're right for it."

"Well, what is it? I can build furniture, repair woodwork, help with your social garden?"

Violet cocked her head. "This requires dexterity and prudence."

He thought about what the job might be. He'd passed the test on discretion with other people. Trouble was, in being judicious he couldn't very well disclose his deeds. He certainly couldn't reveal how the reverend, one of her valued customers, obtained some of the funds she expertly invested for him.

She smiled. "I like that. Your mouth shut."

His eyes widened.

"Come with me. I'll show you everything."

He followed her. Frank swooped over their heads as they stepped off the porch, making Violet duck and squeal.

Tommy supported her. "Frank, be polite."

She squinted up at the bird as it landed on the trellis. "Dear God, that's . . . I heard about your bird, too. I never want to see that thing in either house. Ever."

"Mama said the same," he said.

Miss Violet caught her breath and stalked toward the arborvitae and boxwood that divided the shed area from the fruit trees on her side of the property, Tommy fast on her heels.

They passed Katherine coming out of the kitchen, arms laden with crocks for Mama's and Yale's supper. He stopped and Katherine leaned in and kissed him on the cheek. "Hi there, dear brother. How're things today?"

"Fine, fine, just headed to—"

Miss Violet shot Tommy a look from the porch, warning him about discretion again.

"Errands and chores."

Katherine smiled and headed toward the hole in the hedge. Tommy hurried in front of her and spread the branches so she could get through easier. Mama poked her head outside the door and waved. Tommy said hello and turned back to follow Miss Violet into the house. The kitchen was empty, but with all the dishes scattered and bread in the oven, he knew Katherine would be back soon to finish her work.

Miss Violet held the cellar door open and gestured for Tommy to head down. He hesitated, worried he might have an attack if it was too cramped or if it smelled like earth and filth, the way the Hendersons' had. She nudged him. "Go on."

He drew a deep breath and descended, Miss Violet following. The ceiling was higher than most, the floor covered with wood planks and carpets. He eyed the perimeter, looking for windows. A series of small ones lined the back wall, relieving him, knowing he could open at least a couple if needed.

He turned and offered his hand to steady Miss Violet.

She gripped his hand, steadied herself then took off, swatting cobwebs as she went. She stopped at a workbench at the back of the cellar. He hesitated again, his throat starting to close, worried he'd feel too closed in back there.

"Miss Violet?"

"Don't dawdle, Tommy," she said as she fussed with items on the bench. He squeezed his eyes closed, trying to smooth out his breath, searching for an excuse to not enter the dank room. A loud bang startled him. Light flooded in, reaching him even though he'd stayed back. Air circulated past, and he knew she'd opened a window, that he'd be all right. He exhaled and followed her.

Her back was to him as she spread things on the bench. He joined her there to see rectangular cuts of skins, needles, and thread.

He drew back and removed his hat, unsure of what his job would be.

She loosened her hat strings, let the hat dangle down her back and slapped her gloves onto the bench, pointing at each pile. "Skins, needles, thread." She pulled a small bowl of water closer to the other items.

He bent closer. The items were just as he'd thought at first sight. "You want me to sew? I think you want Katherine for that. Or one of the other ladies."

Miss Violet leaned one hip against the bench and popped a fist on the other. "The ladies in the financial arm of my business are occupied with high-minded things, and Katherine? She's cooking and baking like she was dropped into my kitchen from the heavens. She's much too busy. I need you to ensure my employees have the ability to focus on work. I need you to make . . ."

She looked at the display on the bench.

He glanced at the items, then back at her.

She drew her lips in a straight line. "I'm being demure about a subject that I'm sure you understand well, being a man of your . . . looks . . . Well you must have your pick of pretty girls." She picked up one of the pieces of material.

He adjusted his hat. "Suppose so but, I've no idea what . . ."

Miss Violet stared at him.

He noted the shape of the skins. "You want me to make very tiny stockings?"

"I have to spell this out for you?"

"Suppose so."

She smoothed the shirt seam at his shoulder. "I'm trusting you, Tommy Arthur. If I confide in you then hear one whisper in the wind that you've passed this information along, it'll end badly. For you *and* your family."

He was nervous at what she was threatening, but he was starting to think she might be asking him to do something illegal. Kill someone? Break someone's legs? "Understood. I've got a lock on these lips like the secret vault in the back of the bank."

She exhaled. "All right then. The women who work, study, and live here experience a level of freedom other women don't. They're financially secure, and they're whip-smart. Due to their intelligence and business acumen, they enjoy freedoms and privileges usually reserved for men."

He raised his eyebrows.

She raised hers back at him and talked slowly. "You understand what that means, right?"

He balked. He had a guess, but it didn't quite make sense so kept it to himself.

She collapsed, gripping her chest. "Dear God in heaven, Tommy Arthur. Are you pure as the driven snow? You? Is that possible?"

She pulled his hand and turned him around, smacking him on the bottom. "Look at you. Handsome, storybook handsome. And you're naïve as . . ." She shook her head.

He was still confused. She dropped her head in her hands. "I'm going to have to write this out, aren't I?"

He lifted his shoulders. "Suppose so because I'm not sure what you want me to do."

She held up a skin. "Condoms, Tommy. You're going to make tight-as-a-drum, thin-as-a-man's-skin condoms so when a lady would like to engage freely with a man she's interested in, she can do so and not end up with child. And while some of the men who invest here enjoy the company of a lady now and then, we can't be sure where they've been with their . . ." She glanced at his crotch. "We need to protect our ladies if it comes to this."

Tommy jerked back and shoved his hand through his hair. "Whoa. All right, I understand that." He'd heard plenty of stories from the saloon crowd about painful experiences men had after lying with too many women.

She glared and spoke through gritted teeth. "You're not a holy roller, are you? Did I miss that bit of information at some point?"

He grinned, thinking of the prayers he sold, how good that made him feel earlier, but also of the things he'd stolen over the years. The world was complicated.

Miss Violet palmed Tommy's chest. "'Cause if next thing you do is start praying and telling me you're dragging me to some reverend, I'm going to take one of these needles and poke you through the heart with it. Jam it right into your chest and then bury you," she threw her thumb over her shoulder, "right there inside that wall."

The mention of a reverend made him think of Shaw and his investments with Miss Violet. Surely he wasn't involved with Miss Violet's girls. The man manipulated and stole and ran a stream of boys through Judge Calder's courtroom for profit. But this was different. He shuddered at the thought of Bernice, Olivia, or Helen having to feel Reverend Shaw's flesh against theirs.

Still, Tommy couldn't help but laugh at her threat. Not because he didn't believe Miss Violet would hurt him, but because keeping it secret was not the problem he had with this job.

"What's so all-fire funny?" Miss Violet said.

He shrugged. "I can't sew."

She groaned. "Well, you're gonna sew, and you'll do a first-class job at it because if any of the ladies turn up pregnant or sick, I'm coming to you."

"So you'll pay me extra for this? Outside of room and board owed for all the lighting of fires and hauling water and the rest of whatever chores come up like they do?"

"If you can sew a tight condom and keep everyone without child, you'll be worth your weight in gold."

He straightened up to his full height.

She smacked his shoulder. "Well, not *your* weight. My weight, maybe. Let's just see your work before we discuss bonuses of any sort."

He pulled a piece of paper from his pocket that he kept there for writing lists and Frank's words. "Write the directions and I'll sew you the best condoms the world's ever seen."

"It's a deal, Tommy."

Chapter 15

Father, the word, the person, the thought brought stinging pain. Ever since the letter came heralding his arrival in midsummer, Tommy had begun to segment time in large portions. His father never appeared as planned. Then late summer, early fall, and midfall rolled by without Frank G. Arthur appearing. Conflicted by worry that harm had come to his father and anger and disappointment that he probably just went west, Tommy had begun to pull the death sheet over the eyes of the man he once thought his father was. Not knowing what happened made it all the worse, all the harder to let go. He wasn't even sure what he was letting go of anymore and so he found ways to numb the loss, the betrayal.

Tommy's days were rooted in work for Miss Violet, peppered with prayer sales, and flavored with odd jobs and a return to school.

Katherine had been invited to take her classes in Miss Violet's kitchen, in between her kitchen mistress duties. It surprised Tommy that Katherine agreed to this since her interests had always been more with the arts, history, and reading. But the financial empire Miss Violet was building was certainly worthy of Katherine's time and attention. When she wasn't working, she spent time with the Arthurs' old friend, Aleksey Zurchenko, who was studying law and working on a farm.

Tommy suspected there was romance blooming between the two. If there was any male who Tommy would trust with his sister, with her heart, it would be Aleksey Zurchenko. And so it was reassuring that he came around time to time, giving Tommy one less thing to worry about when it came to Katherine.

Tommy made it to school several times a week, but he often left at lunch. He wanted to please Mama and sometimes even imagined himself as a lawyer or business owner, like those who invested with Miss Violet, but his personality wasn't suited for formal schooling.

His teacher, Miss Hawthorne, threatened to box his ears if he didn't follow her rules more closely, but since he easily completed the work she assigned, she let his afternoon absences slide. When needed he submitted a note from Reverend Shaw stating that he was busy tending the poor and all should be forgiven.

Outside the school, Miss Hawthorne waited for him as he approached. "Thomas Arthur," she said through clenched teeth, "this is the third day this week you've been tardy or absent."

"Talk, talk, talk," Frank said when Tommy approached her at the school steps. Tommy handed her his papers. "I did my essay."

She read a few lines, a smile tugging at one side of her mouth. "Don't dare sneak that beastly bird into the school."

"Aww, he knows more words than Paddy O'Dell. I think Frank's earned a seat."

"Pretty, pretty, pretty," Frank said, startling Miss Hawthorne, who was plain as mud in autumn in Des Moines. Frank went most places with Tommy, yet only Pearl welcomed him into indoor spaces like the post office.

Miss Hawthorne straightened and crossed her arms. "I noticed Frank hidden in your knapsack on Tuesday, his little beak and eyes peeking out sometime during history recitation."

Tommy felt bad for lying to his teacher, but on that day it was raining bullets, and though Frank was built for the outdoors, Tommy couldn't bear the thought of leaving him to be drenched while Tommy memorized dry facts in a building with a hot, cozy fire to warm the students.

"I'm sorry, Miss Hawthorne." Tommy pulled a folded paper out of his pocket and opened it. "But look. Frank's word list grows nearly every day."

Miss Hawthorne took it. "Frank's words: talk, pretty, lady, rose, hello, chew the fat, fat man, hands up, magnificent." She jolted and widened her eyes at Tommy. "Magnificent?"

Tommy nodded.

"Thirty words!" She ran her finger down the paper. "Orotund?" She sighed and stared at the paper even as she was handing it back to Tommy. "You're right, he knows way more than Paddy O'Dell, you're certainly—" She shook her head and straightened, face flushed. "Well, that was inappropriate of me."

"Just the truth, Miss Hawthorne. Frank's exceptional." They let the other half of that hang unsaid—that O'Dell was not.

Her face drooped and took on a pleading expression. "Well, Ginny Pierce'll come undone if she sees a bird in the school after that situation at the river when the woodpecker went at her hair."

"If she stopped wearing those feather hats big enough to house a family of six inside that won't—"

Miss Hawthorne held her hand up. "I appreciate Frank's dedication to language, but he stays outside. Has to."

A crack of thunder startled them. "Another storm," she said. "Come, come." She patted his shoulder.

He thought of the job he'd been hired to do later that day. If it stormed too hard, it would ruin his chance to work for the tannery. His plan to send money the next day to Texas to reduce his father's debt (no matter what excuse Frank Arthur had for not appearing by midsummer, Tommy wanted the debt erased) would be delayed. But if he could work before the storm broke, he'd at least earn some.

Luckily he had something for Miss Hawthorne. He pulled a paper from his pocket. "Can't. But here. Please. If Mama asks, just tell her I was here. I'll do the work. Just like today."

"Your mother paid a great deal for—"

Tommy pushed the paper toward her. "Here. For your troubles."

She frowned.

He pushed it closer. "For your sister, really. To help with the illness you mentioned the day you boxed my ears."

She drew back, hand at her throat. "I'm sorry, I just . . ."

Tommy pushed the prayer toward her again. "Part of the job, I understand. But read it. It's a prayer. I normally sell them for the reverend, but this one's free. For you."

She stared at it.

"'Specially for you."

She took the paper and read silently. Her shoulders softened, and her eyes filled with tears as her reading took on volume. "As you think of your sister, your own prayers and memories reach out, the stars like stepping stones across America, and across time, threading your strength to hers, infusing her poor health with all that is good in you. God . . ." She choked back a sob and shook her head, folding the paper into the little sack she kept around her waist with chalk and pencils. "I'm going to have to read the rest later."

He nodded. "Hope it helps." Satisfied, he sauntered away, Frank taking flight.

"Your assignment!" Miss Hawthorne called after him.

"Plenty of time for that, Miss Hawthorne. Plenty."

He broke into a jog and looked over his shoulder to see Miss Hawthorne's head bowed, the slip of paper in one hand, the other over her mouth, her shoulders shuddering before a rip of thunder sent her running up the school stairs.

**

The clouds roared in, threatening to drop buckets, the air growing thicker and heavier. Tommy bolted further toward the fringes of town to Murray's Tannery to get the barrel, scooper, and rake. He could smell the place before he could see it and was grateful he didn't have to enter the suffocating beamhouse to get his tools. Before hiring him, Mr. Murray gave Tommy a tour of the facility, sizing him up to determine which part of the process would be right for him. Men stood at stations curing, soaking, liming, scudding, bating and pickling skins. Even with Tommy's face covered by a bandanna, the stench of each job turned his stomach, making him vomit twice. More than the odor, seeing the hides manipulated and treated made the work impossible for him. He kept seeing the animals that once wore the pelts and simply couldn't bear it. Murray had shaken his head after Tommy threw up the second time and yanked him out of the beamhouse, toward the shovels and pails.

"Just shovel the shit. The more, the faster, the better."

The waste would be used to bate the skins, and though the collection of bird, dog, cow, and every manner of dung he could find was awful, it was better than what the man who beat it into the hide had to endure.

With tools in hand, he paced himself, shuffling along the road, shoveling and dumping into the barrel he slogged. After two hours or so, pinprick raindrops came, mixing with the feces, lifting the stench as though freshly laid, making Tommy gag with every scoop.

Grateful he'd listened to some of James's prattling on about weather predictions, Tommy could tell that though the clouds were heavy and black, they would crawl by without fully releasing rain, at least not in the buckets that most would suspect.

Tommy circled back toward the tannery as a rumble of thunder shook him. Focused, shoveling and dumping with machine precision, he stopped to catch his breath and looked into the sky. The clouds churned, no longer looking to be the kind that would hold their load. He reminded himself that though the weather could be read to some degree, there was much that didn't follow rules and speculation. The blizzard that killed his brother made that case.

He delivered the waste, collected a fistful of coins, and started home. The storm struck as he was passing into the older section of town, dark sky splitting open like trousers ripping up the back seam. Fat dime-sized raindrops drenched him to the bone. Hot lightning bolts zigged and zagged. One left a steaming black scar on a roadside tree. Raining so hard he could barely see, he worried he might be the next thing struck and ducked under the awning at Churchill's Saloon. A small poster with a tiger trying to get away from something or someone was in the window along with a poster featuring dice and another with a billiard table.

He craned to catch sight of Frank the crow but couldn't see him through the rain that marred his view. He cupped his hands. "Frank!" He strained to hear him, the flap of wings or a word spoken. Nothing. He ran into the street, looking this way and that. "Frank!"

Lightning struck the road ten feet ahead of him, shaking the ground, sending shocks up his spine, propelling him into the saloon.

Chapter 16

Tommy drew deep breaths and removed his hat. His hair stood on end from the lightning striking so close, skin tingling, scalp tickling. He rubbed his neck and looked back out the door. Frank was safe. He had to be.

The stench of beer and whiskey mixed with male body odor, cigars and pipe smoke. The crowd's murmurs were punctuated by the gravelly-voiced faro dealer. "Remove your bets, place your bets, copper your bets, no more bets."

Slap, slap. Two cards dealt followed by a pause, then the wounded roar of losers whose bets had been laid on the wrong cards. The clinking of bone and wooden checks being stacked by the dealer and the coffin keeper sliding clay beads to indicate cards dealt rose above the din.

The dealer said through teeth gripping his pipe, "Remove your bets, place your bets, copper your bets, no more bets."

Wild. The game moved with quick pain or ecstasy.

"Wanna buck the tiger?" a voice from the bar asked. Tommy shook his head as he dripped on the pitted pine floor. He wasn't about to gamble away what he'd earned on a game that resulted in more pain than pleasure for most.

"Chuck-a-luck?" the barkeep said.

Tommy glanced to the far end of the space where a dealer sent an hourglass-shaped chicken wire spinner rotating, three dice inside it tossed and turned. The thunk of billiard balls drew his attention through the thick cigar and pipe smoke.

The barkeep set his revolver on the bar. "Don't recognize you. You with that asshole purity pusher? The one trying to sneak in every other day?"

Tommy thought for a moment.

"You slow or somethin'?"

These puritans inadvertently fed the corrupt system that funneled kids through Judge Calder's courtroom to look as though he was fulfilling his promises. "No." Tommy smacked his hat against his leg to remove the remaining water.

"You a member? Dripping all over my floors like that?" A woman with black hair spiraling down her back moseyed toward him, lifting a glass of amber liquid.

The barkeep wiped down the wood top. "Git that boy a seat at my bar, Dotty, or show him out the door. Looks like he's thinkin' about becoming a member of our proud establishment."

A flash of lightning made everyone jump. Though Tommy had no interest in joining anything, he wasn't going back into the weather. Dotty pulled a stool out from under the bar with her foot. Tommy sat. The barkeep pressed a coin into her palm and kissed her fingers as she wrapped them around the money. She sashayed away, heading back to the door to greet some men coming in. Tommy nodded hello to the man beside him.

The man cringed. "Christ on a cross. You been rollin' in shit, boy?"

Tommy's nose had gotten accustomed to the stench of waste he'd been shoveling. His wet clothing must have amplified the odor. The man grabbed his arm.

"What's yer game?"

Tommy glanced around the room as though the answer to his confusion was somewhere outside of him.

He gripped harder. "That's it, come in here smellin' like hell so you don't have to pay yer fee."

"Fee?"

"Next new guy at the bar buys the guy beside him a drink. That or get yer nose broken."

Tommy shot a look at the bartender, who lifted his shoulders. Tommy tried to leave, but the man readjusted his hand.

"I ain't foolin'."

"I just—"

The man gripped harder, shutting Tommy up. He wanted to shelter until the storm passed, but the seriousness of this demand was clear, and he wasn't in the mood to fight. He pulled some of the coins he'd just earned from his pocket and slid two bits across the bar. The barkeep poured the man a shot of whiskey and he released Tommy's arm.

Tommy exhaled deeply and scratched the back of his neck, relieved to not have to tussle. Another man slid onto the stool next to Tommy and slapped a dollar bill onto the bar.

Tommy lifted his hand to signal the barkeep. "Water, please, kindly."

The barkeep slid a whiskey shot in front of the new man and in front of Tommy. Tommy lifted his hand again. "No whiskey." He *wanted* it all right. The scent of it thrilled him, the desire for it, knowing he shouldn't drink it created electric tension.

No. Too many times he'd selected the booze over common sense.

Anxiety knotted in his belly, and he hoped it wouldn't explode into full-blown panic. Maybe just a sip to relieve the yearning.

He eyed it. *Silly. It's a little glass of liquid.* He reminded himself of all he'd survived. He could certainly say no to a tiny shot of whiskey. Choosing right was the mark of manhood. He thought of Mr. Zurchenko, father of a passel of kids on the prairie. He was the one man Tommy had seen as all-around perfect. Much as he loved his own father and wanted him to return, he saw his struggles, that pain infiltrated him, caused him to have to leave, to make decisions that he wouldn't have if not in such desperate straits.

But Mr. Zurchenko never strayed, not even when sinking into despair over the death of several of his children and sorry prospects. The man barely spoke, but when he did, his words always made Tommy stop, their delivery and meaning reverberating in his chest. "Mark of a man," Mr. Zurchenko said at dinner with all the neighbors, using his hands to clarify, "is his *dorozhka*. Wrong choices happen, yes. But *men* can step onto *new* paths anytime. Repeated choosing, right as can be, or wrong, is what defines a man. *Dorozhka*. Find the right one. Easy." Recalling the strong foreign words, Tommy could hear the bold roll of Mr. Zurchenko's Russian propping up his weaker English, and the feel of the man's purpose, his mentorship came alive as though he were there. Tommy could choose well just like Mr. Zurchenko.

The barkeep glanced at the new patron who slowly turned his gaze on Tommy. Tommy realized the whiskey had been bought for him by the next new guy, as he now understood was custom.

Tommy pushed the glass toward the man who'd bought it for him. "Doesn't sit well with me." He rubbed his belly. It was one thing to take a swig of whiskey to calm a frantic attack, but it was another for Tommy to start flinging back drinks in a saloon. It was too good, too much fun, too much trouble.

The man smiled, his stubbly lips parting to reveal just four yellowed, dangling teeth. "Well, yer stench don't sit well with me." He rubbed his belly in a mocking way. "But I ain't been impolite about it."

The man brushed the glass back toward Tommy with the back of a dirt-encrusted hand. If Tommy hadn't smelled so bad, he was certain this man's odor would have overwhelmed him.

The barkeep leaned onto the bar and looked between Tommy and the new man. "Too early for carousing, boys. Let's just keep with the mannerly fashion of Colt Churchill's fine establishment." He knocked on the bar. "That Mrs. Hillis, running around trying to save the sad and derelict, the purity pushers, the bad masquerading as the good? I ain't in the mood today to have a fight and the police arrive to toss one of you into jail. And I wonder 'bout you, boy." He glared at Tommy. "You better not be the eyes and ears of that man working to clean up the streets at the expense of good businesses like mine."

Tommy put his hands up. "Swear on my life. I'm the last one to side with some sort of purity fella."

The barkeep gestured toward the whiskey; the wisdom of Mr. Zurchenko dissolved while the tension from declining the drink surged. The only way he'd resolve the lure would be to take the drink. Just one. It would settle his nerves and satisfy these bar rules he'd just learned. He tossed back the shot, the hot liquid screaming down his throat. He didn't want to tell them that his real problem was how much he liked to drink, not the opposite.

He straightened on his stool. "Maybe a water now."

The men around Tommy laughed. "No water."

Another man, dressed in fine wool clothing, slid behind the bar and turned a faucet, filling a glass with clear water.

Tommy pointed toward that.

"Ten-cent piece for that. Look at the clear deliciousness," the man beside Tommy said.

Tommy groaned and reached into his pocket for the change he'd earned earlier. His fingers easily avoided his Indian Head penny, and he slapped a ten-cent piece on the bar.

All the men threw their hands up at once. "Ohhhhh, here we go."

Tommy raised his shoulders, unsure what was happening. "What?"

"A new member, fellas."

"Member of what?" Tommy said.

"The club." The finely dressed man turned and opened his arms. "Churchill's Billiards. I'm Colt Churchill."

He'd seen Colt Churchill somewhere before. Heard his name. "Look, I can't afford a club. I just came out of the rain and wanted a water and—"

"This ain't no one-bit joint, my friend. This here requires two bits to join, and then when you come back to visit us, the water's free. It's a great deal, really."

Tommy crossed his arms, knowing it was only a good deal if he was ducking out of storms on a regular basis.

"One-time fee. You sat here long enough that you're obligated to pay."

Tommy recoiled. One of the men pointed to the sign on the far left wall that stated the rules. He blew out some air.

A man slapped Tommy on the back, and the barkeep put another whiskey in front of him. "Can't go back into the storm now anyhow. Might as well."

Tommy nodded but didn't drink the whiskey right off. He signed the membership book with the phony name he used when he needed it—Zachary Taylor. The men began telling tales of adventure and exploits that kept him laughing and unable to remember when exactly he took that next drink. Or the next. Were there more?

When the boozy warmth had him wishing he could take a bottle home to drink in private, he got up to leave.

He towered over most of the men, backing up, waving good-bye to his new club friends. He considered it might be nice to have a place where he could get a drink and chat. He was convinced for that moment that he could manage one whiskey and one water— no, several waters—and enjoy the chance to socialize. "Okay, okay. So if I join, I get water when I need it? I'm in."

The men shrugged. "Well, you know. Mostly."

He backed up further and bumped into the faro dealer, causing him to jostle the spindly game table. The checks sprayed across the board, and men started screaming, heading for Tommy. When they parted, Tommy saw *him* sitting at a table near the billiards.

Judge Calder. Tommy's breath caught as his gaze connected with the judge. The man squinted and scratched his forehead, and Tommy knew Calder was sorting through his memory. Tommy had to get out of there, grateful he'd given his phony name, Zachary Taylor, to the barkeep when signing the club rolls.

A crack of thunder accompanied by a lightning strike froze all the men at once. In the space between startling noise and light, Tommy ran.

As he trotted home, the sky rumbled, rain dumped. He burst into the shed. Leaning against the wall, breathing heavy, he heard a hollow knock at the door. A cawing sound told him it was Frank. But who had knocked? He opened the door to find Frank standing on the porch alone, his feathers glistening with moisture that pearled then rolled off his wings. He had pecked at the door like a person. "That was you?" Tommy asked.

Frank took to the air. Tommy put his hands out and the bird landed in them, rubbing his black head against Tommy's palms, emitting a sound Tommy could only describe as purring like a cat.

Chapter 17

Panic still gripped Tommy after seeing Judge Calder so close up. He reminded himself that if the judge remembered him, it would be from his time in jail and he had given a phony name, so there was no connection to his mother, no real risk of the judge finding Tommy or telling his mother.

Tommy pulled the little dish he kept for Frank's water under the porch trellis so the bird could drink without being doused by rain. He petted Frank's head, the movement allowing relief to settle in, and Tommy calmed. He stripped out of his reeking clothes, needing to soak them immediately to avoid the stench sinking in and having to relegate them to work clothes for good.

The family who'd bought the original property had lived in the shed until they'd built the big house and the servant quarters so there was a large stone fireplace available for warmth and household chores. Tommy hauled water inside, dumping it into the larger pot he'd set up. He lit the kindling and blew on it until the fire roared. He dumped his filthy clothing into the warming water and cleaned himself from head to toe with the soap Katherine had made. He even rinsed his mouth with peppermint water she'd given him for a stomachache, wanting to remove the taste of booze even if he couldn't shake its numbing results.

He pulled on fresh underthings and work clothes that were stained and ratty, but clean. Remembering the trunk the former owners had left behind, he dug through it and found a newsboy hat. As the rain let up, he dragged a rain barrel into the shed and emptied half of it into a large pot.

Leaving the water to heat, Tommy headed to his family's house to get soap flakes and a washboard. He entered the kitchen to find Mama serving a bowl of soup to Mr. Hayes and Yale.

Mama's face brightened. This buoyed him, and he ignored the irritation that the initial trade of tilling for bread had run its course, yet Mr. Hayes was still helping with the garden and often enjoying meals with Tommy's family, as if he were part of it. The two men nodded hello to each other.

"That storm was something else, wasn't it?" Mama said, brushing back Tommy's hair.

"It was." Tommy drew back, unsure whether he'd successfully scrubbed away all traces of whiskey scent.

"Have some potato soup. Katherine made it for Miss Violet's meeting, and there was extra. Bread, too. The cinnamon and raisins melt in your mouth."

Tommy rubbed his growling stomach. He *was* hungry. "Could I take a bowl to the shed? I worked a job for the tannery, and my clothes smell like all heck. I've got a fire started to soak and wash them."

Mama smiled a little smile, eyeing Tommy suspiciously. "You're not troubling me with your filthy clothing? Very mature, Tommy." He liked the compliment, even for something insignificant.

He pulled the cellar door open and peered at the shelf where they stored the soap and other supplies. He picked up the washboard. "Yeah, that stench would curl your hair. Wouldn't do that to you."

He glanced at Mr. Hayes, who was watching mother and son.

"Well, thank you," Jeanie said. "Helps a lot since I have a meeting with Mrs. Hillis and Mr. Hayes."

Tommy set the soap and washboard by his feet. Mrs. Hillis's name had been mentioned in the saloon. She and Mama had been friends before the Arthurs left Des Moines, and she'd talked to Mama since they'd come back, but he was surprised to hear Mrs. Hillis would continue to associate with his mother since so many of her other friends would not.

"What kind of meeting?" He lifted his chin at Mr. Hayes.

"Apparently the masters of our little Des Moines universe are looking to clean up the town, one orphaned child by one desperate child by one wayward boy at a time."

"Shoving them into Glenwood by the dozen," Mr. Hayes said.

Mama and Mr. Hayes shook their heads, the two of them seeming to share additional, silent thoughts.

"Some of the folks at Glenwood have good intentions, but I've seen as much harm as help," Mr. Hayes said. "Every child in Des Moines is threatened with a stay there at some point growing up. But there's a reason it works as a threat."

A crack of thunder shook the windows.

Mr. Hayes turned in his chair, squinting into the yard. "Not sure we should take Yale into the weather tonight. Thought it was past us, but doesn't look like it now."

Mama agreed then patted Tommy's arm. "Could you sit with Yale? People need to see upstanding men at these meetings because half the judges in town are playing half the citizenry against each other, claiming Mrs. Hillis and others like me are raging females set on letting feral children run wild, robbing and stealing and turning the streets brown. As if they're not brown every blessed day of the year anyway."

Tommy squirmed but didn't answer. He was happy to sit with Yale, but the idea that Mr. Hayes and Mama were spending so much time together wrenched his insides.

Mr. Hayes spread butter on a slice of bread. "Some of the aldermen are playing a game, judges, too, shuffling kids in and out of Glenwood and a few workhouses for profit."

"I've heard those same whispers," Jeanie said.

Whispers? Tommy'd heard the booming voices, knew too well Judge Calder's hand in sorting boys in and out of jail and various workhouses to make it appear as if he was tough on crime. Meanwhile, Calder was taking breaks, gambling in saloons, letting boys be beaten in jails, and paying off reverends to supply the boys so he could show a level of rehabilitation that earned him votes and money.

"Tommy?" Mama asked, bringing him back into the conversation. "Could you? Sit with Yale? This is very important to both of us."

"'Course, Mama. For you, anything." He picked up the washboard and soapbox. He should have just walked out to get the laundry going, but he couldn't keep his trap shut. "Why's it so important to you, Mr. Hayes?"

Tommy glanced at Mama to indicate that he was on to Mr. Hayes's interest in her.

"Besides the data collection from the garden work I've been doing with your mother, she and Mrs. Hillis have enlightened me about some of the ills plaguing our growing city. My interest goes toward common societal good, Tommy. I may be studying science, but my doctoral studies at Drake are rounded with a good deal of philosophy and religion."

Tommy raised his eyebrows to keep from rolling his eyes. If Mr. Hayes hadn't been getting too close to Mama, he might have really liked the man. But as it was, Mr. Hayes seemed to be drawing Mama further and further away from thoughts of Frank Arthur.

"Sit, eat, Tommy," Mama said.

He shook his head. "I'll eat when I come back to watch Yale. Give a shout when you're ready to leave."

"Well . . . all right."

He walked out the door, hearing Mama's voice, quieter, full of questions she didn't ask, questions like whether he'd been drinking, why he was so moody. He hated that he so often reacted before thinking through his actions when it came to Mama. Mr. Hayes hanging around, helping, using information from the Arthurs' garden for his studies, didn't seem to bother Mama. Surely a man studying at Drake University wouldn't sully his reputation by taking up with a divorced woman. Yet here he was.

Nothing wrong with Mama helping Mrs. Hillis. Seeing her excited about that and the garden was good, Tommy told himself. Mrs. Hillis was the kind of woman Mama used to be, and so if they were together, Mr. Hayes's influence would be lessened. That, and seeing his mother more like her old self, was something Tommy could live with.

Chapter 18

Tommy and Yale sat on the porch off the kitchen, watching slow, thick raindrops hit the ground. Yale loved the garden as much as Mama, pointing to sections of the yard, naming the plants they'd grown there in the summer.

Frank landed between Tommy and Yale, making her giggle. She got onto her belly, chin resting on the back of one hand as she stroked the black feathers.

"You've got Frank purring like a cat," Tommy said.

The crow dipped his head, brushing it against Yale's hand. "Cat," she said, struggling with words she should be able to say easily by the age of five.

"Bird," the crow said. "Frank, bird."

Yale lifted her head and smiled.

"Pretty, pretty, pretty," Frank said. He and Yale tilted their heads back and forth, mirroring each other.

Tommy brushed his hand over his sister's hair. "You are pretty, sweet Yale. I just wish we knew why . . ." He didn't want to finish the sentence, even though he doubted she'd understand if he did. She was developing far slower than any child he'd ever seen. And he wouldn't be accused of paying too much attention to little ones, but he saw Yale's slowness clear as the springs that fed the well in the back. It had really hit him the first time she and Mama were back in town the year before. Yale clung to Mama like an ivy vine, whimpering for words, still prone to wet herself before she made it to the pot, lethargic.

Yale laid her cheek on one hand, and Frank rubbed his head against her fingers, making her eyes squeeze shut and her shoulders shake with laughter. Before long, she was drifting off to sleep. "Treasure," Frank said.

Tommy petted the bird. "Yes, she is."

The side gate slammed, startling Tommy. Feet crunched over the gravel walkway then stopped. Tommy pressed Yale's back and straightened, craning to hear. Perhaps someone entered the yard by accident. Wheezing. Was it wheezing? The labored breath sounded again along with the always accompanying throat clearing. Tommy stood, anxiety making him clench his jaw.

Bayard appeared with Hank on his heels. Yale didn't flinch, the setting sun reaching under the porch roof, warming her cheek, putting her into slumber.

Frank took flight.

"Hank. Bayard." Tommy wanted them gone. The less they saw of his family and their home the better. He removed his coat and put it over Yale in case she got a chill. He angled down the stairs, trying to box them out of coming onto the porch. "What can I do for you?"

Hank widened his stance and crossed his arms. Bayard leaned against the porch balustrade, causing it to wiggle. Tommy gestured. "That's rickety, Bay. Watch yourself."

"Calling me fat?"

Tommy shook his head, irritated. "What do you want?"

"Message from Judge Calder for Zachary Taylor."

Tommy scratched the back of his neck. "That right? Don't know him."

"That's the name you told him for court, for your club membership, and he recognized you today as such."

Tommy kept his face plain and without emotion. He clenched his jaw. Hank and Bayard were much too far into Tommy's business. "How the hell do you know . . . I don't know what you're talking about."

The boys smirked. "Came in just before you ran out of the saloon like a little . . ." He glanced at Yale. "Girl. Like that."

Tommy felt like the two boys had a leash on him, tethering him to them even when he couldn't see them. "You didn't tell Calder anything, did you?"

Hank smirked. "I keep secrets close like my coins, Tommy. Turns out they're often worth more than money."

"Then *what*? I don't have anything to give you. Just drank up all the money I made shoveling shit for the tannery. Surely the judge mentioned the stench I left behind."

"Yeah, he saw me call to you as you ran away. Wasn't close enough to hear me use your real name. Then I remembered when it comes to the judge, you employ an alternative calling card," Hank said.

Tommy was grateful for that much. "So?" Tommy said.

"Told Judge Calder we'd see to giving Zachary his message," Bayard said.

Tommy looked away.

Hank cleared this throat. "Be at his house next Thursday. Got work for ya."

"Seven a.m., sharp. Work clothes, back garden by the big barn," Hank said.

Tommy scratched his chin. He had school, and he'd missed enough already.

Hank moved toward Tommy as though wanting to intimidate him. Tommy was taller by a lot, but Hank was a scrapper, much stronger than he appeared. "Judge said *you* don't show, then *I'm* headed to Glenwood. That happens? I'll pummel you. Been there twice, ain't goin' back," Hank said.

Tommy drew up. No matter what he did, he couldn't seem to outrun his bad choices. Mr. Zurchenko's words returned. Maybe the path he needed to take was one that led straight out of town. He shook the words off. In that moment, he wondered if there was another *dorozhka* for him. Perhaps he'd already used up all his good opportunities, and the only roads left ran him right past all the wrong choices.

"Cat," Yale said, having opened her eyes, petting Frank's head. Tommy turned his back to her trying to block her from the boys' view. Hank leaned around Tommy and studied her, but didn't comment on her wrong labeling of the bird. Tommy couldn't leave his family again. Even with his current predicament, they needed him. He would have to trust that somehow he could get moving in the right direction without leaving town.

"You didn't breathe a word about my real name?"

They shook their heads.

Hank shoved his hands into his pockets. "Found it's better to save information than spend it at first opportunity."

"Well, thank you for that," Tommy said.

"Someday you'll repay me."

Tommy knew that was true.

"See ya round, Tommy-Zachary," Bayard said as he and Hank disappeared around the house, the wheezing and throat-clearing fading with the slam of the gate.

Tommy pulled Yale onto his lap, the setting sun bringing a crisp chill. He held her tight and rocked, her breath evening out as she fell into slumber again. He brushed her hair back and kissed her forehead, thinking of all the trouble she'd faced in her young life, right from the time she was born, the size of a prairie chicken, in that dugout in Darlington County. "You're safe, Yale, and I'll stay with you and Mama and Katherine to keep it that way. Somehow I'll do that."

He knew the promise was complicated. He searched for ways he might be able to make the secret name not matter anymore. Perhaps he should just own up to the lie, beg forgiveness.

The wind kicked up, carrying autumn crispness. Tommy carried Yale upstairs, where he tucked her into bed. He stood over her and watched her sleep peacefully.

Yale hadn't been born when the family scandal broke, yet she lived its consequences. Even after five years, many folks still held bitter thoughts and feelings for the Arthurs. Luckily the Des Moines population was growing in leaps and bounds with a good influx of people who hadn't been touched by the trouble.

In the back of Tommy's mind was Elizabeth Calder, her quietly hostile treatment of Mama, the money the judge lost when Tommy's grandfather's fragile investments crashed. It had been a mistake, a misjudgment, a series of bad luck incidents. That was different than reckless spending of money, *stealing* money.

Grandfather's suicide should have been enough to satisfy angry investors, to show that he felt so guilty and sorry about the losses that he couldn't go on. But that's not how they saw the act. They believed his death was evidence he'd been cruel and careless with other people's money. Tommy didn't take that memory out to consider very often.

He bent forward, hands on his knees, chest heavy. His father wasn't coming. His breath burned his insides. The realization pulsed with his heartbeat. *He's not coming.* The words curdled in his belly, filling him with grief he'd only reserved for James up till then. Though he thought he'd come to grips with this before, he understood right then, he hadn't. He finally knew how Mama and Katherine felt about Frank Arthur, the man. Betrayed. And the deep wound seeped.

**

Tommy tucked Yale into bed, lit a lamp and went down the darkened staircase that led to the front hall. Heading toward the kitchen, the back door squeaked open. Mama's and Mr. Hayes's voices burst with passion as they entered, words flying from one, the other picking up to finish sentences. They were appalled, determined, and disgusted at whatever they'd just learned at the meeting. Electric. Their tone and fervor could have powered the lamps at Miss Violet's.

Atrocity, cruel, unimaginative solutions, old-fashioned, unhinged.

Their descriptions about the plans the leading citizens of Des Moines proposed were supposed to save the city's children from nefarious villains. But the core of the strategy sickened Mama and Mr. Hayes.

Tommy leaned against the wall, hidden, listening, not wanting to engage. He appreciated and admired Mama's interest in helping children. Did she suspect at all that he might be on the list of wayward boys? It made sense she'd help children given her contributions to the Des Moines Women's Club before the Arthurs left for the prairie. At one point, Mama let out a long sigh and then there was silence, followed by a rustling, then quiet. The stillness was full, as loud as their voices had just been and Tommy had the distinct sense that he shouldn't look in the kitchen, that he would see something he didn't want to.

Then the quiet broke. Chairs moving over wood and papers shuffling allowed him to exhale.

"Let's go over this legislation for Mrs. Hillis one last time," Mr. Hayes said.

"All right. I think I have the energy for it. Suddenly I have the energy for everything, Reed."

Tommy could tell she'd sat at the table, that the two of them were hunkered in, heads probably together as they went over whatever legislation she was talking about. Tommy tiptoed down the hall, away from the kitchen, toward the front door. He wasn't angry that Mr. Hayes was there, not that moment, not like earlier. But their harmonized voices, their mutual goals and plans, hurt. The spark of ardor in their exchange reminded Tommy of the first time he'd met Mr. Hayes in the garden, the blush that had swept over Mama's face at the sight of him, that it had infuriated and worried him.

Now it simply drilled further into the sorrow he felt at his father not showing up midsummer. While Mama was inspired by her developing life, Tommy seemed to be floating away from her, from the life he'd planned, like a balloon attached to a string, to a wrist. He only hoped there was a string connecting him to Mama, that something to rope them together still remained.

Chapter 19

Tommy woke the day after purchasing a membership to Colt Churchill's saloon awash in dread, thinking of his various predicaments. But then just like daylight shot through small cracks in the shed, a glimmer of hope lit his mood. Recounting the night's events he realized he steered clear of the whiskey bottle after leaving Mama and Mr. Hayes to their civic planning. That was good. That was enough. For right then anyway.

The sense that he'd achieved something got him thinking about aspects of life he appreciated. Pearl. She came straight to mind. It'd been a while since Tommy had stopped at the post office.

He washed up, realizing why he'd been avoiding the building like a disease. Face dripping over the basin, he admitted to it. His father wasn't coming to Des Moines and probably wouldn't be writing. It hurt too much to be disappointed over and over. But in avoiding the post office, he missed Pearl, seeing her smile, hearing her news about other people's news, the way her face lit up when she saw Tommy, when she shared a freshly harvested word, when she shared a secret and made him pinkie promise to keep it hidden forever.

After a quick bite of bread, he completed his chores, saw that there were no requests from Miss Violet and swung by the post office before heading to Reverend Shaw's place.

He popped a sprig of grass in his mouth and entered. Inching forward, chomping on the blade, watching Pearl sort envelopes, he felt it was they who were connected, even more than he and Mama.

Pearl shuffled envelopes, her attention steadfast, her emerald eyes, like jewels blazing from across the room, causing Tommy's stomach to flutter.

She glanced up, a smile snapping to her lips. "Prince Aeriel." Her reception electrified him.

"I've been reading that precious fairy-tale book ya give me." She shook her head. "Oh, Tommy. Thank ya again fer it. I added *pages* of words to my list. And the stories, they take me away. Like a prayer. Like I've been given a new life with every story. Prince Aeriel's the one I'm on now. The words!"

She dashed around the counter and tackled him with a tight hug. She squeezed him, her head buried in his chest, shocking him. At first he froze, but then he wrapped her up, hugging right back.

She patted his back, pulled away, and dashed to her side of the counter before he had the chance to memorize how it felt to be latched in her arms, with more than their pinkie fingers locked in a promise.

Tommy's eyes burned; he couldn't speak.

"Give me a sec," Pearl said as she sprang back and forth behind the counter, hands flying, red curls bouncing. He grinned at her excitement, that she'd been too thrilled with the book to correct her grammar like she normally did around him. He'd known she would like the present, but her response was more than he expected. She finished sorting, squaring off seven piles, then wiped her brow and sighed with her whole body.

She dug into her apron pocket and pulled out a paper and shook it at him. "My list! Every single word is wonderful. Each one is fragile or big or bold or stinky! I can actually taste some of 'em. *Ill-shapen, urchin, URCHIN!* Can you believe that word? And then *nuisance, chatterbox.* I love them all. Every single one has a particular sound and shape. Like people."

"I'm so happy you like it, Pearl." Tommy edged forward, sorry that he'd stayed away from her in the attempt to protect himself from his father's letters. His chest pounded with need. He needed her? With two feet of wooden counterspace between them, he was struck by the urge to hop behind the counter and swallow her into his arms the way she had him. The impulse struck him dumb, paralyzing him. To have someone so unabashedly affectionate and excited at the sight of him, made him high, like a switch had been pressed and electricity released right into his veins.

Pearl glanced at him, put her list back into the apron, then started working again, her hands shuffling a new set of envelopes into piles like a card dealer. "Yer ma come in the other day. With that fella. Hayes . . ." She looked at the ceiling, lips pursed. "Yes, Reed Hayes lives at Drake, gets mail from the four corners of the U.S. Yes, indeedy. Can ya fathom that?"

Tommy tapped his foot and looked away.

"Sure's nice ya got that ma of yers, boy, oh boy. Other day, she stopped in—no, *floated* in like a queen, polite and fancy and *lovely* as can be." Pearl straightened her posture and made her fingers dance through the air. "Like someone wrote her right out of her own fairy story, right into that space you're standing in now. They were on an errand to buy special feed fer grass. You folks feeding yer grass? Heard it all now."

He pulled another blade of grass from his pocket and slipped it into his mouth. Tommy was stuck on Hayes. Mama and he were shopping together? Didn't he ever work at the university? "Yeah, yeah, *floating*." Tommy shrugged, knowing Mr. Hayes was the reason for Mama's light step.

Pearl stopped shuffling mail and stared. "Some bear probably squatted right over top of that grass you're chomping. Just this morning. That's disgusting, chewing grass like that."

"Says who?" He couldn't determine exactly why it was that his thoughts seemed to turn to Pearl in the night, when he woke up, and certainly when he passed the post office. His body recognized her before his mind did. He tingled all over, and he imagined his fingers roped through hers. He would waken, his sleeping clothes soaked all over, his body rigid, inflamed in a way he never imagined possible. It was as though she was with him right there, alive in his dreams, making him want to touch her, to kiss her, to have her near him all the time. Not even Miss Violet's investment ladies woke him at night.

It didn't make sense. He knew beauty and refinement. Pearl was raw. Yet her confidence, her jagged humor, honest eyes, heart-shaped face, dirt smudged as it was, made him want to love her.

He nearly choked.

Love.

Yes, that word popped into his head. He pushed that right out. He had no idea what love would have to do with Pearl. He liked her. Surely. Missed her, yes. None of that was close to the definition of love.

Yet.

Her name nearly always brought the word *love* on its tail end.

Pearl squeezed his hand. "Says anyone with a few smarts gathered inside her skull bone."

Tommy's breath caught at her touch.

"What's wrong with you? You look nauseous. Head on out if you're gonna vomit. Can't afford to get sick . . ."

She went back to her envelopes, releasing his hand, letting go of his heart. He gripped his chest, wanting to slow the thumping. He couldn't stop a smile from coming to him as his stomach flipped.

Tommy noticed then her lip was split at the corner and in the middle.

"That Reed Hayes is quite the gentleman. Reminds me of you."

"What happened to your lip?"

She shuddered and pressed fingertips on the lower one. "Well . . . just . . . chapped is all. This fall weather's dried me up like autumn oak leaves."

She angled her body away from him and he considered pressing her on that response, thinking her lip looked more swollen than chapped.

"Anyhow," she said, flipping through the mail. "Mr. Hayes, held the door for yer ma, walked to the store with her, selecting stationery. *Nice* man. Good man."

Tommy felt the blood drain from his face.

She held up two envelopes. "Been meaning to drop these to you, but I took in some sewing and had to hop on that right after work. Kept thinking you'd be in fer 'em."

Tommy eyed the envelopes, wanting them to contain truth, not empty promises.

"I know ya like to collect yer own mail, so I didn't give it over to yer ma. One's from Texas. Other's San Di-eg-o," she said, emphasizing each syllable, savoring them like Christmas sweets.

He reached for the letters, his fingertips brushing hers as she pulled them back.

"San Diego," she said it again, her voice lifting as though saying it could transport her there.

He snatched her wrist before she could pull it back. "You're sure you're all right? Your lip?" He motioned at hers.

Pearl cocked her head and smirked at him, but she didn't flinch. "'Course." They stared at each other. "I know what you're doing with these letters of yers."

She released the envelopes, and he let go of her, knowing she turned the topic on purpose.

"Reading them? That's what people do," Tommy said, now a little embarrassed, sensing that she might be reading them and resealing them. "*You* best not read them, you know. That's an invasion of privacy."

She couldn't possibly know what lurked in the hollows of his yearning for his father, yet the thought that she might was humiliating.

She brushed back her hair, tightening the bun at the back of her head. Her gaze went past Tommy, and he followed it to see that a line was forming behind him.

She cleared her throat and tapped the counter with shaggy nails. "That's it fer today, sir. Give yer ma my regards."

Tommy nodded, shoved the envelopes into his pocket, and drew up straight and tall as he turned to leave, tipping his hat to the folks lined up behind him.

Chapter 20

Tommy didn't rip open the letters and start reading as he normally did. He headed for the river, one of the places he often found a bit of calm. Maybe he wouldn't read the letters at all. Then when his father finally did show up, it'd be a delightful surprise. Delightful surprise? He marveled at the fact he now viewed his father arriving as a casual, surprising appearance, as though a mere acquaintance.

He reached the riverside and pulled the envelopes out. Maybe he should send them sailing away on the sparkling water, not having to be disappointed, or worse, become angry like Mama or disengaged with their father as Katherine was. He could keep the thread of expectation that his father had Des Moines in sight.

The return address indicated it was from the boardinghouse in Texas where his father had been staying at one point, but the writing was female and unfamiliar. Perhaps his father's landlady had gotten Tommy's letter and was sending information about his father's whereabouts. Tommy squatted and dipped a corner of one envelope into the water, a steady current rushing by. Dampness climbed up the paper. *Let it go. Better not to know.* The moisture swallowed the paper, consuming, nearly reaching the address.

He couldn't do it.

He stood and opened the letter from Texas, careful not to tear the sodden parts.

> *To Master Thomas Arthur:*
>
> *Yur father, Frank Arthur, was here but run out on his failed cotton crop and bills, past due. If you catch word uv im afore I do, tell im pay directly. Or you send it, being the son, he indicated you wer to send*

money. You, next of kin, his keeper, as the Bible says, as yur father claimd more than once yur an onerabl son. We beleved im.

Tommy's cheeks burned. He felt as though rheumatic fever gripped his internal organs. Tears stung. He rubbed his eyes with his hat and scolded himself for being a baby. *Baby.* The voice of Mr. Henderson, the cruel miner he'd boarded with, replayed in his mind, and he could feel the blow to the ear that followed. In an instant, the tears evaporated.

He stared at the envelope from San Diego. He would deal with the Texans as soon as he could, unwilling to allow Frank Arthur's name to dangle out in the world with anything else awful attached to it. He held his breath and ripped into the second envelope, fingers quivering, willing it to reveal good news.

Tommy Arthur, your pa stayed with us a piece this winter, then beat a path up north and hired on with a crew to sail to some spot I can't remember as I ain't never heard mention of the place before. Like he made it up or something. If you get word from him, point him back to us. Owes board for a month, and the money is necessary for the keeping of my children. We need to survive, too.

Bile crept up Tommy's throat. He swallowed it, blistering his stomach. How could this be true? His father responsible for another family's trouble? He rubbed his stomach, hoping to dispel the acid. Was this truly the man his father had become? Or always was? Shame followed, guilt for considering these people might have a more accurate view of his father than he did. But that's not the man he knew, the one who had walked the land with him in Dakota Territory, dreaming aloud, sharing all that was possible, making the best of things when the worst happened, when James died.

Tommy stood and went to a bench near a tree and sat, wind biting through his jacket. He closed his eyes, visualizing a map of North America. He pictured California, the path his father took to get there. He reread the letter from San Diego. No.

His father had promised to come north and east to Iowa, but clearly he hadn't done that. He wasn't merely detained and trying to make right with his debt. "I'll be in Des Moines by midsummer." Tommy had read the words in the prior letter a thousand times.

Was he already sailing the Pacific? Every statement and excuse Tommy would have once lent his father had turned into a question, had turned his sense of purpose inside out. Was he no longer tasked with helping bring his father back? He looked at the letter from the Texans. He was not his father's keeper. His father should have been his keeper, provider, protector. It was time to let go. Clearly his father had let go of him.

"Tommy Arthur," Pearl's voice cut through the wind. He looked over his shoulder. She stalked toward him in wide strides, bent forward, feet ducked outward, revealed by her tattered, too-short hem, hands balled into little fists, a force sweeping toward Tommy, making him draw back. The sight of her, the girl who set his stomach to fluttering, at this vulnerable time, turned any excitement into humiliation and anger.

She stood in front of him, fists plugged on hips. He pulled his hat down over his eyes. He couldn't let her see his tears.

He stared at her worn boots, the tips of them nearly touching the toes of his. A faint smell of lemon met his nose, and he wondered if she'd cleaned up before following him. She crossed her arms and tapped her fingers on one arm.

"Go away, Pearl."

"No."

"Please."

She paused and shuffled her feet.

He held his breath.

"I want to warn ya is all."

He exhaled deeply. She wasn't leaving.

"Mr. Nelson reported to me just after you left that Judge Calder, his merry men, and god-awful wife are riled up like hens with a fox cresting the hill. Making blustery threats about impure dealings all over town, women, gambling, con artists, fortune-tellers all settling here. They're not happy about the reputation of our fine city. Some Dreama woman who talks to ghosts and such got everyone's hair set afire. Meetings are set, mobs are forming, and the law's gonna stop her just like they did Madame Smalley."

She breathed deep after unloading the information in one breath.

Tommy pretended to be reading the letter and watched her feet shuffle again. He didn't know what to say.

She shifted her feet. "I seen ya working for the reverend. The wind rushed by my ears saying his boys are up to no good. *You're* up to no good, then, I s'pose?" She balled her fists at her sides. "That's Miss Violet Pendergrass you living next to, right?"

Tommy nodded once.

"Well, she and the rev and such are running some wrong business there. Heard tell you're working for 'em."

Tommy leaned forward, forearms on his legs. "You just heard all this now?"

"Parts of it. I pieced the rest of it together to get me to this point where I see you heading for trouble."

He shook his head. "Miss Violet's as nice a woman as I can name. I do chores for her." He thought of the condoms he'd been tasked with making but dismissed it. "Katherine works the kitchen. Mama works the garden and runs errands. We board in the tiny house next door. Violet keeps a respectable business. I've seen plenty of leading citizens, fine men, there. *Women*, real smart ones just burning through textbooks under her watchful eye. Other women trusting their money with Miss Violet. You've read the articles about her, right?"

"She's up to illegal dealings. She ain't no—"

"*Isn't. Ain't* ain't a word," he said before he could pull the words back into his mouth. He looked her straight in the eye for the first time since she'd arrived.

She drew back, her expression wounded. In that moment, he could see right into her heart, each of his angry words tattooed there. Pearl didn't have the gift of a gambler's face.

The guilt was immediate. "I mean, if you want to talk proper like you say you do. I didn't . . ."

"Well," her voice quivered. She cleared her throat, glanced away, then gathered herself up. "Maybe you oughta trade that book learning for some street smarts before yer tail end gets tossed in the slammer with them boys you pal 'round with."

She had that right. Tommy didn't want to spend any time in jail at all. The stench of urine and perspiration and dirty hair was fresh in his mind, as though he'd been there that day. He thought of the doodads Hank and Bayard had stolen while Tommy was busy delivering the prayers. It was certainly possible people were on to them. Hank and Bayard had starring roles in Judge Calder's clean-up-the-streets scam, where he tossed them into jail for effect and then released them to do it again.

Still, they would've warned him if something was about to happen to him. Wouldn't they? They were the ones who said Tommy was to go to the judge's house to work. Were they sending him right into trouble?

Tommy looked at the letters in his hand. He'd crumpled them into a ball. He didn't like Pearl seeing him like this, in his natural, worrisome state. He'd worked hard to maintain a hard, confident shell. Two letters cracked the façade. Pearl's news kicked the exposed belly. Tommy was the only surviving son. He needed to shoulder the family's burdens in Des Moines, not worry so much about his father's splintered trail.

James never had to work hard at being a moral person in the way the Bible and clergy suggested. Yes, Tommy's moral *dorozhka* was more serrated than straight, but he was still headed in the right direction, choosing the right . . . wasn't he? He was sure if he had to face God the next day, the Great Father wouldn't hold his lifting of items against him. If there was a God, he'd fully understand every action Tommy took to preserve his family. Heck, if James were still alive, even he would've lifted an apple or trinket if it meant staying alive or keeping them together.

But Tommy had to wonder. Were people really talking about his work with the reverend? He had to get away and collect himself before he burst into full, self-pitying tears. Though he knew anything he'd stolen had been for good reason, Pearl wouldn't understand. Her moral path was set in granite. Mr. Zurchenko would love Pearl for just that reason and Tommy couldn't bear seeing disappointment in her face if she knew the truth about him. Her scolding expression said as much.

He pushed past her, jogging away. He glanced back as he headed through the trees.

The last thing he saw was confusion drape Pearl's face. He hated to make her feel bad, but the last thing he needed was her seeing him cry like a baby.

Chapter 21

The Thursday Tommy was due at Judge Calder's home came quicker than he expected. He'd been hoping somehow the day would never arrive or that he could skip over it. His nerves threatened to fire up the panic that was always a whisper away. He calmed himself by repeating that he was arriving as Zachary Taylor, not as Tommy Arthur, who'd spent countless hours and parties at his mother's best friend's house as a child. He'd been ordered to meet the judge at the barn, not the house. Judge Calder hadn't recognized Tommy in large part due to him changing from a boy to a man over the years, but also Jeremy Calder had married Elizabeth when the Arthurs were away on the prairie.

You'll be fine. Just do the work then leave.

He was fairly sure he'd steer clear of Elizabeth Calder since he was to work in the barn. Though she might recognize Tommy on the spot, he was relatively sure she wouldn't. He was out of context for her, no longer dressed in fine wools and the latest fashions. He was fairly certain she wouldn't give him a second glance on his state of dress alone. He'd had several close calls with her since he'd been back in Des Moines, but each time she'd been sufficiently distracted with self-centered preening or, like in the post office, he was simply hidden from view.

He entered the property at the back, a sturdy gate and fence sections having been built since he and his friends used to cut through the property daily to get to school. He jiggled the latch on the gate as Judge Calder came toward him, shouting his name.

He unlocked the gate and waved Tommy into the field.

"Damn thieves have been sneaking off with the hens. Someone stole two cows the other day. The balls on these heathens."

"Awful," Tommy said, following the judge to the barn.

"We have two boys with duties in the house and the outer property, but each was needed for other tasks today. When I saw you at the saloon the other day, I thought you would be perfect to fill in for them."

How often? Tommy swallowed hard. "I have school normally."

"School? Big boy like you? Farm's your future."

Tommy shrugged, not wanting to disclose anything about his breeding that would cause the judge to ask specific questions.

"If you're not in jail half your life."

Tommy winced and glared at Judge Calder, who was surveying his land, seeming satisfied the words were insulting.

Frank circled above the judge and Tommy as they moved toward the barn. He let out a caw and dove toward them, swooping over their heads so close they heard the flap of his wings when he lifted upward. "Bastard," the bird said clear as day, piercing the conversation and the soft wind blowing across the field. Frank did this sometimes, playing with Tommy as they went about their business.

Judge Calder halted and looked into the sky, shielding his eyes against the bright sun. Frank's black body swept in and out of the glare. "That son-of-a bitch bird just breezed my lid."

Tommy stopped breathing for a moment, hoping Frank wouldn't land on his shoulder.

"Did he call you a *bastard*?"

Tommy scratched the back of his neck. *Not me.* "Naw, just the wind making us think we're hearing things. Impossible."

"Crows are smart, you know." Judge Calder puffed his chest out. "Could swear he called you a bastard."

Tommy let the idea that the bird may have called the judge a bastard hang between them.

Judge Calder shrugged and waved Tommy along to follow him as he glanced into the sky now and again, keeping his eye on the circling bird. "If it weren't crazy, I'd say that bird's following us."

"Just looking to break his fast, probably," Tommy said. Now Tommy was the one who was satisfied, amused.

When the judge refocused on the barn, Tommy lifted his arm and signaled Frank to wait in a nearby tree.

"You're going to finish splitting that wood."

Tommy could do that quickly.

"Then you'll haul it inside, and the maid will direct you where to put the logs. Wife's got some hooty-hoot gathering of hens today, and she wants goddamn wood in some fireplaces and coal in the furnace. Replacing it all with steam heat soon. But you're gonna split the wood, nice and pretty so it looks neat when it's piled by the fireplace."

Tommy eyed the wood that had been set to dry under the barn overhang and inside it.

"And as you're swinging that axe, you think about how generous I am to give you this opportunity to work off your debt to society. Could have hauled you off to jail again for gambling like I saw you."

"But—"

Tommy clamped down on the words, *I wasn't gambling. You were*, before he said them.

The judge grabbed Tommy's shoulder. They were the same height, and though no one had deemed Tommy to be slight since he was ten years old, he wasn't as thick as the judge. Judge Calder dug his thumb just under Tommy's collarbone. "Don't start thinking I was at that saloon in a nefarious way. Sometimes a man has to get inside the filthy guts of a problem to clean it up. My work's important, and it gets a little dirty at times."

The judge paused. Tommy nodded, trying to keep from buckling under the extraordinary pain the man's thumb managed to inflict. Tommy bit down on his honest thoughts about what the judge had said.

"I'm providing you an easement to the right side of the road, Zachary. I think you understand what I'm saying. Hank and Bayard—fine young men—*they* understand and swore you would, too. Told them they'd spend their days locked up if you disappointed. Their continued refuge at the church depends on you, Taylor. And though gambling is illegal, your name is now on the board at Churchill's, and you need to pay off your debt there."

Tommy scowled.

"Complicated, I know. Good, bad, legal, and illegal. Just do what you're told. For the sake of your friends."

Tommy nodded. He knew it was for his own sake. If the fellas felt threatened at all, they'd spill all the details to Mama and the judge. He picked up the axe near the barn door. "What will I be paid, then, with all this debt to pay off?"

"Stupid. Maybe you *should* attend school just so you can exhibit a modicum of intelligence." He swung his arm toward tree trunks. "After you split the wood that's dry then get busy cutting those and haul it into the barn. I already paid for your freedom. This job *is* your pay. The opportunity to do honest work. Colt Churchill wanted you to pay the whole shebang a week back. Or see jailtime. I vouched for you." Tommy had lost track of the tab once he'd spent all his tannery money.

"Vouch for me to someone running a—" Tommy bit the inside of his cheek, insulted, but not willing to make things worse.

Judge Calder jerked his head toward the wood and walked away.

Tommy released his anger by cutting the wood at a frantic pace, then hauled it to the back porch of the Calder home, where he would be told how many logs went to which rooms. He knocked on the kitchen door, knowing the help would answer, not Mrs. Calder. Still, being so close to running into her sent his nerves blazing again. The scent of bread, chicken, and even steak filled his nose and made his stomach growl. A gray-haired woman answered the door and waved him in with a meaty hand. She jerked her head toward a door. "Wash up in there."

Tommy glanced at the door, then followed her. "Wash up? I'm supposed to carry wood, I thought."

She turned on her heel, spreading her arms, wild-eyed. Her apron was stained with gravy and meat drippings. "Listen to directions, boy. I ain't got time to train you up like a baby. Hell, ain't even my job to manage the help, but here I is doing it. So shake a leg. Lady of the house don't like no one inside with grubby paws. Wash the hell up without a peep."

Tommy shrugged, annoyed that everyone seemed to think their time was precious and his was for their taking.

He entered the washroom. Pretty, clean, and wallpapered, it was similar to Miss Violet's. He locked the door and lifted the lid on the toilet seat. He exhaled and focused on the wall behind the toilet. What he saw caused him to freeze in the process of relieving himself. Right in front of him was the painting. *The painting.* The one from McCrady's window. In the washroom, above the toilet, covering the entire wall. There it was.

He forced himself to finish using the toilet and flushed. He washed his hands and turned back to the painting, hanging where the help relieved themselves. As angry as he'd been at Judge Calder's condescending threats and arrogance, so sure Tommy was stupid, *this*, the hanging of a valuable painting of his family in the bathroom, enraged him.

He forced his memory back to the day he saved Mama from shooting the people she saw as looters. Images of that day flew through his mind as though he was experiencing the event all over again. Elizabeth Calder had taunted Mama with feigned concern while slipping jewelry into her pockets.

That day he'd been so focused on keeping Mama from killing someone, he hadn't really thought of Elizabeth and what was behind her "concern."

A bang on the washroom door startled Tommy. "Get the lead out, boy," the cook growled.

He glanced over his shoulder at the painting one last time and shut the door behind him. The cook pulled a paper from her pocket. She wafted it open with one hand and read, "Ten logs in each of the indicated rooms. Neatly stacked, then sweep area around logs and pick up any shred of wood or bark on floor."

She looked up from the paper. "Can you read?"

He nodded.

"The missus drew a map of the rooms to show where you put the wood. Last dummy had the whole thing reversed and had to redo it. Don't believe the judge when he says the boys had something else to do. He stuffed them away in a jail cell just for being stupid."

Tommy's eyes widened.

"And don't consider telling Judge Calder I said any of that 'cause he won't believe you, and you'll be in the cell with those other two next."

"But—"

She shoved the paper against his chest, shutting him up. "Don't ask why. Doesn't matter, does it?"

He understood that.

She threw a long swatch of fabric at him. "You look strong. Stack the logs in sets of ten, tie with this, and carry the whole mess. It'll cut your work in half."

He nodded. "Thank you."

He did as the cook said, following the map. He encroached on the cook's time once by asking her to check his work to be sure he'd started with the map in the right direction. She swore and mumbled the whole way to the first room on the list, a bedroom at the far end of the second-floor hall, but she confirmed it was correct. He was free to work as quickly as possible.

"Ms. Calder's lady friends'll arrive just as you finish the front parlor. Make it neater than any pin you've seen or her wrath'll be worse than his. Better to be in jail than at her mercy."

Tommy's breath caught. He couldn't risk anyone at this gathering seeing him face-to-face. He moved quickly. Loading, tying the fabric, hauling it to each room, sweeping up bark and debris. He rushed through the work, wanting to finish long before the ladies arrived, but being careful not to draw Mrs. Calder's attention, having to duck into bedrooms and closets to avoid her twice.

He barely glanced at anything in the rooms until he finished the parlor. Relieved to finally be done, he paid attention to the delicate, ornate furnishings, silver and porcelain objects. Distinctive items made him think of the reverend: a silver pack of elephants, large crystal paperweights, and landscape paintings drew his eye. He suddenly felt as though he were back in his own home. And not because these things *recalled* his former wealth, but because they were the actual items his family once owned. So many things.

He couldn't believe he hadn't thought of this in five years, that when people had taken his family's belongings in legal payment for their losses that he'd ever see them again, that he would ever have to imagine someone else using them. Mama. Her pride, her sorrow in losing her father, their entire standing all at once tore at him, making fresh wounds. The devastation at the time, her trembling hand when he'd held it and led her from the house when they realized there was no point in staying, that there was nothing to protect any longer.

His only solace was knowing his mother didn't have to see this. He picked up one of the elephants, remembering when his father had given them to Mama. He needed to get away from Judge Calder, somehow get the boys to tell the judge that Zachary Taylor had left town and then avoid him for the rest of his life. Or perhaps he should work to move his family out of Des Moines. There were plenty of places to start again, again, again. Always starting over.

But they'd be together and without any of this burden. He set the elephant down and picked up a silver pen, an envelope opener, and a small rattle. He wanted to jam them into his pocket. They were Mama's. The very pen she had used to draft her articles. The Arthurs had paid their debt. Mama deserved these things back. He could tell her he recovered them from McCrady's. He started to shove them into his pocket. No. It would only lead to more trouble.

The sound of the door chimes reverberating through the house startled him. He dropped to the floor to sweep around the logs again and finished as a gaggle of women headed for the parlor. He went to the second opening to the hallway and waited for the women to leave the foyer so he could dash down the hall to the butler's pantry and into the kitchen, unnoticed.

The women grew quiet as they looked around the beautiful parlor, admiring it all. A familiar voice filled his ears. Two familiar voices. He held his breath. It couldn't be true. Not this. Why?

Elizabeth's condescending tone came again. "Jeanie, you're here. It's so . . . Well, you're here. I didn't think you'd actually come."

"She's doing magnificent work for the children. Better than ever, more than ever, isn't that right, Jeanie?" another woman said.

Tommy knew that voice but couldn't place it. He leaned into the hall just enough to see. Mrs. Hillis. Yes. Her. She looped her arm through Mama's, smiling as though their friendship hadn't been impacted by the scandal or divorce, not like it had the others. Tommy's heart quickened at the thought that someone in town, an old acquaintance more than friend, treated Mama with the respect she deserved. His heart contracted at the thought of how she was dressed, her clothing the usual of late—worn, out of fashion, drab. But there was Mrs. Hillis treating Mama like royalty.

Elizabeth ushered the women toward the parlor, then hung back with another woman, covering her mouth, giggling, and pointing at Jeanie, mocking Mama from behind.

Tommy seethed. It was wrong. But the right *dorozhka*. He dismissed any future regret. He wouldn't stay on the wrong path, he wouldn't make it a lifestyle. But hell if he'd let Mama be shamed by a soulless princess as though she were trash.

So, at just the right moment, heart slamming in his chest, Tommy slipped into the hall and down to the butler's pantry. He stopped to collect himself and grabbed hold of one countertop. There it all was. Splayed on several silver platters, as he knew it would be, as it always was in homes where they used it daily, was every manner of silver item ever made. He picked up a knife, far heavier than what he'd held at Mrs. Schultz's place.

Elizabeth Calder's laugh rang out, fueling his anger further. Awful, terrible people. He thought of the painting in the bathroom. He prayed neither Mama, nor anyone else at the gathering, would use that washroom. But then he realized. Elizabeth Calder put it there on purpose, just like she wore

Mama's sapphire necklace around to taunt her. Tommy thought of all the items in the Calder home that had been his family's, the way the judge treated people, and before Tommy knew it, he was slipping silver knives and forks and spoons into his pockets. And he stormed out, unconcerned that the Calders could notice.

But that was the beauty of it. Judge Calder was the kind of awful man whose bold self-worth caused him to believe he was invincible. The judge thought he was being kind and generous in letting Tommy chop and haul wood.

Tommy jumped the fence and stalked across the neighbor's field, indignant.

Chapter 22

Tommy approached McCrady's. He pressed his hand against his pocket to keep the silver from clanging. A girl in a wagon-wheel-sized straw hat sat on the stairs that led to McCrady's porch, face buried in her knees, arms latched around her legs.

Tommy jogged up a couple stairs, eager to unload his silver haul and distance himself from the thieving. The girl let out a funny noise, making him stop.

Tommy looked back but then moved on. Another noise. A sob came from the girl, plucking at something in him, trussing the girl's pain right to him, reminding him of his own deep, heavy desperation. "You lost?" Tommy asked.

She shook her head, not looking up.

Move on.

He couldn't. "Your mama in the store?" He went down a step. "Want me to get her?"

"I'm by myself."

Tommy would've preferred her to be lost so he could return her to grateful parents who might want to reward him for his effort. The silver poked into his thigh, reminding him why he was there. But seeing her, this delicate soul, curled into herself, made it impossible to just walk by. "Everyone's alone in some way. You hurt?"

The girl lifted her head. He drew back, surprised he hadn't recognized her. Her red hair was tucked under the wide-brimmed hat.

Tears trailed down her dusty cheeks, her green eyes glistening. "Pearl?"

She gave a little shrug. Her vulnerability, seeing her delicate and exposed, frightened him. He turned away wanting to run.

No.

His breath stuttered. He gripped his chest, pain swirling there. What was happening? His thoughts ran wild, the secrets she knew about him, how she'd helped him with the deer . . . *Love*. That word kept forming behinds his ribs, then springing to mind.

She stared past him and he visualized how she'd chased him down to warn him about the reverend the other day. Pearl looked out for him. And in that moment, the fear disintegrated and all he wanted was to protect her, to take away whatever caused this pain.

He sat beside her and put his hand on her back, drew it away, then laid it there again, her wiry body quivering under his palm. She cried hard. Her crumpled face and watery eyes made him move closer, his leg against hers. She sniffled and pulled away slightly. He became nervous and pulled his hand away, stuffing it in his lap.

Her tears cut trails through the filth, revealing pink skin. His heart clunked, paining him. He grasped at his chest. He wanted to shield her from whatever this was but didn't know how to get her to confide.

Pearl readjusted her arms around her knees, her skirt pulling up, exposing dirt-covered, bare legs. He started to ask what happened to her stockings but couldn't get the words out. She stared out past the street in front of them.

He patted her back again. "What happened, Pearl?"

She jerked her body so her back was to him. If it had been another girl, he would've gotten up and walked away. Maybe she needed something different than his help.

"Can you do me a favor, Pearl? I need to go inside for a minute, and when I come out you can tell me all about it. But I need a favor."

She sniffled.

Tommy pulled Frank from his pocket and petted the bird's back. "How about you watch my bird, Frank, while I'm in the store? He likes you and I know he'll stay put with you."

She remained quiet.

"Here." He brushed her arm.

She turned toward him, her knees against his, staring at Frank. Her eyes were swollen, the spring-green irises practically swallowing the whites. She turned her palms up and cupped them to accept the bird. Frank settled into her grasp. She wouldn't look at Tommy, and he knew she'd be there when he came back out. He waited for Frank to say something as usual, but he was silent.

Tommy shrugged. "Well. I've got business inside."

She didn't respond but she'd stopped crying. Tommy hopped to his feet. Inside the dark store, musty, dusty, grimy scents—the odors of unloved things—made him choke then breathe through his mouth. Whatever acquisitions had recently been made, the aroma carried the innate filth of a home built right into the side of a hill—the type of home the Arthurs had lived in on the prairie. He scratched his belly, sickened.

"Whatchu need, boy?" A voice from behind a stack of newspapers startled Tommy. He moved around them and saw Mr. McCrady sitting on a stool, legs spread, a piece of wood in his lap as he carved it.

Tommy wiped his palm and then the back of his hand on his pants and stuck it out. "Tommy Arthur. We spoke about silver a while back. For if I ever decided to sell some."

Mr. McCrady grunted.

Agitated, Tommy struggled to steady his voice. "Said you'd take a look. I think this is rare, what I have. Not that ordinary stuff you've seen over the years."

Mr. McCrady grunted again and nicked his knuckle with the knife. He sucked at the cut and stood towering over Tommy, talking around his finger. "Damn it, look at that."

Tommy stepped back. His mind went to other people he might sell the silver to or gift it to for equity in favors. He was interested in easy money, not this hassle. "Well, okay. Thank you." Tommy began to leave the store.

"Now wait a cotton-pickin' minute. Shuffle back here and give me a gander." He gestured with his unharmed hand, looking over the spectacles that slid down his nose. "Grab me that silver book off the counter there."

Tommy felt a surge of glee that his leaving may have evoked the very response he'd been trying for. He handed McCrady the book and pulled the fish fork, knives and teaspoons from his pocket. The silver shone in the dark room like it might have if lodged inside the earth before being freed.

McCrady stopped sucking on his knuckle and paged through the book. "Lay it all out so I can see."

Tommy splayed it in front of McCrady. The man held the fork into a channel of sunlight streaming through a side window. He whistled as he turned the serving fork back and forth. "A beaut all right." He licked his finger and turned pages. "I think I saw this in . . . Yes, here it is." He tapped the name on a page. *Old Orange Blossom.*

"You have more than these pieces?"

Tommy pulled his hat from his back pocket and settled it onto his head. "Well, I have more of a lot of stuff. But you know, I come by these treasures in upstanding, law-abiding ways, so I can't just snap my fingers and—"

"You have more, boy?"

"This is it. For now," Tommy said before he had a chance to play this whole thing to its natural conclusion.

"Well then, I'll give you six bucks for the fancy fork. For the rest, another five. And if you git more of this pattern, I'll give a bonus."

Tommy looked at the page that outlined the pricing for Old Orange Blossom. "That fork alone's worth nearly twenty-two dollars. That one fork."

McCrady sat forward on his stool. "Bring me a place setting. No, *two.* The wife would love some of this here shiny decadence. Even the slop she peddles will be tasty if delivered on these here utensils. And I'll give you a fat bonus."

Tommy wasn't pleased with this plan, but it was more money than he'd had in some time. This amount would allow him to give extra to Mama. "Thank you, sir," he said, considering if he could find his way back into the Calder home to steal more.

Outside the store he stuffed the money into his pocket.

Pearl.

Tommy clomped down the stairs and plopped down next to her. He drew a deep breath. He wasn't comfortable with people watering the landscape with their tears.

We're not crying people. Mama's voice came to mind.

Tommy sighed. He'd come to see that everyone, including Mama, was indeed a crying person if the pain struck deep enough. Pearl's lips quivered again. Tommy took Frank from her and set the bird on his shoulder.

"Can I walk you home?"

She shook her head.

"That boardinghouse on Rose Lane. What's it called again?"

"Rupert's." She wrapped her arms around her shoulders, pulling the neckline of her dress downward, exposing her collarbone. The way it jutted out of her skin, Tommy was sure the girl hadn't much to eat in recent times and probably not much hardy food when she did eat. He never thought of her as needing to secure food after seeing her slice up a deer faster than any man. He never saw her as needing anything.

"Not going back," she said.

He was afraid to ask. "Why?"

"Things happened. Think I found another place. But well, it's that . . ."

"You need money?" he asked.

"Been a day since I last filled my belly."

He thought of Mama's garden, the way she worked tirelessly throughout summer, fussing over her plants like they were children. It had meant they had a steady flow of food even into late fall. Tommy considered the silver he'd just traded, how the money would help his family. Mama was doing well with her extra sewing, gardening, and with Katherine's money when she baked extra for Miss Violet added in, they were doing well. The bills were wadded hard against his leg.

He considered the manhandling he'd suffered when he'd been boarded out, before his luck turned and he got to board with the Babcock family for a time. The sun peeked its head through the clouds and revealed bruising on her exposed collarbone. He studied her, the way she wrapped her arms tight around her naked legs, her shoulders hunched but chin lifted, eyes scanning for . . . threats? Her lips were parted slightly, and it softened her face as he'd never seen it. It was as though his heart were an envelope and her sad face tore it open.

He touched her arm. She shrank away.

Her reaction brought back his own fears. Seeing her frightened made him want to be brave. "Tell me what happened. I can help if you tell me more."

Her throat constricted as she swallowed a lump. She stared straight ahead, tears spilling over her lower lids. He understood her not running her mouth about it, but he was her friend. He'd trusted her. He held out his pinkie. "I won't tell anyone. But you have to tell me."

She kept silent. He was due back home but couldn't let her go on without means. Now that he had no idea if his father was halfway to the bottom of the ocean plucking pearls from oyster bellies or halfway back to Des Moines, he could spare something for his friend.

He pulled the money he'd just been given from his pocket and pushed it toward her. "Go to that women's hotel. On Main. Mama stayed there with Katherine and Yale for a time. It's safe."

She didn't move.

He unlatched one of her hands from her body and pried open her fingers. He smashed the money in her palm and closed her fingers back around it.

"Do not go back to Rupert's."

She shifted toward Tommy, meeting his gaze with tangible force, jarring him. "I gotta get my book. My bag and my things. Gotta go back at some point," she said against his ear, sending quivers through his body.

Tommy wanted to hold her, but couldn't do it, not there. "The fairy tales?"

"Only book I got."

"Well," Tommy said. "Don't fret about that. You go on to the women's hotel. Your safety is most important." He knew what it was like to lose things, but things could be rebought.

"Why're ya doing this?"

He swallowed hard, the words already formed in his mouth, but he wasn't sure he could get them out. She kept his gaze, and he knew he could say them to her and she wouldn't make fun of him. "Because I like you."

Her eyes widened.

"I do."

She tilted her head, tears brimming again. But then she roped her arms around his neck and kissed his cheek. Her lips brushed his ear. "You're like a knight in the book. The one who—the hero." She stopped talking, her breath was warm on his skin. "Thank you, Tommy. Thank you."

She gripped him hard, and he let her hold tight as long as she wanted, this time memorizing exactly how she felt against him. He'd never been anyone's hero before. The thought that he might fail her knocked the wind out of his body.

No. Don't think that way. This is your new story, he told himself.

Chapter 23

Tommy had lost and recovered plenty of money over the course of his life. The losses were always paralyzing, at least for a while. But this time, when he gave Pearl money he'd earmarked for his family, he was empowered, his anger at someone hurting her propelling him to action. At first he started running toward Rupert's boardinghouse, but he forced himself into long, even paces to tamp down his rage, not wanting to run blind into the barrel of a gun.

When he reached Rupert's, he took the stairs by two and banged on the door. A scrawny old man wrenched it open and spit. "What the hell?"

Tommy drew deep breaths, assessing what he saw, telling himself this man was physically small and harmless looking. Tommy dwarfed him by a foot and probably sixty pounds. This couldn't be the right man.

"Looking for Rupert."

The man lifted his chin, his nose crooked from being broken several times. He pulled a shot gun from behind the door and leveled it on Tommy.

He began to sweat. "I'm here to collect Pearl's things."

"Don't know no Pearl." He started to shut the door. Tommy jammed his foot into the gap, ready to duck away if he saw a glimpse of the man's trigger finger moving.

"Give me her book and anything else that's hers. And if she paid ahead, give me that, too."

The man scoffed. "She owes *me*, that trampy thief."

Tommy kicked the door open, making Rupert stumble back and drop the gun. Tommy caught the man before he fell and set him back on his feet. "Pearl's not that."

The man slapped Tommy's steadying hand away. "She's got a thief's heart. Wouldn't be long 'fore she—"

"Does not." Tommy kicked the gun away, his voice lifting the rafters in the shabby room. As dirt covered as Pearl's skin often was, her heart was as bright and pure as the sun rising on a clear summer morning. He thought of how she'd warned Tommy away from bad deeds. She was as far from a thief as anyone he could name.

Rupert crossed his arms and smirked. "Well *you* do, don't ya? No other type would take up with a girl like Pearl. Boys!"

As Tommy surveyed the space, moving toward the gun, boys of all ages crept out of hiding spots and down the front steps as though being lured by a sudden tilt of the earth toward Tommy and Rupert. Two boys carried baseball bats, and suddenly Tommy fully understood Pearl's bruises.

"Give me Pearl's bag now. Her book. Whatever else is hers."

"She don't own nothin' but worthless words on paper. Owes *me* and I'm takin' payment in her stupid papers until that tramp—"

Tommy took one stride toward Rupert and lifted him by his collar.

A war cry rose up and someone hopped onto Tommy's back. Another boy jammed a bat into his stomach. Tommy dropped Rupert and turned just in time to catch a second bat in the midsection. He bent forward, the wind knocked out of him. The boys leapt all over him, pounding away. Tommy curled into a ball to recover his air, and once he had, he unfolded his limbs with a grunt, sitting up, tossing them all across the room. He lumbered to his feet and ripped the bat out of the hands of the last one rushing toward him. He held it up as though waiting for a pitch, still barely able to breathe.

Rupert's face registered fear, and that caused the boys who were cowering or finding their way to their feet to realize that one Tommy Arthur could do more damage than a handful of them.

Tommy grabbed the rifle and held it, realizing why none of the boys had made a move for it.

The trigger was missing. He tossed it aside and pointed the bat at a slip of a boy who hadn't been in the tussle but trembled on the stairs. "You. Show me Pearl's room."

Tommy followed the mop-topped boy upstairs, the steps creaking as they went.

"Leon," Rupert said. "He harms a single thing up there you crack 'im in the head."

One full riser near the top was missing. Tommy finally took in the full extent of the smell—the stale body odors—and his heart broke to know that this was where Pearl had been living. The boy led him to a small room at the end of the hall. It was cold and crowded with mattresses strewn across the floor. "Pearl slept near the closet. Bag's in there."

"Get it, Leon. That's your name, right?"

He nodded and stepped across the mattresses, making Tommy cringe as his filthy shoe bottoms touched where people laid at night. "Where's the other girls? They all right?"

Leon leaned into the closet and pulled a bag out along with the book of fairy tales Tommy had given her. He stepped back across the mattresses. "What girls? Pearl's it for girls. Other than her female dog. But that's it. No girls."

Tommy's breath caught at the thought she had to sleep in the same room with unrelated boys. She never mentioned pets that he could remember. "Where're the pets now?"

Leon shrugged. "And we ain't ever hurt her. Not us boys. Rupert's son. He done it. Pearl's dog wet the floor, and his son went crazy." The boy's voice quivered. "She ain't got no thief's heart neither. Most generous I know."

Tommy nodded, studying the emaciated boy. "She's a good soul."

Leon shivered through his thin undershirt and signaled toward the fairy-tale collection. "She reads me stories from this here boulder of a book. Can't even believe all the ideas locked up tight inside of it."

Tommy smiled feeling bad for Leon, pleased that Pearl had shared her stories, knowing that doing so would have been satisfying to her. "Where's your shirt?"

The boy appeared confused and looked down. "This *is* my shirt."

Tommy exhaled, wanting to give Leon something that would help keep him warm as winter neared. He set Pearl's things down. The boy flew back into the closet.

"I'm not gonna hurt you." Tommy took off his coat and plaid work shirt. "Here. It's too big for you, but hide it away so Rupert doesn't see it's from me. Then trade for something that fits."

The boy's mouth fell open, and he reached for the shirt. He held it against him, gasping. He finally met Tommy's gaze. "Thank you."

Tommy yanked his coat back on, blanching from pain. "Welcome." He buttoned it up on the off chance someone might notice his shirt had gone missing.

Tommy stuffed Pearl's book into the bag, jammed it under one arm, and picked up the bat.

"Tell her see-ya for me." Leon's voice cracked.

Tommy nodded. "I will." Tommy touched the boy's shoulder and he got a distinct sense of goodness from him, despite his current situation. "You'd better come down so Rupert doesn't suspect you have a sweet spot for Pearl or were nice to me. Might use it against you somehow."

Leon balled up the shirt, stuck it into the back corner of the closet, and followed. Tommy swung the bat as he descended, hiding the pain that came with each stairstep. The other boys had mean, strong swings and bony fists, and Tommy could feel the broken vessels spilling into bruises.

Tommy hoped he wouldn't have to hit his way out of the boardinghouse, but he wanted to be clear. He raised the bat. "Don't ever bother with Pearl again."

Rupert pressed his back up against the wall near the door and lifted the other baseball bat in response. "Sure thing, Prince

Charming. Best not've lifted anything from up there. Leon? He take anything not Pearl's?"

The boy shook his head and squared his shoulders, trying to make himself look big, as though to repel any sense of alliance that may have formed while Tommy retrieved Pearl's things.

"Prince Charming?" Tommy stared at Rupert.

"Pearl always squawkin' 'bout life with princes and fairies and men who rescue girls." Rupert scoffed. "Told her a million times *I'm* her prince. Good as it gets."

Tommy wanted to strangle the man.

"But here you are. First, that nosy battle-axe Hillis in her fancy coat and feather hat. Now you. Prince. Rescue. Whole goddamn thing."

Tommy shook his head, not knowing if Pearl found a nice room at the women's hotel, but sure wherever she was, had to have been a million times better than this.

Chapter 24

Tommy returned to the shed with Pearl's things, hoping she made it to the hotel safely. A note from Katherine was tacked to the door.

1. Haul water to third floor. Leave outside bath door.
2. Check on Yale. Napping. Mama on errands.

He set the bag on the table near the fireplace then went to the house to see about Yale. She was asleep in Mama's and Katherine's bed, tucked into a tight ball, breathing deep and heavy. Back in the kitchen garden, Tommy cut through the hedge to Miss Violet's property. He was forced into a limp with his back and stomach muscles tightening up. He pressed his belly and sucked back air, remembering he was now without long sleeves under his coat. He skimmed leaves and sticks off the top of the rain barrel and hauled it up the back stairs, wincing all the way.

As he neared the bathroom, his grip loosened and the barrel clanked to the floor, water splashing over the rim. "Damn it."

The bathroom door swung open, and Tommy looked up to see Katherine standing there, her shirtwaist pulled out of her skirt. "Tommy?"

He breathed hard. "You? I'm hauling water up these stairs, my back half-broken, so you can have a day-break?"

Katherine's eyes went wide, and she started rattling off her defense of why it made sense that she, the kitchen mistress, was readying for a bath in the middle of the day.

Miss Violet came into the hall and walked toward them. "Now, Tommy. Your sister's congested and courting a chest cold. I cannot have her infecting my clients' food with some contagious disease. Her health is of the utmost concern." Violet yammered

152

on and on about eucalyptus and tea and whatever else would help get Katherine better. Katherine came back to the door and opened it wider so Tommy could lug the water to the stove in the corner to heat it. He'd thought that once the weather turned cold that would be the end of hauling rainwater to the third floor, but Violet had solved the problem by installing a stove. Better she'd installed a pulley system to bring the water up.

Tommy turned. "If a bath'll help, then by all means, do it. Mama wouldn't want you sick either. Maybe you should rest after the bath."

Katherine nodded, looking relieved. "I'm sure I'll feel much better after this. Bathing is rest enough."

Miss Violet patted Tommy's arm. "Don't worry your mama with this, Tommy. She's got enough to think about. Katherine mixed up the herbs herself, and I'm sure she'll be right as rain after this healing bath."

Tommy wouldn't add more to his mother's concerns. "I surely won't."

Katherine coughed and nearly doubled over as Miss Violet added drops of something to the tub water. He could hear the phlegm in her chest loud and clear.

"Don't forget about Yale," Katherine said. "Should be dead asleep, but just to be sure . . . Mama'll be back any time now. Keep Yale with you if she wakes."

"I know, I know." He rubbed his side, the ache turning into a stabbing pain. Katherine appeared to be feeling a mix of exhaustion and serenity. Tommy thought of all Katherine had been through in the past five years—thought of all he knew about anyway. When she'd arrived in Des Moines the year before, she was a blend of woman and waif. She was taller, beautiful, her movements always drawing the eye of any man she passed despite her ragged clothing and much-too-thin build. It had to have been as hard for her to have been without the family as it had been for him. This made him think of Pearl, her recent living conditions. He hoped Katherine hadn't suffered anything like that. He couldn't think about that, imagine it, talk about it. While he could fix Pearl's situation, he could not go back in time and fix Katherine's.

She deserved a few moments of restful bliss, a chance to stave off illness if it was trying to settle upon her. And though he didn't know many specific details of the years they'd been apart, he was quite certain she'd probably had no peace—not to mention sweet bathing opportunities. He realized for the first time that he'd been so busy surviving that he'd accepted as fact that Katherine's boarding experiences had all been suitable—good, in fact. And now, thinking of just how bad things might have been for her, his blood turned cold.

**

Tommy wanted to wake Yale and take her with him to deliver Pearl's bag to the women's hotel, hoping she'd found a room there. But when he went to rouse his sister from her nap, she simply rolled over, her even, deep inhalations telling him she was far from waking. Tommy calculated the time it would take to run the bag to the hotel and make it back if he left Yale. Thirty-five minutes, maybe. He shook Yale again to no avail. Katherine said Mama would return anytime. Despite his sore muscles, he was antsy, wanting to get Pearl her things so she could settle into her new place. Yale would be hungry when she woke, so if Tommy took the bag now, he could be back to feed her if Mama hadn't returned.

He reached the hotel and was told by the desk clerk, Virginia, that it was full and Pearl had been turned away. She had no idea where Pearl went or even in what direction. Tommy swung by the post office to find another woman working there, and she had no idea where Pearl was either. "It's her day off. I ain't her keeper," she said with a shrug.

Tommy returned home and dropped Pearl's sack in the shed as Miss Violet was ringing the bell to call her ladies to dinner before clients arrived. Tommy entered Mama's kitchen. She and Yale were there eating. Mama's face was bloodless, as though overwhelmed with great dread, taking Tommy back to the hours soon after James had died.

"Mama." He knelt before her. "What's the matter?"

She grabbed Tommy to her, squishing Yale between them. "Yale nearly died."

Tommy froze, fear rushing through him. "I checked on her a little bit ago and she was sound asleep. I covered her and . . ."

Tommy's voice cracked as he looked Yale over, checking her for injury. He'd been so concerned about getting to Pearl. Had he neglected something? "I did the same as always, Mama. She was fine, asleep when I left."

"You should have stayed." Mama's voice was rough, cutting. "We can't do like we used to with her. She's up and about when she wakes. She's not—"

Tommy saw that now. He pulled away and checked over his sister, squeezing her arms and legs and cheeks, his light touch eventually making her giggle. She flung her arms around his neck and squeezed, stronger and more aggressive than he'd ever seen her. Relief replaced his fear, and he exhaled. She was fine.

But Tommy was mortified. He never imagined Yale would waken and explore. She rarely left where she was set down, let alone to go looking for someone.

"Mama. I'm so sorry. I didn't think she would . . . What *happened?*" He ran his quaking hand through his hair, trying to determine if Yale was injured where he couldn't see.

"Maybe you don't realize how she wanders now. Just silently shows up behind me." Mama's words tumbled out. "I missed stepping on her in the garden by a hair yesterday. And today she got out of bed and was digging into . . . I walked in, and she was elbow-deep in powder under the dry sink. I should have stressed how much she'd been into trouble lately. I should have told you."

"She does love playing under the dry sink."

Mama's lips quivered. "I thought she'd gotten into rat poison. I panicked and started screaming, and Katherine came running. It was powdered sugar."

"Thank God."

Mama stood and set Yale on the seat and started pacing. "It took me right back to losing James. I can't . . . Listen, Tommy. I explained this to Katherine, too. I've been to meetings where lawyers and judges and business owners all want the streets cleaned up. They want any child who appears the least bit unkempt or imbecile or . . ."

Tommy could see these words, thinking them, saying them, sickened Mama.

"They're sweeping half these poor souls into wagons and hauling them off to Glenwood. The other half are stuffed in people's attics or cellars. I won't do that to Yale. I know she's—" Mama stopped pacing and covered Yale's ears. "I know she's an imbecile." She whispered the word, barely getting it out, as though admitting such a thing was as painful as death.

He leaned forward, grabbing her hand. "No. No. She's catching up now. So many words and..." He sighed. Frank knew more than Yale.

Mama straightened in her chair, bracing against her own words. "Mrs. Hillis is a saving grace. She understands children can develop beyond what people expect. She's a voice for all who are vulnerable. People actually listen to her. And, she understands why I can't just send Yale off like an animal to be cared for in an asylum where children are abused and . . ."

Mama took Tommy's shoulders. "We have to be more careful. She's growing and finally learning, but if anything happened to her, I would just—"

Tommy put his hand up. Not wanting her to finish her sentence. "I know. When I think how her life started and all that happened since then . . . I'm sorry. I am so sorry."

He pulled Yale onto his lap. "Katherine and I will do a better job when you're not here."

Mama sat. "And I'll take her with me more. She doesn't need to nap so much. Being busier, out and about with adults, will help her develop even faster."

Tommy agreed.

"But when we take her out, we have to keep her close. You've no idea what happens to children in asylums at the hands of these cruel but powerful people. And that's what some of these important men have decided needs to happen in order to *clean things up*. Can you imagine? That's how they term it. As though fragile children are *things*."

He squeezed Yale harder and kissed the top of her head. "We'll keep you safe. Always and forever. I'm sorry I let you down."

She looked up and put her palm against Tommy's cheek silently conveying pure, sweet love and faith in her brother. His whole body sighed, thankful she was safe, hoping he deserved even a pinch of Yale's trust.

Chapter 25

Night put an end to the day that brought such fear for Tommy—seeing Pearl in tears and homeless and then the incident with Yale wandering. He was too unsettled to eat and glad that he would soon sleep.

Back at the shed, Tommy fluffed his mattress. He gasped with each reach and pull, the movement agitating the bruises given to him at Rupert's. He pulled the spare quilt Mama had traded seeds for the other day over the mattress, liking the homey look, his privacy, and the proximity to his family.

Soft clanging noises from outside drew his attention. The sound stopped, and he kicked out of his boots. He opened the loft door and called Frank inside. The bird landed on the edge of the window. "Inside. Time to sleep," Tommy said, petting Frank's feathers.

"Up, up." Tommy jerked his head toward the rafters. Frank flew away, settling into the old nest Tommy had put up there for him. Finally Tommy snuggled into his bed. He pulled the quilt to his chin, the cold night air seeping into his bones as he relaxed into the straw bed.

Drifting toward sleep, the jangling from outside started again, growing louder, closer. He pushed up on his elbow, straining to discern what would make that sound outside. He pushed the loft window open, listening, peering into the yard. Flashes of light came near the hedges, then the arborvitae rustled and spread as lantern light pushed through, followed by a head and the rest of a body. It didn't take long to know who it was. In the glow of the lamp and moonlight, red hair dangled from its pinnings, shining. A thrill trembled through him.

Pearl.

She straightened and pulled on a rope. "Come on, girl," she said clicking her tongue. A dog appeared, and she patted its head. Pearl moved closer to the shed, the clanking tin bowls were attached to a rope around her waist. Tommy's heart beat harder at the sight of her.

"Psst," he said. He knew the darkness hid him.

Frank landed on Tommy's back. "The girl," he squawked. Pearl raised the lantern and her gaze shifted up toward Tommy. The dog whined and sat on her owner's feet.

"Tommy?" Pearl squinted. "That yer bird? That Frank? You up there?"

He nearly giggled at the sight of her, exhilarated and relieved that she was all right. "Pearl! You'll wake the dead with that racket."

She pulled something out of her smock pocket and thrust it into the air. "Got another letter fer ya."

Tommy got to his knees, the movement making him gasp. "Another?" He yanked on his boots, scrambled down the ladder, and was out the door as quickly as his pain would allow. So soon? Maybe his father was nearly back to town and he had been waiting to let him know he was done with the seven seas. The dog growled and Tommy stopped short, hands in the air in surrender.

"Fern, no. Tommy's good people. Fine young man." The dog took that as direction to lay on the ground and roll over. Tommy petted her belly, and Frank landed on Tommy's shoulder. Fern lifted her head.

"No, Fern. Frank's a pet, not dinner," Pearl said.

"Definitely not dinner," Tommy said. He looked Pearl up and down, noticing that she seemed sturdy again, like her old self. She pulled the loose end of a wool shawl tighter against her body.

"She won't bother Frank none," Pearl said. "Fern's got manners. She's a lady. Like your ma."

"My ma, er, Mama? Comparing a dog to my mama?"

"In a good way."

Tommy chuckled. His blood pounded through his body, and his nerves lit with what he knew to be affection, not simply

159

attraction. The sight of Pearl soothed him even amidst the excitement she sparked in him. His chest warmed, as though his innards were lit like candles. Pearl was so strong, determined to make a better, particular life for herself. Seeing her feeling better made him feel stronger, like maybe he could be the knight she thought he was. There was something so open about her, forgiving, forgetting. She saw everything in him that no one else ever had.

"You're safe," Tommy said.

"'Course." She spread her stance and lifted her chin. Tommy wondered if he'd imagined her tearful, fragile demeanor at McCrady's earlier. He wiped his hands on the front of his night pants, then grasped his ribs.

"Heard what you did," Pearl said.

Tommy nodded toward the shed. "Got your bag in there."

"Leon said as much."

"So you're all right?"

"Right as raindrops in April." Pearl handed him an envelope. "Stopped at the post office after I saw ya."

Tommy studied her again, searching for signs of the vulnerability he'd worried about all day. "You're not going back to Rupert's, are you?"

She lifted her arms to emphasize the load she was carrying. "Nope."

"So then—"

"San Diego," she blurted out.

"What?"

She stared at the letter in his hand. "The letter. Best read it."

He turned it into the lantern light and noted the postmark. He started to walk away. "Thanks, Pearl. San Diego again, I see."

He strode up the porch, eager to dig into the letter. Pearl let out a big sigh, causing her things to jingle again.

"Well, you *ain't* a princely gentleman. Not one bit. I dang near . . . Well, I thought you were a good man. And for a mother fancy as yours and—"

"Fancy?" Tommy turned. Mama hadn't been fancy in years.

"Mannerly. A society woman."

Tommy admired again how Pearl could see beyond a person's dress to a deeper kind of worth. He smiled and stared at Pearl, suddenly wanting to tease her like he always did when his heart raced too fast in her presence. "I asked if you were all right. You said you were dandy. How am I not a gentleman?"

"You ain't even offered to quench my thirst."

"Ohhh. Right. And your bag. You need that. Come on. I forgot you required an engraved invitation."

She scoffed. "Hardy har," she said clanging behind him.

He poured water into a tin cup and gestured to one of the chairs at the tiny round table near the fire. "That chair rocks due to a short leg. And these two are missing slats, so until I fix them, it's really more of a stool. Help yourself."

She tried the wiggly seat and then hopped to one of the slatless ones staying put. She sipped her water. "Read me your letter?"

He stopped midway through ripping into the envelope. "That's what you want?"

"Please?"

Tommy rubbed his forehead considering the risk. She'd shared something private with him earlier. He could trust her. Yet baring family wounds still seemed impossible.

She lifted her hands and dropped them, making the dog dishes reverberate. "Got my entire wealth, minus the bag you rescued, and I still managed to personally deliver your letter. I deserve to hear it."

"Pearl."

"Tommy."

"You really all right? When I saw you—"

She shushed him.

"I saw Rupert's place and where you had to sleep, and Leon said—"

"Shush. Better I leave the thoughts of that place back there. Luxury of sadness isn't mine no more than fox-fur coats and summer silks."

Her eyes shone with tears he knew she didn't want to cry. Tommy felt another rush of admiration for the strength that must have filled her from the inside out. She was like no one he'd ever known. Special. Like an angel sent to him . . . Or had he been sent to her? He shook his head.

He could at least read her a letter. He could trust her. He sat on the shaky chair, set the lantern on the table. The fire crackled sending sparks up the chimney. He blew out his air.

"Dear Tommy, thinking of you as I set off. Soon as I have my treasure, I'll return. Love to Katherine and the others, for I do indeed . . ." Tommy glanced up at Pearl. Her head was cocked to the side and her hands clasped in her lap as though she was trying to will the letter to say the words Tommy needed to hear. He shifted, making the chair wobble in the silence.

"Love you all."

Tommy folded the letter, empty. He cleared his throat. Pearl didn't move. Yes, he felt good that his father loved them all, but the lack of information, the letters from those holding his debt, that his father had told them to contact his son for payment, his foolishness that he had believed in him when Katherine and Mama had not, stung as much as anything he could imagine.

He immediately thought that he would write back and tell his father to come now, that they could solve his problems together, that there was another man sniffing around their family and Tommy needed him. He shivered. He held the letter against his chest and focused on the line about loving all of them. All this did was confuse Tommy, especially in regard to Mr. Hayes. The longer Father was gone, the more this man slid into their family.

Yet Tommy's own feelings had changed toward his father. He'd been disappointed too many times. The lack of that sense of desperately believing his father was just a week or two from showing up in Des Moines left a crater in him that he wasn't sure would ever be filled. He never imagined he could feel worse than he had in anticipating his father's arrival, always worried for the man's safety.

Pearl didn't press him to discuss the letter. She straightened and pushed her hand into her pocket and pulled another letter out. "Read this one."

"Whose? Pearl." He eyed the envelope. "No. Are you crazy?"

"She's dead. The woman the letter came to." Pearl shrugged. "No harm in reading dead people's mail, is there?"

Tommy searched her face for some clue as to what this all meant to her. He crossed his arms making the chair rock. "Return to sender."

"Already did. Came back again. Meant for me. Wouldn't you say?"

Tommy sighed, though he welcomed the distraction. "You already have an arm's-length list of words and places to go. Do you really need more illegally gotten letters?"

She gaped at him, a smile coming, bringing her even more back to her former self. "I ain't . . . I mean, I haven't even begun to gather enough words for my future ladyship."

"Ladyship? That a word?" He liked that they could lighten the mood, together.

She shrugged. "Someday I'm gonna be a lady like your ma, like Mrs. Calder, like . . . Well, reading these letters, it's like studying. I hear their fancy, polite voices in my head, I learn about all the ways a woman of means should—"

"It's against the law."

"You keep saying that. But I ain't the only one breaking laws round here."

Tommy drew back.

"Now," Pearl said with a forced, but soft voice. "Read it like, well, read like you talk when you run into Mr. Hathaway, the way you talk when you forget you ain't rich and important anymore."

Tommy pulled the envelope toward him. He didn't realize how obvious it was that his language and manners shifted according to who he was with. Gone were the days when high manners and perfect discourse were the only way he interacted. And the trappings of that life, the food, the warm beds and white-glove service right in his own home . . . It did hurt when he allowed himself to consider the way his life had been before, when they had everything.

He understood why Mama had forced him not to tread in too many thoughts of the old days. Submerging in thoughts of everything you lost made living with what you had even harder. What struck him was that Pearl, who never had anything, seemed to be inspired by tales of excess, not depressed by them. "Feels creepy reading a dead lady's mail."

Pearl shrugged, stood and motioned for Tommy to stand. "Switch chairs with me."

He shrugged. "All right, Goldilocks." She settled into the wobbly chair, her head to the side as Tommy's reading washed over her.

When he finished, she looked directly at him. "I want to go to school."

"Sounds like a good plan."

"Well, all my money from clerking at the post office went to room and board at Rupert's. Couldn't save enough to pay for two weeks of high school, let alone years."

Tommy reimagined the room with all the mattresses and the boys who slept there with her.

"Can't go back there," she said. "Got to make new plans."

Tommy nodded.

"Thinking I might sleep in the woods." Pearl's words dropped from her lips as sleep began to take hold of her. "Like you did a ways back. That spot by the beaver dam to hide meat. Something 'bout that place draws me there in the summer. Should be fine for winter as well."

"You'll freeze first night in."

She shrugged. "You don't understand what it's like to have nothing worth having. Suppose I could ask that Miss Violet next door to your house if I could have a room."

"No." Tommy bit the inside of his mouth, surprised at his forceful response. Miss Violet was providing his family with a clean, safe place to live, but something gave him pause about the bathing ladies who lived in the rooms on the third floor of Miss Violet's, the condoms they used when "needed."

Pearl straightened, narrowing her eyes on Tommy. "It's clean. She's smart and training women in finance. Don't you see the write-ups about her and the ladies in the paper?"

Tommy leaned forward, gasping with pain. He patted his ribs. "Whoa, there. You said Miss Violet might be up to no good. And I—"

Pearl leaned forward. "I was mistaken. Des Moines's leading citizens are taken with her. Even her competition's stumbling over their feet to compliment her work. Maybe that's a good choice for me. She can give me my schooling. I won't have to pay the school system that way. Overheard Miss Olivia talking at the post office the other day."

"No." Tommy covered her hand with his.

She snatched it away, pushing both her fists into her armpits. "Ya don't think I'm good 'nough to work fer her."

He shook his head, exhausted, unsure of exactly what he did think. Being with Pearl tangled his thoughts, making what he believed feel different every time she came down his path. But whatever he labeled his feelings for her, they grew more intense, slowly over time, then instantly when he saw her at McCrady's. "Here," he said.

"Here, what?"

"Stay here. There's room upstairs, it's warm. Until a room at the women's hotel opens."

She smiled and took the letter from Tommy, folding it into her pocket. She handed him the money he'd given her to spend at the women's hotel. "Thank you, Tommy Arthur. I knew you were a gentleman. A true prince. Like Prince Aeriel in that there book you brung me."

Tommy nodded and picked up the sack he'd carried from Rupert's with her things. "Book's in here with whatever Leon put in it."

She took it from him.

"Dog stays outside."

"That bird of yers stays inside, I'll bet ya."

Tommy shrugged, making him wince. "He's house-trained."

"So's Fern."

Tommy looked at the dog lying at Pearl's feet, the firelight dancing on her dark fur. She did seem sweet. He sighed and led Fern toward the ladder to the loft. Fern put her front feet on the ladder and tried to step up, but the rungs were too narrow.

Tommy glanced at Pearl. She gestured upward.

"You want me to carry her? She's a hundred pounds."

She shrugged and looked around. "Nah, wouldn't want her to fall trying to come down. Pearl squatted and rubbed Fern behind the ears. "How 'bout you sleep by the fire and keep us all safe?"

Fern closed her eyes, falling into the comfort of Pearl's scratching. "Well, all right. That's our plan."

Tommy climbed up the ladder and readjusted the quilt.

Pearl appeared over the edge of the loft and surveyed the space. "You'll take one side of the mattress. I'll take the other."

She stared at the mattress.

He held his hands up in surrender. "I'm a gentleman, Pearl. All the way."

"I know it," she said.

She went back down to untie her rope with the bowls attached and removed her shawl. Back in the loft, she lay down stiff as a board, not removing anything, not even her boots. Tommy acted as though it were perfectly normal. He'd slept plenty of nights fully clothed, knowing he might need to run or wake up fighting.

He pulled Mama's quilt over Pearl and tucked it around every inch of her. "Sleep here. Save your money for proper schooling, if that's what you're after. Good to have goals."

He closed the loft door, laid down on his side, and pulled his coat over him for a blanket. Pearl turned her head to face him, her eyes lighting the space between them. "Thank ya, Tommy," she whispered.

Tommy was about to say you're welcome, but instead he leaned forward and kissed her forehead. She stared at the ceiling, a sliver of a smile pulling at her lips.

A surge of protectiveness like he'd felt earlier that day filled Tommy. Frank landed on him and brushed his head against Tommy's hand. Tommy stroked the bird for a bit. "Up, up, Frank. Time to sleep."

Tommy took a final look at Pearl, her relaxed expression, the sweet slope of her nose over parted lips. He tucked the blanket around her again, then turned his back to her, falling asleep content to know he now had Frank the crow and Pearl to care for, filling him with a sense of worth that made him glad to be alive. He was no longer alone, a lost bird himself. And though he yearned for the way things used to be, before . . . he felt good moving forward in life. Mama and the girls were near, but he was beginning to see that the past he'd been glorifying wasn't allowing him to really grow up the way he wanted. No. It was time to accept the world had moved on, and so should he.

Chapter 26

Tommy rose before the sun, Pearl's body adding heat to the loft space. He crept to the ladder and paused at the top before descending. She was curled into an impossibly small bud, the quilt tucked around every inch of her except for her nose and eyes. Her breath came soft but deep and he knew she must not have slept well for days and he was proud that he could give her a warm safe place to mend.

Downstairs he let Fern and Frank outside into the just-turning-sapphire sky.

Before taking on his usual chores, he lit a lantern and sat on the porch in the chilly air to make a list—coal for Miss Violet, wood for the stove at Mama's, cows, prayers for sale, get Mama into a cottage, watch for silent Yale. Tommy added *keep Pearl safe* to his list of things to do.

He tapped the paper thinking of all the things he lacked and also possessed. For the first time the sting of having almost nothing was lessened. Pearl. It had to be her arrival. He felt optimistic, motivated, generous. And this made him think of the family his father had stuck without paying what they needed for their children. Tommy resented his father reporting his name as someone to contact to help, but he was indignant about there being a family, children out there suffering because of his father.

He underlined the word cottage several times and stared into the distance, Frank the crow circling over the kitchen garden in smooth swooping loops. With Pearl returning the money he'd given her earlier, he knew what he had to do. That money was ill-gotten and though he still felt justified in stealing to spite the woman who was mocking Mama, he knew he couldn't keep it all. Maybe not any of it.

He'd send a portion of it to the family his father had left in a lurch in San Diego. He'd send two dollars and request the full amount of money his father owed.

"Thanks, Tommy," Pearl said from behind him, startling him. She sat beside him on the step, her shoulder against his arm, that tiny connection filling him. She wrapped the quilt tight, her hair trailing over her shoulders.

He leaned closer. "Slept all right?"

She nodded.

"Listen." He folded his list and tucked it into his shirt pocket. "Stay as long as you want. But Mama wouldn't—"

"I know. She's carrying a ton. Won't add to that load." She lifted her pinkie. "Promise. She'll never hear a peep or see evidence of me here."

Tommy looped his pinkie around hers. "She never comes back here. She won't know."

Pearl smiled.

They shook their fingers gently and just before she pulled hers from his he memorized how it felt, that exact bit of weathered skin against his.

"Sometimes that Professor Hayes who helps with the garden and is writing about it for his dissertation or some nonsense . . . every once in while I see him poke his head through the hedges keeping an eye on me or something. Stay out of his sight."

Pearl nodded, then her brow furrowed. "Hear that?"

Tommy cocked his head and listened. "The wind?"

Pearl strained to hear whatever it was that had drawn her attention. This time Tommy heard it. A soft mewling.

Pearl followed the sound, and Tommy stole along the porch after her. Behind the shed they stopped to listen. The mewling came again, taking them to the boxwood that divided them from Miss Violet's back property. Pearl bent down and dug into the bushy limbs. She pulled a teeny, delicate kitten out. She clutched it to her chest. "Oh, Tommy. Look at him. Look." Her voice was thin and gentle.

"I see." He ran his finger gently over its head. The kitten was bones with a large head it could barely hold up. Tommy's heart seized at the thought this kitten wouldn't last long in this shape, without a mother. Pearl clomped away, snuggling the cat against her chest. "He'll be fine, Tommy. I can feel you doubting. Lots of stuff you know . . . This is what I know. Inside me."

Tommy followed. "Pearl. It's not going to—"

"He."

"He what?"

"The kitten's a he, not an it."

"I don't want you to get your hopes up. Look at it—him, I mean."

"Light the fire, Tommy."

She cradled the kitten and entered the shed, full of strength and a knowing he didn't want to question. And so he did exactly what he was told.

Chapter 27

Tommy worked one last shift at the tannery before he and the other part-timers were replaced by full-time workers. Luckily he had a steady string of prayer buyers who were often willing to pay a little extra when he added a personalized prayer at the end of a session as he'd started to do since Mrs. Schultz had been so receptive and generous with small tips. Every bit made a difference to his savings.

When Tommy arrived at Mrs. Arbuckle's with prayer in hand, her butler blocked his entrance. Tommy's heart stuck in his throat. Had they figured out Hank took a silver thimble the last time they were there? Tommy looked over his shoulder, hoping a police officer wasn't coming up behind him, knowing Tommy had an appointment that day and time.

"Mrs. Arbuckle won't need your services, Mr. Arthur."

Tommy cleared his throat. "Can I ask why?"

"None of your business."

"Well, I wrote one especially for her—"

"Invite the boy in at least, Charles," Mrs. Arbuckle said from the foyer.

The butler sighed and opened the door to let Tommy inside.

Mrs. Arbuckle took Tommy by the shoulders. "You're a very nice boy, Tommy. Perfectly crafted prayers and sweet. Always a comfort."

Tommy held up a slip of paper. "I wrote you a new one. In regard to your worry about your brother and his journey to the afterlife. I've covered it all with scripture and the reverend's seal of approval."

She shook her head and stepped away from Tommy.

"What's wrong?" His heart beat in his ears. He got ready to run if he had to.

She glanced at the butler and waved him away. "Always has his nose in my business."

Tommy agreed. That's what butlers did.

"I don't want to offend you, but with my age and my family's finances, I only have so much to devote to my spirituality and religion, and I tithe a good deal to the reverend. The prayers were insurance, extra."

Tommy nodded.

"And now there's this Dreama in town. You've heard of her?"

Tommy thought back to a newspaper article he'd seen, one that mentioned she had come to town to be a medium between the living and dead. And he'd heard her name mentioned at Miss Violet's, known that she'd been there to visit, but was confused. "I read something but . . ."

Mrs. Arbuckle closed her eyes and took a deep breath before refocusing on Tommy. "She's *remarkable*." Mrs. Arbuckle's rheumy eyes looked up to the ceiling as though this Dreama was up there. "You must have been to see her by now? A spiritual soul like yourself?"

"I've read about her. Heard her name mentioned."

"Well, I met with her, and she connected me with Robert. I *felt* him, I heard his voice like it was in my own head, and I left with the peace of mind that nothing, no one else has given me."

"But this . . ." Tommy held up the paper. "This is a special prayer, sure to ease your worry. And you can keep it and reread it and—"

She grasped Tommy's hand. "Your work is done here. I'm going to consult with Dreama from now on. I'm sorry."

Tommy shook his head, thinking maybe he should visit Dreama to see exactly what she was offering that he wasn't.

"You told me about your dead brother," Mrs. Arbuckle said. "Go see Dreama. She's a godsend. You understood my pain. But Dreama *relieves* pain, and she could remove yours. Go see her." Mrs. Arbuckle picked up a newspaper and shook it at him. "Says she's doing a night for mothers and meeting privately at Miss Violet Pendergrass's offices . . ."

Tommy held up his hand; hearing her gush over the person who siphoned off his business was painful.

"Take this. Read up on her." She shoved the morning paper into his hands. The front page screamed, "Pennies from Heaven: Dreama Sees into Souls and Heals and Cashes in Big."

He read testimony after testimony from people in the article whose lives had been changed by Dreama. "I can sleep again." "Made amends with my brother after twenty years of not speaking." "Record harvest after Dreama told me where to plant my crop this year." All of this was accompanied by illustrations depicting a veiled woman sitting among clients, her slight build looking like anyone else aside from the veil. But the people sitting with her were in awe, their faces enraptured—that was clear.

It seemed like magic.

Another headline caught his eye. "Miss V. Pendergrass. Too Good to Be True?" He sighed. Surely not. Miss Violet's reports indicated her success and wealth fanned out to clients and now seeing articles about Dreama, she seemed to be the only person challenging the height of Miss Violet's achievements.

But he was confident most people found peace in the old reliable Bible, something they could revisit. So off he went to the rest of his prayer appointments. Perhaps he could get Mrs. Johnson to buy an extra prayer or invite him back a second time that week to recoup the loss of Mrs. Arbuckle's fee.

Tommy plodded to each home.

Slam. Slam. Slam.

Every last client dismissed Tommy and his prayers. Each had decided Dreama delivered comfort he could not. Tommy was so worried about the loss of funds that he didn't even notice that Frank had kept to a distance.

At one point, the bird landed on Tommy's shoulder and rubbed his head into Tommy's neck. "Oh, Frank, this isn't good." Maybe he should hire onto the tannery full-time. He'd been doing most of his high school work from afar anyway. With his enthusiasm damp and gray, he headed back to Miss Violet's where he'd retrieve his afternoon chore list.

Nothing on the list would lead to Tommy making more money. More work—same money.

Trudging along he considered the articles detailing the money and fame funneling toward Dreama. Now her success was undercutting his. He shook his head and picked up his pace. Partway home he thought of Mrs. Schultz. She liked him more than any regular prayer client. He wasn't due to see her until later in the week, but perhaps she might be able to point him to friends of hers who might want his services.

When he arrived at her home, the lady's maid answered the door. Her face dropped, then lit up, and she pulled Tommy into the foyer. He exhaled, a good feeling sweeping through him.

"I'm not supposed to deliver Mrs. Schultz's prayers until the end of the week, but—"

"She's gone." The maid held up her forefinger, then dug through a drawer in the desk near the door. "Where is it, where is it?" She opened the next drawer and finally spun around, holding an envelope. "For you."

He took it from her. His name was written in blocky print. "Gone? Where?"

The maid moved toward the door and opened it for him to exit. "Back up north with her son. I'll join her there next week. She said your words, your reassurance, led her back there to her children, where she should have gone years ago. You'll see in the envelope that she wanted to give you something extra. And she had me write a note."

A chilly breeze whipped through the door, fluttering one end of the envelope in his hand. "She left because?" Tommy asked.

"Because you did a good job and shone a light into the darkness of her life. She took what you gave her and did something with it."

Tommy drew back at the sentiment, reaching to recall the exact prayers he'd sold her recently. "She believed what I said?"

She pointed at the envelope. "Same words are in the note there. You'll see for yourself. She didn't believe what you said. She believed in *you*."

He tipped his hat and exited. Then, before the door could shut, he jammed his foot into the opening. The maid peered at him, her eyes wide.

"Tell her thank you. For believing."

The maid lifted her hand to wave. "I will."

The mix of the day's disappointment combined with the thrill of finding out someone took his prayers far beyond her heart and into action made his heart leap. Only one person felt like that, but it felt monumental, as though something shifted, like when Pearl needed him.

Was he good at what he did? Not as good as Dreama, apparently. But . . . Mrs. Schultz. She believed. Her departure dissolved a steady income source, but still, what she said . . . He opened the envelope, read the appreciative words, and saw two dollars inside. Grateful for those dollars since sending money off to San Diego, he began to think giving away money had brought some to him. He shook his head. Silly thought. That wasn't how the world worked. Clearly not. All the canceled appointments were evidence of that. But he basked in the pride that Mrs. Schultz's letter brought him. He'd done a good job and changed someone's life. That was worth more than any money he might have lost that day.

Chapter 28

Tommy bounded into Miss Violet's kitchen to find bread cooling and stew on the stove, among other things. No sign of Katherine, Violet, or any of the girls. That was better. His conversation with Miss Violet needed to be done in private. He took the back stairs two at a time and rushed down the hall to Miss Violet's private rooms. He knocked, telling himself to breathe evenly, to be calm and grown-up when he spoke.

No answer. Noise came from the third floor, where the ladies had rooms. He headed up the stairs, following the voices. He could see through the spindles as he rose upward. Several women were in the dressing room area near the back of the house at the top of the stairs. Golden sunrays spilled through the window and Tommy paused, remembering he'd been told that he shouldn't enter these rooms without permission since sometimes the ladies were changing clothes.

A tall woman was dressing in a ruffled dress. A lace veil trailed down her back. She was facing the window. Tommy squinted, the sun burning his eyes, and he continued upward against his better judgment. He held the railing, moving slower. That dress, the veil. He'd seen it in newspaper photos.

Dreama.

He swelled with anger that this woman had caused him to lose significant income. Every single client gone. He didn't want to miss the chance to let her know just that. He hit the landing right in front of the open door, and she turned. The front of the veil was folded back over her head, revealing her face to him for the first time. His breath caught.

"Olivia." He shook his head, as though doing so would clear up his muddled thoughts. One of Miss Violet's finance students?

His mind immediately went to Madame Smalley, the fortune-teller arrested for setting up illusions, cons. He knew it. Dreama was a fraud.

She glanced away, and Miss Violet filled the doorway, her face warped with anger. "Get the hell downstairs, Tommy Arthur. How *dare* you."

Her face flamed red, and she flew down the steps on his heels. When he hit the second floor, she grabbed his arm so hard her nails cut into his skin. He turned.

Her chest heaved. "I told you never to come to the third floor unless invited. How dare you—"

"How dare *you*," Tommy said slowly, reminding himself to watch his tone with Miss Violet too late.

"You have no idea—"

"*You* have no idea. That *Dreama*, that fraud you have up there is cutting into my prayer business. Olivia? Dreama is Olivia. She's a nice girl and all, but there's nothing about her that would—"

"You work for me. That's enough income."

"It's not enough. I'm saving for my mama, my sister. My father. He has plans to return, and he's depending on me." It shocked him that those words flowed out as if he hadn't come to the conclusion his father wasn't returning anytime soon.

"No one else in your family wants your father back here, Tommy. Wise up. Grow up. Your sister's moved on from childish dreams like that. Your mother certainly has. Have you even noticed?"

Tommy couldn't believe the cruelty Miss Violet wielded like a weapon. His eyes burned, and he was afraid he might burst into tears. Mama and Katherine certainly didn't believe in Frank Arthur the way Tommy had—wait. He thought of the letters, what his mother and sister had said about them, his father's broken promises, that he'd started to see the very same thing. Yet Miss Violet's nastiness stung worse than the bruises he'd gotten at Rupert's. Every breath he took at that moment caused pain in his ribs, pain in his heart, even if for different reasons.

177

"You're running a game with Olivia acting as Dreama, and it's causing me to lose prayer money. Every single customer turned me away for Dreama today. It's like you're trapping us here. Is that what you're doing?" Tommy's anger had run away with his sense. He could very well be making the whole thing worse.

Miss Violet loosened her grip on Tommy and then hugged him close, making him gasp from pain and surprise. She pulled him down to her and whispered in his ear. "Please, Tommy. Let me get through this night, and we'll figure out the financial aspects of this. You've done a fine job with your work for me. You've been discreet and . . . Give me a chance to make this up to you. I never imagined that Dreama could be the force in town that she is. People are excited about her and fearful of her and loving her and hating her, and the whole stew of it has created a sensation."

Miss Violet's sudden shift in delivery shocked him dumb. The news articles surely indicated that. Miss Violet released him and patted his arm where her nails had dug in. "Please. Forgive my reaction. I was afraid. Fear can do powerful things to people."

Tommy nodded, unsettled further by the swing back to kindness, patience.

"You understand the need for even more discretion than before? With the condoms, with Dreama, Olivia, all of it? You understand, don't you? You're a good soul, Tommy. I know that. But you cannot breathe a word of what you just saw to anyone. Your family depends on me—you do, too. I know you want to protect your family, so please don't let on that Olivia is Dreama. The less they know, the better. You must understand that. I know you understand. You are wiser than most, and I was wrong to say what I did. It's important I keep all aspects of my business separate. Most women can't manage to remain steadfast in their work when they begin to wonder what is happening in other areas. My ladies are very smart, but still I deal with their womanliness. I manage it, and I can't have anything crossing over."

Tommy thought of Mama and Katherine and Yale, all of them warm and together in a home for the first time in years. He could not put that at risk. "I understand, yes, yes."

She angled her body against his again, painful ribs making him suck back his breath.

"Thank you, Tommy," she said. "Thank you. Here, take this."

She pulled three dollars from her apron pocket. "I have more for you. It's coming. Don't be impatient or short-sighted and ruin this for your family."

Tommy was willing to protect Mama and his family, but he had to agree his anger had taken hold. He reminded himself to control it, not to let his emotions rule him. "Thanks, Miss Violet."

She led him by the hand. "You're still agitated. I don't want that, Tommy. Wait here."

She returned from one of the rooms with a mug. "This'll make you feel better. More relaxed. Your sister found the recipe in that book of hers. Calms the nerves and sharpens the mind. We all need that, right? Let's worry about new income streams tomorrow. Right now, just relax."

"What is it?" Tommy sniffed it. The scent was sweet and sour.

Miss Violet lifted her shoulders. "Katherine's a genius with her cures. I don't even ask anymore. I trust her completely."

Tommy was relieved that Katherine had made herself so useful, that his missteps, like coming upstairs uninvited, might be overlooked because of it.

"Drink it," she said.

Tommy sipped the warm liquid, trying to decipher what was in it. After a few sips, he found that he was practically chugging it down.

"There, there." Violet took the mug and looped her arm through his. "Help me down the stairs, won't you?"

Tommy felt the drink expand in his body, warming him, calming him just as Miss Violet said it would. Almost like when he had a few sips of whiskey, just before a few slid to a dozen.

They went downstairs slowly, and by the time she was guiding him through the kitchen and out the door, his state of mind had changed quite a bit.

"Well, then. Remember, this is just between us, Tommy. Reward comes in quiet faith and kept promises. I need that from you, and I will return it tenfold."

Tommy nodded and exhaled. "Sure, sure."

"Not a word about Olivia being Dreama. I need your vow. For your family's sake. They've been through enough."

Tommy nodded. "Yes."

And out the door he went.

Chapter 29

Tommy drifted back toward the shed. The drink dulled his anger, but a heavy sense of worry replaced it. He thought about what he'd experienced with his prayer business and seen at Miss Violet's and how it impacted his ability to earn money. Miss Violet was intelligent and successful. His job making condoms was evidence she was independent, and so were her employees. But he also knew there were murmurs about what went on there, as Pearl had told him. Dreama's impact on Des Moines had been far greater than he imagined. But until he lost his work selling prayers because of it, he hadn't really considered her. *Olivia.*

Pretending to communicate with the dead. Miss Violet had neither confirmed nor denied that Olivia was a fraud. But if she wasn't capable of communicating with the dead, she was good at convincing others she did. The soothing drink had to work hard to keep anger about that from taking over.

One article he'd read in the paper indicated not everyone was pleased with Dreama. She'd been lumped into the barrel of ne'er-do-wells by the purity pushers, judges, and leading citizens who were trying to clean up the community. Or pretending to do so. He thought of all the prominent men who'd been at Miss Violet's—had they all sat with Dreama there?

He hoped Olivia would be safe with those men, inches away when she did her readings. If they decided to make an example of her like they did with Madame Smalley, he couldn't imagine she'd do well in jail.

Perhaps he should focus on his own loss at Dreama's hands rather than worry what might happen if her identity were discovered. Evidently Olivia was not in need of his worries. She was just fine.

He scooped up an armful of logs from the porch and hauled them into the shed. Fern greeted him, and Frank swooped onto his shoulder. He set the wood in the iron holder and petted Fern behind the ears. He let her out and noticed the kitten bundled up by the nearly extinguished fire.

Pearl. Thinking of her—her sweetness edged with roughness—made him wonder where she was. Tommy picked up the kitten and found his breath more shallow than in the morning. Katherine, with all her knowledge of herbs and cures, would be able to do something. He tucked the kitten into his pocket, put Fern back inside, and left for Mama's, the effects of the drink fully taking hold of his mind, playing with his vision just a little, making him smile at the numbness that dulled the pain in every inch of him. He'd definitely have to get that recipe from his sister because he needed it, more than he could have thought.

**

Mama's kitchen windows glowed with evening lantern light. She was at the table with her sewing, holding Yale and talking to Katherine. Tommy patted the kitten. Mama didn't like animals, but this sick, harmless soul might turn her in another direction. Still, he'd have to be gentle with how he showed the kitten to her.

Just as he got to the stairs leading to the back porch, Mr. Hayes slid into view through the window. He bent forward, tickling Yale, making her giggle. Then he locked eyes with Mama, the two of them lost in each other in a way that shocked Tommy, hardening the edges the sweet drink had dulled.

Have you even noticed? Miss Violet's words came back to him. Was this what she meant? Mama and Mr. Hayes were more than friends? Tommy pushed into the kitchen.

"Hello, Tommy," Mr. Hayes said.

Tommy grunted and began to sort through the jars of herbs that Katherine had organized since harvesting and drying them.

Mama kissed his cheek. "Remember your manners," she whispered.

"Forgot them, yes."

Those were the last words Tommy could remember when he woke later that night. He lifted his shirt and squinted down to see bandages and dried poultice wrapped around his midsection. What on earth? Who had prepared him a poultice? It had to be Katherine but . . . He squeezed his eyes closed, remembering going into Mama's kitchen, seeing her and Yale and Mr. Hayes, and yes, Katherine. She'd kept coughing.

He felt as though he'd been dropped into someone else's life. He hobbled down the loft ladder and added wood to the dying fire. As he poked it and opened the flue more, he heard mewling. He looked at the stone hearth. The kitten wiggled and stretched.

Tommy scratched his chin. The kitten. That's why he went to Mama's earlier. To have Katherine cure it. He reswaddled it like he'd seen Pearl do earlier and stood, noticing a note on the table.

Had to irn at Mrs. Randolfs. Plese water and feed Fern. And Tedde the kittn. Think hes goin to live. Thanks for having yer sweet sis give medcin. You fell rite aslep aftr brung Tedde bak. I herd yu yel at yer ma and that man. Be nicer. Yer family is good. Luv em hard, but dont be hard yerself.

Tommy smiled at the chicken-scratch writing, smiled that she'd named the kitten, not waiting to confirm if he would in fact live. Her words reminded him of Mrs. Schultz when she told him though he was big he didn't have to be hard.

He collapsed into a chair at the table, pounding head in hand. Why couldn't he remember anything Pearl talked about in that letter? He was mean to Mama and Mr. Hayes? Pearl was there? He shook his head, rolling back through time. He'd lost his prayer sales, gone to Miss Violet's, seen Olivia dressed as Dreama... The drink. Then he took the kitten for Katherine to help.

He squeezed his eyes closed trying to remember details beyond arriving at Mama's. Yale, Katherine, and Mr. Hayes had been there . . . He shook his head.

According to Pearl, he had succeeded in getting a cure for the kitten, but apparently had also been very rude? It must have been that drink. A warm gush of goodness followed by a dizzying loss of memory. Good God, what else had he done that he couldn't remember?

At the bottom of the note was a word. *Equipage. P. 67. Has me stumpt. Help!*

He smiled at the open book of fairy tales. *"Leander on his arrival had the finest equipage prepared that was ever seen . . ."* He didn't need to finish reading. He knew it meant a prince's people and all the trappings of a regal life even as the character traveled. He remembered the story. He thought of Pearl, her love of words and other worlds, the way she seemed to tell everyone of her fairy-tale dreams and her desire for a prince. He may not be able to offer a princely life, but he could give her a story of one.

He opened her bag and fished through a load of things for paper. He pulled out several sheets. He took a blank piece and saw the one under it was covered in her hand. "Letters to Heaven," it said at the top.

Dear Ma…

When he realized he was reading Pearl's private thoughts, that she might be writing to the mother who abandoned her or was dead, he felt intrusive and he tucked the papers back inside, keeping a blank piece out.

He shaved some wood from the pencil he and Pearl shared to reveal more lead, and scratched some sentences onto it. *Once upon a time there was a girl.* He shook his head. No, that wasn't right. Girl didn't fit. Woman? No, that evoked images of people like his mother. *Mama. Pearl's ma.*

The thought of both mothers dampened his creative thoughts. He needed to apologize for his behavior even if he couldn't remember it. He folded the paper and tucked it under some tools that had been stored in one of the trunks when he moved in. He'd write more later, but he was unsettled. He checked on Teddy, let Fern out, and had Frank come down from his roost.

The bird landed on Tommy's shoulder and dropped something at his feet. The clink of metal and shine of silver made Tommy scrutinize Frank. The bird dropped a second item. Two quarters. He looked at Frank again, who cocked his head.

"You found these?"

"Money. Money," Frank said.

The weight of coins in his hand reminded him of the day he'd ducked into Colt Churchill's saloon to get out of the storm. He was stung by quiet loneliness. He'd once frequented the dances held by the riverside, populated by musicians and artists who played all night, allowing dancers to revel around a fire. He could go there . . . But no, he reminded himself. He had Pearl. He wasn't alone anymore, though the residue of isolation stuck somehow, surprising him that he had to make an effort to recall that he now had a purpose larger than his immediate family—protect Pearl, watch over Frank the crow.

Lonely, he thought perhaps Katherine wanted company. He could apologize for, according to Pearl's letter, being ill-tempered to all involved. He could also ask about the drink Miss Violet had given him and suggest Katherine make it a little weaker next time. But when he reached the house, his sister was gone, working the party Miss Violet was holding for Dreama—"Olivia dressed as Dreama," Tommy said aloud to no one. He knew better than to bother anyone at Miss Violet's while she worked, and he wasn't about to try the drink again, not when it left him unable to recall swaths of time.

Shuffling back to the shed, Frank lifted off Tommy's shoulder. The numbness from the drink and poultice completely gone, allowed the return of stabbing pain in his ribs. Frank returned with a third quarter. Tommy scanned the night sky, trying to discern exactly where Frank had gotten the money.

He had to do something about the pain because then he'd be able to think straight and make a plan for a new job that might provide enough to get his savings for Mama's cottage back on track.

Whiskey.

It worked well to relieve his panic attacks. He thought perhaps it would work the same on physical pain. He entered the shed and dug through the dusty trunk for the whiskey bottle. He popped the cork and emptied the last few swigs down his throat.

Numbness eased closer, like rivertide reaching for the shore, but this low tide wasn't enough. He considered the money Frank had brought. He'd be careful with it, pay his debt at Churchill's and have plenty for a small bottle of whiskey to bring back for medicine. He'd just sip it occasionally when things got to be too much, until the pain of his ribs was gone.

He scratched a note for Pearl saying he'd be gone for a bit but he'd see her soon.

Chapter 30

Tommy entered Churchill's and hobbled to the bar. Scattered groups of men played billiards, chuck-a-luck, faro, and poker. Fiddle music narrated the action, and the scent of beer filled his nose, familiar, evoking a sense of home. A distinct floating happiness came, and he wondered how that was possible for smells and sounds to conjure powerful, immediate feelings. When the barkeep sidled up, Tommy gestured toward the board with the name Zachary Taylor written on it. "I'd like to pay that debt," Tommy said. "Get a small bottle of whiskey to go home. For medicine."

The barkeep dried glasses with dishwater-gray rags. "Medicine." He wiggled his eyebrows. "Only heard that a couple hundred times this week."

Tommy raised his shoulders, making his ribs scream. "Please."

"Have to wait on Mr. Churchill. He's the only one who can erase the board. He'll be back any second. He's at a meetin'."

Tommy sighed, hoping that was the case. He hadn't been there long when someone sat down next to him.

"Say, Tommy," Hank said. "How 'bout a swig for you as is custom here?"

Tommy's first reaction was exhilaration that someone he knew arrived, but then he remembered Hank seemed to show up most reliably when he needed something or to bring Tommy trouble.

"Zachary Taylor." Tommy put his hand out to remind Hank that, in the saloon, that was his name.

Hank winked, grasping what Tommy meant. "Prayers dried up like prairie dust, ain't they?" He signaled the barkeep for two shots.

Tommy drank the whiskey he'd been given and nodded. "Sure have."

Hank lifted his glass toward the door behind the bar. "Know what's happenin' in the back room?"

Tommy shrugged. "Storage?"

"Baths, Zachary-Tommy. *Bathers.*"

Tommy scoffed. "Bathers?"

"You take your two bits, you go back there, and they change it out for a warm sudsing by a lady. And she don't just git ya under the arms."

Tommy understood. The current drive to clean up everything deemed impure and imperfect in Des Moines must have missed the path to Churchill's Saloon. Judge Calder belonged here, so he obviously knew they were giving "baths" in the back room.

"Baths. Imagine that." Tommy thought of the ladies at Miss Violet's and the steady flow of rainwater up their rear stairs courtesy of his back. Maybe he should have himself a bath, a few moments of relaxation in the back room. "Could use a hot dip, but no. Have other plans for my money."

A whoop from the game tables made him turn. The two faro boards were covered with checks. Men lined the perimeter of each, faces full of laughter and angst, arms thrust into the air, patting each other on the backs in celebration or consolation. The sense of companionship lured him. Merriment. It wouldn't last. But . . . Maybe he could join?

The whiskey bit away at his determination. One game. Just while he waited for Colt.

He edged toward one faro table and stood between two men who threw their arms up and groaned or cheered just about every other time. The odds could be nearly fifty-fifty for the bank or the punters who played against the bank, but Tommy knew there was usually a trick on the bank's behalf. Still, a pattern emerged, making Tommy think maybe he could beat the dealer's system.

A man at the table elbowed Tommy, making him grab his bruised side.

"Been lucky all night. Slide in, friend. Share some good fortune."

Tommy shook his head and stuffed his hands in his pockets.

The next round brought winners for every man but one.

Another round, more big wins.

Keep your hands in your pockets.

He glanced over his shoulder, looking for Colt Churchill.

"Deal ya in, son?" the dealer with close-set eyes said as the coffin keeper slid the beads to show which cards had just been played with that round. Tommy eyed it. Half the deck had been played.

"Remove your bets, set your bets, copper your bets. No more bets."

He thought of Pearl wanting to go to school, Mama's cottage. Every other hand won, then three losses for the players. Same pattern every time.

Keep your hands in your pockets.

The dealer hesitated and looked at Tommy. "Jumpin' in?"

Tommy shook his head and made a move toward the bar, now thinking it better to just drink away his found money from Frank, but a saloon girl cut him off, handing him a shot, and dropping whiskey in front of the other men. "On the house, fellas!"

Tommy studied her.

"Drink up. Ya just got lucky," she said.

"Remove your bets, place your bets, copper your bets," the dealer said.

The man beside Tommy jostled him. Thoughts of his goals, the debt, anything other than his desire to win against the house disappeared. Tommy exchanged his two bits for checks and started to put them on the ace, but then shifted it over to the queen, for luck, thinking of Pearl and her stories of royalty and fortune. He set it smack in the middle of the card since he'd seen a man put his too close to the edge and then be accused of having placed it between two cards, causing him to lose.

"No more bets."

Tommy won.

Another shot in front of him, another down his throat. The drinks further eased his aching ribs and muscles. The sound of the cards cracking against each other as they were shuffled and slid into the box to be dealt two at a time punctuated the screeching fiddler's music. Like a dance, a winner and a loser were dealt and the copper that could change a winner from a loser punctuated the rhythm of the game, its music. The booze filtered out the conversation around him.

When Bayard joined Hank at the next table, Tommy was finished checking with himself to see if he was keeping track of what he was doing. Tommy's buddies toasted one another in between games, and a swell of comradery wrapped him tight.

He snapped his fingers at the girl, and she delivered another shot. Tommy swayed, gripped the table, and threw back the shot, his stomach lurching for a moment. He pressed his gut, the searing booze threatening to burn through.

The fuzzy sensation disconcerted and pleased all at once. His problems with Mama, money, his father, faded into the background. He suddenly had control. He could plan his fate, not be a slave to it. He nodded at the thought as though he'd said it aloud.

Enjoy the miracle, the sensation of floating away . . . He was floating, wasn't he? He deserved it after all he'd been through. Why had he resisted drinking regularly? It cured everything from his aches and pains to his worries to his attacks. It was medicine when used properly. It wasn't like laudanum.

Hank sauntered over. "Tommy, my friend. Let me git ya home. Ya drank too much too fast. Bonafide lightweight. Ya never had a drink before? I know better."

Tommy sat back in his chair but kept gripping the table. "Nah. Just got here."

Hank came around the table and grabbed Tommy around the waist, walking him toward the exit. "Let's git you home. You've had 'nough fun tonight."

Tommy struggled to see through his muddy vision. "That's funny. I'm funny! You're funny!" Tommy said as Hank dragged him toward the door. Tommy's feet tangled, and he stumbled. Hank lost his grip, but another patron caught Tommy around the midsection and righted him. The pain it caused his ribs blurred his vision more. Even with the numbing booze, being caught up by the man sent searing pain through his body.

He tried to even out his breath to stop the pain and looked up to thank the person who helped him. The black hat and white collar startled him.

"Reverend Shaw." Tommy staggered toward him and poked at his chest. "My prayers dried up, and I have a mother and sisters and . . . Miss Violet Pendergrass told me . . . She had me . . ."

"Tommy Arthur." The reverend grabbed Tommy's wrist. "Shut your mouth."

A familiar voice boomed from an unseen source. "Tommy Arthur?"

Tommy struggled to balance while he scanned the space.

"Jeanie and Frank's son?"

Tommy turned slowly, finally realizing who the resounding voice belonged to. He straightened and balled his fists. The vision of Judge Calder sharpened and blurred as Tommy swayed.

"Well, well, well. Zachary Taylor?" The judge looked Tommy up and down.

Tommy spread his legs to steady himself. He held up two fingers. "Both! I'm two…" He stumbled and caught himself. "Two names. Right boys?" He elbowed Hank. His drunken bluster diminished his sense of self-preservation. "Two people. I am."

"A little coffin varnish has a way of reducing mental function, doesn't it, Tommy Arthur?" Judge Calder stalked forward. "*Tommy Arthur.*" Judge Calder's movement silenced the room; only the flap of the faro dealer shuffling cards rang out. Judge Calder shook his finger. "So you're a thief. Just like your grandfather. Like your daddy."

It had been years since Tommy heard those words spoken aloud about his family, weaponized.

Judge Calder spit, narrowly missing Tommy's leg. "Apple doesn't fall far from the tree. Can't believe I didn't see it that first day in court." He grabbed the back of Tommy's neck, yanking him up like he was cut from paper. "Over a year ago, wasn't it? Your stay in my jail?"

Tommy choked as the judge tightened his grip on the collar.

He squeezed Tommy so tight it numbed his feet. "*You were in my house.* This information, this little *twist,*" his words took on a hissing quality, "so much news here, well, it's handy. I've a lot to consider, young Tommy. Your mother, your sisters . . ." He looked to the ceiling as though this was the most important information he'd ever been told. He let Tommy go.

Tommy lurched and rubbed his sore ribs, his mind focusing on the mention of Mama and his sisters. "Leave my family out of this. They haven't done a thing wrong. Ever." His alcohol-fattened tongue softened his words.

He chuckled. "Can't be sure about that, can you?"

"I'm sure."

The judge scoffed. "Shut up, *Thomas.* For now, you keep doing as Reverend Shaw has outlined. I mean, I take it if you're occupied with Hank and Bayard here, you understand the game you're playing?"

Judge Calder cackled, sounding half like a wounded animal and half like an insane patient at Glenwood, his eyes wild and wide.

Tommy balled his fists, wanting to pummel the judge. He stepped toward him again, staggering then straightening, then staggering, before falling forward.

Hank and Bayard caught him under his arms. "That's enough," Hank said. Through the front windows, a crowd of people swept by, pointing at someone and screaming. Two policemen followed behind.

The judge took Hank and Bayard by the backs of their collars. "Out the back, Hank. Get this one home. Get on out before—" As Hank and Bayard dragged Tommy toward the back room, the front door opened. Women's voices mixed with a pastor's rantings.

Tommy pulled out of Bayard's grip and stumbled, falling behind the bar. Hank and Bayard dropped right behind him.

"Officers," Judge Calder bellowed. "Arrest these men for gambling and drinking. You men don't understand the meaning of the word 'temperance'?"

The men playing faro groaned but didn't appear frightened, as Tommy would have been.

Tommy strained to hear, his drunkenness reducing his hearing. The pastor raised his hands and prayed, and Tommy caught a glimpse of Mrs. Hillis. His heart sped even faster. Was Mama there, too? Wasn't she always with Mrs. Hillis? Tommy's mind swirled as the officer put a man's hands behind his back, roping them. The man winked at the judge, and the judge put his finger to his lips.

"I saw some young men, boys, in here, Judge," the pastor said. "I want any young men tossed in jail before their souls are irreparably damaged by Satan himself. Won't be long before a den of sin like this hosts every bodily sin in the book if we don't shut it down now. Children cannot be party to such dealings."

Tommy held his breath.

Judge Calder had opened his arms, and he slowly rotated in place. "I don't see any boys here. We're cleaning this town up, to be sure."

"Well, what are *you* doing here, Judge?" one of the men in the crowd asked.

The judge drew back and shuffled his feet. "I'm doing the work of lazy officers, I suppose. Just happened by and—"

The pastor shouldered past the judge. "I saw young men in here. I recognized one boy from a workhouse near the riverbend. Know I did." He put his hands on his hips and looked around as though he thought Tommy and his cohorts might be ducked under a table, nearly in plain sight.

Tommy surveyed the space behind the bar. "Hey," he said.

Hank slapped his hand over Tommy's mouth. "Shush. My God, shut up."

The barkeep remained calm, drying the glasses, seemingly uninterested in the chaos. He added the name Tommy Arthur to the chalkboard and scribbled $6 next to it. Hank pulled Tommy's sleeve. "Let's go."

Tommy froze, the angry voices on the other side of the bar getting closer. He raised up and peered over it, peeking between half-full glasses.

Another man entered the bar and joined the purity pusher. Hank yanked Tommy down.

"We're thinking the same, you and I, Stevens. I thought I saw young men in here, too. But if there were children in here," Judge Calder said, "these two gentlemen will give them up and I will deal with them, for I agree young men need guidance, and without a doubt it's becoming clearer my role in helping such types." The judge's gaze drilled a hole in the bar where the boys were hidden.

They crouched lower. Hank signaled for them to follow and they crawled toward a small, hidden door that opened out of the wainscoting in the wall behind the bar.

Once in the backroom, Tommy's hands and knees wet from crawling past the tubs now abandoned by saloon girls and patrons, the three boys scarpered through the darkened storage room and into the alley. Tommy's legs wobbly and soft, he shuffled and teetered into the main road, hoping his drunkenness wouldn't keep him from outrunning a man charged with cleaning up all that was evil in Des Moines.

Chapter 31

Tommy arrived at the shed. Empty. Even Fern and Teddy were gone. His stomach growled. There must be something left from dinner at Mama's. His head still buzzing, he entered the kitchen and slammed the door, rattling the windows. His bird gripped his shoulder tighter. "Hi, lady," Frank squawked at Mama.

Tommy fell back against the door and propped himself there, arms across his chest. Reed Hayes stared at Tommy, his mouth slack. Tommy scowled, irritated at the man's presence. He touched his ribs, the swelling increasing. He'd had enough fighting for the night.

He wouldn't have gone there at all had he not been desperate to fill his belly and soak up the firewater he'd been served. It was as though he'd drunk something that changed him completely in a matter of a few servings. He'd never felt so out of control, numb—but alive—at once. The acid turned his stomach, but the scent of bread, chicken, and potatoes reminded him why he was there.

"Tommy, what's the matter? You've been out of sorts since this evening. Look at you. What've you been doing?" Mama went to him, taking his face in her hands, stealing glances at his bird. She examined Tommy as though he were a plant with leaf rot and she were trying to determine how best to treat the ailment. The bird pecked toward Mama. She backed away.

"I'm hungry, but I'll be out of your hair in a minute." He glowered in the direction of Mr. Hayes.

Mama took his chin and turned his face back and forth. "What's wrong with you?"

He didn't answer.

She sniffed. "You've been drinking."

He looked away.

Mama's mouth fell open, her eyes filled with disappointment. "You know better than anyone that you can't drink like this. Is that what had you so awfully rude earlier?" Her lips went into a hard line. "*Not* after what your father went through with the laudanum. You've been drunk all day?"

Apple doesn't fall far from the tree . . . Judge Calder's words floated back, filling him with rage.

"'Course not. I wasn't feeling well earlier. I tried a cure and . . . Never mind. What's it matter? Bad day is all."

His vision wavered between focused and blurred. He wiggled away from Mama and went to the stove, where there was a pot of potatoes. He grabbed a fork and began to eat right out of the pot.

Mama took a plate from the cabinet. She pushed it in front of him, and he loaded it heavy, clanging the fork. He stopped for a moment. Mama's expression was sad and searching, the way she'd looked at his father when the curtain of laudanum dropped over him.

Now he understood his father better than ever. The man may have used laudanum to numb away his life, having to deal with his mother, who clearly turned disappointed easily. Her sad expression made Tommy want to slam back another glass of red-eye.

Mama took the fork from him and added chicken to his plate. He fell into a chair and leaned his forearms on the table.

"Glad you're home safe, Tommy," Mr. Hayes said with all his feigned friendliness.

Tommy gnawed on the words that he wanted to say but shouldn't. Then he gave them their legs. "So friendly. Mr. Friendly. Right here in my kitchen."

Mr. Hayes gave what Tommy was sure was a chuckle before gathering himself. "Maybe Katherine has some headache powder? You're going to have a mean one," Mr. Hayes said.

"How 'bout this, Mr. Smart. I already got myself a blazing headache. Beat ya to it." Tommy didn't want anything from him, least of all his concern. "What on earth are you doing, Mr. Reed

Hayes? Haven't you had your fill of putting your hands in my family garden? Haven't you gotten enough articles and dissertations out of us for now?"

Mama set the plate on the table and clamped onto his shoulder. "Stop it. Mr. Hayes has done nothing but be helpful and kind."

She slid into the chair next to Tommy. "You can't drink whiskey, Tommy. Yes, people get drunk by accident. But that's why you can't drink at all. *Not one drink.* It's like a family curse or something—" She lifted and dropped her shoulders. "One round," she said through clenched teeth. "One round to lose all sense. It's in our blood, like a rule we can't break. Your father, your grandfather . . ."

Tommy snorted, shoveling food down his throat. She was the one who broke sacred rules. She'd gotten divorced. She'd made his father leave and shamed them all. Who was she to tell Tommy what to do with his free time?

He pointed his fork at Mr. Hayes then Mama. "You two in the garden this summer. Laughing and writing in that blasted book and digging and composting and bent over those roses like the two of you birthed them. It's *wrong.* My father might not be here," Tommy pointed his fork at his heart, "but he's here. He belongs to us, with us, and he's coming back just as soon as . . . I don't know. But soon."

Mr. Hayes stood, scooped up Yale, and headed for the stairs. "I'll put Yale to bed and leave you two to discuss this alone."

Yale put her head on Mr. Hayes's shoulder, and the sight crumbled what was left of Tommy's good sense. Mama moved closer to Tommy, whispering in a taut tone, "Mr. Hayes is a friend of our family. You need to respect your elders. I've taught you—"

"Nothing, Mama." Tommy tossed his fork onto the plate. "I've learned nothing from you except I have to depend on myself."

"Tommy!" She grasped his shoulders. "Who in their right mind served you this . . . whatever it is you drank to turn you into the devil? If you stumble into the street like this and the police see you, they'll toss you in jail. You don't want to know . . . It's awful what happens to boys in jail."

Tommy shrank, glad that she didn't know he was plenty acquainted with what it was like in jail. He clenched his jaw. "I've been on my own long enough to decide when to have a sip of joy-juice."

"Really? This is joy to you?"

"Yes."

"You won't mind jail? Frigid cells, brutish men who will be more than happy to give you a beating just for fun. Or worse. Surely you realize that?"

He shrugged. Mama's brow creased with sadness and confusion. She grasped Tommy's face and pulled him toward her, kissing his forehead.

"You'll ruin your opportunity to shape your life in a meaningful way, in a way that provides a comfortable home, one that allows for a solid life, a wife someday, children."

"It's already ruined." He moved Mama's hands from his cheeks. "My father left because it's so bad with us. He left us, Mama, and that's why I'm like this. You made him leave. That's why I need things like a beer once in a while. Or a whiskey for medicine."

Her mouth dropped open.

Her stunned expression reflected back at him, shocked at what he was saying, but he couldn't stop himself, the words loosened by alcohol. "You ruined our life, Mama. You."

She drew back, looking as though he'd run her down with a wagon. She put her quivering hands in her lap. Tommy breathed heavily, nauseated. He hadn't realized how angry he'd been with her, how much resentment had curdled inside, waiting to unfurl, veiling both of them. It felt good to let it out. Then he saw her absorb the pain, the silent flinch before she looked away.

Finally she met his gaze hard. "You can do anything you want, Tommy." Her voice was strong, not weak, as he'd expected it to be after what he just said. She balled a fist and set it on the table. "You're in school; you're working for Reverend Shaw. You can build up what you see as destroyed. Carousing, running away doesn't solve anything. You're old enough to claim your life choices and not blame others."

"I'm not the one who ran away from everything that mattered. *You* ran, and my father just did what you told him to do—leave. You ran away. You sent him away."

Her face reddened. Tommy braced himself, thinking she might hit him. The tendon in her neck tensed a cord snaking down, disappearing into her collar.

"We can reshape our lives. I'm doing that. Katherine is. You can, too. But if you're falling into drink, then you are most surely running away, even if you never lift a foot to leave Des Moines." She pulled him into her arms. He was stunned that she didn't strike him, that he let her hold him.

She kissed his forehead again and rocked him. "Your life could be grand, Tommy. Finish high school, be a draftsman, a lawyer, anything. You're just as smart as James. Never forget that." Mama's voice caught. Had she ever said that before?

He *was* as smart as James, just not in the way that James was smart. His mother didn't understand Tommy's intelligence. "I'm not James, Mama." Tommy pulled away. "And I'll never like that Mr. Hayes. No matter how much you do."

"But—"

"You know why?" Tommy said. The resentment reared up again, his ability to stifle it, gone.

Mama shook her head.

"Because Mr. Hayes isn't my father and I'm not James. James would love Mr. Hayes. But not me. And as much as I miss my brother, I have to say the only reason I wish he was here is so that you wouldn't have to press the memory of him, the shape of him into me. If he was here, I'd be free. His death was like a house falling in on me. I'm forever trapped by him—what he was and what I'll never be."

"Tommy, no." Her voice was thin. He'd hurt her good; he could see that plain as if they shared broken, half-beating hearts.

"I know you were never like James, and that wasn't bad. That was wonderful. It was—"

Tommy pushed his plate away, the entire thing clean. "I'm done, Mama."

He hopped up and ran out the door with Frank squawking, "Bye, lady," as the door slammed behind them. Into the night, he stomped through the kitchen garden and he finally felt empty of all the fear and worry and guilt and anger. Trouble was, the emptiness, it sat there yawning, ulcerous, filling right back up with all that turned his soul rancid in the first place.

Chapter 32

No more whiskey. A few days passed, and Tommy's stomach still churned at the thought of it. His insides remembered what his mind couldn't. He'd forbidden himself from accepting unidentified concoctions meant to calm and numb. No more coffin varnish. If he needed to soothe a panic, he'd have a gentle, quiet beer, something that softened his edges instead of sharpening them, instead of turning him into a soulless tornado.

Thick disgust for how he'd treated Mama sat heavy in his belly. He kept apologizing and she kept accepting, but he didn't trust that he'd ever stop seeing his unleashed cruelness in her eyes every time she looked at him. He had to do something to show he was sorry, to force things to evolve.

He'd also apologized to Katherine, whom he'd been told he was also rude to that same night. She'd hugged him tight saying she simply wanted him to be safe and stay out of the bottle. She had been fighting off a cough for some time, and he told her to take care of herself as much as she worried about him. None of them could afford to be ill or drunk if they intended to create a better life. The line between having enough to survive and being dragged into despair was simply too thin and at points, invisible. Purpose, the right path . . . Attention on it was required to avoid desperation.

"I'm all right, Tommy. Even with this awful cold I can't shake. Aleksey's been coming around . . ." Her gaze slipped toward the horizon and a peaceful expression spread over her face.

Dorozhka. "Aleksey's on a good path," Tommy said.

She had agreed.

"Like his father always said to us."

"Yes, they are such kind people. So . . . I am just so happy he's here. I never expected to see him again after everything." She looked at her hands, her pinkie finger that had to be amputated after frostbite got to it during the blizzard when Aleksey saved her life.

Tommy wished he could take all the awful behavior back from the night he'd fought with Mama. It was as though his mouth had been working independent of his brain, the words propelled with deep anger that had overtaken him. No—pain. It was as though saying what had hurt him so much could relieve it, but it only made things worse. What if Mama didn't really forgive him deep down? Perhaps he didn't deserve it.

**

Odd stretches of freezing rain alternating with quick melting snows, then short, but warm days made Tommy patch sections of the shed that had lost too much plaster, that would soon allow critters inside as winter arrived and tightened around them. He spread the thick mortar and considered the work ahead. He was due for a night-lighting of the furnaces at Miss Violet's. He'd also been hired to perform what Miss Violet termed "listening duties" for Dreama's readings that night.

"Very, very important tonight, Tommy. We need to capture what is said," Miss Violet had told him. He barely kept from rolling his eyes, but wanted a closer look at what Dreama did that was so wonderful that he'd lost every single prayer client.

Miss Violet explained that the individual readings were done in the company of an audience, but often Dreama spoke quietly, and the others in the room might be distracted by their own drinking and finance consultations.

He daubed the plaster and smoothed it into the holes at the front of the shed. The sound of a shovel digging into the ground drew Tommy's attention. With nightfall coming, Mama should be settling in, not breaking ground in the kitchen garden.

Tommy followed the noise and stopped halfway through the hedge. Reed Hayes. Digging along the border near the fence.

"Does my mama know you're digging up her garden?" Tommy wanted to be nicer to this man even though he seemed the perfect target for the ever-filling anger. "I mean . . . Is that the plan?"

Mr. Hayes leaned on his shovel and squinted at Tommy. "Matter of fact, your mama doesn't know. She's out buying buttons and stays for Mrs. Calder. Mother-of-pearl buttons she said—only the best will do for Mrs. Calder. And this work won't keep. Crazy weather, isn't it?"

"She could ask me for help." Tommy's guilt at the way he'd treated his mother the other evening was banished by his distaste for Mr. Hayes.

"Can we talk?" Mr. Hayes asked.

"No." Tommy headed away from Mr. Hayes, back toward his shed.

Mr. Hayes followed and took him by the arm. "We're going to talk."

Tommy shook his arm free and sat on the broken-down porch.

Mr. Hayes knocked on the pillar that held up the trellis above. "Rotted. It'll need replacing."

Tommy shrugged.

Mr. Hayes sat beside him. "Your mother loves you like no one I've ever seen. Wants what's best for you."

Tommy squinted at Mr. Hayes. "You're an expert on mothers loving sons?"

Mr. Hayes's gaze penetrated Tommy, making him squirm.

"You hurt her bad the other night."

Tommy's stomach lurched. What bothered him most was that he might not even remember everything he'd said, that Mr. Hayes was witness to the emotional rampage. He couldn't argue with Mr. Hayes on this point. "I know it." He despised this man for noting it.

"Saloon juice'll rot you from the inside out," Mr. Hayes said.

Frank landed on Tommy's shoulder. He considered this. The first couple whiskeys never tasted right to him, but then as it filled him up, the sensation that came was glorious, numbing his soul to perfection. When he drank, he carried no worries, no pain, no sadness during the splurge.

The next day was another story. Until recently, Tommy had barely even carried a next-morning headache, as though he and whiskey were made for one another. But the other night, when his anger ripped him open, spewing all over Mama, it scared the hell out of him. Tommy had been awful, but he didn't need Mr. Hayes to tell him so. Rotten was correct. And, he'd make it up to Mama, but he didn't have to explain that to this stranger.

"Listen," Mr. Hayes said, "my parents died when I was twelve, and I kept five younger siblings in good health. I know what it's like to fall into the bottle now and again. Like tumbling into a canyon, the pain swallowing you up." Mr. Hayes tapped his chest. "Inside and out. And I just want to help. That's all. I can—"

Tommy drew away and cackled. "That's just beautiful. You, the rev, the judge, the world is full of folks wanting to help, apparently, but—"

Mr. Hayes stood and planted his shovel into the ground. "Maybe you should start taking the help."

"I won't *ever* take your help. And my mama doesn't need it either."

Mr. Hayes shook his head. "Well. If you're gonna stay deep in a bottle—"

"I swore off the whiskey, if you have to know."

"Good." Mr. Hayes scratched his chin. "Good. And if you want me to help—if you need anything—just ask."

Tommy nodded. Mr. Hayes walked back toward the hedge that separated the fruit garden from the kitchen garden.

"Don't you have some science to do or some student to teach? You spend more time in our garden than at Drake University. People are talking. I saw that article questioning your Christian ways, digging and planting in the garden of a divorced woman."

Mr. Hayes turned. "Like I said, if you change your mind . . ." He disappeared beyond the hedgerow. Crisp icy rain ticked at the earth, at Tommy's skin. Knifing his cheeks, he let the frozen shards hit him, accepting it as a reprimand from God or some force of the universe.

The rain came faster, accompanying Mr. Hayes's shovel speed. Tommy thought he heard the man grunt. Good. Tommy had angered the man. Good. Wasn't fair if he kept all the hostility for himself.

Chapter 33

With the bigger holes in the shed patched, Tommy completed the evening chores. He shoveled coal into the furnace in Miss Violet's cellar and thought about Mr. Hayes. Tommy refused to accept that man's offer to "help" him. The nerve, the bluster. What right did that do-gooder interloper have to be so solicitous? Tommy could dismiss that part of his conversation with Mr. Hayes, but the part about how Tommy hurt his mother—that he could not ignore.

When he thought of Mama and the way he loved her, he thought of his affection as existing in layers, like the earth. Some layers were rich and full of goodness, and other layers were near useless and hard. Mama never said a word to him about special feelings for Mr. Hayes, just that they traded services, but Tommy could see plain as the sun rising in the east that she wanted that man for herself.

Her lack of disclosure was like how she never explained why she pushed his father away, never even said a word about being sorry she hurt him when she made him leave, when she didn't even try to get him to stay when he came back for them so many years ago.

Tommy set the shovel against the coal bin and went to the sink. He rinsed his sweaty face and wiped under his arms, changing his shirt and readying for Miss Violet's next job—the new one.

He climbed the steps that led into the kitchen. Miss Olivia met him there and guided him to the spot where he was to take notes on everything Dreama said and how the men responded. He wanted to ask Olivia if she was conning everyone as Dreama or if she had an inclination for reaching the dead, but he'd had enough trouble for a few days.

"Right here," Olivia said, pulling a hidden set of velvet portieres from behind the ones that fronted the room. "Miss Violet said not to make a peep and stay still as marble. I'll be downstairs for a while, and then I'll leave. Dreama will make her appearance then. Keep your ears peeled because there's no telling exactly when she'll start reading for a client."

Tommy scratched the pencil on the paper. "Got it."

"And when it's over, you head through the door right there." She pointed to a section of the woodwork and popped it open. A cool breeze filtered through, and he was relieved he'd have moving air when behind the heavy curtain. "Take the passage all the way to the kitchen. Once you're through the door it's big enough to stand and walk upright. No one'll ever see you, and you won't see anyone. Just listen and take notes."

Miss Violet joined Olivia and Tommy and stared at him with sharp eyes, digging into him deep, making it clear to him that this job was important.

"You're simply backing up the conversation in case one of the clients forgets what was said during the session. There will be business talk, then Dreama will entertain the gentlemen with her reading of their spiritual lives, and then there will be talk of finance again. Olivia has very important work tonight."

Miss Violet held up her finger, the pink polish glimmering in the candlelight, apple lotion fresh on her skin. "Capture every word you can. But you are not to peek. You'll panic the clients if you're seen."

**

When the evening started, Tommy put all his focus into listening. At first he tried to catch all the chatter so he would know when Dreama was starting to read, but then he realized the financial talk might go on for some time. Soon the room grew quiet, as though it had emptied. No peeking. But he needed to see what was happening so he wouldn't miss anything important. He pulled the edge of the thick portiere to the side, just enough to get a look at the people in one half of the room.

Miss Olivia sat with Mr. Renfrew, her dainty hands folded around one of his. After a bit, she got up and went upstairs, leaving Mr. Renfrew with a paper to read. Tommy assumed her exit meant she'd change into the costume and Dreama would appear very soon. He quietly shifted to see another part of the room and noticed Reverend Shaw near the front door. Miss Helen slipped into Tommy's view and patted Reverend Shaw's shoulder before trailing her fingers down his chest.

What on earth was the reverend doing, letting this woman rub his chest? Helen worked her fingers through the space between the buttons, then downward, between his legs and back up again. Tommy held his breath, not believing what he was seeing. He knew Reverend Shaw was crooked, but something about this part of his warped ways repulsed Tommy more than anything else. How were the rest of these men watching this, as though it were perfectly acceptable? Tommy had thought he, Hank, and Bayard were the extent of the people who were privy to the reverend's behavior, but apparently the circle was much wider and encompassed so much more.

Tommy closed his eyes for a moment. Sadness filled him, as though his disappointment in religion hadn't been fully saturated. How many lies, how many things could this man do wrong while still telling others to be good?

He peeked again. Miss Bernice came into the room with refreshments on a silver tray, and all eyes turned in her direction as she stood near the portiere. He knew the thickness and length of the fabric hid him, but Tommy was suddenly vulnerable. The form of a large man came into view, his shoulders the size of a cornfield, his hair familiar. When Miss Violet sashayed to the man, threading her delicate hands around his neck, he leaned into her upturned face and swung her around. His hands roamed her backside, and his identity was confirmed as he pulled out of the kiss.

Judge Calder.

Tommy's mouth went dry. His heart sped up. *They can't see me, they can't see me.* He squeezed his eyes shut.

Miss Violet had been earnest in Tommy's need to be discreet and to keep to himself any information he learned. Sweat poured down his face, and he wished for the evening to rush by so he could get out. Surely next time he wouldn't have to get into place so early, as the small talk wasn't what Miss Violet wanted him to record anyway.

Miss Helen swept by with a tray of half-eaten patty shells and half-drunk tea, and Tommy thought of Katherine and her baking for Miss Violet. At first Tommy was frightened that Katherine would be exposed to such things, but then he reassured himself that if he was naïve enough to not know what was happening here until this moment, then his sister, relegated to the kitchen, was certainly green enough to overlook any sort of clue that Miss Violet's financial dealings might include her own affection for a married man.

Tommy told himself all of what he witnessed was none of his business. He certainly had no room to judge.

Miss Violet announced Dreama's arrival. He strained to capture every detail, reminded of how Mrs. Schultz praised his ability to listen, to hear beyond words spoken. For this, he was only required to write exact wording, no interpretation. And so he did. A mash of voices rang out as the partygoers welcomed Dreama.

The noise dissipated and Dreama began her work. Her voice was quiet and whispery, like the papers had described. Tommy closed his eyes to try to home in on the words, anticipate what was coming so he didn't miss anything. He scribbled notes. Dreama suggesting certain dead people were in the room and then having the clients leap to conclusions from what she said, reminded him of his brother, James, reading the clouds and then suggesting what the coming weather would be. It was accurate sometimes, but only sometimes. Dreama's talk of spirits and guides and angels without the underpinnings of scripture bothered him.

Focus.

Dreama suggested that Mr. Renfrew's spirit guide wanted him to begin to sell off stock in his lumber company, which seemed strange to Tommy, but her claim that his dead daughter's spirit was with them, and that she wanted to fly kites with him again, shocked Tommy and Mr. Renfrew. *Scribble, scribble.* Tommy leaned forward trying to hear Dreama's soft, scratchy words clearly. Renfrew's reaction to Dreama's information, his sob and acknowledgment that she had contacted his daughter, made the hair on Tommy's arms lift. Could Oliva be this good of a con?

**

When Dreama was whisked away by Miss Violet and the guests went back to boozy socializing, Tommy snuck through the hidden door and put the notes under the vase in the hall outside the kitchen, as directed earlier. He hauled water from the rain barrels up the back stairs to the water closet and felt saddened that the women were so free with their kisses. It didn't bother him when he thought they were privately entertaining men, but publicly touching and kissing and . . . who knew what else? And the judge. Miss Violet had to have known the judge was married. Miss Helen had to know the reverend was, well, on the outside at least, a man of God.

While tucked behind the curtain, Tommy had begun to suspect that perhaps these women were not only enjoying sex and free love, but that it was tied to the advising they were doing. It didn't make sense that the financial works were a front for a brothel. The newspapers were clear for the most part—Miss Violet was better than anyone in increasing investment returns. These men might not have the morals he once thought, but they weren't dumb either; they weren't interested in losing money.

There were other articles. Those always yelling about purity, pointing at mediums, a jailed fortune-teller named Madame Smalley, juveniles, single women fraternizing with men in saloons. There were a smattering of articles about Miss Violet possibly not being on the up-and-up. He imagined his mother discovering something so heinous as prostitution occurring in the house next door, separated by only a hedge of boxwood and arborvitae.

Mama couldn't find out. It would crush her, and they'd be on the move again. But as he took his time, delivering the water, firing the bathroom stove, lurking about, watching, listening from the landing upstairs, all he heard were people enjoying chocolate cake and coffee and talk of stocks and banks and trustworthy businesses.

Chapter 34

Tommy and Pearl stood in Mama's kitchen, each on either side of the tub, gripping a side, leaning over the center. Their eyes met and they grinned, excited for their plan. He imagined Mama's face when she saw it, the way her tense shoulders would soften at the sight. She would take his face in her hands and cover it with kisses that he would pretend to not want at all. And at least there would be an opening for Mama to begin to forgive him. He knew it would take more than a bath, but he hoped she felt the gesture deep in her heart.

"Can't believe McCrady said you could borrow it."

"Rent. I paid a handsome fee."

Pearl put her hands on her hips. "Two bits for it and the wagon isn't too much fer yer ma. Deserves it every day of the year, way I see it. And you threw in a prayer. That was really nice of ya."

He nodded. "Let's fill it," Tommy said, turning to the stove. "The other day I dropped prayers to some of the ladies who stopped hiring me."

"They paid?"

He shrugged. "Nah. I just kept thinking about them and their troubles, and the words just flowed onto paper, and what am I going to do? Keep them for myself? So I delivered them. Mrs. Hamilton even refused it because she'd spent all her prayer funds on Dreama, but I put it through her mail slot. Just in case it's helpful to her."

Pearl ran her finger along the edge of the tin tub, the blue paint along the outside bright and cheerful. "That's . . . exactly what I'd expect from ya."

Tommy adjusted the flue on the stove. "Thanks, Pearl."

"And," she said, "this's the prettiest tub I ever seen. Saw, I mean, saw."

Tommy nodded. "Same here. Even the large tub at Miss Violet's isn't as good-looking as this."

"If I ever have a tub so nice, I'm gonna put it right in the center of my home, on permanent display."

Tommy glanced at the clock above the dry sink. Nearly six o'clock. Where was Mama? She should have been back from Mrs. Hillis's panel discussion hours back. They were probably caught up in the crowd, waiting for the trolley.

"You listening, Tommy?"

"Yes, Pearl. But the other day you very clearly illustrated that you were going to have a house with six bedrooms and indoor plumbing. So naturally you'd put your tub right in the same room with your toilet. Or your bedroom. Houses like the one you'll have don't boast tubs in the parlor."

Pearl shrugged. "Changed my mind. This here blue tub is pretty 'nough for it to be displayed in public rooms."

Tommy got an image of Pearl as a grown woman sitting in a full tub in front of her front parlor window, callers coming by and visiting right there while she bathed. He laughed out loud. "You put me in stitches, Pearl, you really do."

She grinned, her cheeks flushing red.

Tommy enjoyed every moment with Pearl. He often thought of her meeting his father who would adore her because she had spirit. Pearl had dreams, air-castles, like his father regularly built. Mama sometimes called them ridiculous when she was frustrated with Father.

But Tommy thought what Pearl built in her mind, her plans, were wonderful. When he caught Pearl staring at him, her upturned face full of warmth, it was as though she saw all the good in him, only the good, and that just made him wonder if Mama had ever loved his father at all. And if so, was Tommy unlovable? Perhaps a mother forced her affection on the children who weren't quite a fit in the family out of duty, not really out of love at all. Maybe that's why Tommy and Mama seemed to have to try so hard with each other.

Much as his father disappointed him, his father wouldn't mind Pearl being grimy around the edges or that her words often came in jagged, truncated bits when she wasn't concentrating on sounding fancy or rich, as she termed it. He imagined his father loving the idea of a tub in the front parlor. Tommy could hear his father's laughter at the sight, a small chuckle growing into rolling laughter as he let it take hold and humor him fully, laughing with his whole body.

"Let's at least heat the water," Tommy said. "Mama'll be exhausted when she gets home, and I'd like to treat her to peace and quiet and warm water the minute she walks in."

Pearl nodded. "And tea and those biscuits yer sister brung over."

They hoisted a large bucket of water onto the stove.

"Still think the water would warm faster if we heated small amounts," Pearl said.

Tommy shrugged. "Half-dozen one, six the other. Small amounts will take longer."

Pearl craned her neck studying the water.

"Watched water never boils," Tommy said.

She turned, the lantern light from the table casting her face angelic gold, hiding her grimy skin. Tommy had never seen a girl so perfectly beautiful, naturally so, without any of the fixings that the ladies next door used to greet clients. He couldn't take his eyes from her. She sashayed back to the table and sat.

"Tell me again 'bout Christmas morning when you lived in the house on the hill."

He sat beside her, his shoulder rubbing against hers, wondering again why it felt so much worse to talk about things he used to have than it was for her to imagine things she'd never had.

"Tell me how your ma made sure you each got exactly what you wanted and some things you didn't even know you wanted."

"I told you that?"

"Why yes, you did. When you got back from your meeting with Hank and Bayard. When you got that shiner?"

Tommy shrugged. He must have been drunker than he thought that night. He was surprised he'd lied to Pearl or that she believed it. Tommy's leg rubbed against Pearl's as he shifted in his seat. She moved closer to him, the warmth of her body exciting. He was growing fonder of her every moment they were together.

"I went to the library the other day and read up on some of yer ma's columns from before you went west. Boy, oh boy, she knew how to run a house. And everything just right. Pretty, too? Right?"

Tommy nodded. He supposed so. Nothing was as dirty as the dugout on the prairie. By those standards, a coal mine was clean.

Pearl lifted her hand and, with fingers spread, swept it through the air in front of them before flipping it palm up and wiggling her fingers as she dropped it to the table. "I could see every flower arrangement in my mind. And the roasted rosemary chicken? I could smell it. Taste it." Her hand was in the air again, flitting in the lantern light.

"And the sheer summer curtains wafting in the cool breezes, curling and dancing back and forth while you took visitors and sipped lemonade so sour I bet your little lips tightened up just before you swallowed. You know she always wrote about you in the articles, Tommy. You really were something. She doted on you like you were carved from sugar cubes and might melt in the rain if she wasn't careful enough with you."

Tommy listened to her retelling of articles he'd never read, but he could envision, as he'd lived it. Except for the doting. "No, you must have misread. James was the one she doted on. And Katherine."

"Well, maybe she favored them in this way or that, but the way I see it, a ma's got enough favoring for each child. It's the way it works. 'Specially yer ma."

Tommy thought of Pearl's Letters to Heaven that he'd seen when he borrowed paper from her bag. He'd never pressed her to discuss her family situation, not wanting to embarrass her for being orphaned, living in awful circumstances, but that night he felt as though he could, that he should. "Where's your mama, Pearl?"

She pushed the cuticle back on her thumb. "No idea. Never knew her for even a second. Been told my papa dropped me at Widow Fontell's. Suspect my ma died giving birth to me. Or somethin'. Don't know. Sometimes I wonder if I even came from a mother, or if I was just cobbled from the dirty earth, a tree, river-clay, stone . . . somethin' other than a soft, warm ma." She wet two fingers and rubbed at the back of her hand, scrubbing the dirt. "Nah, I'm joshing. You know how I love my fairy stories. I can feel a ma, my ma somewhere. She's . . ." She shrugged.

Tommy tried to imagine never having known Mama. "So how do you know so much about mothering, then?"

She squinted. "Suppose it's something I learned just being in my mama's belly. She must have been a good woman fer me to know such things. Suppose it's that." She squeezed her eyes shut. "Yeah, when I really think on it, I'm sure. Mine must've been a lot like yers—exquisite. I'm sure if I knew my ma, she'd be like yers. I mean, I hope so." She touched her lips. "I'm positive I got my good teeth from her. Leastways, that."

Tommy was surprised by Pearl's view of what her mama would have been like. She was normally practical and saw right into the grit of life, unafraid. Even her love of fairy tales didn't color the way she saw everyday limitations. He considered his mama. She *was* special. He just wished she recognized *his* value. But maybe, like he was slow to see hers, she was slow to see his. This would help, this tub. "What about your father?"

She wafted her hand, making a *pfft* sound. "My papa? I rarely give men a thought in terms of fathering. Ms. Fontell at the orphanage said he dropped me off like a sack of potatoes, with a couple a pearl-handled knives and a box to my name. Suppose that's something. Those things are precious to me. They've seen me through hard times, that bowie knife 'specially." She turned and glared at Tommy. "Have ya paid much attention to men and their fatherin'?"

"Well, my father, yes."

She shook her head. "I'd trade all the fathers and their lofty perches in the world, how easy it is to be a man. My papa dropped me off with a sack of things and left." Her voice was tight. "I'd trade one hundred papas for the arms of just one ma."

Tommy was stunned. He pushed his hand through his hair. "You just haven't worked at imagining hard enough what a father can do. A good father is everything. It makes the world right. I'd know. I used to have both together, and now look: one's gone and one's here so . . ."

He could feel Pearl staring at him.

"Both is what I want. Mamas can't be everything, that's all I mean."

Pearl smoothed her hand over the pine table. "True. All men aren't all like those I met up till now. Take you. You're not a thing like the others."

Tommy straightened in his chair, feeling proud. "Well, that's because I've a father who taught me to be a man, Pearl." Even as the words were out of his mouth, they turned his saliva bitter. That's what he wanted to be true, but he was wondering more now than ever if he'd even see his father again, let alone learn anything more from him.

Pearl's heavy gaze warmed his cheeks.

"Suppose you're right, Tommy Arthur. I probably haven't considered papas in just the right way."

Tommy smiled. Her blaze-green eyes turned slightly up at the outside corners, making her always appear kind and sweet, even when she was scolding him. Looking at her, sitting that close in the lantern light, staring right into her fine-featured face, he wanted to kiss the corners of her eyes, brush his lips against her skin. The stirrings started, his body tingling and hardening, but he'd never felt this overwhelming urge to just kiss someone and hold her and never let her go.

"I feel like I was born to something bigger than that orphanage, bigger than Rupert's, too. But look at me. Ordinary, dirty, barely getting by."

"Maybe you were born to grow into something bigger. Americans don't have to be born *into* something big." He wanted to encourage her, to keep her thinking, dreaming. "Yeah. You're headed to something special. Like all those tales you read. I'm sure of it."

"Yeah," Pearl whispered. She shifted to face Tommy directly. "I feel like you really understand me . . . and my stories. You really understand."

He watched her lips move as she talked and found himself leaning in, wanting to feel his lips on hers. She looked away, explaining how Prince Aeriel was good-looking and the hero of the story and Furiban was ugly and bad.

Tommy inched closer to her, unable to make sense of her words as he wondered if he should take a chance and hold her in his arms.

"Maybe." She shook her finger at Tommy. "That's it."

"What's it?" he asked as he jerked back.

"You should write something to yer ma to go with the tub apology. You could turn out the sorrowful contents of yer heart onto paper, and then she could savor it and keep it in her handbag or stuffed under the mattress or stowed in an old trunk. Or in her pocket. It would be there, with her for always. Like the prayers you sell and leave for people to comfort them later."

Tommy cocked his head and slid his arm around Pearl's shoulder squeezing it. She shifted closer, her entire leg touching his from hip to knee.

"Maybe I should do just that, Pearl."

The bubbling water on the stove made them hop up, ready to pour it. He found a piece of paper and pencil and recorded his very sorry thoughts on his behavior the other night.

**

Tommy wrote his note, and he and Pearl had filled the tub and even reheated some of the water several times before they heard footsteps on the porch stairs. Tommy couldn't wait. He flung the door open. Mama's eyes went wide, Yale wrapped in her arms, asleep on her shoulder.

"Shhh. Yale's sleeping."

"Where were you?"

"Women's club meeting."

Mama looked past Tommy. He turned to see Pearl had stepped behind him.

"Hello, Pearl," Mama said.

Pearl gave one of her curtsies she seemed to do every time she saw his mama. "Hello, Mrs. Arthur." Pearl put her hand out. Mama juggled Yale and shook Pearl's hand, then looked over her shoulder.

"Mama?" Tommy said. "I have a surprise for you. I know it will take a lifetime to apologize for my behavior when I was so cruel. But I wanted to do something to show you right this second how sorry I am." He pulled her into the house. She looked over her shoulder again.

"Tommy, wait." She went back on the porch. Tommy followed her out as Reed Hayes started up the first stair. He backed away and sighed. He removed his hat. "Good evening, Tommy."

Like gas being lit, Tommy's recently muted anger flared. He glared at Mama. He told himself to just leave the house before he said something spiteful again. "Him? You're with Mr. Hayes again? I spent all day orchestrating this big apology for you. And this is what you were doing? You were with him?"

"We've brought dinner from the meeting, Tommy. Sit with us. And thank you for the beautiful bath—"

"He can't stay if you're enjoying your bath. So he can go."

"Let him eat and then he'll go. Look at this beautiful tub. You remembered how much I love a bath. Thank you."

Tommy glowered at Mr. Hayes, waiting for the man to politely dismiss himself.

"The water'll be cold if you don't—"

"We can reheat it again," Pearl said.

Mr. Hayes backed out of the kitchen and went into the yard. Mama followed. "At least take your food, Reed."

Tommy's breath grew shallow.

Pearl took Tommy's arm. Enraged, all he could see or think about was the man who ruined everything. He wrenched away from Pearl and loped across the porch, leaping down the stairs and tackling Mr. Hayes to the ground. Tommy pinned the man's hands. Mama and Pearl screamed for Tommy to stop. He looked over his shoulder, letting up on Mr. Hayes. The older man, large, but spry, took advantage of Tommy's distracted moment and flipped him to his back, holding him down. Tommy kicked his legs, flailing as Mr. Hayes restrained him.

"I'm going to let you up, Tommy. But you calm down. We aren't doing anything wrong. Your mother's a friend, and there is nothing wrong with that. We had a meeting and were going to have a meal here, with you and whomever else. That's it."

Tommy squirmed more, testing to see if he had a shot at reversing his situation.

"Now you stay calm." Mr. Hayes hopped up and dusted off his trousers. "Let's get inside and talk this out."

Tommy stood, heaving for breath. Mama had Yale in one arm and Pearl wrapped in her other. Humiliation bloated his insides. He looked at Mr. Hayes, who was retucking his shirt. He straightened and extended his hand to Tommy.

Tommy glanced at all of them. Who'd they think they were?

"What's wrong with you? Come inside. Please," Mama said, coming down the steps. He might have gone in with her, but she let Mr. Hayes take her elbow, helping her down the stairs into the yard. Tommy knew it was over. Mama had made her choice. She didn't appreciate any little bit of him. Not even when he tried.

Pearl looked at him with a sad face. "Please. Just listen."

Tommy shook his head. Listen . . . Mrs. Schultz had said how gifted Tommy was at hearing . . . But this, he didn't want to hear the secrets, the private lives woven into Mama and Mr. Hayes's words. And, now Pearl . . . siding with Mama. He leapt the fence and took off down the street, not sure where he was going but needing to leave all of them behind.

Chapter 35

Mama's half-hearted response to the tub surprise, choosing Mr. Hayes, Pearl staying behind—all of it sat thick, betrayal deepening after Tommy thought he'd been successful in moving past such negativity. Back at the shed it didn't take long for Tommy to empty the two bottles of beer he'd secured in case of emergency. He'd kept to his vow not to drink whiskey, but instead of savoring small sips of beer like he promised himself he would, he chugged each bottle down. When there was no sign of Pearl returning, he put up a tiny fight against the urge to dig into his savings and go drinking at Churchill's Saloon.

He'd had enough humiliation and it all felt fresh. The sorrow that had seeded when he began to recognize his father wasn't coming was now in full sprout inside him. He deserved a drink for both his pain and for his good deed of sending payment to the family his father was indebted to.

He bounced some coins in his palm. Mama. The cottage. He shoved money into his pocket. If she was going to choose Mr. Hayes, well, she could wait a little longer for her beloved cottage. Tommy belonged to a club, and he was ready to drink and have some fun, like all the men who went there every single night.

He arrived at the saloon and peacocked in, shoulders back, owning his space and anything that came into arm's reach. He'd had enough of being tentative.

"Beer! Get me a beer, barkeep! And you have one, too!" he said, feeling sure that he could control his behavior if he stayed away from hard booze. The barkeep pulled a face then poured a beer into a chilled mug for Tommy.

"You there!" Tommy gestured at a man at one of the tables beside the bar. "Have a beer on me! Drink up!"

The man's face brightened and he mumbled a drunken thank you as he guzzled the last of the beer he already had.

All evening, Tommy was charming and fun, overdoing it by buying drinks for every fella through the door. He burned through his money, and the barkeep added hashmarks by Tommy's name to keep track of his tab.

A finely dressed man slid behind the bar. Colt Churchill.

"Have a beer, Mr. Churchill!"

Colt raised a glass to Tommy and gave the barkeep permission to keep serving up beers, saying Tommy looked good for it.

Tommy raised his glass back. "I am good for it." His tongue was fat with beer, slow to work right. "Ask the little family in San Diego for a recommendation on me being good for it!"

"Add another hashmark!" Tommy sucked it down.

A crew of men entered and Tommy made fast friends with them, trading stories of narrowly missing the police, singing drinking songs.

He became especially friendly with a man called Hamhock. "Oh, tipped the wagon the other day and tossed my brother clean off . . . Still won't talk to me."

Tommy slapped his back. "What? Little fun's no good for your brother?"

Hamhock staggered into Tommy. "Jesus, he survived the crash. You're *alive*, I says to him. Little wagon tip makes you appreciate your life all the more. Broken leg kept him from seeing it that way."

"You should hear about my brother."

"Didn't appreciate my comment or the dumping he took," Hamhock slurred.

Tommy was no longer really listening. "Never a minute of fun." He chugged the half a beer he had left. Teasing about his brother felt rotten, only made Tommy want his brother to walk through those doors, years older than when he died. So he shut up about James and turned his thoughts elsewhere.

He and Hamhock kept at it, one upping each other with tales true and fantastic, and eventually found themselves falling off the stools, laughing so hard they couldn't breathe.

Hamhock swayed and bobbed his way out of the saloon and Tommy staggered to the faro game. But instead of playing, he yelled out who was cheating whom, exposing the coffin keeper's trick in helping the bank by attaching thread to a chip to pull it in the direction that gave the bank a win.

When the dealer rushed at Tommy, he flipped the table, sending all the checks and cards flying. The spindly table legs broke off, and Tommy wobbled out of the saloon, where one foot caught on the other and he tumbled into the street.

Strong arms kept him upright. His rescuer grunted under Tommy's weight while Tommy swung punches at him, unable to make hard contact or get his feet stable. Tommy pushed against the man and sent him tumbling into the road.

A policeman rode up in his rig.

Tommy waved at the officer, pulled the fella up and then leaned on him.

"You want to stuff that young man into my wagon? I'll take him right to the courthouse."

"I've got him, thank you, Officer." The baritone was familiar. Tommy finally stumbled away from the man far enough to study his face.

"Mr. Hayes." Tommy staggered back before catching his balance. "Jesus Christ. You."

Mr. Hayes hooked Tommy under the arms.

"You know that jackass?"

Tommy and Mr. Hayes looked at each other, and Mr. Hayes said yes at the same time Tommy said no.

"If he's your son, he can go with you. Otherwise dump him into the wagon, and I'll bundle his wrists."

Tommy finally stood still, even if swaying. Mr. Hayes put a hand on his shoulder. "You want to spend a night in jail?"

A chill rolled through Tommy. He shook his head, defeated.

"I'll get my son home. Having a hard time of it lately."

The policeman narrowed his gaze on them. "Best get him under control, then. Citizen groups are hot to lasso heathen men and wayward children. Cons and thieves. Hell, they might just drag me in one of these days if I don't watch myself."

Mr. Hayes latched his arm around Tommy's waist. "Understood."

The officer paused, staring at them.

"I'll toss ya both in the clink if I see this mess again."

Mr. Hayes doffed his hat. "Won't see us again. On my honor."

The wagon pulled away.

Tommy shrugged Mr. Hayes's hand off.

"You need to stop, Tommy. Your mother needs you, and I know you understand that. But you can't be pickled and—"

Tommy didn't need a lecture. He brushed at Mr. Hayes's shoulder. "You got some manure there." He slurred and spittled as he talked.

"This way," Mr. Hayes said, hands in pockets.

Tommy took one last glance at Mr. Hayes and beat a dusty path home, half stumbling, full-up with misery.

**

The journey home took longer than usual due to his mood, gait, and a fall at the side of the road where he suspected he may have napped for a bit before getting up and making his final way home. The walk, mixed with cold air, helped sober him. He entered the shed, expecting to see Pearl tucked into the bed in the loft. The fire was lit, Fern stretched beside it. At the washtub he scrubbed his face with oat soap and his teeth with a rag and peppermint water.

Could Pearl still be at Mama's? He went back outside through the hedges. Lantern light shone from Mama's kitchen. He knew tomorrow Mr. Hayes would tell her everything that happened, so he had to confide his side first.

Nervous to admit another round of bad behavior, he crept up the back stairs and peeked through the window. The lantern sat near the tub. If Mama was relaxing in the apology tub, perhaps she'd be open to hearing his reasons for drinking himself stupid and he could beg for forgiveness yet again.

He opened the door. "Mama!"

She turned.

Pearl.

She sank under the water up to her chin. "Tommy Arthur, you scared the wits clean out of me."

"Sorry, Pearl." The lantern light lit on Pearl's face in the way he loved, creating a golden, angelic glow around her.

"I uh . . ."

"Ain't never had a bath before," she said, her hands culling the surface of the water. "Believe that?"

Tommy wiped his sweaty palms on his pants, trying not to stare, knowing she was naked under the dark water. "I should go."

"No. Stay."

He licked his lips. He should go.

She held up her hand, fingers spread. "Once read a letter written by Miss Simpson from Paradise, North Carolina, to Mr. Marks on Cornell Street, Des Moines. She described her pruny fingertips, puffy with swirls and whirls from bathing in fancy hotels as she waited for her family home to be built on some grand mountaintop." She turned her hand back and forth. "Now I know what it means to be pruny."

Tommy put his palm to hers, the sensation sending sparks through him. He met her gaze, his heartbeat calming just being near her. She'd been in the tub a while but still had dirt on her cheeks and near her lip.

"Why're you in such a dark mood?" she asked.

Tommy blew out his air. "A misunderstanding."

They stared at each other. "You have a mighty lot of misunderstandings, Tommy Arthur."

Tommy went to the pie safe and took a cotton cloth from the drawer. He squatted and held the cloth up. "A smudge." He brushed his fingers past his cheekbone to show her what he meant.

She cowered.

"All right? If I clean that spot?"

She nodded and closed her eyes.

He got closer and held the linen to her delicate cheek. "Sure it's all right?"

She nodded.

He dipped the cloth in the water, wrung it out, and patted the spot between her nose and cheek, blotting away the dirt patches. "We do plenty of talking, Pearl, but I don't even know your last name." He shook his head, marveling at this fact, his lingering drunkenness making him slow to remember that she might not want to discuss family names.

"Riverside."

"Riverside. That's quite a name. Pearl Riverside of Des Moines? Of Dubuque?"

She closed her eyes as he dabbed at her skin and rewet and dabbed some more. "That's what old Mrs. Fontell said 'fore she died and they released me from the orphanage and into the wild. Whole place shut down when she went into the ground. Me and the rest of the kids scattered like dust in the wind."

"Pearl Riverside. I like that," Tommy said, following the line of dirt along her cheekbone.

She smiled. Tommy dipped the rag again. The moon shifted into the window and cast its shine right through the glass, splashing over Pearl. Tommy inhaled at the sight.

"What?" she asked.

He put his attention on wetting and wringing out the cloth. He couldn't really say what he thought, that word *love* had been forming in his sozzled mind and playing on his lips. He twisted the cloth until not one bit of dripping water gathered in the folds.

"Tell me," she said.

He turned her face and dabbed at her other cheek. "The moonbeam's falling on you as bright as a sunray. But . . ." His stomach flipped, and he dipped and wrung out the cloth. She kept his gaze, water droplets crowning her lashes.

"It's like you're lighting the moon, not the other way around."

"Tommy." She looked away, but not before he saw her smile widen. The kitchen was silent except for the crackling fire and the sound of water dripping when Tommy wrung the cloth. He traced the clean path he'd made on her skin, daubing her chin and every plane and valley of her fine face, taking as long as he possibly could to keep these moments from passing, half-wondering if they were real or alcohol-fueled dreams.

"Tilt your head." He washed under her jawline, back toward her ear, and down her neck. He could barely keep from diving into the tub with her. He worked the rag over her collarbone, and his breath caught. Not only at the sight of her beauty, in response to his attraction, but he realized then the depths of what her presence did for him. She always accepted him as he was. No—she saw him as greater than he was at that moment, as though she intuited his past and believed in his future. He circled the cloth around her shoulder, and for the first time his eyes dropped to the waterline, searching for a view of the rest of her. The shadows obscured her beneath the water, but he wanted to see, wanted to touch her without the cloth between his fingers and her skin.

No.

He dropped the cloth in the water and put his back to the tub, sitting against it. The tin warmed him through his shirt.

Pearl touched the top of his head, water droplets working down to his scalp.

"Didn't mean to be ungentlemanly, Pearl."

She curled his hair around her fingers, sending thrills through him.

"You can touch me any way you want."

He looked over his shoulder at her. What was she saying?

"Ain't I pretty enough?"

Oh, how wrong that was. "'Course you are."

She tapped the end of his nose with her forefinger.

"Not smart enough."

"You're brilliant. An uncut diamond."

She shifted and started to rise out of the water, her shoulders coming into view, then her chest, her skin shimmering. "You can touch me. You can."

He turned his back to the tub and knocked his head against it as he adjusted the crotch of his pants.

"No, Pearl." Could he touch her? She wanted him to. What would be so bad if he just turned and touched her below the water, if he just kissed her a little bit? The thought excited him so much he couldn't move.

The sound of the water shifting told him she'd sunk back into the tub. He exhaled.

"You'd be the first," she said, twirling his hair through her fingers again, lighting him on fire.

"Your husband should be first." Tommy rubbed his temples.

"Not what I meant." She shifted again, sloshing water over the edge, drenching Tommy's shoulders.

He looked over his shoulder. Pearl's chin rested on her hands. Their connected gaze was almost too much for him to bear, the closeness like nothing he'd ever experienced.

"I mean you'd be the first *not* to touch me just because you wanted to."

Tommy turned away. His insides turned cold. He brushed at his shirt as though he could flick away the water that had splattered over him. He'd known Pearl's life had been hard. No parents, Rupert's place. So alone. She was uneducated, unclean, and coarse, but the sweetness and optimism at her core like a miracle, had made him assume she'd managed to stave off anyone who pressed her, even if she got some bruising in the process. He looked back at her. "Oh, Pearl."

She shrugged.

"It's not right that it happened to you."

"Not right doesn't make it not so."

He nodded, dazed. She was stunning but fragile, her long hair floating on the water surface. He was proud to be the one who didn't, who wouldn't press her to let him touch her. The one thing he'd done right that day. He dipped the cloth in the water again, wiping at her cheek. "Missed a spot."

She leaned toward him, arms on the side of the tub, her forehead pressed to his. She cupped his cheek and brushed back his hair. He couldn't breathe. "You ain't missed a thing, Tommy Arthur. Not one thing."

He clasped his hand over hers and gently put it back with her other. He wanted to scoop her up and lay her near the stove and warm her with his body.

He brushed his lips over hers then drew back. He couldn't do this.

He handed her the cloth. "Get your legs and feet while you're in there. Nothing like a first bath, I imagine," he said.

"Right, so . . . I will."

He exhaled and stood, unfolded the sheet that had been set aside for her to dry off and held it up so she could step into it without him seeing her. He wrapped her in it, her back to him. With his arms finally around her, with the sheet between them, he felt relief. He walked her toward the stove, keeping her tight against him.

He kissed the top of her head. She wormed one hand out of the sheet, laid her head back against him, and played with the hair at the nape of his neck.

"Thank you, Tommy Arthur. You're a great, great man. A good soul. No matter what else is wrong or going bad, you are *good* at your core. So very good."

Tommy nearly fell over with the power of her faith in him. The strength of what she said scared him, making him unsure he could be who she thought he was. "Get dressed. You'll catch pleurisy if you stand around in a wet sheet all night."

Tommy left her there to dress while he headed back to the shed to stoke the fire. Trudging through the dormant garden, hands in his pockets, the crisp air stung his cheeks. He looked over his shoulder and saw Pearl in the window. He stopped, his heart kicking at the sight. He let what just happened in the kitchen settle into his body, good and sure. That girl, with her word collection and places she wanted to travel to, what she'd said about him, well, it was as though she reached right inside him and put that kitchen lantern on his heart, waking it up like a mother wakes her child, and the child realizes for the first time he's alive.

She pulled her chemise over her head, her slight body shadowed, ethereal. He grabbed his chest, his heart beating against his hand.

Pearl.

She gave him hope that he really was the good man he always claimed to be. Perhaps Tommy didn't need a mother. Perhaps all he needed was Pearl.

Chapter 36

Tommy rolled to his side, every muscle aching. Even without his eyes open he knew it was morning. He rolled back and groaned, feeling like a house had fallen on him in the night. Banging came from downstairs. He reached beside him for Pearl. Her spot was cool, and she'd pulled up her blanket, neatly made.

"Pearl?" he said but barely louder than a whisper. He heard tinkling, the sound of... a bell? He must still be dreaming.

No answer, no stirring from pets. Tommy rubbed his forehead. A pounding headache moved through his skull in waves.

"Tommy!"

Mama. Tommy sat up. He couldn't talk to her right then, not with the way he felt. He didn't think she'd ever set foot in the shed except for the day they moved in. He'd managed to make sure she, Katherine and Miss Violet didn't know Pearl was living there.

Please keep on past, Mama.

He sorted through the events of the day before, how he ended up feeling as though he'd slept in a vice grip. He assumed there were holes in his memory, but pieced together being at the saloon. He exhaled. The knocking stopped. Silence except his breath.

Water.

Tommy started down the rickety loft ladder, mouth parched, rancid.

"Tommy?" Yale's muffled voice came through the door with the sound of more tinkling. Definitely bells. Tommy froze.

"Tommy!" Yale's sweet call came again, and Mama pushed the door open.

Tommy sighed then staggered the rest of the way down.

Mama released Yale's hand and covered her mouth. He pushed his hand through his hair. Did he look that bad?

"One day you're wincing in pain, another you're drunk . . . You're white as a sheet." She inched closer.

He straightened, holding his breath to stave off the pain, keeping one arm against his midsection. "Tired."

"Here, sit." Mama slipped her arm around his waist and guided him to the wobbly chair by the table. Tommy glanced around the shed, noticing for the first time that, although Pearl lived there, she didn't leave a single belonging in plain sight. She packed all her things together each morning as though she might need to run.

Mama tossed a log into the dying fire and knelt in front of Tommy. Yale climbed onto his lap, snuggling against his chest, chair thumping back and forth on its uneven legs. It was then he saw the source of the bells he'd heard. Yale had them strung around her wrist and dangling from a button on her dress. He rocked and smoothed her hair back, each movement prodding tender muscles.

Thump, thump, the chair echoed. The bells jingled.

"What pretty jewelry, Yale," he said hoping to change the subject before they even started on it.

"Katherine strung those so we could keep track of her better. After the powdered sugar thing, and how she kept ending up underfoot, well, this helps us keep track of her better," Mama said.

"Like a cat," Tommy said, amused, but also full of new regret and guilt as he remembered the day Yale wandered under his watch.

"Yes," Mama said.

"Cat." Yale smiled up at Tommy and he squeezed her tight despite the hug causing fresh pain to course through him.

Mama wiped her hands on her apron, studying Tommy. "I didn't know you were so bad off. He didn't say . . ."

Tommy's eyes flew open. *He.* A vision of tussling with Mr. Hayes came to mind. The police . . . he needed more time to put it all in order. But she knew? Mr. Hayes must have gotten to her. "Mama—"

"Judge Calder told me everything. Or at least I thought he had."

Tommy exhaled and looked away. So it wasn't Mr. Hayes. He didn't know which was worse. Would the judge have told Mama about his time in jail, about the lies he told the court and his family?

"What did you do? Jeremy didn't have all the details."

Tommy tilted his head to the side. He didn't know exactly which facts she was reaching for.

"What did you do?"

Thump. Jingle.

"Nothing."

"People don't get tossed out of saloons for nothing, Tommy. What happened?"

Ahh. Yes. The faro game, hours of drinking with new friends. He squinted trying to call up the rest. "I was walking by the saloon."

"Walking by?" Mama rubbed her temples.

He nodded. "I just wanted a glass of water. I was walking, clearing my head, and I got mixed up in a brawl. I wasn't part of it; I was swept into it like dirt into a dustpan." He couldn't tell her the truth. It was bad enough he felt his own shame that he'd been drinking and gambling, but he didn't want her to have to share his shame.

Mama shook her head.

"I'm . . ." He was going to apologize but wasn't exactly sure of the list of things he should be sorry for . . . He massaged between his eyes. If he could only remember. What was he even doing at the saloon?

"Where's that bird?"

"Frank?"

Wobble, thump, wobble. Jingle, jingle.

Yale giggled and wiggled so the chair and bells would make a rhythm she liked.

"The *crow*, yes. When I left the house earlier, he dropped a barrette at my feet. It's got Elizabeth Calder's monogram on it. A *diamond* barrette. Is *that* what you've been doing?"

Tommy smiled, remembering the quarters Frank had brought him. Still, it seemed impossible that the bird could target items from specific people.

"That's crazy." Yale put her fingers into her mouth and Mama gently tugged them out. So many little things he couldn't remember. He was beginning to think Reed Hayes was right about him having a problem with drinking. "I swear. I didn't take it. Frank must have found it somewhere."

"We have to give it back."

Tommy wasn't sure how Frank's stealing fit into the morality scheme he'd constructed since coming back to Des Moines, but in his mind Elizabeth Calder could live without the barrette. He hadn't been back to the Calders' for more ornate silver pieces yet, but . . . Frank stealing? The crow went back? Impossible. But foolproof. He wished he'd dreamed it up himself.

He thought of the Arthur family painting hanging in the Calder bathroom, of all the Arthur family belongings littered around the Calder home. Had Mama seen them when she was there? She must've. And as shamed as he felt for drinking and gambling and being cruel to Mama, the anger at what Elizabeth Calder did to Mama sparked hot and easily. "Elizabeth Calder stole all *your* stuff, Mama. Waltzing around in that sapphire necklace of yours."

Mama cringed.

He couldn't tell her he'd been there when Mama had attended the women's club meeting, that he stole silver that day. He wouldn't degrade her by asking if she'd been in the bathroom and seen the portrait of them over the toilet. "And so what? If Frank so easily stumbled upon her barrette, she was too stupid or careless with her things. Can you imagine? Diamonds just lying around for a silly bird to find?"

Mama exhaled and stiffened. "I hate seeing my belongings in her possession. I do. But taking things, whether they've been tossed aside or not, will get you sent to a workhouse. It's like you haven't heard a word I've said about the work I'm doing with Mrs. Hillis and Mr. Hayes."

Tommy wished he could explain he knew exactly what her work was all about but didn't know how to explain what Judge Calder was up to without angering and disappointing Mama further about his own behavior.

"You can't afford to get in trouble, Tommy. People like us, who we are now, who get in trouble, can't get out. Look at you." She shook her head as a sob escaped her throat. She looked away from him. "Please stop drinking and stealing, and please don't gamble. Stay out of that saloon."

"Who said anything about gambling?"

Mama cocked her head. "Judge Calder said this wasn't your first stop at the saloon. And that you spent a night in his jail."

Wasn't the judge just a little chatterbox?

"I'm trying to make things right, Mama, I am. I don't know what happened last night that . . ."

"If you're not stealing or gambling, how'd you end up garnering Judge Calder's attention?"

Tommy thought of Reed Hayes and him being there when Tommy ran out of the saloon. How much did he know?

"You were in the saloon, Tommy. I know that. Not just walking by."

"Some other boy, Hank—you've met him. He waved me into the saloon for a water, and I wouldn't pay for it. It was water, Mama. The barkeep snapped like old wood and went nuts."

Mama studied him. A cold sweat drenched him as he silently begged her to *want* to believe him, to choose to accept his lie.

"So you haven't been stealing—the crow really found that himself?"

He wiped his brow with his forearm and leaned forward, grimacing, thinking of all the things he'd stolen over the years. "I swear. Frank found that all by himself."

She took his face in her hands and turned his head side to side, staring into his eyes, searching. "I want to believe you, Tommy. I want to dismiss hard evidence to the contrary. I want to just take flight with your stories."

She released his face and gently brushed his cheek. He rubbed his jaw where she'd been gripping him.

"I think you've done more than you admit. And I'm telling you right now you need to stop it. No matter what happens to us, we can't do what's wrong. The truth always comes out. And Judge Calder's not a good man. There's a lot you don't know about him."

Yale slid off Tommy's lap. He buried his face in his hands, rubbing his temples. He knew plenty.

"What you said to me the other night—"

He felt her words like a punch. He looked up. "I am so sorry for that, Mama. That's why I brought the tub. Just a beginning of the ways I'll say sorry."

She swallowed hard.

"You didn't even get to enjoy your bath. It made me mad and seeing him . . . always *here* . . . I'm not . . ."

"I know. And I'll use it before you take it back. I know you were trying to do something nice. But you need to get yourself lined up straight. You need to keep schooling in the forefront of your mind. I know you've been skipping. Nothing else should matter right now. Education and a good career after. College."

Tommy had stopped even trying to keep up with assignments when he missed class.

"And you need to let go of this anger. You're not a cruel person, yet you were vindictive. You get so angry. Your face doesn't even look the same when you're like that."

Tommy nodded, dishonored.

Mama smoothed her bun. "I did wrong in recent years. But there are things you don't know that caused me to make certain decisions. Things better kept between a husband and wife."

Tommy wanted to know what Mama meant, but knew it was no use asking at that moment.

She pressed her fist to her chest. "We all have to move forward from all that awful—everything."

Mr. Hayes. That was her moving forward. Her desire to do that felt as though the connection between them was straining. He wasn't her husband. Why did it hurt so much to think Mama could move on when Tommy could not?

She was right that it was time to move on, to bury old aspirations that would not come to fruition no matter how much they wished for them to be. "Well, if I'm going to move on. Then I'll just say it. I don't need school. I pass the stupid tests without even studying. I'm quitting so we don't waste the money."

She stared at him, her face flushing. "Quitting to do what? Sell prayers to old women who'd rather hand money over to that charlatan Dreama? Run the streets? Get tossed in jail? *Look at you.* You're hurt, you're lost, you're a mess."

Tommy flinched with each sentiment. She was right, but wrong about how to fix it all.

Mama tensed and pointed to her chest. "I've suffered enough indignity, Tommy. Disgrace has tried to ruin all the good that's left after whatever your father, and my father did."

"You don't have to be ashamed of me. I'm making money." He swallowed the words halfway out of his mouth, as the memory of him emptying his coins into every throat in the saloon rushed back. "I had a sack of coins I was saving for the cottage, but I—" He nearly confessed sending money to the family in San Diego, but she wouldn't see the kindness in that.

"You what?"

He might as well get it all out, to stop the festering. "Well, I did save a lot and then I helped my father a little and . . . Last night . . . I'll save more. I promise."

She shook her head and paced. Yale toddled around the shed, humming to herself. "You sent money after your father? Where on earth did you mail it? God knows what type of debt he's racking up behind him. You'll be cleaning up for him for the rest of your life."

That was true. "I was trying to help a family who needed it."

"That will never end."

Tommy had finally come to agree with Mama about his father, but he couldn't verbalize that. Though he'd been disappointed repeatedly, he couldn't betray his father by agreeing out loud with the terrible truth. His father needed someone to keep a little faith in him, someone out there in the universe. "He just needs a little help, Mama. It was a misunderstanding that grew his debt, but I think—"

"Bad decisions are not misunderstandings. Selfishness is *not* a misunderstanding."

Tommy felt as though the comment was pointed at him, especially in light of what Pearl had said about his string of misunderstandings. "Not everything is on purpose." He knew how ridiculous that sounded.

Mama heaved for breath, her face red. He'd never seen her so angry. "A terrible provider, Tommy. Always walking into trouble and away from the people who have to clean it up. Before we left Des Moines, it didn't matter. We had money and more money."

"Don't say that."

Jingle, jingle, jingle.

Yale pulled on Mama's skirt and shook her wrist. Mama took her hand.

"Privy," Yale said, smiling.

Mama moved toward the door, shaking her head. "We'll discuss this later, Tommy. But do not send another dime in your father's direction until we get a home of our own, where we are safe and no one has to consider illicit behavior as a solution to problems or to salve wounds or save lives." She opened the door, and a gust of wind sent dead leaves swirling into the shed, making Tommy sneeze and double over with the pain that caused.

Mama was right. Worse. What she said was also right about him. Father may have betrayed them, but he was seeing clearly that Mama saw Tommy as ineffectual just like him. And though Tommy had proven exactly that lately, he was convinced she never saw him in any other way. He merely fulfilled what she'd seen as true since he was young.

He almost kept it in . . . but why? At this point what would hiding the truth do except rot him further? "I'm just like him, Mama. Every time you say something about Father, you're saying it about me. That's the truth."

She stopped.

"I'm a dreamer and a failure. I build air-castles. Just like him."

Jingle, jingle. Yale tugged Mama's hand, but she stayed put, looking into the yard. Tommy waited for Mama to agree. Why do anything other than that at this point?

Her voice quieted, calmed. "You *aren't* like him, Tommy. Not like you think you are. You're better in every single way. And I expect you to start living *that* truth from this moment on."

Mama scooped Yale into her arms and took off toward the privy.

The tension release fell over him, sudden silence cut only by the fading tinkling and jingling of frantic bells, leaving him to wonder if he was no longer the son who embodied his father's best as she'd said before. Had Mama never seen any of Frank Arthur as good? And if not, what did that mean for Tommy—dreamer, failure, air-castle builder?

Chapter 37

Tommy was on a hunt to find a job that would allow him to make substantial changes in his life. Since making a slow slide into melancholy upon realizing his father's limitations, realizing Mama was moving on in her life, sending money to the family in San Diego, and quitting school, Tommy finally began to feel as though he was emerging from a mud pit.

Pearl came home from work to let the dog out and have an apple for supper. She set her bag on the table. "Never guess who came into the post office this morning."

Tommy washed his hands at the basin. Before he could venture a guess she was talking again. "Aleksey Zurchenko and your sister."

"That's nice." He dried his hands and hung the cloth near the fire.

Pearl pulled her word list and a pencil out of her bag. "Two of 'em were snug as bugs, but without the rug. 'Course, so *in love* they didn't need a rug to wrap them up tight. The magic between 'em kept 'em tight as anything. Beautiful pair, those two. Love flooding all over the place. Like when summer sunrays lift off wood planks in heat waves. Like that. I felt it."

"They're just pals . . ."

She put her hand up. "Didn't have the chance to ask about their status since he helped Mrs. Ryan out with her packages. But didn't look like pals to me," Pearl said. "Looks like they're meant to be, like two plants with crisscrossed roots. That's it. They're rooted together, their happy green leaves all intertwined."

She'd been reading a lot of fairy tales if this was how she was thinking about them. But it made Tommy think. Maybe their friendship had turned into something else. "They did go through a lot when we were on the prairie. A lot."

241

"Tell me." She perched on the slatless chair.

He recounted how Katherine had painstakingly taught Russian-born Aleksey to read on the prairie. "Not just to read, but he devoured our science and literature and philosophy books. He liked it all so much she gave them to him to do the job when she wasn't there to teach. Mythology, *everything*. I shunned it. Isn't that strange? I was born to it and turned away. He couldn't get enough."

"Hunger for what ya don't have'll do that."

Tommy agreed. "And then there was Anzehla, Aleksey's sister. She got lost in the high grass and disappeared when Aleksey and Katherine were watching her."

Pearl's eyes teared up and she mouthed the word, no.

"Happened on the prairie frequently." He hadn't thought about that in years. Now the weight of it sat heavy on him. "And there was when Aleksey saved Katherine and Yale during the blizzard that killed James and so many of the Zurchenko brothers and other neighbors. Only thing Katherine lost was part of her finger to the cold. Aleksey was . . ." He shook his head.

"Her hero," Pearl said.

Tommy added wood to the fire.

Pearl's face alight, she put her hands to her cheeks as she took it all in. "They have so much history, don't they? No wonder they've fallen in love quick as the dickens. The love's been living between them for years, even if they were miles and miles apart. A true-life fairy tale."

Tommy sighed and sat at the table. He took Pearl's hand and stroked the back of it. "Now that I look at it, yes. The Zurchenko family saved the lives of the Arthurs a bunch of times. Why, Mrs. Zurchenko was even there when Yale was born early. Too small, like a hairless prairie chicken. We didn't think the little bird would make it."

"Yet here she is," Pearl said.

"Yes." All of this moving on for his family sank in, and he decided to reset his goals. His path. It was time to be intentional about which one he took. What Mama said was right. He needed to let go of sending money to rescue his father. He couldn't make up for what his father was doing.

"Time to get back to the post office for afternoon shift," Pearl said.

Tommy stood. "I've got chores at Miss Violet's."

The two of them stood there for a moment, an awkwardness between them that he'd never noticed before. When he'd taken her hand it felt natural, but now . . .

"Well," he went past her. "See you later."

**

Tommy entered Miss Violet's cellar, a full set of condom materials waiting for him. He made short work of them, having mastered tiny stitches despite stabbing himself a few times, but they were works of art. Not one bit of test water seeped through. Miss Violet had been pleased with that, but she had also been angry that Tommy hadn't told Katherine not to come to work that day.

When had she asked him to tell her not to come? Had he run into her when drunk?

"I'm sorry. I . . . I drank too much last night and . . ."

Miss Violet grabbed his arm. "I'm doing my best to protect her, to keep her innocence in every way. But if I can't depend on you to help me then I'm not sure if this will work, you all staying here. And I can't protect you either if I can't trust you."

She pulled herself up tall, a bit of spittle at the corner of her mouth. He almost wiped it away but decided not to push the boundaries of polite behavior even if he was tasked with impolite work.

"Heard you were at the saloon again." She paced. "Colt Churchill told me. You get blind drunk and next thing you know you're compromised and forced to give up information."

"What information?"

She grew frustrated with him, calling him naïve.

"Yet you have a girl in the back. There's that. It's all an act, isn't it? We all have secrets . . ." She rolled on and on without even really waiting for a defense from him, as though she preferred holding Tommy's secret rather than not. "Trust is everything."

It was true that Tommy knew Olivia played as Dreama, something the public was scrambling to know. He'd seen Judge Calder there for a reading, kissing and hugging Miss Violet, and he knew about the condoms, but he had no intention of revealing any of that information to anyone. He'd explained he doubted whether she could trust the judge, but she felt fully invested with trust in the big, oppressive man. Tommy left it at that, knowing if anyone could manage him, it would be Miss Violet. He wondered who would win in a battle, Miss Violet or Mrs. Calder. Both were iron strong. Tommy did his best to convey his loyalty as he didn't want to be on Miss Violet's bad side. He was looking to earn more money, not less. He'd dropped the entire conversation just as soon as she'd let him.

"Trust, trust, trust," she'd kept repeating. And though he liked Miss Violet, appreciated the home she let them board in, that he could use the shed, he felt cold when she exposed her mean streak that told him he couldn't completely trust her, not when there were many puzzle pieces missing to her work, even if he wasn't sure what he didn't know.

"I understand," he'd said when she harped on trust again. She'd twisted and manipulated him, and by agreeing to continue to work for her, he was agreeing to let her do that. So which of them was truly more calculating? Who could be trusted, really?

Tommy was beginning to wonder if anyone besides Pearl was worth the word.

Chapter 38

It wasn't long after deciding Pearl was the most trustworthy person in the world that a sliver of mistrust slipped into Tommy's heart. He'd gone for wood at Miss Violet's then caught and followed the scent of bread and patty shells into the kitchen. When he entered, not only did he find Katherine looking pale, gaunt, and coughing, but she was surrounded by easels and paintings by the dozen, not baking supplies.

She seemed to be entranced. He shook her a few times to get her to pay attention to him, to really pay attention.

Then he saw it. The painting of a boy and a dead deer, the boy's face wracked with sorrow as he knelt by it with his gun. And off to the far side was a girl coming toward the boy . . .

The sight of it choked him, angered him, confused him. It was the exact scenario that had happened between him and Pearl the day she dressed the deer when he couldn't. When they made their first pinkie promise. And here was the entire tale, all of it illustrated in beautiful brushstrokes, executed by his own sister, courtesy of Pearl?

Had Pearl divulged their secret and Katherine went ahead and cast it in paint and canvas?

He tried to ask that question without giving too much information, but ended up making Katherine scold him about being nice to Pearl.

"I haven't been?"

"That's not what I meant."

That really got him thinking that Katherine had been commiserating with Pearl, talking about him. Had Pearl revealed to Katherine that she was living in the shed? After the first night she stayed there he hadn't even thought to ask if she was moving out. Miss Violet knew about Pearl . . . Maybe she'd told Katherine when she broke the pinkie promise?

"What is all this? All these paintings?"

"I just paint things that come to me. Half the time I feel like I'm in a dream. I feel calm and lost in this creative world."

Tommy could understand that. He experienced it when he wrote an especially good prayer or sometimes when he worked with wood.

"Why does the painting with the boy bother you so much?"

He confided the story he'd wanted to keep hidden, that he felt so guilty about shooting the deer that he would have sworn it had a soul, felt like he had practically murdered a person.

As he knew she wouldn't, Katherine didn't mock him for this, but instead went on talking about how all animals have souls, that she had tried to tell him that she could sense dead people several times since they were little, that it was no different with animals.

She sounded a little too understanding, making him think of the articles about Dreama and Madame Smalley and their mediumships. He was frightened for Olivia playing Dreama, especially after Madame Smalley's comeuppance. He suggested Katherine not say too loudly what she had about animals and souls and the dead, sensing them. The last thing he wanted was his sister tossed in jail or Glenwood for claiming to speak to the dead.

Yet he was full of questions he didn't really want answers to. It was not realistic to think this way—that she could see or hear the unseen or whatever she thought she could do. No, the painting was a coincidence. He put his trust in Pearl above all, and that was the only possible answer. He thought of how Katherine said he was lucky to have Pearl. That he knew, but soon his mind was tangled around everything Katherine was saying, and he couldn't follow her logic. "Pearl told you about the deer, didn't she?"

Tommy never got his answer to that because Miss Violet interrupted them right then and sent Tommy away.

He went into Miss Violet's yard, wading through the naked blueberry, raspberry, and chokeberry bushes, threading his way into her social garden, that hadn't been used since weather turned chilly, to get wood. He pulled logs from the pile. Much as he wanted to believe Pearl kept his secret, it was clear that Katherine had been talking to Pearl. Pinkie promise. Pearl wasn't keeping their secrets at all. She had to have told Katherine about the day with the deer. Nothing else made common sense.

By the time Tommy had gathered the wood, delivered it to the shed, and chopped more to replace what he'd taken, he was ready to tuck into bed. As he cut through the hedges, he ran into a hulking man.

"Tommy!"

Tommy recognized the voice. He smiled at the sight of him.

"Aleksey." He put his hand out, and they shook.

"Nice to see you. Just dropped some extra squash from Mr. Palmer's farm for your family. Katherine said she could make a soup."

Tommy sighed. "She can make anything."

Aleksey tilted his head. "What's wrong?"

He looked over his shoulder at the opening through the hedge. "Nothing. She's just working so hard, seems a little pale . . ." He didn't want to add that she might be sounding crazy, the way she talked about angels and dead people. "That cough she can't shake, just thinking about that."

Aleksey adjusted his hat. "Agreed. She works so much, more than me even, with all my law studies."

"Yeah, good work for you." Tommy's face flooded hot, glad the color would be obscured in the darkness. "She looks up to you so much."

"I surely hope so. I would never have been able to study the law if not for her. All because of her."

Tommy considered Aleksey. "You both did a lot for each other, didn't you? Before, I mean. You really like her, don't you?"

He put his hands in his pockets. "More than I could have imagined. Before I ran into her at the grocer's, I never thought I'd see any of you again."

"Felt the same about your family, Aleksey. Your father. I think about him often, what he said about choosing a right path—" Tommy choked on the rest of what he thought about the Zurchenko brothers, sisters, their mother, Greta. Tommy hadn't realized how much they all meant to him until he had a chance to more fully reflect on what they lost those years ago, too. "Well, I've got to get to sleep. I'm glad you have your eye on Katherine. She's so strong, but sometimes a feeling comes over me that makes me just worry."

"Being twins, I imagine that's so. I'm hoping to see her after work tonight."

They passed some small talk about Aleksey's studies and work on the farm and then they parted ways.

"Lots to do tomorrow," Tommy said. "Looking for work, trying to keep out of trouble."

"Definitely stay out of trouble. From what I'm learning about the law and seeing at the courthouse, I'd have to say paramount. We should all live by that mandate, right?"

Tommy recommitted to doing just that.

Chapter 39

Des Moines bustled with news that Dreama would be reading for people at an event called *The Night for Mothers*. It would be held at a grand theater in town. Instead of small readings at private homes or at Miss Violet's, Dreama was going to pull individuals from an audience of hundreds, all watching, all hoping to be one of the lucky ones brought on stage.

Every newspaper burst with articles, both for and against Dreama and her abilities. Some articles claimed her to be as much a fraud as Madame Smalley had been with her act. The charlatan had hidden assistants under tables and behind thick curtains, embedded them in lines of people waiting to see her to then give information to lure the clients to unload more and more money until their purses were empty.

The part about the assistant hiding behind a curtain was particularly unsettling since Tommy had hidden like that during one of Dreama's readings. Not that he did anything other than collect information, but he shuddered to think someone might have ripped the curtain aside and revealed him as part of a scam.

Still. He wasn't so sure Olivia was a scam. He'd felt the connection between her and Mr. Renfrew. As much as he held resentment and a smidge of jealousy regarding Olivia acting as Dreama and her allure for his former prayer customers, he had to admit he'd felt something powerful when he was hidden in the room.

On the morning of *The Night for Mothers*, Tommy saw Olivia and Violet. They'd been bubbling over, discussing the money that would come in, organizing their fancy clothing, and rehashing the plan to usher people into seats according to the amount they paid.

Even Pearl had caught Dreama Fever. She was going to the event, hoping to be singled out, to learn something about her parents. She said she often spoke to them in her mind, and sometimes she thought she felt their presence. This sensation caused her to wonder if one of them had just walked right past her on the street alive and well or if she'd experienced something otherworldly, their ghostly presence.

"I just want to know what they look like, what they were like, why they . . ." She shrugged. "I just need to know."

Tommy sighed when she said that. He thought of her Letters to Heaven. He didn't want to stomp out her hope that she might receive a message from parents who may or may not be deceased. He nearly revealed to her that Olivia was performing as Dreama, and while he was sure he'd felt something powerful during the Renfrew reading, he still didn't fully believe it was anything more than the mood of the night, the setup, the game.

It surprised him that he thought of it that way, as a game. He wondered if people like Mrs. Schultz's butler had considered the prayers Tommy wrote for her to be a game, too. There were certainly enough religious phonies to go around.

Tommy surmised that the event, the fact that most people would not be "read for," and Olivia's/Dreama's con would be revealed and Pearl would see that such things were not reliable paths to serenity, that her future didn't depend on her past.

He scoffed at himself. He'd been tying his future to his past for years. He gently tucked away that little piece of advice, knowing that maybe Pearl just wasn't quite ready to let go of her parents yet.

He watched her prepare for the post office that day, brushing her hair, knotting it tight at the nape of her neck. "Like your ma wears it. Parted on the side." She turned to show him. He smiled and nodded.

"Cleaning up extra nice so I can go straight to the theater after work. Want to look nice if my parents are there to see me."

He nodded. "Sure, Pearl. You look . . ."

She stopped smoothing her hair and turned to him.

Heat rushed up his neck and face. "Pretty. Real pretty."

Tommy fully understood the trouble with letting go. And so earlier, with his work completed, with the idea of moving forward, his vow to find his next right path, Tommy suggested a business idea to Miss Violet. He argued that with Dreama siphoning off so much of his prayer business, he thought he could stand in the lobby waiting for saddened, unselected, attendees to exit and provide them comforting prayers.

Miss Violet sneered.

Even when he mentioned they could double their money, she shot the idea out of the sky like a straight-shot cowboy, her head nearly spinning off her neck. "Don't mess with my night for mothers, Tommy. Not one bit."

He held up his hands. "All right, all right. Just an idea."

Chapter 40

With his newly made vow to change his life, Tommy spent the afternoon ticking his way through want ads and walking the town, applying anywhere there was a help-wanted sign. He even tried the steel mill, thinking that its mindless work for burly men would be perfect for him to sort through his next steps, but he stepped too close to the furnace and melted the bottoms of his already-worn shoes.

"Come back when you've got work boots," the man said and sent him on his way. If only he had the money to rush off and buy a pair. If only.

Nothing else panned out. With the city growing in population, it seemed Tommy was missing every opportunity by seconds. Heading back through town, he glimpsed Aleksey Zurchenko walking with an older man he assumed was his boss. Both carried leather cases like the ones he'd seen his father and grandfather use before the scandal. Aleksey had come so far, from immigrant non-English speaker to studying the law. And there Tommy was, born with every advantage, and he'd traded on none of it.

He felt a momentary surge of resentment but then derided himself. It was his fault. It was time for him to take responsibility and use the skills he had to make his life better.

Though he was good with his hands, Tommy's real talents may have resided in his mind, as his mother had suggested all along. He may not have been the curious intellectual that James was, but with the conversation with Aleksey the other night plus the series of failures at odd jobs that should have been simple to get and keep, it became clear—he shouldn't have quit school, and he should have seen that he could find a way through life on the intellectual path his parents had originally set for him. Mama had been right. His last stop before heading home was at the schoolhouse to beg Miss Hawthorne to let him back into school. She relented with Tommy's promise to provide a steady stream of prayers for her.

Once home, he found Mama elbow-deep in material, Yale on the kitchen floor playing with a doll. He rushed to Mama and swallowed her into his arms. She gasped, stiff, then she softened and gripped him back. They sat at the kitchen table, talking. He crossed one foot over his knee. Mama looked at his feet twice and then grabbed his ankle.

"What on earth? What happened to your shoes?"

He felt a half second of self-consciousness, the inclination to hide his failure, but then he shrugged. She'd already seen his failures and still opened her arms and heart to him. "I looked all day for work. Even went to the mill thinking I could easily work there, and first thing I did was walk too close to slag and," he lifted his foot to emphasize, "melted the soles on the spot."

"You're burned?" She pulled his foot onto her knee to examine the sole. Yale crawled over to investigate. She reached for his foot like Mama, the bells attached to her wrist jingling.

Tommy brushed his finger against the bell. "Just red skin, not burnt."

Mama untied his shoe and she and Yale wiggled it off together, the bell tinkling, as Yale "helped." Mama reached for the other shoe.

Katherine's bells, strung onto Yale's wrist, had been the perfect solution to her newfound independence.

He was embarrassed but wanted to make sure Mama knew he was trying to change. "You were right, Mama."

She froze and lifted her gaze to him.

"I'm more suited for school and all those pursuits. All that stuff you always talked about with my riches in my mind, all that you taught me, all of us." He drew a deep breath. "So I went to Miss Hawthorne and begged to get back into school. She said yes."

Mama tilted her head and patted his leg. "Just because of the melted shoes? Maybe I was wrong in making you follow in James's . . ." She looked down and smiled. "Shoes."

They giggled as Yale went back to her doll. "I'm not like James in lots of ways, and the shoes aren't the only reason for me seeing I need schooling, it's just that the incident at the mill gave me a chance to think and to see and really know I don't want a job like the ones I tried for. You were right."

She engulfed him into her arms, hugging him so tight he couldn't breathe. In that moment, he felt his loneliness lift a little, enough that he noticed it, realized he had a hand in their difficult relationship. When she let go of him, she prepared one of Katherine's poultices and wrapped his feet in soaked cloths.

They read the newspaper together, dissecting the articles that praised and criticized Dreama, neither of them sure what was really happening with the woman, afraid to doubt completely, but knowing that frauds were everywhere when mothers wanted to know their children were safe in the afterlife. He nearly told her about Olivia but stopped himself—what if she *wasn't* a con?

"Katherine's always telling me James is with us. And while I want to tell her I believe that, because I think I actually do, I don't want her believing it too much. She told me about angels and . . . The thought lends her serenity, so I don't want to tell her to stop saying that to people, but then I think of . . ." She gestured toward the papers. "All the craziness that happens when a woman claims she knows the dead. It's just too much and too dangerous. There are groups forming, trying to get to the bottom of how Dreama's succeeding in helping people."

"I agree." Tommy nodded, thinking of the painting Katherine had done that seemed to depict Tommy on the day Pearl had found him crying over the deer he'd shot, unable to dress it. Katherine claimed she just painted it without realizing it had anything to do with Tommy. It reminded him of how his prayers came to him. Perhaps it was just an artistic path, unexplainable.

Katherine had always been especially sensitive. "Remember the fire on the prairie, and she said she saw someone while we were in the bee-tree and it turned out that a boy had been buried under it? I think about that sometimes. The luck we did have even when I didn't think we were fortunate. And maybe it's like when I write prayers to sell along with the reverend's. The words just come to me without me even thinking them. I wrote some good ones."

Mama's eyebrows shot up. "You did?"

"It's like I'm recording a voice inside me. Like for this woman, Mrs. Schultz."

"I'm not surprised you have a way with prayers. You read the Bible nonstop before . . . well, before everything."

He folded the newspaper. "It was the other stuff I wrote, beyond the scripture. Anyone can copy scripture. I think I actually am good at that, but then I think of all the bad religious stuff and—"

Yale grabbed her belly, declaring her hunger. Mama scooped the child into her lap, resting her cheek on the top of Yale's head, rocking her.

"You look so peaceful holding her, Mama. So beautiful."

"Thank you. A child in my arms is the best feeling. For that moment, I know exactly what I need to do—is the child happy? In pain? Safe?"

"Hungry," Yale said, looking up at Mama.

Mama grinned. "Hungry. Yes. Let me get busy."

"I'll help." Tommy stood, making Mama's eyes go wide yet again.

Mama and Tommy made toast and eggs for dinner, letting Yale help butter the crisp bread. He couldn't remember a nicer time he'd had with his family, even with his feet smarting.

She handed him money. "New shoes."

He pushed the money away. "No. That's your savings. Katherine's working so much for Miss Violet and has school. And she's painting there . . . and that cough. She looks tired and pale, doesn't she? The sooner we get into a cottage, the better. So no. I think the soles look bad, but they melted in a way that covered the holes that were there. Katherine might need some new shoes."

Mama put the money back and moved Katherine's cure book to the side. "Aleksey's spending a lot of time with her. I trust him. His family was so good to us. He's keeping an eye on her, too."

"I know. I saw him the other night," Tommy said.

"He stopped by earlier today to say his mama might be in town to see Dreama and that they'd stop by. Said he hadn't known she was coming, but got a letter saying so."

"Well, that's nice. You must miss her."

"I do, I really do."

She kissed his forehead. "I'm so glad you're going back to school. And keep looking for a small job. The right thing'll come along and fit with your schooling. I know that. Deep down, you do, too. Whether it's prayers or whatever that Dreama does—if she's doing anything—or Katherine's belief in angels, there are things at work in the universe, and I believe there is good for you, Tommy. It's coming your way if you just believe."

Tommy breathed deep, relieved.

He removed the want ads from several issues and took them to the shed to tend the fire and the dog. He wondered how Pearl was, if she was finding solace at *The Night for Mothers*. He knew Katherine would be baking or helping to usher people around at the theater, collecting money for Miss Violet.

He stoked the fire and let Fern out. Teddy scratched in his box and then settled on the hearth to warm himself. Frank dropped onto Tommy's shoulder and released a silver coin into Tommy's lap.

Tommy sighed. "Where'd you get this?"

"House. House."

Tommy chuckled. That could be anywhere, but he wondered if it was Judge Calder's again. He tucked the coin into the old nail box and saw the folded piece of paper on which he'd begun to write a story about Pearl. He pulled it out and reread the one and only line: *Once upon a time there was a girl* . . . He had put a line through girl, and he remembered that he had decided *girl* didn't fit a story starring Pearl Riverside. He looked up and smiled. Just having her name on his lips gave him pleasure.

But then he thought of Pearl and Katherine together, discussing his secrets, that Pearl lived in the shed, the painting. Pearl was the only one who knew about the deer. Was Pearl as loyal as he believed? She was enamored with him, he knew that much, but he wondered if to her he was just someone to use. No, he couldn't believe that idea even came to mind. He remembered the night in the kitchen when Pearl was bathing. The softness hidden inside her rugged shell—that was real. He knew he could trust her.

Once upon a time, he wrote, *there was a force of nature who came with flaming hair—no, she came with wings and emerald eyes. Her name was Pearl. But most people never even saw her. Tiny, ordinary to most, but to the boy who knew her strength and her softness, she was everything . . .*

He shook his head at what he wrote. Ridiculous. Still, he kept on with the story. He wrote until his ideas were laid out, spent. He refolded the paper and put it in the trunk with the few coins he had left and waited for Pearl to return. The night stretched long, and Tommy worked on the loft ladder, changing the angle and widening each step to create stair-like treads so Fern could join them at night.

It was getting nearly impossible to keep from pulling Pearl close in the night when he woke with urges. If Fern slept between them, it would keep Pearl from ever having to push him away, or worse, allowing advances. He didn't want to do that. He wasn't ready to take on a wife and all it entailed. And so a barrier was required, and who better for that than Fern?

Chapter 41

Pearl returned from *The Night for Mothers*, her face flush with excitement. She sat in front of the fireplace with Teddy in her lap, but hopped up intermittently and sat back down, crossing her legs, thrilled with her evening, story tumbling out like water down a fall.

"It was amazing!" Her arms flew up, and she spread her fingers wide. "I barely had enough money for entrance. I had to stand in the back with the rest of the poor folks. Could barely see the stage, but that was fine. I could hear."

Tommy smiled.

"Dreama connected a woman with her dead babies and then a husband who'd hid away treasure for the family, and then the last family . . . Dreama soothed the mother's soul, but then something happened. I couldn't see what exactly, but she just stopped talking to the mother and son—a big fella, but the shadows and a pillar hid him away from my sight so I couldn't see his reaction. But the mother. She was tall, but frail and… anyway. They sat at the table. Dreama started breathing hard, like she was in pain or something, then she just up and ran away. Her white dress fluttering behind like a bird. She left out the back, I s'ppose. Treasure, Tommy. Do you think it's possible there's treasure for me somewhere? That my parents are desperately trying to tell me where it is?"

Tommy tried not to laugh. He certainly wished for his share of treasure, but this was different. "Possible, I guess."

She drew a deep breath and expressed it, talking with her hands again. "The whole audience rushed the stage, surrounding the family to ask what happened. Dreama had dropped her glove and her crystals—she left it all behind when she ran. People were grabbing for it all, just wanting a piece of the magic."

Tommy had been told security would be there for Dreama, and he assumed Olivia had gotten away without anyone discovering her true identity. The rushing crowd worried him though.

"You're okay?" He stepped closer, checking her over with his gaze.

"Oh yes. It was beautiful." Pearl's words came like a sigh as she closed her eyes and hugged herself. "Hundreds of people drop-dead silent, just feeling Dreama's revelations like a warm coat."

"So she did this for three people? That's it? Hundreds paid, and she dashed away without you getting anything from her?"

Pearl pursed her lips and plugged her fists on her hips the way she did so often. "Don't rain on my parade, Tommy Arthur."

He sat on the stairs to the loft that he'd been shoring up, not wanting to hurt Pearl. He patted the ladder risers. "Like what I did? Widened and deepened them so Fern can come up in the loft with us."

Her dark expression lightened, and she went to Tommy, sitting on the step below him. She ran her hand over the stair.

"Not yet smooth," Tommy said, "but I got a lot done. Even added some curlicues along the sides, like the stairs in Miss Violet's." He didn't want to confess the reason for wanting Fern in the loft between them because he didn't want Pearl to worry that she'd have to bat him off.

"Oh." She ran her fingers along the moldings. "The nicest thing anyone's ever done for Fern."

"Glad you like it. Fern got up and down fine."

She removed her hat and leaned back against Tommy's legs. He brushed his hand over her curls once but then stopped himself. "So you felt comforted even though she didn't do anything for you? Like all the others say?"

She nodded. "I did. I know it's odd. Like your prayers, maybe?"

He thought of the way his words had calmed people before everyone wanted Dreama instead. "Maybe. Maybe it's that."

**

Tommy and Pearl lay upstairs in the loft, Fern between them, her head on Pearl's stomach, her body warming Tommy's leg as the fire was dying out. Frank sat on the window ledge; an old robin's nest stuffed with cotton was his bed.

"Tell me about it again, Tommy."

Tommy lifted his head to meet her gaze, but she was staring off into the shadows. "Go to sleep, Pearl. I've early work with the reverend." He wanted to tell her about the painting Katherine had done and ask her if she'd been disloyal and told Katherine about the deer. There was no other answer. Yet he didn't want Pearl's lie or her truth on the matter. He wanted to pretend he had no idea she'd been talking to Katherine and revealed something she'd promised not to.

"Please."

Tommy rubbed his stomach.

"You're awful cranky all of a sudden. Orders for prayers got you riled like this? Thought you'd be glad to have some after yer dry spell."

Tommy sighed. If he told her he suspected she'd been disloyal, they would argue, and then Pearl would be off into the night—or he would. And that wasn't what he wanted. "Nothing. It's nothing."

"Try me."

"I'd rather tell you stories again."

"Suit yerself, grumpy. But if you tell me stories, talk proper. Christmas morning. Tell that one."

"Geez, Pearl, mighty demanding. No, before I tell you a story, you tell me one."

She seemed to be holding her breath. "I don't have stories like you."

"You must have stories of some sort."

"Well, my life ain't like yours with family to remember what I forget, with people who love me and keep after me. So I write letters to heaven. For my parents."

He turned to his side and propped up on one elbow. "You send them?"

She swatted his shoulder. "'Course not. There's no real heaven. This is it, right? I just like using that title. Lends some hope to what I'm writing."

Tommy was surprised to hear her say that. "You don't believe in God?"

"Didn't say that."

"Well, then?"

"Don't know exactly. There's greatness right here. In between awfulness, the tramping of bad people over good, around good, instead of good . . . There are such great, kind people in the world. I believe that. I've seen them. I know them."

Pearl grasped his hand and squeezed. Fern knocked their hands apart with her head. "Tell about the mansion and all that came with it. I swear I once lived in a mansion. I can feel it like I feel my blood running through my body. Or maybe like you said, I'm going to live in a house like that someday. Maybe that."

"Ah, okay." He was thankful Fern was between them to help keep him from sliding closer, from acting on his desire for her. Not even the doubt that his conversation with Katherine had sown had stopped him from wanting to pull her into his arms. There was something about her listening to his old stories that made him think it could actually happen again, that he could have a beautiful home and life and all the wondrous Christmas cheer that came with it.

"Go on ahead," Pearl said. "Start when you would wake."

"Jasper the butler would shake me—"

"Gently shake."

"Yes, gently shake me awake. I'd slide my feet into wool slippers and shrug on a toasty robe Jasper had warmed by the recently lit fire across from the foot of the bed."

"Don't forget the pine swags yer ma hung rafter to rafter. And how she'd meet ya in the hall with a Christmas kiss and clasp your face." Pearl put her hands to her own cheeks. "And plant smooches on yer forehead and cheeks and nose."

"I'm getting there, Pearl."

Tommy moved his feet toward hers, sharing heat through their stockings. Pearl lay her hand back on Tommy's. Her slender fingers slipped between his, making Tommy's belly flip over. These moments with Pearl, much as he wasn't in the mood to keep up the chatter, comforted him like nothing he could ever recall.

He imagined what Pearl might look like in fine silk dresses and hats and gloves that matched. And shoes. She'd never had a pair of shoes made to fit her feet, made to be as beautiful as a dress. She would appreciate such things like no one else he'd ever met. Perhaps the two of them could make a life together. Maybe someday when he built something, he could look at her that way.

"You think I'll ever be a lady, Tommy? Like yer ma?"

"Your manners are good sometimes. Maybe a little rough when you forget to pay attention to them, but you're smart and—"

"But a *real lady* like yer ma and Katherine, and Mrs. Calder and Mrs. Hillis? Miss Violet? Like them?"

Tommy sighed. He didn't know how to answer her.

"Think on it." Pearl got up on her elbows. "Your ma's in rags no better than mine." She sat up, cross-legged. Fern shifted in her sleep. Pearl pulled Tommy's hand into her belly, petting it. Her eyes sparkled in the dark. "But your mother, the way she carries herself—her posture, the lift of her chin, the way her words flow pretty as a picture, sweet as roses, pointed as the thorns, but just . . . magnificent." Pearl's head fell forward, shoulders slumped. "I could just die to be like her. It don't matter one little lick what a lady's dress is like if she's already a lady underneath."

Tommy sat up, crossing his legs, his knee butting into Pearl's. He scratched his chin and considered what Pearl said, pictured his mother, the way she behaved, what she always said about carrying riches in her mind. He thought of Pearl's way of carrying herself, the way she bolted across a street, arms pumping, face crimped in concentration on some matter no one else was privy to.

"You can learn all that stuff, walking like Mama. That's just parental instruction."

"It's *money* first. Maybe after you acquire such lady-hood you can carry it into the poorhouse, but I'm not sure a girl can learn to be a lady without the means to do so. That keeps me up at night sometimes. What if this is all there is for me? Bunking here and there. Dragging my animals around. Nothing more. I'm trying to remake myself, to find the right path to the place I know I belong. Those letters I read—"

"I know."

She laid down, hand flung over her eyes. "Sometimes when I think of the future, I nearly crumble up like a dry leaf and blow away."

"You'll do fine, Pearl. I'm sure of it. You're saving money staying here. Maybe you can start school soon."

"Yes. Schooling first. But what about you, Tommy? You quit school."

"Miss Hawthorne let me back in. I asked her today."

She sat up. "Fan-tas-tic! That's exactly what you ought to be doing. I was thinking, how's Tommy gonna move outta here and tread down a solid, good path if he don't finish his schooling? You don't seem inclined toward the farm or such. And you ain't got enough bank to get out of trouble like you been getting into."

"I have bank."

"Not enough. But you have riches, mountains of it, in your mind. Just like your ma said."

"I've yet to see a man pay his saloon tab or gambling debt with riches he plucked from his head."

"It's everything, Tommy. Knowledge is everything."

"Look, do you want to practice talking rich or not? It's more than money in the pocket, though I agree I wish I had more. I do, I wish it deep down to the bottoms of my scorched feet. But I'm trying to see beyond my wallet. After what happened when I went looking for jobs today and coming up empty, I see it now."

"Your ma could use that money that you're collecting to bring back your pa."

Tommy considered not saying it, but then decided he ought to. "I spent it, Pearl. I'm ashamed and trying to fix that."

She shook her head and lay back down. "Good. You should trust your ma more."

Tommy stiffened. "You think you know so much about my mama, but you don't. You know her outside appearance. But you haven't seen her like I have."

"She wants to protect you."

"She wants to control me." He thought of how he'd made up with Mama earlier. He turned toward Pearl and ran his hand down Fern's back. "Maybe you're right. It sometimes, it doesn't feel that way and all of a sudden I'm reacting so poorly."

"She loves you. I see it in the way she looks at you and always finds a reason to put her hand on your shoulder, or brush dust from your cheek or muss your hair."

"She loved my brother most."

"You're jealous of your dead brother."

"What do you know?"

"See it every time you mention him."

Tommy clenched his jaw. "You don't understand."

"No. *You* don't understand. Mamas love every child, even if they love each differently."

He didn't want to argue. Every time they discussed Mama, Pearl's dander rose, and she turned snippy, accusatory. Tommy couldn't win that argument because Pearl didn't have to contend with parents who didn't love her enough. Still, he felt too . . . Well, he didn't know what he felt toward Pearl, but whatever it was wouldn't allow him to hurt her by discussing the topic of parents. So he remained silent, open to the idea she'd just let him fall asleep.

Pearl rolled to her side. Tommy could feel her gaze on him in the dark. "Talk like you're rich and tell me about Christmas breakfast again. The pancakes . . ."

"No. This time tell me what's in your bag there. Letters to heaven, your pearl-handled knife—"

"Knives. Mother-of-pearl knives and a box . . . and . . . I can't say more. It's personal."

Tommy shifted so his body touched as much of hers as possible even with Fern there. "Okay, Pearl. Go to sleep then.

Sleep tight as can be. I'll tell you the story long as you fall asleep while I'm telling it so it keeps the magic."

Tommy drew back. *Keeps the magic.* Words his mother had spoken before she read the last story of the night when he was small. He'd forgotten, yet here were the words in him, as sure as his blood and organs.

Fern stood and settled so that her head was on Tommy's belly. Pearl clasped his hand over the back of Fern, and he smiled, wondering how on earth Pearl came to be the person he trusted more than anyone, even being certain that she told Katherine about his deer hunting, wondering how in heaven he'd manage if she suddenly wasn't part of his world. For now, the possibility she broke a promise didn't matter. They were together, separated by daytime obligations, but moored in their loft by night. Slumber finally came and settled him into the place where awake met asleep, and in that slice of time and place, in between, beside Pearl, he passed right through a tiny bit of heaven.

Chapter 42

Well. The excitement of Dreama and *The Night for Mothers* did not end with Pearl leaving with the crowd. Mama poured Tommy coffee and gave him corn bread while she explained.

"Not only did Greta come to town, but she stopped here after seeing Dreama."

"Oh, Mama, that's so wonderful."

"She brought me a beautiful seed box with specimens from the prairie. I can't wait to plant them in memory of James and the little things that were good that year, like my friendship with Greta."

"That's really nice. So Dreama read for Mrs. Zurchenko?"

Mama nodded. "She was pleased as she could be with the results, said she felt healed, that Dreama said the children were warm and safe. And then Dreama just got up and blew away—leaving a glove behind and her crystals, and it was mayhem after that, apparently. Katherine and the girls all got home safe. She was here with Aleksey as a matter of fact. I thought the two of them went out back to get you, but they were just talking, apparently."

Tommy puffed his cheeks, then blew out the air, thinking of Pearl and her retelling of what happened with Dreama and the last family she read for. She had said the son was big, but couldn't see him with the pillar and the shadowy stage lighting. "Well, I suppose the Zurchenkos got their money's worth, right? Of all of those who went."

Mama shook her head, hands on hips. "Suppose so. I wouldn't have imagined someone as practical as Greta could be moved by such a thing. Even Katherine and her angels . . . I just don't know. Town's even more riled up since Dreama ran from the hall, a frenzy of both anger and also admiration. Quite a stew of interest, I'd say."

"Lots of money, I suppose."

"Oh." Mama shook her finger. "Greta brought one of our trunks that we left behind when we abandoned the dugout. Drag it back to the shed when you have a chance. I can't bear to go through it. Not yet, even after all these years."

"I will."

"And today's the day I need you to take Yale to that picnic and fair the women's club is hosting."

He adjusted his shirt tail. "Sounds good. I think Yale's ready for this kind of thing. I remember one of the events we went to when I was little—an elephant. Remember they had one to ride?"

"I sure do. Took us months to arrange for that."

Silence hung between them. Tommy knew they were both thinking, *So much has changed since then.*

**

When Pearl came home from the post office, she volunteered to take Yale to the party. "You can keep looking for a job," she said as she washed her face at the bowl.

"No. I want to go. I want to see Yale's face when she meets exotic animals and new people—children her age. And I promised Mama I would."

As they reached the park, Tommy explained that the gathering was sponsored by the women's club and the Society for Social Action and given for children who had everything in life and those who had nothing. Mrs. Hillis believed that joining children from all types of families would be what changed the least of society, what would allow them to transform and participate in the community in ways that were productive, not criminal or desperate.

Mama was busy that day organizing news articles for Mrs. Hillis. Tommy was proud of Mama, that she was writing again and that doing so lit her up, reminding him of her before they first left Des Moines.

They reached the tree-covered picnic grove. There were pony rides, bobbing for apples, foot races, tiny cakes frosted pink and white, candies, oranges, and paper for children to paint and draw on.

It was as though every decadent experience from his former childhood had been laid out before him. When it was Yale's turn to ride, he walked alongside the pony, holding her hand, the jingling bells on her wrist, providing harmony for every step the animal took.

Tommy swelled with love and satisfaction that his sister was experiencing a sliver of what he had for the first ten years of his life. It made him think of how she'd been born, in that dugout on the prairie, early, just a sack of stick-bones with loose, see-through skin, her veins and arteries mapping her little arms and legs. And now here she was riding a pony. Impossible to imagine, he would have said at the time she was born. She smiled as she bobbed along with every step the pony took, but she grasped Tommy's hand, clamping on with an iron grip.

Tommy loved seeing her happy, engaged with the world, wearing her best blue-checked dress, redone from a larger, worn frock. It was as though he'd been taken back in time. He was happier than he could have imagined to be charged with accompanying Yale to such an affair. Adding to his delight was Pearl's reaction. Fifteen years old, she'd never experienced such decadence. Her dress was dingy, as always, but she'd scrubbed her cheeks clean and wiped strawberries along her lips to redden them, a smattering of freckles trailing across her nose.

When Yale was done with the pony, Tommy and Pearl walked her to the trees, where children were climbing. Pearl grabbed Tommy's hand. "Thank you, Tommy. For bringing me."

"You're welcome. You look pretty with your scrubbed cheeks."

She smiled at him from under the brim of her hat.

He squeezed her hand wanting to say more about how much he liked her.

Yale pointed to one of the smaller trees. "Sit."

Tommy and Pearl exchanged a glance and took her closer. He held her up, unsure what she meant. She grasped for the tree, fingers brushing low-hanging leaves.

"Sit on the branch?" Tommy asked.

She nodded and kicked her legs, muddy shoes leaving marks on Tommy's chest. "All this icy rain. Wish we'd get a blizzard to freeze all the mud." Tommy set Yale on the branch above him, keeping a hand on her. There was a second branch just above it, running parallel to Yale's chest. She grabbed on, leaning into it for support and swung her feet, mud flying. Tommy put his hand at Yale's back. "Wheee," she said as a soft breeze lifted her hair, her hand moving just enough to make the tinkling bells lift on the wind. Pearl stood at the other side, reaching up to keep a hand on Yale's back, too.

That moment of bliss came to a sharp end when someone tapped Tommy on the shoulder. He turned and faced Reverend Shaw. The man leaned in close to Tommy's ear.

"You've been very, very bad, Master Arthur."

Tommy glanced over his shoulder. Pearl was confused, staring at him. Tommy shook his head and waved her off. "Stay with Yale."

Tommy was stunned that the minister's grip was so strong. "You've been skimming extra from the prayer earnings, and that money belongs to the poor and wretched souls I serve at the church."

"Hardly." Tommy's voice rose. He lowered the volume down to a strained whisper, embarrassed, but noticing that most people were engrossed with their party activity. "Any prayer business I had, dried up with the arrival of Dreama."

Tommy remembered Reverend Shaw being at Dreama's reading when he was tasked with taking notes, that the reverend had his hand down Helen's bodice. He was frightened by what Shaw had against him and others he cared about, but he felt as though offense might at least give him some distance from the man. "You know Dreama, Miss Violet, her employees, their *assets*.

You've met all of them. Certainly you haven't forgotten Dreama took the entire prayer business right out from under us. Certainly you haven't forgotten your time with Helen."

Tommy glanced back at Yale and Pearl. He could tell Pearl was trying to coax Yale from the tree. She had to get on her toes to reach Yale to pull her down. Tommy shook his head. "Stay there," he shouted. "It's fine."

Jingle, jingle. The sound of bells carried to his ears.

"That's right," Reverend Shaw said. "But I'm not sure you were honest when you told me the prayers dried up. I heard you get special requests for your prayers. They don't want mine. They want the extras. The second set of prayers they get when *you* visit. You're providing extras that I'm not compensated for."

"If you must know, I've dropped a few free prayers to former customers, yes. But no one paid me. I didn't take a thing from you."

"Free prayers for no reason?"

Tommy stuffed his hands into his pockets. "Maybe I earned a little satisfaction from it. Contentment that I helped someone. You know . . ." Tommy pondered what he was about to say, that he suddenly saw himself in a different light. "Like a minister should. Self-sacrificing. Do you feel that way when you pray with someone, for someone?"

Reverend Shaw's face screwed up, reddening. "*Selfish*, like all the boys I help. Always taking. Thieves, all."

Tommy didn't want to argue about other boys or state the obvious reason Reverend Shaw chose thieving boys to "help," not right then. Tommy may have known the truth about Reverend Shaw, but he understood his word wouldn't stand up against the minister's in public. Yet, he felt the power shift between the two.

Jingle, jingle. For his sister, it was time for Tommy to be a man.

"So I'll ask again," Tommy said. "You haven't noticed that Dreama's the one stealing our prayer opportunities? Whatever extra I do is nothing compared to what she's siphoned off. None of the addresses you give me are good. Everyone's waiting to sit with Dreama."

"I want what's owed me."

"I don't have anything to give you. Unless you want the remnants of my free prayers. I imagine at some point in time you believed in prayer for real? You didn't start off being a lying fraud, did you?"

"You think you can make accusations like this, that you—"

"Yes. I do."

"You're no different than me," Reverend Shaw said.

Tommy felt himself straighten against a man he was afraid of. Tommy wouldn't push against him publicly, but he wouldn't be pushed in private any longer.

Reverend Shaw poked Tommy's chest, stepping closer. "You owe fourteen dollars at *least* to Colt Churchill. And you owe what you stole from me. Slinging mud at your benefactors isn't going to persuade me to help you."

Tommy grabbed the reverend's arm, folding it back against his chest. "Don't wait for me to ask for help. I've made plenty of mistakes. I'm not . . . Well, I'm far beyond not perfect; I'm troubled and lost and all the things you say about me and the boys you help."

Dorozhka. Mr. Zurchenko's voice came to Tommy.

"But I'm going to change. I am. But for now, I'm the poor you claim to help."

"And yet you claim not to need me." The reverend wrenched away and surveyed the party; Tommy followed his gaze to Yale and Pearl.

Yale was getting antsy, kicking her feet hard, too hard. Pearl rose onto her toes, reaching up for Yale. Tommy jogged toward the tree.

"Don't push me, Arthur." The reverend's voice made Tommy stop and turn back to him. A stiff wind blew the reverend's hat off. He shoved it back on, stalking after Tommy. "Town's ripe for a sacrificial lamb, someone for the mob to claim they caught. You'd be the perfect scapegoat to get things going—to show the judge isn't letting people slide through the system without consequences. Gambling, taking advantage of grieving widows, stealing, too? All I have to do is tell people how hard I've been working to wrench you back on the righteous path, that you're resisting despite my generous overtures."

Tommy's thoughts tied into useless knots. He whirled back. "I'll spill all *your* dirty deeds. Everyone knows you sent me to sell prayers. I did nothing wrong."

"They won't believe you, Tommy. You must be joking. Your name's all over the saloon. You've been in jail, using phony names . . . There's even a question of stolen items at each and every home you've visited, including the judge's the day you cut wood. Or maybe your mother lifted the items. She was there that day, wasn't she? Maybe it's she who should do a turn in the clink."

Jingle, jingle.

Tommy clenched his fists at his side. He wanted to pummel the reverend but knew that was a bad choice for several reasons. Tommy had surely done plenty that would be punishable under the law, even if for good reason. But he wasn't going to let this phony do-gooder rule him any longer. A juggler caught Tommy's eye, and he knew Yale would love to watch that act. "A juggler, Reverend. I'm sure you understand my sister would love to see him."

"You're bold, Tommy. But naïve. It's like you don't even see beyond your own little nose."

Tommy backed away from the reverend and was just about to turn and run toward the tree where Yale was sitting when he heard a scream.

Pearl's and then Yale's.

Chapter 43

Tommy and Pearl knelt beside a wailing Yale. Her face was folded in pain, her arm caught at an unnatural angle, obviously broken, the bell bracelet quivering as she writhed. Tommy pressed Yale's abdomen to keep her from flailing. "Please, Yale, sweet Yale. Doctor's coming. He'll see to you, and you'll be good as new . . ."

Tommy glanced up to see Pearl hauled to her feet by a police officer. Someone yanked him away as well, and the doctor got down beside Yale, her screaming intensifying. Tommy struggled toward her, but a policeman pulled him back.

"That's my sister."

"Should've been watching her, then, wouldn't you say?" the policeman said.

"Get this girl to the doctor's office," Judge Calder's voice came. Tommy turned toward him, shocked that the judge was helping, but grateful. Judge Smythton and two others were there as well, watching, working to get care for Yale.

Tommy struggled toward Judge Calder wanting to say thank you, but the policeman held him back.

Judge Calder crossed his arms, widening his stance. "Looks like you've got a prime example of what we've been seeing all over town, Alderman O'Hara." His tone turned Tommy's blood cold. Judge Calder wouldn't look at him.

Another alderman leaned in to look closer at Yale who was writhing, but quieting as shock set in.

"Yep. Sure enough that's what we got here. Glenwood. You were right, Judge Calder."

Tommy's throat closed. "What'd you say?" He stopped struggling so he could hear clearly.

Judge Smythton drew closer. "I've seen this girl at the community meetings. She's an idiot. Or an imbecile. I forget which they said she was. I was assured she was well cared for."

"Belongs in Glenwood. That's why it's there," a woman said, staring, huffing. "I hear her mother leashes her outside. And the bells. Look. Like an animal, she needs warning bells."

Tommy's stomach clenched. He ripped out of the policeman's grip and went to Yale's side. Her sobs slowed when he knelt beside her and smoothed her matted hair away from her eyes. "You'll be all right, Yale. The doc'll fix you up, then you'll come home. I'll stay with you."

Pearl was released, and she dropped beside Yale. "I'm so sorry, Yale. I tried to hold you."

"It's not your fault, Pearl." Tommy looked at her. "I should've—" He looked up to see Reverend Shaw watching them with a satisfied smirk.

The doctor's assistants brought a makeshift stretcher, and they heaved Yale onto it, the movement causing her to lose consciousness.

"Back away, Arthur. She's going with the doc, and then you can take this up in court," the reverend said.

"What? You can't be serious. I'm going with her. You can't—"

"Tommy. Please. Begging is beneath an Arthur, isn't it? I prefer to be paid for favors." Judge Calder elbowed Reverend Shaw playfully.

Tommy eyed Judge Smythton and the aldermen. Had they just heard that? They all knew the judge and Reverend Shaw were crooked?

"Why?" Tommy asked, unable to believe the one time he took Yale out for the day that she'd been injured and stolen away.

Judge Smythton followed the stretcher and turned back. "I'll handle the paperwork."

The bells went silent as they got farther away, leaving Tommy to wonder if Yale passed out or if they were just too far to hear anymore.

The other officials left, but Judge Calder sneered.

"Why?" Tommy asked. The silence suffocating him.

Judge Calder narrowed his eyes on Tommy.

Tommy spread his arms open. "Why?"

Judge Calder shrugged and smiled. "Why not?"

Chapter 44

Tommy sent Pearl to get Mama and Katherine while he ran for the courthouse. He needed to stop whatever paperwork Judge Smythton was about to write up then get Yale. He tried to block out her face as she was being carried away, her good arm stretched toward him, reminding him of the day Katherine was boarded out, reaching for their mother as she was hauled away.

He'd felt helpless plenty of times in his life, but never like this, never on behalf of someone else. Even when he'd seen Mama at her broken worst, when he'd left to ease her burden by making his own way, he'd known she'd be all right. He couldn't say the same for Yale. She had no defenses, thriving only recently in the embrace of the tiny house next to Miss Violet with her siblings and mother always nearby. And now this. Now Tommy had failed like he never thought possible.

He burst into the courthouse, past the clerk outside of Judge Calder's chambers. The office was empty. He ran down both sides of the hallway until he reached Judge Smythton's chambers. He ignored the clerk's protests and threw open the door. "Where's my sister?"

Judge Smythton's eyes widened.

"What is going on?"

The judge pointed at the door. "Out. It's a court matter. You'll be notified when you have a date."

Tommy turned to see Mama bursting through the door.

"Judge. My daughter. Something happened?" She put her arm around Tommy. "What is it? She fell, Mrs. Thompson said?"

Tommy nodded. "I'm so sorry, Mama. We had the best day with the ponies and the apples, and then she wanted to climb a tree. Can you believe it? She was sitting in it, her feet swinging and smiling and . . ."

Mama's face cracked with a smile and tears at the same time.

"Judge Smythton," Mama said, holding her voice steady. Tommy put his arm around her, holding her up. "You *know* I'm a good mother. My son is a good brother. Surely you remember me. I met you through the work I'm doing with Mrs. Hillis. For the children. Yale's loved, cared for. Please. You need to let us see Yale right this moment."

Judge Smythton swiped his hand through the air. "Enough."

A policeman and the clerk entered.

"Get them out."

Mama's jaw dropped as the judge turned his back on them. Her knees buckled, and Tommy caught her. The policeman pulled out his gun. Tommy guided her toward the door. "Let's go, Mama. We'll get her back."

As they exited the judge's chambers, the clerk and policeman followed. "The judge will see you in court. Not here, not like this," the policeman said.

Tommy held Mama up as they moved into the hallway. Katherine came toward them, Pearl close behind. Katherine was as colorless as Mama, her face collapsed in worry. "We'll get her back, Mama. We will," Katherine said as she pulled their shaking mother into her arms.

Chapter 45

Night came while Tommy and his family continued to fight to see Yale, to get her home. When it became clear she was no longer theirs, that the courts had custody, they returned home, snow and icy rain freezing them nearly solid. Tommy paced the shed, unable to form coherent thoughts. The guilt, the worry collapsed inside him. Pearl tried to calm him and even plied him with a beer in order to ease his attack. He couldn't breathe, he couldn't see straight, and he didn't know how to set things right.

"It was me, Tommy. I was standing there with her. I should have called you over to get her when I couldn't reach high enough."

He rubbed her shoulder. "It wasn't you, Pearl. It's that damn reverend, and that's my doing, not yours."

He and Pearl discussed what she knew about the judge and Reverend Shaw, how it was convenient that just as Yale was in the tree the reverend distracted Tommy.

No, that was crazy. It's not as though they could have depended on Yale falling. Pearl lifted her arms. "Look at me, Tommy. Dressed in my best rags. Yale, slow and . . . Well, you know. Maybe it was already a plan to take her when she was with just me? Yale fell because I was too short to latch on to her tight, but what if they were planning to take her no matter what? What if the fall just made things easier?"

Tommy shook his head. "That's insane. There are so many ways he could ruin me. This is destroying me, but it's Mama who won't be able to get through this. Not after James's death."

Tommy pushed his hand through his hair.

Pearl lifted her eyebrows.

They sat quiet with their thoughts for a few minutes.

"Mama." He shook his finger. "You think it's *her* the judge was trying to hurt?" Tommy asked.

Pearl shook her head. "I see the worst in those men. Always have. But hurting your ma? We have to be mistaken, Tommy. Why on earth would a human being do such a thing to another? That can't be right. Maybe they just really believe Yale belongs in Glenwood. I certainly ran away from my share of those goons mistaking me for an idiot just because my rags are raggedy."

Tommy grew nauseous at the mention of the asylum. "Let's check on Mama, and then I'm going back to the courthouse. Maybe the night judge'll be reasonable. This can't happen."

He and Pearl found Mama and Katherine in the kitchen, Mama numb and rocking in her seat, her empty arms clutching her waist.

"Get me some whiskey, Tommy," Katherine said. "I'll put it in her tea. She's got to sleep, and her body just won't let her."

She shoved money into his hand. Tommy nodded and left for the saloon.

Because he owed so much money at Churchill's, he bypassed it and entered Mack's Tavern. Nerves shattered, Tommy drank two shots and then left with a jar half-full of whiskey for Mama.

Chapter 46

Tommy delivered the whiskey to Katherine, who added it to a mixture she was stirring. Katherine's coloring and cough were so bad he sat her down and prepared a honeyed tea for her. She actually fell asleep at the table, head on her arms, in the time it took him to fuss with the kettle at the stove. She stirred and woke when he set the fragrant tea in front of her, but her eyes were slits. She ran her fingers along her neck. "Glands are swollen. Fighting something."

"I can't leave you like this," Tommy said.

She waved him off. "Go. I'm fine. The drink will help."

He stared at her, blue veins visible beneath her pale skin. "Go, Tommy. Please. It won't help for you to stand here staring at me. Tea will perk me up."

"No, rest while I'm gone, when Mama sleeps."

"I'll rest when I'm dead," she said with a half smile.

"No. No more dying."

"I've eighty more years to live, at least . . ."

"Let's hope we both do."

He knew Katherine was right; staying there, watching Mama sleep and Katherine worry would be useless. He left for the courthouse before dawn cracked at the horizon. The hearing for Yale wasn't until later, but he wasn't willing to wait for a public display to demand answers. Judge Calder arrived and stopped at the sight of Tommy. "I'm not the judge of record, Tommy. Smythton is."

Tommy followed him into his chambers.

"Get out," Judge Calder said.

"I know things about you, Judge. If you think you're just going to roll right over Yale and hurt her because she's already vulnerable, you're the idiot you think she is."

"That's going to help you? Coming in here, chest pushed out, insulting me?"

Tommy felt his powerlessness like a boulder on the chest. Like with the reverend, Tommy could certainly tell everyone everything the judge was up to, but people either wouldn't believe him or would be too afraid to cross the judge. "Don't send Yale away. Please. Mama will . . . *Please*. For all the years you knew us before I showed up in your courtroom, when your wife and Mama were friends. *You* were my parents' friend. I'll do whatever you want to make it up to you. I'll work for free for you . . . forever." Tommy shrugged. "Whatever you want."

"You can't give me what I want, Tommy. Don't be a stupid asshole. I'll have to commit you into Glenwood along with your sister if you keep it up with this absurdity, thinking you have *anything* I want."

"Then what? Why're you doing this? Because my dead grandfather lost your money more than half a decade ago? You look to be doing fine to me."

Judge Calder loosened his tie and retied it. "The mysteries of the universe, Arthur. They're really something when they have you by the balls. He's not the only Arthur I have business with."

The clerk stuck his head into the judge's chambers. "All right?"

The judge scoffed. "'Course I'm all right." He stared at Tommy. "You'll have your day in court. Out."

Tommy couldn't move. "Please."

The judge turned away, a policeman entered the chambers and marched Tommy out.

Chapter 47

Tommy returned home via the saloon. The night temperatures dropped, freezing his cheeks and ears. Winter was finally fully upon them, the drenching rains that had come off and on had finally turned. Snow fell, a dusting hitting the dirt roads, melting as soon as they hit, followed by snow dumping like rain. He was desperate to numb his fears and quiet his thoughts so he could sort out a plan. He stopped at Churchill's. His pity story about his sister being taken and his distraught mama who needed whiskey to cope earned him a larger tab since Colt wasn't there. He hated seeing the barkeep add more slashes next to his name to signify two jars of whiskey, but he couldn't imagine not having something to help him or his mother if she'd already worked her way through the half jar he'd taken her the night before. Despite his craving for alcohol to numb his guilt and fear over Yale, he kept from drinking it. Somehow, he managed.

Pearl was already in the loft with Fern beside her. He laid down to sleep and heard Pearl sniffling.

"I'm so sorry, Tommy, so sorry."

He moved Fern out of the way and pulled Pearl close, spooning her, holding her tight. "It's my fault, not yours, Pearl. You're a good soul who never harms a flea. So you just don't feel one more smidge of guilt over this. Because the only thing that turns a person rotten faster than not forgiving others is not forgiving yourself. I know."

She cried in his arms, eventually falling asleep. Yes, he knew too well what it did when guilt and resentment seeded in your gut and he couldn't think of anything he wanted less for Pearl than for that to happen.

**

The next morning he woke to find Pearl already gone to work. He took one whiskey jar to Mama's. She wasn't in the kitchen, but there was chicken soup simmering on the stove. He set the whiskey near the lavender and honey on the shelf above the countertop. Katherine would see it there if she wanted to add it to Mama's tea later. He heard a cry from upstairs above the kitchen.

He flew up to the bedroom and found Mama kneeling beside the bed. For a moment, his heart leapt for joy thinking she'd gotten Yale back and was tucking her into bed for a warm nap. But when he approached the bed, Katherine came into view, her face bloodless, her breathing shallow.

He thought of her cough, how exhausted she'd looked for weeks. Now he fully recognized her unsteadiness and sickly appearance as symptoms of illness, not just exhaustion or worry with the taking of Yale.

He touched Mama's shoulders. She looked up, her eyes wet.

"What happened?"

"She collapsed next door at Miss Violet's."

"I should have made her go to bed when I saw how tired she was. She looked awful yesterday," Tommy said.

"She has for some time. I should have made her take a break from all that work and studying."

Tommy thought of Katherine's frenzied painting, all the canvases scattered around Miss Violet's kitchen. He should have demanded she rest way back on that night when she'd looked so tired.

Mama looked just as ashen as Katherine. He knelt beside the bed, and Mama collapsed into his arms. "I can't, Tommy. Yale and now Katherine."

"I'll get a doctor," Tommy said.

"Already had one come. Another's coming soon."

"More blankets."

"Miss Violet's bringing extras over."

He nodded, helpless. "What's wrong with her?"

"First doctor said maybe pneumonia then left without doing anything much. Mr. Hayes was here when Katherine collapsed. He went for another doctor."

Mama held Katherine's hands as she bowed her head and said prayers that Tommy hadn't heard leave her lips in half a decade. Tommy pressed her back. "You're sure another doctor's coming?"

She nodded but didn't look up.

He held Mama close. "I'll be back, Mama. There has to be something I can do."

Chapter 48

Tommy couldn't heal Katherine, but he could get Yale back. He raced to the shed and jotted down every compromising thing he'd seen Judge Calder and Reverend Shaw engage in. He considered writing down the things Miss Violet had done, too, but didn't. He had to keep an ally in case his plan went wrong.

When he finished writing, a piece of paper fluttered to the ground. As he bent down to pick it up, something glittering from across the room caught his eye. He crawled toward the object that caught the little bit of sunlight coming through the small window near the door. When he got close, he saw it was a cross made from mother-of-pearl. The creamy base was swirled with pinks and blues that made it appear as if made of liquid. Frank landed next to the cross, startling him.

"You brought this?"

Frank pushed the cross toward Tommy with his beak.

Tommy picked it up and ran his thumb over its smooth surface, tracing the shape. He thought of all the mother-of-pearl things Pearl owned and wondered if it was hers.

The quiet moment gave him a chance to feel the full weight of Yale's loss. The pain in his chest was like fire, alive. He thought of Mama praying at Katherine's side. He clutched the cross, taking huge, choking breaths spurred by desperation. A fresh bout of it not fueled by past captivity, but by pure sadness. He reached for the trunk where he kept his booze. He slid over to it and flipped the latch.

No.

He shook his head. Not that. Breathing heavily, he couldn't think of anything that would take away this trouble except a miracle.

He went back to the table, took another piece of paper, and wrote a prayer.

Please, God. A miracle. Something for us. Something small, something to let me know it's possible that Yale will come back to us. Please. I won't even pretend I have something to offer of the same value in exchange. This will have to be pure grace from you to us. I don't deserve it, but Yale does. She is pure goodness, and for her, please help me.

Tommy couldn't believe he'd just written his own prayer, not bothering with scripture or bargains, that something in him wanted to believe in a force greater than himself. He traced the cross Frank had brought him onto the paper and folded it up in thirds, tucking it and the cross into his pocket.

Once he'd done that, he felt a release, a whisper of faith that allowed him to breathe, to move.

Action.

He ran to the courthouse, where he paid a little boy a couple pennies to distract Judge Calder's clerk. Tommy slipped into the chambers, closing the door with a soft click that made the judge look up from his desk. He yelled for his clerk, but Tommy knew the man couldn't hear him.

Tommy whipped the list of sins out of his shirt. "This should be enough for you to bring Yale back here. She's innocent, loved, and wanted, and what you've done in taking her is beyond any trouble between us."

The judge leaned back in his chair and put his hands behind his head.

"Let me see that list," the judge said. Tommy handed it over, and Calder laughed as he read each item. "Gambling, adultery, abuse . . . That's it?" He shook his head and tossed the paper on his desk. Tommy snatched it up.

"*You're* involved in all those crimes," Calder smirked. "You think I don't have reams of notes on you? You think there's one person in this town who'd verify your accusations against me?

You'd appear as crazy as Bayard and Hank, the purity pushers, Madame Smalley, every shrill housewife we put away. You'll be tossed in jail in seconds."

"Mrs. Hillis," Tommy said. "She'd believe me, I know it. She knows people are up to no good."

Judge Calder leaned forward, clasping his hands on his desk. "She's in Louisiana. Sick sister or aunt or something. Amazing how things worked out as though *God Himself* or maybe that Dreama, some*thing* or some*one* intervened to create the perfect situation for all this to transpire. It's out of my hands, this business with Yale."

"I'll tell the papers."

Judge Calder leaned forward onto this desk, a flash of fear coming over him for once. "That sin list of yours? It's not nearly complete as far as what the Arthur family is up to, Tommy. You think you're the only poorly behaved Arthur? You burn that goddamn list or you'll find the rest of your family tossed in the clink with you. Then Yale'll be lost forever."

Tommy swallowed hard. What was the man talking about? The scandal? That was hardly news. He couldn't chance that the judge was telling the truth, that Calder could make it appear as if Mama and Katherine were involved in something illicit. He nearly said Katherine was sick, that the judge should stay away from them, but he didn't want to offer any information that might be used against them.

"Out of my chambers. And if you ever come back, I'll take it as a request for a jail stay."

Tommy had nothing else to threaten with or use as a weapon. He thought of the prayer in his pocket with the cross. The surrender it took to write it nearly made him want to curse his idiocy. Nothing he had to offer was worth anything to the judge, or anyone who had control of his life at that moment, including God himself.

**

Tommy fled into the hall and ran right into Aleksey Zurchenko.

"You all right?" Aleksey stopped Tommy from passing by him.

Tommy grimaced, embarrassed on top of everything else. Aleksey put his hand out to him. He took it. The sight of Aleksey relieved Tommy, buoyed him in much the same way that he'd been after writing the prayer.

He grabbed Aleksey's arm. "Yale's been taken to Glenwood. Katherine's sick."

Aleksey's face flashed with fear. "What's wrong with Katherine?"

Tommy wished he knew exactly. "Not really sure, but one doctor said maybe pneumonia."

Aleksey suggested he could get a doctor to the house, but Tommy told him there was already a second doctor on the way.

"She need anything at all?"

"A magic wand. You have that?"

Aleksey gave a little smile along with his concerned expression. "You look awful."

Tommy thought of all he'd been doing wrong, how it must have been seeping into his skin, putrefying him from the inside. "Mine's my own making," he said.

Aleksey explained that he was working with his boss, Mr. Stevens, and anyone else he could find to help Yale. "Saw her name on a list for Glenwood, and I nearly fell over."

Tommy straightened. Aleksey was helping? Tommy was embarrassed at his failings, but most of all he was reassured. In the same way Aleksey's father had lent strength and reassurance all those years ago, Tommy felt that from Aleksey now.

"My boss thinks there's a way to move things along for Yale at Glenwood."

Tommy had never been so glad to know a person studying the law. "I just took my eyes off Yale for one second. She was sitting on a tree limb, and she fell in a blink, and her arm . . . I just can't . . ."

Aleksey grabbed Tommy's shoulder. "Take care of yourself so you don't get sick. I'll be to your house just as soon as I can get some answers."

"I can't thank you enough," Tommy said.

Aleksey tilted his head in confusion. He scratched the back of his neck. "If you were standing there, why'd they take Yale away?"

Tommy could have handed over his list of terrible deeds, explained that the judge hated him, that he deserved derision to some degree. But the conversation he'd just had with Calder led Tommy to believe the taking of Yale had a bigger motivation than he was aware of.

He shook his head and finally gave a big shrug. "I don't know. I've surely made my own messes from time to time, but this . . . I've no idea."

It may have been Pearl standing closest to Yale when she fell, but it was Tommy's fault, that he knew deep in his bones.

**

Tommy started for home. He stopped under a streetlight and took out his prayer. Snowflakes dotted his list. *A miracle.* Aleksey Zurchenko having the resources to look into Yale's situation was about as close to a miracle as Tommy could imagine. The prayer had worked. The prayer had put Aleksey right in Tommy's path when he needed him.

But action. That was part of prayer, as Tommy saw it. Why was he relying on the judge or even Aleksey to get Yale back? She was his sister. Her predicament was his fault. He should solve the problem. As he passed a boardinghouse, he noticed two horses hitched out front. What was he waiting for? He looked into the sky, pincushion stars glimmering down on him, even with snowflakes popping into existence, the stars shone between clouds, evidence a person's worst darkness contained light of some sort. Pearl, Aleksey, people like them. They were light in the face of darkness.

God, please, help me. Make me useful for once.

No sweet words, just a simple request whispered into the wind. One of the horses whinnied, nosing him, encouraging him to pet her.

He almost hopped on it and rode it away, justifying the "borrowing" as being okay in this one situation, this emergency. But as he grabbed the reins, the horse whinnied again.

Please, God.

He would do this right. Tommy entered the boardinghouse and explained the situation to the owner without revealing anything damaging to the players involved. He sounded as though he himself should be admitted into Glenwood. As the owner listened, his face changed from interest to surprise to anger, but then he shook his head. Of course the businessman wouldn't just lend out a horse to a penniless man, even with the story Tommy had told. The man pointed to the door, making Tommy's eyes fill with the sorrow that pulsed in his chest.

Tommy backed away as the owner's wife stepped into the room from a darkened hall. She pushed her husband's hand down and told Tommy to take the black horse, the friendly one. "Clover's her name. Great in snow. The brown one's horrible once it freezes."

"Just a little snow. It's not bad right now."

The woman looked past Tommy who then turned to see snow cascading like water.

He doffed his hat and promised to repay them for the inconvenience, for the borrowing, for whatever they wanted as he backed out the door.

Outside, Clover whinnied again, and Tommy slipped the reins from the post and took off in the direction of Glenwood. He was going to get his sister.

Chapter 49

Snow fell hard and fast, making Tommy squint into swirling winds. When he reached Glenwood, he tied up Clover and stormed the door, throwing his shoulder against it, bursting in. "Yale!" he screamed, out of control as his voice echoed in the marble foyer. The fineness of the space startled him, and he told himself to tamp it down, to remember that he was in an asylum and shouldn't act similar to many of the patients.

As he started toward a doorway to his left, the sound of a shotgun cocking stopped him, drawing his attention to the backside of the foyer. Standing behind a desk, a man leveled his gun at Tommy.

"Stop there, fella."

Tommy knew instantly he wasn't the first person to arrive wanting to break someone out, or possibly the gun was more often used to keep people in. He put his hands up and inched forward. "I'm unarmed, and I don't want to hurt anyone."

The man lowered the gun for a second, then raised it right back.

"Please." Tommy stepped forward. "My sister's here. She shouldn't be. She broke her arm, she's four, turning five, and she's slow, but she doesn't belong here."

"Same old story," the man said. "You know how many people come here looking for loved ones? Looking for kids they pretend are loved ones? Then sell 'em off to work farms? You know how many people come by here every blessed day?"

Tommy inched forward, every step allowing him to see more of the man hidden by a shadow cast from the landing above the desk. He was younger than Tommy had thought, and he realized he recognized him from somewhere.

They sized each other up.

"I know you," Tommy said.

The boy leaned further into the light, peering. "And I know you."

It took Tommy a moment, running the boy's face through his mind. Jail? Church? Somewhere with Hank and Bayard? He started to shake his head, but then a flash of recognition struck.

"Rupert's," they both said at the same time.

Leon. The boy Tommy had given his shirt to.

Leon lowered the gun. "How's Pearl?" His whole demeanor softened, and he looked more like the thin boy Tommy remembered.

Tommy couldn't stop the smile from coming. "Pearl's fine, fine. You should visit her at the post office."

He nodded. "Work here, live here now. And I only get a whack when I don't do my job. Got my own cot. Three meals a day." He looked down at himself.

"You filled out, for sure. Barely recognized you."

"Steady food'll do that. But I can't shirk my work. Not for nothing." Leon's eyes sparkled with tears as though pained. "Not even for you."

"You must know that some of these people *don't* belong here."

Leon's breath stuttered. "I do. Started as an inmate myself."

Tommy eyed Leon's rifle. "I won't hurt you or anyone. I promise. Least of all my sister Yale. She needs me. I need to get her home."

Leon shook his head. "Can't let her leave. But you can see her. I owe you as much as I can do, and that's it for now. They won't let it pass if she went missing. There's no excuse except the death of a patient for someone leaving without permission from the docs or courts."

He led Tommy to the back rooms and stopped in front of a slim door, opening it. The light from Leon's lantern illuminated Yale's sleeping body. Tommy rushed to her side and knelt.

He pressed the back of his hand against her head. Cool. Her breathing was normal, but she barely stirred. "Yale." He brushed her cheek with the back of his fingers.

"They give her sleepin' juice."

Tommy lifted her splinted arm, her bell bracelet gone.

"Heard 'em say clean break, splint's good. She'll be fine, they said. Maybe a crooked arm's all. But they drug 'em all to keep 'em quiet until they decide what to do with 'em."

Tommy shook his head. He stood, lifting Yale's featherweight body. He turned toward the door.

Leon set the gun on him again. "Put her down."

Tommy shook his head.

"Haven't shot anyone in a week. Finger's itchy."

Tommy looked at him caressing the trigger, remembering Rupert's gun had a broken trigger. This one looked intact. "After what . . ." Tommy knew giving someone a shirt was hardly payment for his life if that's really what would happen.

"People like me disappear. No one notices," Leon scoffed. "So easy when no one cares, when ya ain't got family or anyone to come charging through the door in the night to rush ya back home. Like ya did for Pearl, like yer doin' now."

Tommy understood, having felt like that when he was shoved in the cellar at the Hendersons'. No one would ever have known if he'd died there. Still, that didn't change what Yale needed. "I have to take her back. Her mama's sick about her. I'm sick about her."

Leon kept the gun steady. "Think about why I knew who ya came here fer."

Tommy froze.

"Five hundred patients, and I knew exactly who ya wanted."

Tommy understood. Leon had been warned someone was coming.

"Yer not the first person asking questions about yer sister."

Tommy exhaled at the protective way Leon sounded when he described Yale. "All the more reason to get her home to our mama."

He nodded. "Put her down. She's safe fer now."

Tommy swallowed. "You're watching over her?"

"You watchin' over my Pearl?"

"'Course I am."

Tommy looked down at Yale's placid face, so quiet and peaceful compared to when she'd been carried away on the stretcher. Tommy feared she would be hurt like so many were in Glenwood.

Yet Leon . . . Something about him made Tommy trust him. He felt it deeply that the boy would continue to keep an eye out for Yale.

"Snow started again. Best git back or you'll get caught up, freeze to death. Then yer mama will be short another kid."

Tommy thought of Katherine being sick, that no one knew where he'd gone.

He set Yale back in bed and smoothed the blanket over her. He kissed her forehead and clasped his hands. "Please, God, take care of her." His simple prayer gave Tommy an idea.

He got up and followed Leon back to the entrance.

Leon dug through a drawer and pulled out a piece of paper. "This here paper's the one they keep askin' fer when the doctors arrive. Notes on yer sister, I think."

Tommy glanced at the report. "*It* was wild. *It* needs a diaper." He couldn't read anymore. "It?" Tommy's voice cracked. "They call her *it*?"

Leon nodded. "They still call me *it* half the time, even as they hand me a gun. But I see beyond that. I see *her*."

"Thank you." Tommy felt a surge of gratitude and trust.

"You have to git." Leon gestured to the window. "Snow's dumping heavy."

"Just a minute." Tommy pulled a sheet of paper toward him. "Can I use this?" He lifted the pen from the inkwell.

"Suppose." Leon's brow furrowed.

Tommy drew a deep breath and bent over the paper, letting what he felt was God or just some sort of universal understanding sweep through him. "You're safe in the arms of your creator. In your generosity for others, you'll find God returns his gaze tenfold. Courageous love for your fellow sisters and brothers is worth more than anything else you can own. You're brave and kept in the hearts of those you help."

He tapped the paper trying to call up the right scripture. The words wouldn't come, as he fought the urge to rush back to Yale and pull her out of that bed. He tore the paper in half and wrote a second piece. "Yale, child of strength and sorrow, your face lights up and shines on the world like sunrise in summer. We will be back for you. You are safe and loved."

Tommy folded the first paper and handed it to Leon.

Leon furrowed his brow as he stared at the paper, making Tommy suddenly realize Leon probably couldn't read. It made sense given his past and current circumstances. He grabbed Leon's hand. "It says thank you for your endless well of kindness for those who need it. This one's for Yale. Hide it away until someone you trust can read it to her. Please." Tommy thought of all the small things that happened since he'd tucked a prayer away earlier that day: Aleksey promised to help, the boardinghouse couple lent the horse, and now Leon.

Leon pushed the note away. "They catch me with those, they'll tie me up."

Tommy felt the weight of that statement. But he felt another flood of warmth, of trust in something he couldn't name. "I understand. Just remember what it says then, and if you think you shouldn't keep it, burn it. God . . . something bigger than us will protect you. I know it sounds ridiculous, but . . ." Tommy wanted to say over and over how grateful he was that it was Leon at the desk when he'd arrived.

Leon started to say something but stopped.

"What?"

He exhaled deeply. "Don't really believe in God. Not with my life. But right now, seeing ya again like this, I can't help thinking someone... I don't know how, but something pulled us together twice."

Tommy melted inside. He felt the same. "You being here is a miracle."

Leon took the papers. "You're Pearl's miracle. I wanted to be, but ya were. Ya are."

"You're a good soul, Leon," Tommy said. Besides Pearl, Leon was the first person he'd met in a long time who he thought of as good, not looking for a way to take advantage of anyone else. Looking back, Tommy had thought the same thing at Rupert's when they met, but he'd been so angry at how life was going he hadn't held the recognition of good with him beyond those moments. Now he saw. Now he held these little things tight.

"Same to you," Leon said.

"Keep her safe," Tommy said, and he left, planning to gather everything the Arthurs owned so he could get Yale and leave, all of them together, even Leon, if they had to take him, too.

Chapter 50

Tommy rode as fast as the horse could go. He patted and encouraged Clover to move quickly, every contraction and release of her muscles as she pushed through the weather told Tommy she understood. He reached the boardinghouse just as the sun was rising. He watered Clover and wrapped his arms around her neck. He limped toward the entry to the boardinghouse. The snow had slowed his progress, freezing his feet as the stirrups brushed over cold piles of rising snow.

The boardinghouse wife sent a young boy to tend to Clover and helped Tommy into the house, insisting he stay to eat. They listened to his story, enraptured with every detail. Again, Tommy obscured information that would hurt his family or threaten their freedom if his hosts decided to reveal any of it to the authorities.

When he finished the steak and eggs, the wife insisted he get out of his clothes so she could dry his stockings and shoes by the fire. She gave over the bed at the back of the house where the husband sometimes slept when they needed security with rowdy guests.

Tommy protested, wondering if he would owe them more than he already did, if they might have created a ruse of kindness to trick him out of his . . . his what? His ratty clothing? He jammed his hands in his pockets and pulled out the Indian Head, rubbing it, then looked at the mother-of-pearl cross. They were the only items of value he had, and that was hardly something worth stealing.

The wife covered him with a down blanket, wrapping him tight to keep the warm air in. "Just for a minute. Then I have to go."

He woke as the winter sun was setting on a gray day. Was it setting or rising? Disoriented, he pieced together the events of the last day and panicked, knowing his family had no idea where he'd been. He had no idea how Katherine was, and the fear that she might have worsened settled in deep.

He stood as the wife entered holding his stockings and pants.

"Thought I heard you rustling."

The husband followed with a cup of coffee. "Drink this before you set out. Looks like some good paths have been cut through the snow. You should get home without much trouble."

Tommy looked at them, overwhelmed with gratitude. "Thank you for all of this. I don't know how to thank you. All this kindness. I'll repay you. I will."

The husband shook his head. "Not required."

The wife handed him the stockings.

Tommy's eyes stung at the thought of them just giving, not requiring, not demanding, not asking for a thing. "Like you're angels in the flesh, earth angels or something."

"Wouldn't that be something, Tommy? Angels in the flesh," the husband said, setting the mug of coffee on the table near the fireplace. "Drink that up. I've got chores."

Tommy dressed and drank a few sips of the coffee before setting out on his way. Back by the front desk, he stopped to say good-bye to his benefactors. A couple entered the foyer and went upstairs, heads bowed in private conversation.

Tommy rang the bell on the counter, but no one came. He couldn't imagine leaving without thanking them again. But when minutes stretched on and there was no sign of them, he simply said thank you into the air.

He reached into his pocket. He had to have something to give them. He pulled out the mother-of-pearl cross and his lucky penny. If he left the penny, they wouldn't understand that it was lucky, and they'd spend it and the luck would be gone, spinning out into the world, with no one to recognize its worth. He pushed that back into his pocket.

He set the cross on the guestbook, knowing they'd see it, knowing it was from someone who appreciated them more than words could say.

Chapter 51

Tommy made it home, running, walking, slipping and sliding in the ruts from the wagons. But he made decent time considering the conditions. The kitchen door was locked, so Tommy went to the front of the house. A warm glow in the window made him stop before entering.

He peeked inside. Katherine reclined on a makeshift bed near the fireplace. Mama knelt on one side of her. Pearl hovered on the other side dipping cloths in water, laying one on Katherine's forehead, and dragging the others up and down her arms and legs. Tommy gripped the window casing, enthralled by Pearl's gentle doting. There was a golden glow in the room, the fire blazing bright, radiating around Pearl. For a moment, Tommy thought he may have stepped into one of Katherine's paintings.

He put his head against the pane.

Please, God, heal Katherine and give me any discomfort and sickness you want to give. But please make her better. He thought of Mama having been moved to prayers the day before. *Please let Katherine live.* Mama reached out toward Pearl, talking to her, then brushing Katherine's hair back, her lips moving in what Tommy assumed were more prayers. *I'll be a better person if you just bring both my sisters back to health and back home. I don't deserve it, but they do. Mama does.*

He tried to open the front door, but it was locked, too. He searched for the hidden key, but it was gone. He knocked gently, and Aleksey opened it.

Mama came into the hall and pulled Tommy close, her voice coming with shallow breaths. "Where've you been? You all right?"

He took off his hat. "I'll tell you all about it, but first—what's Katherine doing down here?"

Mama explained that the second doctor who came to see Katherine was useless, suggesting she sleep with frigid, snowy air blasting in on her, that there was nothing left for them to do to save her, that her lungs had filled past the point of them ever draining. The doctor had grown angry when Mama questioned that thinking, and he'd opened the window with such force that it broke right off its track and shattered.

"When he was gone, Aleksey and I moved Katherine down here. Aleksey has been just . . . I don't know what I'd do if not for him."

"I think she turned a corner," Aleksey said.

Tommy felt his whole body exhale in relief at the sight of Katherine peacefully sleeping. "She's better? Really?"

Aleksey and Mama hugged, and Aleksey kept asking about the *other girls* who'd been there with Pearl to help Katherine. But Mama had no idea what he meant.

Pearl came into the hall and smiled at Tommy, keeping her distance before springing at him, wrapping him in a hug. Tommy knew he should have resisted holding her longer than would be friendly in front of Mama, but he couldn't push Pearl away. In her arms was exactly where he needed to be. Just like that.

Aleksey turned to Pearl and asked again about the girls, concerned and confused.

Pearl didn't know what he was talking about either.

Aleksey mumbled that it must have been some of the girls from Miss Violet's who came to help and offered to retrieve fresh cloths from the kitchen.

Tommy and Pearl sat beside Katherine. Pearl gazed at him and brushed hair from his face. "She was asking fer ya."

Tommy slipped his arm around her waist and pulled her close. "Thank you, Pearl."

"For what?"

The way she looked when he saw her through the window, the picture of love and affection. "For being here. For caring."

Tommy started to tell Mama about his ride to Glenwood, but she'd already laid her head on Katherine's chest, falling into a deep sleep.

Chapter 52

The next day Tommy woke from a fitful night's rest, having followed Katherine's breath from shallow and choppy at times to deep and quiet at others. Tommy yawned and added logs to the fire, running his hand down Pearl's arm as she slept, curled into a ball beside the fireplace. Mama stretched and slid out from under the blanket she'd been sharing with Katherine.

Tommy and Mama checked Katherine's breathing. Satisfied her chest was improved and clearing they went to the kitchen, leaving the front room door open to hear if Katherine or Pearl called out.

Tommy lit the stove and adjusted the flue as Mama filled the kettle with the last of the water in the pitcher and put it on the stovetop.

"What happened to you? You disappeared, and if we hadn't been so occupied caring for Katherine—the doctor was convinced she wasn't going to make it—I might've thought you'd been snatched up like Yale. Aleksey and Pearl have been wonderful. Aleksey said he saw you at the courthouse and then . . . nothing."

"That's where it started. I went to the courthouse to try to get to the bottom of why Yale had been taken and get her back. Went right to Judge Calder."

Mama gave an almost imperceptible nod and turned to her kettle, sliding it to the middle of the stovetop.

Tommy shuffled old newspapers on the table, making room for them to sit. "Nothing I said convinced him to give me information or release Yale. Not one bit of help from that . . ." He shook his head. "I left and ran into Aleksey. Told him about Katherine, and he told me he was working on getting Yale released with his boss. I felt really good about that, but then I thought about how this whole mess is my fault. I shouldn't have left Yale in the tree when I talked to Reverend Shaw. I should've just told him to wait and gotten her down. Pearl was too short to reach Yale easily and keep her steady. So as good as I felt knowing Aleksey was putting that education of his to use for Yale, I wanted to *do* something. So I borrowed a horse and rode her right to Glenwood."

Mama's eyes went wide. "You went to Glenwood? In all this snow?"

He nodded. "Rode right up to the door."

Mama inched closer, and Tommy pulled a chair out for her. He readied the coffee grounds as he told her the whole story, about the couple at the boardinghouse, about Leon, about Yale.

Mama listened, fear, worry, and relief shifting over her face as he explained that he trusted Leon to keep her safe until they could get there.

"Some boy?" Her face hardened as she balled her fists. "Just some boy?"

"He's some boy, yes. I met him before, and I helped him and he helped Pearl while she lived at . . . I know it's crazy, but I trust him. Deep inside, without knowing him well at all, I trust him like, well, like I trust Pearl. And I know that doesn't make sense to trust anyone but ourselves given all we've experienced in the last few years, but—"

"Like I trust Mr. Hayes," she said so quietly Tommy nearly missed the words.

He thought of how difficult life had been for Mama, how difficult Tommy had made it for her. He squeezed his eyes shut. He choked on the sense of cruelness—his actions. He hadn't grasped the extent that she trusted Mr. Hayes that she might need to be gifted that opportunity from someone like him. He opened his eyes to see her wiping tears away. In that moment he fully understood her inexplicable trust of Mr. Hayes, even if he didn't feel it about the man himself. "Yes. Like that."

She met his gaze. "If you think so, then I trust you to say so."

He thought of the prayers, the string of good luck he'd had. "I do." He pressed his chest. "Something changed." Like he thought he'd feel the day his father walked back into their lives, sure of things again. Confident.

Mama pushed back from the table, putting her hands to her hair, smoothing it. "I need to meet with Judge Calder."

Tommy poured coffee for both of them. "I'll take you. Have coffee first."

"No. I need to clean up and speak to him alone. Aleksey needs to meet with his boss. Said he'll take me."

Tommy recalled the judge's words last time he saw him, the threat that he could harm the Arthurs in a multitude of ways, that it wouldn't be hard to do.

"No." Tommy stood. "I don't want you talking to him. He's mad at all of us. Still angry over the investments. I don't trust him as far as I can—"

Mama tensed and pressed her hand against him. "There's a lot you don't remember or never knew; you were too young before we went to the prairie." She straightened. "I can handle Jeremy Calder like no one else. And I need you here with Katherine. Pearl needs more sleep. So please. Just stay with Katherine."

Tommy's instinct to insist she stay away from the judge flared. "No. You don't know how awful that man is."

"I know enough. I won't argue this. You stay here."

Tommy didn't like it. "Aleksey'll be there?"

She nodded, then pulled clean cloths from under the dry sink. "Pearl's been incredible. Katherine responds to her, her voice, her presence. You should have seen it last night. It was as though a shroud of peace just lay upon us once Pearl started with the cloths and the eucalyptus water." Mama looked upward. "I can't explain it other than to say it's a miracle. I sound like one of those Sunday service hanky-wringers, but . . . it's true, even if I can't explain the weight of it, what happened once Pearl came."

Tommy refilled the kettle and set it on the stovetop. "I know exactly what you mean. Like with the boardinghouse and the horse and Aleksey and Leon, all these people in just the right place at the right time . . . We both sound . . . unhinged."

Mama drew a stuttered breath, as if she were holding back more tears.

"I don't want you to see the judge alone, Mama. He's lying about things and . . . I think he wants Yale in Glenwood, that it wasn't just a clerical error or some act of kindness by people who think they're doing something nice for her and the other kids who got lassoed up with her and dropped at Glenwood."

Her eyes widened.

"I wanted to break her out last night. But Leon was frightened for his life, and I believed, I felt the fear . . ."

She covered her mouth, nodding.

"If I'd taken Yale with me I would've made things worse. And Judge Calder is not to be messed with."

"But you think she's all right, really?"

"I held her. She didn't wake, but she was peaceful," Tommy said, leaving out the part that she'd been given a drug in case that would increase Mama's worry. "Her arm was wrapped tight."

Mama's face regained some color at hearing that. "Thank you, Tommy. That is more reassuring than I can tell you. But Judge Calder is going to see me today. And Aleksey will do what he can, too."

Chapter 53

Tommy explained again where he'd been the night before as he and Pearl mixed more of the cure from Katherine's book. They drew eucalyptus-soaked cloths over Katherine's arms and packed her chest with a poultice that made their eyes water. When Katherine was snug but not too hot, Tommy stoked the fire and sat beside Pearl.

"That was amazing, last night," Pearl said, hands folded on her lap.

Tommy nodded. "Mama said Katherine turned quick after you made the cures, that she felt it like a shift in the air once you came and applied them. Your future may lie in healing people, not shuffling mail or even school. Mama said Katherine was near death?"

"Oh." Pearl drew back. "I didn't heal her."

"You know what I mean," Tommy said. "Katherine won't be surprised to hear her own recipes did the trick. But Mama said Katherine responded to you, your presence, your gentleness. Mama's so grateful you were here."

Pearl clasped her hand over Tommy's. "Wasn't any of that." She hesitated and looked away before latching on to his gaze. "It was the angels. I brung 'em with me. 'Least I think I did. Didn't see 'em, but I *feel* like I did. Sounds like your ma felt it, too."

Tommy put his arm around Pearl and pulled her close. "That's a nice thought. I prayed so hard. Mama, too. I can't remember the last time I saw her praying."

Pearl looked up, eyes narrowed.

"What?" Tommy asked.

"There are things that have power that are unseen. I know you understand or you wouldn't have kept writing those prayerful notes and dropping them at people's houses when they didn't ask fer 'em, didn't pay fer 'em. You wouldn't have prayed so hard if you didn't believe in unseen goodness."

Tommy thought for a moment. "You mean God. I don't think . . ."

She raised her eyebrows, lips pursed.

"What?" Tommy said.

"Angels. It's all part of God, I suppose, but different."

"You think you actually brought angels with you? That you healed my sister just by . . . bringing *angels*? As though you asked a friend to come with you? I know you love fairy tales, but you really have been falling for all that Dreama stuff, haven't you?"

Pearl flung his arm off her shoulder and moved away, talking in a tight whisper. "Don't be so hostile 'bout *her*."

"Hostile? To who?"

"Dreama."

Tommy exhaled deeply.

"Don't patronize me."

"I didn't patronize you. I simply *exhaled*. How's that patronizing?" He wanted to tease her for the new word she used, but sensed she was too exhausted to find humor in it.

"It's the way you breathed."

Tommy shrugged. He was tired and not in the mood to be picked at by anyone, not even Pearl.

"I don't know," she said, her words clear, concise, clipped even, making him pay close attention. "Don't know if I can be with you if you are going to *mock* me with your breathing."

"That's ridiculous." A flicker of a smile came to him, and he knew he was helping to make her point.

"Is it?"

"Is what?"

Pearl glanced at Katherine and put her finger to her lips to signal him to be quiet. She whispered, "You make fun of me having angels."

"Where's this coming from?" He gestured to Katherine. "She's getting better, Pearl. The cures you made from her book worked. What's the matter?"

"I didn't believe it either. Before, I mean."

"Before what?"

She crossed her arms and pushed her chin out. "A while back Katherine told me I have angels. Then last night, I was so desperate for her that I prayed real hard and asked my angels to come with me to heal Katherine. I prayed and begged right over the bowls and pots while I made the healing water and poultice."

Tommy thought of what Katherine had told him about the painting she made of him hunting. He also thought of the beautiful scene the night before when he arrived to see Pearl beside Katherine through the window, the glow from the fire surrounding her, his mother leaning in, both of them caring for Katherine. Still, angels were a different matter. The fact that Pearl had told Katherine about the deer came back.

"I can have my own ideas about God and all of that. Your sister makes sense to me."

Tommy felt as though Pearl was discounting what he might think.

"You ain't the only expert in matters of God and angels and mysteries of the universe and such."

That stung from the inside out. He tried to hide his flinching at her words. He took it personally with all his prayer success and then failure. Maybe Pearl and his sister had even decided Dreama was a better choice, too, like all the people who sat with her rather than buy Tommy's prayers. He hadn't realized just how protective he'd become of what he thought of as his skill—prayer writing. The painting of him with the deer was evidence of how close Pearl and Katherine had become, making him feel like an outsider.

"You two are quite the pair, aren't you?"

"What's that mean?"

"Well, I didn't want to say anything before because I didn't want to believe it, but hearing this, I can see I was not in the know about you two. You told Katherine about the deer. You pinkie promised to never tell a soul about me blubbering about shooting the deer, not being able to dress it, and my own sister paints a painting of me and the deer. Don't get me wrong. It's a beaut. She got every detail. *You're* even in it. Just a teeny, blurred figure in the corner, but you're there, too, a little bit of flame-red hair painted in. How else could she know all that if you didn't tell her?"

Pearl looked down. He could see her eyes sparkling as tears wet her lashes. "I'd *never* break that promise. Not to you. Not ever."

"How can I believe that?"

"Because it's me saying I wouldn't."

"So the information just crystalized in Katherine's brain and she painted it?"

Pearl met his gaze. "That's 'bout how she describes it."

Katherine had told him something similar about her experience with her paintings. "That's stupid, Pearl."

"Stupid as your prayers? You take them plenty serious."

Tommy glared. "That's completely different."

"Why? Because you scribble 'em down on paper, full of Bible words? 'Cause some minister says they work? That makes 'em better? Dreama's busy healing lives without writing anything, without that Bible to help her, or any big, bossy men."

Tommy threw his hands up. "What's that got to do with it? Suddenly you're throwing all my failures at me? Dreama stole my business, yes, but if you think I'm careless with people, with my prayers, then you should know that Dreama's a million times worse. At least I give people something when they pay. Not like that fraud they've got over there."

"She's not a fraud."

"Because you saw her talk to three people after three hundred paid at *The Night for Mothers*? My God, I'd be a rich man if I ran that scam. How stupid of me to be caring and intentional with my prayers for those in need, for being polite when a phony . . . No, not a phony, a true-blue con artist stole my business?"

Pearl pulled him out of the room, into the hall so they could still see Katherine.

"She'll hear you, and you'll stop her from healing if you keep putting out all this disbelief."

"Olivia's not even here. How could she hear?"

Pearl pointed toward Katherine. "I mean Katherine."

"What would she care? She's finally in a deep sleep, and luckily Miss Violet's kept her far out of the fraud they're running next door. Have you read what they're writing about Dreama lately? The mobs, angry ministers . . . If anything it'll help Katherine heal to know she's *not* involved with Dreama."

Pearl locked on his eyes and drew a deep breath.

Tommy stared at her, nausea sweeping through him for some reason.

She shook her head then fixed her gaze on him again. "She *is* Dreama."

Tommy narrowed his eyes. He rubbed his belly, the swirl of bitter acid threatening. "Olivia."

Pearl shook her head slowly. "No, Tommy. Katherine is."

Chapter 54

Tommy would never have guessed those two would turn on him. Pearl and Katherine—one he'd shared a womb with, and the other, his loft. When Tommy refused to argue anymore, Pearl stormed back to the shed. Tommy sat by Katherine, wondering if this could actually be possible. Was he the only fool who didn't know? Mama? How could Katherine not have confided in him? Dreama, the person who cut into his business, was his sister.

Aleksey entered the room and sat beside Tommy, taking Katherine's hand. Tommy watched their old friend lovingly tuck Katherine's quilt around her, brush her hair back from her eyes. He loved her. Like Pearl had said before, it was as though the time they were apart, the years, made no difference in the depth of knowing they shared. Whatever love bloomed when they returned to Des Moines, Tommy understood that it had been seeded years before. But what if Aleksey ran from Katherine when he found out about Dreama? Tommy sighed and dragged a cloth through a dish of the healing water. What if Aleksey already knew? It seemed Tommy was the only one who didn't.

Tommy whispered, "I don't know how to ask you this. I mean, I can see how you care for Katherine, all that's happened over the years. But I'm worried about her. And I trust you to keep this tight if I say it."

Aleksey's brow furrowed.

"And I beg you not to let what I have to say color how you feel for Katherine. Please."

Aleksey nodded slowly, his face questioning. "Sure."

Tommy pointed to his chest. "I don't believe this. I don't think so anyway. I mean, I *can't* believe it, but if she's in danger, then I need to do something. The newspapers are on fire with stories about Dreama. I know this is confusing, but bear with me. Let me start with everything I know about this woman, Dreama."

Aleksey squeezed Tommy's shoulder. "You know?"

Tommy stared at Aleksey—were they talking about the same thing? "*You* know?"

"Found out by accident."

"About—"

"Katherine and Dreama. Yes."

Pearl waltzed into the room. "Can't sleep anymore."

She said hello to Aleksey and butted him and Tommy out of the way. "Katherine." She cocked her head and studied Katherine's face as though she were divining information from it. "Doctor sent word to start waking her during the day to get her nights and days back in order."

She pressed Katherine's forehead and cheeks with the back of her hand. "Tommy, bring the fresh cloths and warm some water."

Tommy had been pleased with Pearl's investment in Katherine at first, but now he was irritated by her bossiness.

She looked over her shoulder at Tommy and Aleksey. "Once overheard a doctor who was picking up his mail discuss the importance of keeping sick folks clean. Her hands are nearly black. Look at her nails."

Tommy wasn't so sure Pearl heard right, but he fetched what she demanded anyway. "And bring me some tea. Please."

He'd never minded when she ordered him around either. Until she betrayed him. The secrets she and Katherine exchanged set him outside the relationship he'd had with each. He brought the water and cloths to Pearl. She went to work on Katherine's hands, washing, patting them dry, massaging them with lanolin. She added the lanolin to Katherine's lips and brushed her hair. Pearl never spent anywhere near this much care on her own self, but she preened and groomed Katherine as though the very act of freshening his sister's skin would completely clear the last of the mucus from her pneumonic lungs.

When Pearl had brushed several sections of Katherine's hair one hundred and thirteen times each, Tommy wondered if Pearl cared about Katherine more than anyone in the world. And for that moment, for Katherine, that was good. Betrayal or not, he was grateful.

**

Over the next few days, Tommy helped nurse Katherine to relative alertness, her strength building enough that she could sit on the settee for short periods. Mama and Aleksey both returned from the courthouse daily, reporting no solid progress for getting Yale out, but determined to find a path. Tommy watched over Katherine when Mama or Aleksey couldn't. He spooned bland chicken broth, water, and an endless stream of jokes, talking to her as though she was a full participant in their conversations, even when keeping her eyes open was the extent of her talking.

Finally Katherine advanced to sitting upright for hours at a time between naps. Pearl prepared poultices and herbal waters to encourage continued healing. Pearl and Tommy had done a fine job of ignoring each other, tolerating each other for the sake of Katherine, but neither engaging in their usual banter or discussion of words, work and dreams for the future.

Tommy resisted confiding Katherine's secret to Mama, not wanting to make things harder for her, not wanting her to feel betrayed by Katherine's secret either. Yet, as he read the papers and saw the escalating adoration and hate for Dreama, he could only feel relieved that Katherine was getting better slowly and well out of the public eye. For that he was grateful.

Chapter 55

Tommy was there for Katherine over the time it took her lungs to clear enough that she could be up and around for portions of the day. Seeing her sick, nearly dying, he'd been shocked by the fear it put into his heart, that he couldn't simply ignore his worry about her like when they were boarded out. Perhaps it was that he was older.

Mama nursed Katherine, too, losing every extra pound of weight she carried on her already slender build. She received a letter from Mr. Hayes saying he'd been held up at a conference in Ames. Tommy saw this saddened her, but he didn't say anything. He merely put his arm around her and kissed her cheek, hoping it eased her sense of longing.

His sorrow at seeing Mama disappointed surprised him. He hadn't considered that Mr. Hayes's absence would evoke anything but satisfaction in him. In the quiet moments he had to launder Katherine's linens and the cloths they used in the healing water, he considered Mama's divorced status. It must be part of why Mr. Hayes hadn't been around much. As soon as he was done with his doctoral work and Mama was no longer part of his study, he would probably be completely done with her.

Tommy kept after Mama to rest and eat, and he helped her sew the coats that Mrs. Calder had ordered before Katherine had gotten sick and Yale had been taken. "You can sew?" Mama asked.

Tommy sighed. "I can. I've learned a lot the past few years." He thought of his experience sewing condoms but didn't reveal that.

When Mama became exhausted to the point she fell asleep at the stove, setting her sleeve on fire, Tommy took over.

Still, every day, after a rest, Mama would head to the courthouse to make contact with various judges, to find a way to have her voice heard on the matter of Yale. She had yet to be granted time before the court in a formal way.

When Mama would go into town, Miss Violet and some of the girls next door would visit Katherine, always bringing their sad attempts at baked treats to try to show her they were fine without her, that she should focus on getting better, not on what wasn't going well next door.

Between his hours at work and appearances in court, Aleksey watched over them all.

One day after all the other visitors and helpers slipped back out of the house, Tommy sat beside Katherine and took her hands in his. Her coloring was pink, and her eyes were lit with the beautiful light that made her appearance move well past attractive to beautiful. Katherine knew Tommy knew she was Dreama and this barrier removed from their relationship made their conversations more personal.

She squeezed his hands three times.

"Why do you always do that?"

"What?"

"Squeeze three times."

"It means 'I love you.' Doesn't Mama do that to you?"

"Do what?"

"Squeeze three times—a silent 'I love you'."

Tommy drew back and shrugged, hurt. "No. She doesn't."

Katherine squeezed again. "Well, now you're in the know."

He lifted his chin and broke her gaze. He stopped himself from feeling hurt about this. He shook his head. "Truthfully, looking back, Mama could've told me about that and I was so clueless I just forgot."

Katherine nodded and scooted back, sitting straighter in the chair. "Thank you, Tommy."

"For what?"

"Bringing me Pearl."

Tommy let out a little laugh. "I think she just busted in. I'm not sure I brought her anywhere."

Katherine pulled her knees into her body, latching her arms around her legs. "You know what I mean. Pearl brought her angels that one night. *She's* a living angel. An earth angel. And she didn't betray you. You have to believe that."

Tommy believed it at that point, knowing that whatever Katherine was able to sense about the universe, it was a different type of knowing than most experienced. But this idea that Pearl had angels? That she could summon them?

An earth angel. That part he understood. The phrase made him think of the night the couple at the boardinghouse gave him the horse, when Leon was at Glenwood, when . . . so many instances.

Katherine spread her fingers in front of her, wiggling them. "Pearl's special. Like no one else I've met. With the warm light that follows her."

Tommy nodded. He'd seen it the night Katherine started to get better, through the window.

"Angels exist and she's got a slew of them. And she believes in me. And Aleksey, finally he does. He's keeping Mama sane with news from the courthouse. I haven't told her yet about any of this, but I think she saw the angels, too, that night with Pearl. And she told me about when you went to try to get Yale. Heavenly angels, earth angels."

The guilt was searing every time he thought of Yale being imprisoned.

Katherine nodded. "They can't do this to Yale. Mama will get her back."

The statement hung in the air between them. "There was a time that would've been true." Both knew full well Mama might not be capable of getting them back together now.

"That's what's so confusing," Katherine said. "I see changes in her since we all split up. She's softer, sometimes even fragile. She believes in whatever miracle put all those good people in your path, she checks clouds, thinking James is talking to her through the weather. But yet, when I told her once that he's with her, she didn't understand. Like she didn't *want* to understand. Times like that, she's distant, spiky, brittle. Like she'll break from giving or accepting any love at all."

"James is with her?" Part of him still fought against Katherine's ability, yet he wanted it to be true now. He wanted to have this same faith in . . . What? He wasn't sure. His breath felt like it had been socked out of his body. "Is James with me?"

Katherine smiled.

"I mean, *ever* with me? I don't suspect he'd be with me *all* the time, but . . ."

"He is." Katherine pulled Tommy's arms, bringing him in for a hug.

Tommy exhaled, pleased, but not sure if she was just trying to make him feel better. It was the sort of thing he thought an intuitive person could do—read the living human being in front of her, not really see spirits.

"James adored you, Tommy. I know he admired your spirit, your impulsiveness, even your faith at the time. Remember when you believed everything about God and you loved the Quaker services on the prairie? And for a moment I thought you even believed me about the boy at the tree during the fire. But James loved your spirit, thought someday you'd be a minister."

"The same things Mama hates about me."

His eyes burned, and he hoped the tears would recede before they dropped down his cheeks. He coughed into his hand and wiped them away before Katherine saw.

"I'm not sure I'm a good fit in the family anymore. So much changed and, well, I just don't know what to think. I never want to be boarded out again, out of control like that, but I'm not sure we all fit together anymore. Not like before."

"I feel the same," Katherine said.

"Mama loves everything about you, Katherine. There's nothing you could do to disappoint her. Not even this Dreama thing."

"I don't know about that. I want to surprise her with the money I'm earning. She's practical, like you. The money will soften her toward the idea, and I know I can convince her that this gift, though unexplainable, is as true as her having given birth to us. I want her proud of me, not to tolerate me. I want to see her face light up at the sight of me. And you. Pearl told me about your prayer writing and how powerful it was."

"Until—"

She put her hand up. "I know, I know. I didn't mean for Dreama to take your work away. I know you understand scripture, and I'm sure you did so much for people."

"Well, it wasn't the scripture that did it. It was the listening." He thought of Mrs. Schultz and what she taught him about himself. "Then I could make the prayers my own, tailor them to what each person needed."

"Like me. I listen, and the calming comes, and I just share it with whomever needs it."

Tommy nodded.

"You *could* be a minister, Tommy. If that's what you wanted."

"I used to want that."

"When we were little."

He scoffed. "Not with what I've learned about ministers since then—Reverend Shaw's a scoundrel."

She sighed. "And the pastors I met when I stayed with the Christoffs. Pure evil."

He shrugged. "So, no, then. Seems as though eventually any good a minister does drowns in bad. Greed and power gets them every time."

She shook her head. "I don't believe that. People make poor decisions, but they can change."

"Ministers are different. They should be better than us. I'm not better than anyone."

"I disagree."

Tommy's heart filled. "Right now I just want you healthy and to get Yale back."

"And get Mr. Hayes back," Katherine said. "Where is that man? I could barely blink without him walking through the door before, and now with all this going on, he's not here."

Tommy inhaled sharply as he leaned over to retie his shoe. "Some conference and then he had to stay longer? Mama mentioned it but I can't remember."

"What's wrong, Tommy?"

"Just things to do."

"Well, move along, then. We both have work to do."

And so Tommy went to the shed to let Fern out and check on Frank. He pulled out his writing paper. He wrote a prayer for Katherine, knowing she didn't need his prayers since she had all those angels and . . . well . . . whatever else she had, but he was compelled to write one anyway, something to capture his hope that she'd be safe, that he believed someone even stronger than Aleksey was keeping watch over her. God. That was the only one he could imagine who could embody her angels, her calming, her love, Aleksey, all of it together as one pure force for good. He slipped the prayer into his pocket, knowing he'd have time to give it to her later, if the time was right.

Chapter 56

Tommy set off to Mr. Hayes's place with good intentions. First, he wanted to know what the man planned to do in regard to Mama. Even if it turned out he was done spending time with her, it would be helpful if an upstanding professor put in a good word for her current standing in the community, how she was much more than a divorcee with few resources. Mr. Hayes was certainly witness to her being an exemplary mother to a daughter who was slow.

Tommy didn't allow himself to go too deep into thoughts of Mr. Hayes's affection for Mama because the result was an immediate pounding in his chest from pain that appeared like spring buds on oak trees—bursting out everywhere. But Tommy admitted he'd been rotten to Mr. Hayes.

His father had disappointed Mama. He'd disappointed them all. They'd all lied to each other. Were any of them trustworthy? But Mr. Hayes. All he'd been was nice.

Despite Tommy's shortcomings, he gave himself leeway for bad deeds, only stealing when necessary, only being cruel when lashing out from his own pain. Perhaps he ought to lend others the same luxury of their lives splintering and struggling to piece them back together?

Perhaps Mr. Hayes was simply a kind soul, delivered to Mama in her most needy moments, like the couple and the horse, like Leon, like Pearl. The man merely worked the garden and went to meetings with Mama. Meetings that should have resulted in Des Moines being a better place for all who lived there.

Tommy had no resources to draw from to help protect his family except for intangible ones, like a connection to Mr. Hayes or Mrs. Hillis. He'd scribbled a letter to Mrs. Hillis in the post office and sent a letter to her family in Louisiana where she was staying.

Tommy's mind went to Pearl. He still felt protective of her despite her not really needing him for much other than shelter and the retelling of stories using proper English.

He stomped onto the Drake University campus, hoping that Mr. Hayes had returned from the conference finally. Tommy wove his way to the Hillshire building where the information desk and main offices were housed.

"Mr. Hayes," Tommy said to the receptionist. "I believe he keeps a room here on campus somewhere."

The woman pulled one corner of her mouth up as she stared at Tommy. "Your business with him?"

Please be here. For Mama.

"I'm a student."

"Well, surely you would know he is now *Dr.* Hayes."

"Oh yes, of course. I misspoke." Tommy tried to soften the knifelike words. No one had told him Mr. Hayes had finished and defended his dissertation. He wasn't even sure if Mama knew. "So he's back from the conference."

She adjusted her glasses, studying Tommy, not answering. "Little young to be a student, aren't you?"

Tommy straightened his shoulders and removed his hat. "Old enough."

"Well, you'll need an escort. Only faculty's permitted in that residence hall alone."

Tommy was relieved Mr. Hayes was back. He twirled his hand at her, knowing he was being rude. He drew a deep breath, put on his best pitiful puss and leaned into her. Everyone liked to be on the good end of a secret, to help someone they clearly looked up to. "Look. I'm here on church business. I deliver prayers, and I have a handful for the good professor. I didn't mean to be rude, but I was told it's dire. And being church business, it's confidential. Reverend Shaw was explicit."

She leaned in, her hand at her neck. Tommy could smell the cinnamon tea that sat between them. "Oh no. Well, of course, you were protecting him. You're a good soul."

Tommy nodded, straightening, putting his hat back on, unsure whether she was stating a fact or asking a question.

She called a student from a back office to escort Tommy and inside of ten minutes he was standing at Dr. Hayes's door, pounding on it.

The door opened.

"Dr. Hayes, I hear congratulations are in order. You're officially a doctor, now."

Dr. Hayes registered surprise and stepped back from the door. "Come in. Yes. Defended my dissertation a few days back."

Tommy entered and removed his hat. A single bed was pushed against the wall, a desk at the end of it, and from top to bottom were bookshelves even surrounding the windows. Tommy stepped over a stack to get further inside.

"Is Katherine still growing stronger? I haven't been by much lately due to my defense and that conference. I dropped a gift for your mother and some broth for Katherine in between my defense presentations. You were out . . . working, probably? How's everyone?"

Tommy hadn't heard about this visit or a gift. He fought the habit of being smart with his response. Dr. Hayes had only been kind to Tommy and his family. He needed to at least attempt to be polite if he was going to ask for a favor. "Katherine's getting better every day. Mama is . . . Well, with Yale gone, it's hard to celebrate Katherine's recovery completely."

"I imagine."

"Looks like you're packing." Tommy glanced at the duffel bag on the bed, unsure that the man cared about Mama and the family that much after all.

"My sister's ill and can't care for her children, so I'm headed out again. Not sure how long I'll be gone, but when I get back, I'll do whatever your mother needs. In fact, I just delivered the coats she made for Elizabeth Calder to her home."

"So you're really leaving." Tommy was conflicted about this news. Was he finally getting what he wanted? He wondered if Mama could take another someone leaving.

Dr. Hayes closed the door and pushed his hands into his pockets. "I know it's hard for you, that you've been through a lot."

"Yeah."

Dr. Hayes pulled out his watch and shoved it back in his pocket. "I want to say this to you, though I hesitate because I'm not at the top of your advisor list."

Tommy felt ashamed that he'd made that so clear to the man.

"But being a man isn't fulfilling some big dream or forcing the world to bend in your desired direction. It's all the little things a man does each day to make his life work, to make it good. Small kindnesses, realizing what he *does* have even when he's lost everything. A man can be strong, but not hard-hearted."

Mrs. Schultz's words came back to Tommy again.

His eyes began to burn with tears. He wanted to run from what he was hearing. Dr. Hayes' words were powerful. Tommy told himself to bend so that he wouldn't break, that he didn't have to case his heart in plaster. He looked away from Dr. Hayes.

"You *are* kind, Tommy."

This made Tommy turn his attention back.

"I see how you are with Pearl and Yale, Katherine, that bird, of all things, Pearl's pets. Your prayers. Several women mentioned to your mother at a meeting how helpful they were to them."

Tommy smiled at that, the compliment filling him. He turned and wiped a tear away, pretending to scratch under his eye.

"And I know you love your mother deeply. You've made mistakes, but I see your love for her, and I know you want to take care of her. But it's like you don't see yourself, your goodness, that you're *already* a good man. You're just trying hard to take some path around what is good about you to do some job—some big thing. You help others and continuously hurt yourself. Just be who you are inside . . . put all of that where people can see it." Dr. Hayes shrugged.

Tommy couldn't breathe. He nodded, his throat so tight he couldn't speak.

Dr. Hayes sighed and pulled the watch out of his pocket again. "I can't miss this train. Bess is counting on me. Her children are too young to be alone."

Tommy wanted to thank Dr. Hayes for what he'd just said, for believing such things about him after how awful Tommy had treated him. His mind flew through every rancid interaction.

Dr. Hayes shuffled across the floor and pulled a piece of paper from a box and dipped his pen in ink. "What is it you came for? How can I help?"

Tommy cleared his throat and found his voice. "I wanted to ask you if you could put in a good word for Mama. With every stinking person in town who might care. You have standing that we don't. I'm sure she's explained all that."

Dr. Hayes kept scratching away on the paper. He waved his hand over it to dry it.

"Already did that, Tommy. Spoke to three judges, the newspapers, and sent word to Mrs. Hillis in Louisiana. Not sure any of it can get the job done, though."

"Thank you for that." Frustration that this man had no further favors to cash in on or muscle to make something actually happen weighed heavy. But Dr. Hayes had tried. He'd already done everything Tommy came to ask.

"Could you do me a favor, Tommy?"

"Yes." He was surprised at how easy the response came to him.

"I know it's hard—"

"My father's coming back."

"How soon?"

Tommy looked at the ceiling. What was he doing? *Grow up.* "He's not. I don't know why I said that. I wish, but . . ."

Dr. Hayes exhaled, his eyes conveying sincerity, and for once Tommy didn't feel mocked or small in Dr. Hayes's presence. "I can see you understand the world is full of shadows and shades of gray and only the occasional day is spent in full light and sunshine."

Tommy felt choked by this man's gentleness. No matter how rude Tommy was, how short or biting his tone, Dr. Hayes treated Tommy with a gentlemanliness that Tommy could only hope to entertain someday. For as hard as it had been watching a man step into Mama's life, Tommy had to admit he himself hadn't been there to do what she needed. Somehow Dr. Hayes saw past all the selfish, childish behavior and knew Tommy was good beyond all that.

"Thank you, Dr. Hayes."

Dr. Hayes looked startled.

"For everything you just said. And I'm sorry for ... everything."

He held his hand out. "You're welcome."

Tommy shook his hand as a knock came at the door.

The receptionist stood there. "Your carriage is ready. Says he's got two others with him to drop off, so time to pull foot."

Dr. Hayes scratched his chin, the stubble sounding like sandpaper. "Can we summon a later carriage? I'd like to stop by the courthouse on my way out."

She shook her head. "No, sir. If you miss this, you're not making the train, and there's not another soon enough to get you to your nieces and nephews in time."

Dr. Hayes grabbed his suitcase. He and Tommy considered each other, Tommy unsure of what to say next.

"Dr. Hayes," the receptionist said, stepping into the hall. "The carriage."

The three started down the hall. "Please take this note to your mama, Tommy. I'll write as soon as I have everyone at my sister's managed."

Tommy took the note and put it into his coat pocket.

They continued down the hall to the stairwell. "Tell your mother she inspired me to make my own prognosticator." Dr. Hayes droned on and on about how sailors used these storm glasses to predict the weather and that he'd given one to her earlier as a gift, thinking she would love it, seeing how she had such an interest in the weather because of James. When they exited into the lobby, Dr. Hayes stopped. "Your mother is . . . She is like no one I've ever met. And I hold her dear and thereby hold you all dear. I—"

"Dr. Hayes, please. The driver's about to pull away."

Dr. Hayes gripped Tommy's shoulder. "The note. It's important, Tommy. I'm counting on you." And with that, Tommy felt party both to the final demise of his parents' marriage and also the bridge to Mama's survival.

**

Tommy passed the saloon, running so not to be pulled in and hassled about his debt. He wasn't sure how he'd pay it off for good, but he could chip away at it with steady amounts if he just concentrated on that. At the shed he lurched through the door. Pearl sat at the table. The fire blazed, lighting her shape as she read something.

"He's home. Tommy's home," Frank squawked.

Pearl looked up. "Well, hello, Tommy Arthur. You're home! '*Home! How sweet the word is. What a dear little home we will have some day, then there will be no more longing and no more pain for our home, will be an Eden with the love that will fill it*.'"

Tommy didn't know why she was reading aloud to him, sounding like she was doing a performance. He stroked Frank's beautiful black feathers.

"I found that quote in a very sweet letter from a woman to her future husband."

He was happy to see Pearl and went to her, swallowing her in his arms. She stiffened, reminding him that they hadn't been talking since they'd argued. She finally relaxed into his embrace. "Tommy?" She pulled away, a confused look on her face. That was when he saw the letters she must have been referencing, scattered on the table, all addressed from his mother to his father, the ones she used to read that year on the prairie at night, the ones that seemed to hearten her.

"You're reading my *mama's* letters?" Tommy shook his head. "Where'd you get those?"

"In that trunk the Zurchenkos brought when they came."

Seeing the letters twisted Tommy's insides. He was letting go of his father, of the idea his family would ever be reunited, but he didn't expect to see the innards of how his parents' relationship began scattered all over the shed. Pearl's gaze flitted to the table. He didn't want to be mean to her. He controlled his voice as he said, "Shouldn't be reading folks' mail. You know it's against the law."

She crossed her arms and tapped her foot.

"Like I said prior, once the mail's delivered and opened, it's not illegal." She opened her hands as though pleading. "Reading your ma's letters, the beautiful, love-filled letters. It's hopeful to see. Makes me think love is possible. It's everywhere."

Tommy was exhausted from nursing Katherine back to health, the heavy guilt about Yale, the final demise of his parents' marriage. And looking at Pearl trying her best to be better, to be what she thought society wanted, he was suddenly sure he could never be the prince she wanted him to be. He felt it deep as the hurt that started back in 1887.

The idea he might disappoint Pearl was too much. Now was the time to make it clear he was not her future. "You'll find a good man to marry you, a farmer who won't expect you to be fancy. He'll want you in the way you want him, too—simple and plain. People are as people are. Why waste your time with this trying to be different?"

Pearl stood and crossed her arms. "Maybe I don't need a man at all. Maybe I just want to be a lady for myself. Yer ma ain't— *doesn't* have a husband, and she's doing fine. Look-it Miss Violet. Works in finance, for goodness' sake. Look-it what she's done with yer sister as Dreama. People come from all over the nation for the chance to sit with her. *Your sister.* And Miss Violet got everyone to know about her. I'm thinkin', er, *thinking* I'll have enough money to go to school this fall. Maybe I'll be lucky enough for Miss Violet to take me under her wing like she does those other ladies. Just today I spoke to her about it. And she told me to keep cleaning up my language. And she even taught me to walk with a book for my posture."

Tommy shrugged. He didn't want Pearl anywhere near Miss Violet's school, but he thought arguing with her might push her in that direction to prove her point.

Pearl reached for his hand. He stepped toward her, attracted, his body moving without him even giving it permission.

"I just want to be good enough."

Tommy snatched his hand back. He didn't ask for whom she wanted to be good enough, and she didn't say it. Perhaps she knew it as well as he. He would never be the man she thought he was.

"Stop saying that. You are who you are. That's just . . . It's *good*. You're just fine. You don't have to keep doing this, Pearl. I'm too tired. Get the idea that my mama is perfect out of your head and you can free yourself from this idea you should be like her."

Pearl's mouth slammed shut. Tommy thought he could see her mind winding around what he just said. He knew what was coming next—*you don't think I'm good enough* and all that nonsense girls said. He steeled himself for a fight.

"Well, Tommy Arthur. You may not recognize what a wonderful woman yer ma is, but it's just not right you talkin', er, *talking* like this. She is a queen. And if you don't see it, you don't deserve her. And the same goes fer me."

Pearl's view of things was narrow. There was so much he'd never told her. It wasn't her fault that she saw Mama the way she did. "Nothing in those letters from Mama to my father tells you the truth, so don't suppose you know it or her. She pushed my father out of our family. She made it so hard for him to live with us that he had no choice but to leave. He was brokenhearted over James, and he couldn't do . . . Well, she was cruel to him."

Tommy chewed on the anger that still sat inside him about the breakup. He'd moved past this, but Pearl brought it all back with the letters and her misunderstandings. "My father came back to us after James died, all buckled over in tears. Can you imagine a man bawling like a baby? Mama humiliated him and divorced him, causing us to scatter hither and yon. She tore us apart. And I—why would you force me to say all of that aloud? I don't want to think about that anymore. I'm—"

Pearl stomped her foot. "Well *she's* here. Your pa ain't!" Her voice rose, her upset taking away her ability to monitor her proper language choices.

"I know that, Pearl." He said her name with a growl, with it caught between his teeth.

She swept her arm up. "I don't care what tales of adventure and woe he pens in them letters of black pearls and Tahiti. If he cared, he'd be here. Like she is. You need to see the truth. You aren't being the person you can be. You owe a hundred apologies for your behavior."

Anger gripped him, exhaustion spreading into the anger. Why was she doing this now? "You don't know everything. I just went to Mr.—no, *Doctor* Hayes and told him I was sorry. Well, sort of. I thanked him for trying to help with Yale. And now you're beating me up. Isn't it enough that Yale's gone because of us? Can't it be enough that we have to get her back? Don't you understand that none of what you're talking about even matters?"

Pearl looked as if he'd punched her in the belly. Tommy could feel the impact, but he couldn't take it back.

Her eyes filled with tears even as she pushed her chin at him. "I knew you blamed me. I didn't mean to let her fall. You said you knew that."

Tommy swallowed. "I do know. I didn't mean it that way, not the way it sounded." He took her hand. "I'm sorry, Pearl, I didn't mean—"

She snatched her hand away. "You meant it. You have no idea what life is about, Tommy Arthur. You make me look like a college scholar, you dummy." She ran out of the shed, Fern following on her heels. She pushed through the boxwoods, but then paced back toward him, shaking her finger. "And you meant it, Tommy. You said *us*, but you meant *me*. And just so you know, I'm not some pet for you to keep."

"I know. Please let me... I didn't mean to . . . let me help you."
He felt as though he was more like his father, or the way his
mother saw his father, in that moment than he ever could have
imagined. And the sense of awful that came to him turned his
stomach. Had his father hurt his mother like he'd just hurt Pearl?

Pearl clenched her jaw and crossed her arms. "Ya don't know
nothin' at all 'bout help. Rough as I am, I know deep inside I've
saved *you* way more than you ever saved me." She stomped away,
the rustling of the hedges filling his ears as she disappeared.

"Pearl!" She didn't answer or come back. Tommy jogged to
the hedges to follow her, but just as he spread the branches to go
through, a door slammed in the distance and he stopped. He
backed away from the hedges, assessing how he felt, his heart rate
slowing, calming. He nodded. Better to let her go. Much as it hurt
to see her leave, to hear that she didn't need him, if she stayed it
would be worse when she eventually went her own way, when
their relationship crumbled as relationships always did.

Back in the shed he climbed into the loft. He lay there and
tossed and turned. Before even realizing it, he would stretch his
hand by his side, hoping to feel Fern's fur against his skin, to catch
Pearl's hand the way he'd done since she'd taken up sleeping there,
their fingers laced.

He hadn't realized how accustomed he'd come to her.

An ache formed in his chest and then pulsed, traveling with
his blood. He thought he'd been better, not drinking, not stealing,
feeling the power of his prayers, that God existed. What was
happening? Why had he been so cruel to Pearl? Maybe he *should*
be a minister. He certainly seemed able to weave a web of malice
that the job required.

Chapter 57

Tommy woke extra early and completed his chores for Mama and Miss Violet before the winter sun hinted at its rising. He spent the rest of the morning selling prayers. He managed to get two housewives and a farmer to buy, but his sentiments lacked verve. His pay reflected it. Perhaps he'd been fooling himself thinking he had a special way with soothing words.

On the way home he stopped at the post office. He was shocked to discover that Pearl no longer worked there. She'd quit without mentioning it. And the next shock came with the news that there was a postcard from Leon. The card said: *All's well so far.* That was it. It wasn't much, but he gave the information to Mama, who was as relieved as he.

He returned to the shed, hoping to be able to apologize to Pearl, to swear he'd shape up and prove that he was worth her initial trust, her constant belief in him until he caused that to waver. But she wasn't there. He wasn't unburdened with her absence, he was unmoored. He went to Miss Violet's to see if Katherine might know where Pearl went and to give her the prayer he'd written for her. But when he entered, instead of Katherine he found Pearl.

She stood with a wooden spoon in one hand, her other balled on her hip. "Katherine's still having tired spells. I took over the kitchen. I'm fully employed with Miss Violet." She tapped a book on the table. "And yer name ain't listed there as allowed to enter."

"I do half the chores in the house, Pearl."

"Well, Miss Violet's sick as a dog. And you ain't listed as allowed access other than first light and last light of the day. So go on. I won't be fired for your stubbornness. Out."

He sighed and left.

He needed to prove himself, and part of that was paying his debts. Though it unnerved him, he did it. He went to Churchill's Saloon barely registering new posters in the window, ads for a "Sophisticated Soiree."

He offered the few coins he'd earned from prayers that day and convinced the barkeep to let him work off his debt. He even threw in a prayer for the man's dying mother to clinch the deal. Tommy spent the rest of the day tending bar, resisting the urge to sneak shots, ignoring the lure of using booze to ease the tangle of nerves that kept up a steady surge of pain at having lost Pearl on top of everything else.

He erased five of the ten hashmarks next to his name when he was done working at the saloon and shuffled home, grateful not to have gotten lured into playing faro or poker, thankful Hank and Bayard hadn't shown up, that the reverend hadn't caught word he'd freelanced selling prayers earlier that day.

The shed was empty. No Pearl. No Fern. No Frank. This was the last thing he thought of when he fell into a dark sleep, the silence, his own breath, little reassurance that the next day could be better at all.

He woke with the evening having fallen, dark and thick. The fire illuminated the space enough for him to light the lantern and decide he needed to find something to eat for dinner. Thinking of Pearl, of Frank the crow, of everything that pained him, part of him would have been fine never getting out of bed.

The only thing that kept him from worrying Miss Violet might encourage Pearl to put those lambskins to use was that she wouldn't put up with such an idea. She would leave if it came to that—wouldn't she? He told himself she would.

His head pounded with indefatigable anxiety. He looked to his left and saw a glass of water. Pearl must have put it there. He leaned over the edge of the loft. Fern laid by the fire with a full bowl of water. Frank had his own little dish on the mantel.

"Pearl," Tommy said aloud.

Frank took off from the mantel and landed on Tommy's shoulder, rubbing his feathered head against Tommy's cheek.

"Angel," Frank purred the word.

Tommy startled then stared at Frank. "She is." He stroked Frank's back, marveling at him.

Angel. Frank flew away, settling between Fern's paws, under her chin. Tommy's guilt at how he treated Pearl deepened. He was devastated that he'd been mean, that he formed such awful thoughts, harbored the deep resentment, that he allowed the words out of his mouth.

He chugged the glass of water and saw there was a note half tucked under her side of the mattress. His hands shook as he read.

> *Dearest Tommy,*
> *A few days past sinse we spoke. I wont speak to ya anymor. Ya muddeed my afecshun with yer unwarented anger.*

Tommy ran his hand through his hair.

> *Stop gamblin and stop swipin things wile sellin prayers if ya still ar. I dont wanna speek, but I don't wanna see ya in jail, beat to all hek. I took werk at the saloon in addishun to kitchen duties. If I see ya there, I'll tell em toss ya out on yer tale. For ya I'll do that.*
> *Yer welcum.*
> *Pearl*

The letter tore at him. He was angry with her but tickled at the sight of her pretty writing, even if her spelling was worse than ever. He was so confused. Part of him wanted to tell her what he felt for her. Part of him wanted to yell at her for being so high and mighty. Leaving him water like he was one of the animals. Telling him what to do in her gently, but directly written letter.

But the saloon? Had she been hired before he was given the chance to barkeep or after?

Tommy got dressed, fed the pets, then started toward Churchill's. A newspaper boy caught his attention, shouting about Dreama and mobs forming to get to the bottom of her dealings.

He cut across the street and told the boy to hold the paper up so he could look at the front page without buying it.

"My boss'll have my head if'n he catches me lettin' ya do this."

Tommy nodded. "I just need to see this one story."

The paper indicated that questions were accumulating around Miss Violet's business practices. Judge Calder and the reverend were quoted, giving their full voices to supporting her.

He cocked his head to get a better view of a second article. The boy shifted it away. Tommy gave him two pennies for the glimpse. Another article indicated a shift in Dreama's readings. A chill ran through Tommy. Katherine was still weak, too weak even to work in Miss Violet's kitchen. Surely she wouldn't try to hold readings as Dreama again. Katherine might have been intuitive—something clearly informed her ability to comfort others and connect in a way that was otherworldly—but five articles on page one of the *Register* indicated groups were swirling with anger, questions, demands that Dreama prove her ability, maybe even in front of the courts. One article intimated there were powerful forces at work with Dreama, but not the kindly, celestial type. Powerful men and wealthy women held answers to Miss Violet's success, and one reporter would not let go of that idea. He listed establishments that he deemed associated with the unnamed power brokers, and one of them was Churchill's Saloon.

Tommy checked the date on the paper again since he was so used to reading old papers.

"Hot off the presses," the newsboy said.

Tommy got a strange feeling in his gut about Pearl. He didn't like the idea of her working at the saloon at all, but seeing Colt Churchill's name listed in the paper made him wonder if it would soon be part of one of the judge's phony "clean up the town" campaigns. Phony or not, time in jail was as real as his beating heart.

He ran to the saloon and peered into the windows, dimly lit from the inside. He searched for a flash of red hair or a girl pumping her arms as she moved across the room to wipe down tables or something. Just a couple of blondes. He scooted to the next window. It gave a better view through widely parted drapes. He saw Judge Calder and drew back. Tommy forced himself to look again. Calder was often at Miss Violet's meetings, but something seemed different. Yes, it was a social gathering, not business. Judge Calder pulled one of the blondes into his lap and kissed her hard. She straddled him and ground into him, arching her back, hair washing back and forth.

Tommy was surprised he could still be stunned by that man. He shifted and peered through the curtains at another angle, straining to catch sight of Pearl.

A cellist, violinist, and pianist played, and more women dressed in gowns mingled with men. A new atmosphere for the saloon. There had been signs this event would be happening when he worked there the day before. It looked as though they had taken a gathering intended for the sophisticated group that normally met at Miss Violet's and moved it to the saloon.

The reverend stepped into view. He was looking all the ladies over. A flash of red caught his eye. Pearl. She held a tray of fluted glasses toward the reverend. Her face appeared nervous, as Tommy would have expected. She was new at serving. The reverend pushed the tray aside, and another woman took it from Pearl.

The world seemed to slow down as Tommy watched the reverend take Pearl around the waist with one arm and pull her into him. She jerked back, knocking the drink tray out of the woman's hands. Reverend Shaw hiked up Pearl's dress, his hand clawing up her leg.

Pearl struggled, turning her face away from him. Tommy burst into the saloon and stormed toward the reverend. The older man straightened, looking at Tommy, eyes wide. Judge Calder stepped in between them.

Pearl pulled and twisted against the reverend's grip.

"Leave, Arthur. This is a private event."

"I belong to this club," Tommy said.

"Well, your debt puts you on probation."

Tommy eyed the board. The hashmarks he'd erased the day before were back. "Let her go, Reverend."

The reverend leaned into Pearl, holding her tighter, his fingers caressing Pearl's leg, moving higher. Tommy jerked to the side to get around the judge who reacted quickly, blocking him.

Anger swelled, and Tommy balled his fist and swung at the judge, connecting with his jaw. The large man stumbled back, and Tommy leapt. The reverend's eyes went wide again and his grip on Pearl loosened as Tommy charged. He grabbed Pearl's hand and pushed the reverend onto his ass as they barreled past him.

They were out the door, running, their breath loud in the quiet evening. It didn't take long before the judge was close behind, exceptionally fast for his large size. Tommy and Pearl bolted past closed storefronts and swerved between wagons.

But as they were taking one corner close, hoping he'd run right by them, Pearl tripped. She flew face-first into the muddy street, knocking the wind out of herself.

She looked up at Tommy and formed the word "Go" without any air to carry it to his ears. Tommy shook his head. He reached for her as she reached for him, their hands clasped.

Tommy was grabbed from behind. He held tight to Pearl as he was wrenched and yanked. She rose to her knees, holding his hand tight. But the judge tugged Tommy hard, and he lost his grip on Pearl, his fingers slipping over hers, their fingertips the last thing to separate before the judge called to two policemen from across the street.

As the policemen pulled Tommy away, he saw Pearl on her knees, the fancy dress covered in filth as she stared after him, her outstretched hand reaching, her face pleading, as he was dragged around a corner and out of sight.

Chapter 58

From behind bars, Tommy could hear Mama begging the officer to let her see him. He wanted to tell her not to bother, to close off the part of her heart that held Tommy in it. It would be easier that way.

"Please, Officer," Mama said. "You know the women's club is raising money for parole officers. That would be a much nicer position for someone like you. I saw your name on the list of men being considered. I'll put in a good word for you if you let me see my son, let me talk to him."

The officer laughed.

"Let her see her son," Judge Calder's voice came. "She's having a rough time of it, this one."

The judge's words cut across Tommy's skin like tiny knives. What was Calder doing there?

"If you say so, Judge," the officer said.

"Thank you," Mama replied.

"We'll talk later, Jeanie," Judge Calder said. His familiarity with Mama chilled Tommy further. "So much to discuss, to do. Isn't there? But let me make this clear . . ."

Tommy fought the urge to scream that she shouldn't see Judge Calder, ever. Their voices dropped, murmuring and Tommy could no longer hear what the two were saying. Soon, Judge Calder's heavy gait sounded in the corridor, growing quieter as the man left.

"This way," the officer said.

Mama came into view. She grasped the bars, wavering at the sight of him.

"That bad?" The officers had worked him over at the judge's request once they reached the privacy of the jail cell at the back of the building.

She just stared.

The officer unlocked the cell and allowed Mama to enter the urine-scented room. She covered her mouth with a shaking hand. The officer lit a lantern, and the cell brightened enough that Tommy could see Mama's eyes filling. She took Tommy in her arms, every bit of him smarting even under her gentle touch.

"I'll get you out of here."

He didn't know how she'd manage to do that. Not after Tommy had humiliated the judge in front of the entire saloon.

She grabbed his hands. "This is exactly what Mrs. Hillis was talking about." She looked around. "Children don't belong with adults who are truly criminal. Even if . . . Why, Tommy? You know better, and you promised."

"I was trying to help Pearl. She was . . ."

Mama rubbed his back, holding him. His shoulders shuddered with sobs.

"The reverend was attacking her. I hit Judge Calder because he tried to stop me from getting her away. He's never going to let me out of here, and I'm worried they'll grab Pearl."

Mama leaned closer. "I can get you out. I can."

Tommy held his aching side. "It's not just that, Mama."

She pushed his hair out of his eyes.

He thought of the headline that claimed Dreama was performing that night. He was hoping Olivia was pretending to be Dreama. "Katherine's safe, right? She's at home? Aleksey's with her?"

Mama nodded. "Yes, yes. It's you I'm worried about right now. Judge Calder said you owe enormous debt at Churchill's."

Tommy did owe money there, but he also knew the judge could increase his arrears equal to the United States debt if he chose.

"Why'd you go there?"

"This time I went for Pearl. She was working there and . . . Before that, I worked there to erase my debt, but they just keep putting the amount I paid off, back up."

She smoothed his hair again and touched every inch of him that she could. "I'll fix this, Tommy."

"No. Don't. I can leave and then . . . stay away from Judge Calder."

Mama started to say something, but the officer latched on to her arm and pulled her away.

"I'm not done. This isn't right. You have no idea what happened. He's too young to keep here."

"Yeah, yeah, yeah, come on, lady. He's fifteen. That's a man where I come from."

Tommy lifted his head to see his mother being pulled away. He forced a smile and raised his hand to wave. "Mama, make sure Katherine doesn't work for Miss Violet anymore. Don't let her go back there."

"What do you mean?"

"Let's go, ma'am. Family time is over."

"Tommy?"

A second officer pulled Tommy up under the arms, making him screech with pain before he could say another word.

Mama was yanked out of sight. "Hang on, Tommy. I'll get you out of here," she called as she was escorted out of the jail.

**

In that holding cell, Tommy was alone. He knew when they took him downstairs he would be sausaged into a cell with older men, that these were his last few minutes of peace even if the space was cold. He was slouched against the wall below the window when he heard a sound above him. He looked up and saw nothing. Then he heard it again. A pinging, then a barrage of pings. He stood and looked out the window. Pearl stood below. She was dressed in her normal clothing again, tossing stones at the building. Fern sat at her feet, and Frank perched on her shoulder.

Tommy put his hand to the window. Pearl raised hers. Her mouth moved, and her voice rose upward, muffled. He tried the latch on the window. It worked, but there was a metal bar welded into place so that the bottom sash could only slide up about five inches. He pushed it up as far as it would go and stuck his hand through the space.

Frank lifted off of Pearl's shoulder and landed on Tommy's outstretched palm. He had a tiny rolled-up piece of paper in his beak. Tommy took it with his free hand and stroked Frank's soft black feathers.

"Frank!" Pearl yelled from below, and she took off running. Frank flew off, following her. Tommy started to yell good-bye to her when he saw Judge Calder pacing her direction. Tommy ducked out of sight when Judge Calder looked up. He sat against the cold plaster and could only hope that Pearl got away, that she'd be waiting for him if he ever got out alive. He realized he was still holding the rolled-up paper. He opened his palm and stared at it. He spread his thumb and forefinger, opening the roll. There in the palm of his hand was Pearl's pretty writing.

Love forgives all,
Love, love, love,
Pearl

Tommy released the paper and let it roll back up in his palm. He put his head against the wall and closed his eyes. He thought perhaps Pearl was the first person in the world who ever really loved him without hesitation, only with a small pause that he deserved entirely. So grateful for her, he hoped he'd have a chance to love her right, too. He loved her. In that moment he knew without a doubt, he'd loved her since she first pledged to keep a secret and wrapped her pinkie around his, tying her heart to his for life.

Chapter 59

Tommy sat curled into one corner of his cell. He pulled the memory of Frank the crow and Pearl through his mind, back and forth. He replayed her smiling face, the way she loved him so fiercely he could feel it two stories up.

As he was moved into another holding cell with several men, Tommy was searched. He handed over his unsold prayers, the note from Dr. Hayes he'd forgotten about, the Indian Head penny, and the note from Pearl.

"For you." Tommy handed him one of the spare prayers.

The officer smirked.

"A prayer. Go on. Read it."

The officer read it silently, and for a moment Tommy thought he might get on that man's good side.

The officer smiled. "Not worth the paper it's written on."

Tommy's mind flashed to the penny, and he nearly begged for it back. The officer looked over his shoulder to see the second officer had his back to them. He slipped the penny into his pocket. "This though . . ."

Tommy thought about what that penny had meant to him for so long, the promises and luck it was to have delivered, his father's useless promises. "Keep it."

The officer swept the papers into his palm and balled them up. Tommy reached for them. "Let me have those. Please."

The officer smirked and shrugged. "Bunch of scrap paper with stupid prayers? Sure. Keep 'em."

And with that, even as Tommy was being stowed in the next cell with three strange men, he felt safer having those prayers and notes in his pocket than the penny had ever made him feel. The Indian Head? Its going missing no longer meant a thing to him.

**

While Tommy waited, thoughts of Pearl were his succor against what the other men in his holding cell were doing— urinating in one corner and fighting in another. He pulled the feel of Frank's silken wing over him like a cover, blocking out the violent sounds.

He would be moved one more time before they locked him in the belly of the building. As evening stretched on, Tommy found himself talking to the men in the cell with him. Two never looked his way, but a third was chatty, explaining how his hard times led him to his fourth jail stint in four weeks. Tommy understood how things could careen like that and said so.

"Hey," Benny said. "What was that you gave the officer?"

"The penny?"

"No. The paper. You said it was a prayer."

Tommy nodded.

"Think I could have that?"

Tommy pulled the wad of papers from his pocket and dug through for just the right one.

The man couldn't read, so Tommy read it for him.

With a big sigh, the man reached for the paper and ran his finger over it. "Sure wish I could believe this."

Tommy reached to take it back.

"Can I keep it?"

Tommy almost said it was for sale, but he knew how silly that was.

"Don't have no coin. Can't read it, but . . . maybe I could keep it?"

"You can pay for it."

And even as the man was repeating that he had no money, Tommy was working through the payment plan.

Chapter 60

The moment would present itself. Tommy knew. These policemen were creatures of habit, though not necessarily disciplined. And when they took him out the final time, Tommy would make his escape, because if he didn't, he didn't believe he'd live through the next few days.

His weakness, him curled into the corner, appearing as vulnerable as possible, would be what might work to save him. His cowering and whimpering would ensure they didn't believe he had it in him to run. His back was covered in his cellmate's spray, the disgusting filthy way these men marked their dominance. As the cold air met his wet back, he shivered. He pushed his head against the plaster, trying to reduce the throbbing as his brain pulsed against his skull. He was back where he'd started almost two years before. In jail, promising himself he'd never go back. This time he knew he could keep the promise.

"Arthur, Harmon, Ridley. Shopshire—you're staying till you get sprung."

Tommy eyed Benny Shopshire, and he winked back. It was happening just as they'd thought it would. Benny had an attorney who owed him for throwing a boxing match so he could collect a significant amount of money on his loss. He wouldn't have to go into the cellar cells. He would simply wait for this lawyer to arrive with cash.

Though the plan seemed solid, Tommy's heart raced. If he didn't get away during this transition, he'd be tucked into the cellar. The time in the cell made it clear that, although he wanted to protect his mother, Pearl, Katherine, Yale, his father, he needed to escape and then leave Des Moines. The idea broke his heart, but he saw no other way. They'd all worked so hard to make it back to each other, worked so hard for the little cottage, but staying in Des Moines would not be the answer any longer. Hearing the whispered conversation that hid information between Mama and Judge Calder made him sure. Living in town with the judge would not be an option. He'd be stowed away in a workhouse or Glenwood, drugged, unable to act other than to allow himself to be abused.

If he stayed and fought the judge . . . Tommy chortled. Fought the judge? All the judges? Were any of them *not* crooked? No. In order to save himself, Mama, all of them, he'd have to leave town.

An officer called two prisoners. Tommy straightened and turned knowing Ben and he would be left with the second officer. A light forced his eyes closed again, and those two men shuffled toward the door.

Tommy's mind began to clear, and he readied himself.

A second officer came and he and the first tied the two prisoners' hands behind them. As they were finishing the knots on the second man, Tommy's breath turned shallow. This was it. He scanned the hall beyond the officers to see if any other policemen were around. He wasn't sure he could do it. But this was it. He had to get his family out of Des Moines.

He tossed himself onto the floor and began to fake a convulsion. At first one officer circled him, staring, a surprised look on his face. Tommy rolled his eyes back as far as he could and jerked with stiff arms and legs.

"You deal with that shit. I'll get these two downstairs." The second officer took Harmon and Ridley down the hall. Tommy, still shaking, focused just enough to see the officer disappear into the stairwell with the two men, and Tommy was left with the first officer. He raised his hand toward Benny, as planned, and on cue Benny managed to make himself vomit.

"Sweet mother of God, what's wrong with you heathens tonight?" the officer groaned.

Tommy jerked and flopped. The officer yelled for someone, but no one came, and somehow Benny kept the vomit spewing. Soon the officer was tending to him with his back to Tommy.

Tommy leapt to his feet and rushed down the hall to the front door. The officer in the reception area was gone, and Tommy made the cleanest escape he ever could have imagined.

Chapter 61

When Tommy exited the jail, torrential rains batted at him. He felt alive again despite his predicament, despite the storm. Although he'd become convinced jail was the front parlor of hell, he couldn't figure the chill that it held, thinking it should be hotter, like the rest of the underworld must be. He knew he smelled like a toilet and wanted to change clothes, get Pearl, Mama, Katherine, and Yale and head west. Or maybe east. Just away from Des Moines. He no longer saw the path for his family, for himself, as ending in Des Moines. He needed to leave town, and as much as it was to run from their troubles, it was also to move toward something. The life he wanted, deserved, and could give his family.

The officers he'd tricked were dumb and lazy, but Judge Calder would not suffer Tommy's insolence. He'd make Tommy pay for creating idiots out of his police force.

Tommy knew Pearl would help him. But he had to move quickly.

He ran the entire way home, passing a crowd that was marching down the street. Despite the drenching rains, they were spirited, chanting, "Clean up Des Moines" and "Dreama is the Devil." Clusters of men and women passed him, and he caught clips of their conversations between wind gusts and rain plucking his cheeks. They confirmed what Tommy'd read in the paper earlier. Dreama was performing, and they were going to put an end to the mystery of her and the sin of her stealing from grieving people. "Dreama's performing tonight. Let's get her!"

A tree blew in the wind, bending nearly over before its roots let go and the entire thing crashed to its side, sending the vigilantes scrambling, screaming. Maybe that would put an end to their plans.

Tommy knew Katherine had been so ill that she hadn't performed as Dreama in some time. He also knew her absence had stoked significant interest. Tommy knew Aleksey had promised he would keep Katherine safe and barely left her side. Katherine couldn't be performing that night. She wouldn't have chanced it even if she was capable of connecting with the dead. It was more likely that Olivia was dressing as Dreama and running a con that night. He hadn't realized he'd begun to think of what Katherine did as Dreama as real and Olivia's part, when she performed it, as running a ruse.

He felt dirty and ashamed, but inside him there was a flinty, optimistic sensation, a notion that he could make things right in his life. He just needed to get his family out, as fast as he could, as far as they could go.

When he reached home, Miss Violet's place was lit like Christmas, yet the emptiness it exuded was dark, sorrowful. He thought of the articles he'd read about the mobs, the people he'd just passed, and the fact that Judge Calder had held a party at the saloon. Clearly Dreama hadn't performed at Miss Violet's that night. His heart surged at the thought of seeing Mama again and convincing her that he would make up for his poor deeds. He hurdled the wooden fence and crashed through the boxwood, nearly falling as his feet met the loose gravel path. He ran toward the shed, praying that Pearl was there so they could arrange their leaving.

Firelight glowed through the shed window. He looked inside before entering. Pearl sat at the table beside the fire in the rocking chair. He rushed inside, startling her and causing the distinct sound of an angry bird to raise goose pimples on his arms. Frank dove for him, then pulled up as he announced himself.

"It's me! I'm out." He stood dripping, shivering from the cold, wet weather.

Pearl's hands curled around the arms of the chair, a slate in her lap, mouth gaping. Frank landed on Tommy's shoulder and nuzzled his cheek with his head. Tommy ran his finger down the back of the bird, and it cooed back at him, sounding more like a cat.

Tommy looked at Pearl. "You look like you've seen a ghost! Whatcha got there?"

Pearl's body seemed as though it had turned to marble, still as a corpse. Tommy went to her and knelt down by her feet. He wanted to touch her, oh he wanted to hold her. But she appeared so frightened he didn't move.

"Pearl? What's wrong?"

His hand hovered over hers, afraid to touch her, afraid of the feelings inside him. "I know I stink, and I'm soaked, I know." Tommy shook his shoulder to signal Frank to lift off. He ripped off his rancid shirt, leaving him kneeling there half-naked.

Pearl dropped her chin to her chest, and her shoulders bounced.

"You crying?" Tommy felt pain rip through him as though he could share the exact hurt that caused tears to drop from her eyes onto her paper.

"You're writing those letters to heaven again, to your ma? Your tears are blurring all that fine lettering."

She'd said she loved him in her note, hadn't she? Maybe he'd misunderstood and she'd been talking about Mama or Katherine loving him, not her.

She nodded but wouldn't make eye contact. It reminded him of the day he saw her at McCrady's, the day he gave her money to try and rent a room at the women's boardinghouse. Suddenly he wanted her to look at him; he needed her to see him. He took her chin between his finger and thumb, not wanting to scare her. He leaned in and whispered, "Please, I know I'm a fright, that I don't deserve you. But please look at me."

Pearl let him lift her chin, and when her eyes met his, he could not stop himself from wrapping her up. He held on to her, and she grabbed him right back, as though the embrace was the only thing keeping each alive.

"I didn't think you were coming back," Pearl said. "Your sister's gone. Your ma's out of sorts, full of upset that she won't explain. Half the town's already run through Miss Violet's place. I never felt such fear. After what you done to the judge . . . I thought for sure you wouldn't walk out of there. That's why I had to send the note with Frank. I had to make sure you knew I loved you if they . . ."

He felt sobs rising up in him, but he pushed them back down. "I got the note. I got it. And . . ." He squeezed her tighter. "I love you, Pearl."

"So bad it hurts," she said. "I'm nearly dead with the love I feel for you."

"I'm sorry for what I said. All of it, all the things I did wrong. And over and over. The day we fought. I don't know what's wrong with me."

"You saved me, Tommy. I won't ever forget that."

"No. You saved me. Every single day since we met."

She nodded.

He heard far-off yelling, but it was close enough to make him jump. "I have to leave."

Pearl's face fell.

"What? You won't go with me?"

She looked as though she was considering the idea. "Yes. I'll go with you. But you have to talk to your ma."

"Talk to her? We're taking her with us, and we're breaking Yale out, too."

Chapter 62

Tommy left the shed while Pearl stayed back to pack a few things in her bag. He saw through Miss Violet's windows that the mob must have circled back and were storming her house again. He snuck along the edges to Mama's house and entered.

"Mama! Pearl said Katherine's gone?"

Mama squeezed him so tight it pushed his air right out of him. "You're free." She covered her eyes with her hand. "He followed through with his promise."

"Whose promise? Who followed through on what? I escaped."

"They didn't *let* you out?"

"No, they were getting ready to haul me away, down to the cellar cells, when I saw an opening and ran. And we have to go. All of us. My debt and troubles are too big. Pearl's packing some things, and then we'll go."

Mama leaned back against the dry sink, looking confused. "Oh no, no. I paid your debt. I did. At the saloon with the cottage money. But you're free. They won't bother you. Your name's off that board . . ."

Tommy put his arm around her. "I'm so sorry, Mama. But we have to go. The judge'll never let this be. Where did Katherine go to? We can pick her up."

"Aleksey took her to his mama, to the farm. He'll keep her safe. Yale'll be released. I managed a few favors. I can breathe on that count. But you . . . you're right. You can't stay, Tommy. Judge Calder'll never let you be if you escaped."

Tommy pulled away from Mama and took her hands.

"We can't trust these people. We've got to get Yale ourselves."

Mama's mouth drew up at one corner. She looked away. "Not like that. I made arrangements for Yale."

"We'll get her on the way out of town."

"We can't just snatch her out of Glenwood. I need to get her through proper channels. And I've secured that process."

"You trust some process after all of this?"

She nodded. "You need to trust me. If I'd have known you could escape, it might be different, but I've already traded on some very old—"

The sound of policemen shouting, threatening to arrest people next door startled them. "You have to go," she said. "Meet Katherine at the Zurchenkos. I'll send word that you're coming, and once I get Yale, we'll join you and clear your name."

She ladled water into the kettle, her hand shaking.

Tommy felt his mother's body tense from across the room.

"I'm so sorry, Mama. This is all my fault. All this running and lying and Yale . . . I should have kept better watch over Katherine."

She stepped toward him and took his hands. "I know things are a mess, but if you're safe, knowing Katherine is, I can settle the rest of it."

"Come with me."

She shook her head, fear in her eyes. He held her the way she'd squeezed him earlier. "I love you, Mama. I love you, but you have to leave with us. It's not safe."

She sobbed into him, then gathered herself, pulling away, wiping tears and steadying her breath.

She pulled a gold money clip from a pocket hidden in her skirt. "This was my father's. I came across it at McCrady's and bought it back because I thought it might be good luck to have it, the prospect of filling it with scads of money someday. It's empty, but I know you'll fill it . . ."

Her voice trailed off in a way that reminded him of Pearl when she was shy about her shortcomings.

The kitchen door swung open. Pearl appeared, sopping wet, the dark night lit with lightning bolts behind her. Fern shook off the rain and Frank, on her shoulder, lifted his wings and shuddered as well.

"Pearl," Mama said. Tommy saw relief flash across his mother's face.

"I'm ready."

Mama wiped more tears away. "I'll take good care of them until we meet up." She held her hand up as though taking an oath.

"Take care of who?" Tommy asked.

"Fern, Teddy, and Frank."

Tommy nearly fell over.

Pearl pulled Teddy out of the pocket of her coat—one of Mama's worn ones. Mama must have given it to her at some point. "Thank you for the coat, Mrs. Arthur. Thank you for caring for my precious animals."

Tommy was glad Mama and Pearl had been talking, but surprised.

"I secured the trunk in the back with all your things the Zurchenkos brought," Pearl said.

Mama nodded. "I'll get it out of the shed later."

Pearl knelt down and hugged Fern around the neck. Her shoulders shook as she began to cry. Tommy pulled her up. "We have to go."

Pearl stood and held out the rope to Jeanie. She took it and drew Pearl into a hug. Tommy heard his mother's hushed words. "I'll watch the animals, and you watch my Tommy." Pearl nodded without pulling away. "'Course I will."

Pearl unloaded all the gear that went with her animals, bowls clanging, tears dripping down her cheeks.

Tommy kissed his mother's cheek and held her tight. He squeezed her three times, for the first time using the secret code for *I love you*. She started to cry, squeezing him back three times.

His eyes filled. He was overwhelmed with love and regret. "I love you, Mama. I'll make you proud." Saying that reminded him of Dr. Hayes. He dug into his pocket and pulled out the note he'd promised to deliver. She took it and swallowed him up for one more hug. "We'll be back," he said.

"Not until it's safe," she said.

"Immediately thereafter."

And before he heard a word she had left to say, he left, taking Pearl's hand.

Chapter 63

They hugged the side of buildings, squinting into the storm, camouflaged by it as they headed for the train station, watching for officers who might be on the lookout for him. He had never felt so good to leave a place, not even the Hendersons'.

He stole a few looks at Pearl and couldn't help thinking she and Mama had a closeness he hadn't been aware of before. He knew how much Pearl admired her, but that had been from afar. The hug in the kitchen, the coat—something about those moments indicated their embrace was about more than just he and Pearl leaving.

When they reached the station, a freight train was pulling out. They waited for what appeared to be an empty car to jump into. They were down to just three more to go when Tommy grabbed Pearl and threw her into the opening. He tossed the knapsacks and then finally made a leap into the train himself.

Splayed on the floor of the car, the rhythmic bounce and sound of wheels on rails, steam, and whistle call mixed with heavy rain, turning to ice, plucking at the roof, making as beautiful a chorus as any spring birdsong ever had.

They caught their breath, shook out their coats, moving to the corner to hide and get as warm as possible. When they got to the far side, Pearl leaned in and turned with a book and some matches in hand.

"Someone left this behind along with newspapers and kindling. Look," she pointed upward. "Says to build the fire under that vent."

"What luck," he whispered.

They lit the fire and opened the book to find a story had been started, chronicling the people who'd hopped that train car. The leather book was half-full of people and their tales.

Pearl shook her head. "Maybe it's not luck."

He slipped his arm around her shoulder and pulled her close. "Angels? Good people. Angels on earth? Angels, the golden, invisible-to-me kind?"

"Maybe it was your prayers, Tommy. Maybe it's you who can make people see God, even if you can't see his angels."

He remembered the prayer he'd written for Katherine and pulled it and the other papers from his pocket. He spread them out, flattening the wrinkles.

"Oh no," he said.

"What?" Pearl said, her eyes shutting and fluttering back open.

He stared at the envelope in his hand. It was the note he was supposed to have given Mama from Dr. Hayes. His heart sank at the thought she might be even more saddened by his absence than she already was.

"Read it to me. We'll send it to her from Yankton."

He shook his head.

She covered his hand with hers. "Then I'll read it." He let her take it.

"Pearl, no. Don't. It's not right."

"You don't want to know what it says? That he loves your ma, that…" She stopped and sighed, seeming to know that she should tread easy on that path. "Well, I'll just take a glance to be sure it's not a matter of life and death or… well, the end of a fantastic fairy story."

He rubbed his temples but didn't encourage or discourage her. He heard the envelope rustle, paper being unfolded, silence as Pearl must have been reading and then a gasp.

"Oh," she said through a sigh. "Oh, my." She cleared her throat and when he heard the paper being refolded he finally looked back at her. She bit her lip, smiling as she tucked it into her satchel. "We'll mail it as soon as we can. Because she needs to—" She shook her head. "He sent more letters for Yale."

She looked at Tommy. He knew she was keeping back anything that indicated love to be kind to him, knowing how sensitive he was about Mama and Mr. Hayes as a romantic couple.

"Thank you. I'm glad he's trying to help. That settles my mind a little more." Tommy knew without seeing the details of the letter that Dr. Hayes had every intention of staying in Mama's life. He knew it from Pearl's reaction.

With the letter safely stored away, she slumped into Tommy. He put his arm around her, hugging her close. He kissed the top of her head.

"A happy ending, happy for now," she said, words thin and soft, and within seconds her breath fell deep and even, and he knew she was asleep.

Tommy removed a linen blanket from one backpack and covered Pearl. Too antsy to rest, he dug through the knapsack.

Pearl had packed the book of fairy tales. Inside it were her lists of words and places to go and more of her letters to heaven, to her dead parents. And the story Tommy had started to write about her. She must have found it hidden away and included it in their things.

Once upon a time . . .

He thought of their story, the deep love he felt for her, how it grew slowly, unnoticed by him until it was nearly too late.

He brushed his hand over her hair. "I love you, Pearl."

He'd never felt anything like it before. It made him think of Mama. Of his father, what they'd had and then lost.

Pearl inched closer to Tommy in her sleep, her hand finding his like it had every night they'd been together in the loft.

So much sorrow, but Pearl beside him, knowing Mama had arranged to get Yale, that Katherine was safe with Aleksey, that—

Dr. Hayes's words came back to him. *You're already a good man.* Was he? Could he turn his inclination for writing comforting prayers into something bigger? A life of caring for others, a life as a minister? He shook his head, thinking of Reverend Shaw, of the ministers Katherine told him about. Even the judges and the police were untrustworthy. Was he like them?

Good, ordinary people had helped him along the way recently. None of them were labeled as men of God or elected or court-appointed power brokers—the people who should have been good but weren't. Tommy was more like the men he despised than the earth angels he'd encountered.

You're already good.

He breathed deep, feeling decency inside, letting himself notice it, letting himself admit it was there. He didn't have to chase it. Just like Dr. Hayes had said—it's all the small things, small kindnesses.

And Tommy felt full, sure that somehow he'd stepped onto the right path, finally, that his prayers might just be the thing that saved him and Pearl after all. He pulled out the leather book where the others who'd ridden that car before had told their stories, and drew the pencil out of the binding. He thought of when things had really changed for him and Pearl, when he'd found her crying at McCrady's. Over time, from that point, she'd stolen his heart—that she wanted his love at all was a miracle. He wrote *The Thief's Heart* at the top of the first empty page.

> *Once upon a time there was a thief alone in the world. He stole to keep alive, just to get by. But one day someone stole from him, and that's when his life really began . . .*

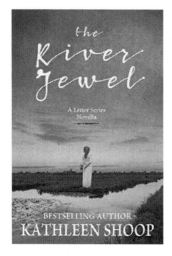

The River Jewel
A Letter Series Novel

Before there was a last letter, before the Arthurs lost everything, before they knew a girl named Pearl....

Meet Tilly Rabel, a proud oyster-woman, and Landon Lockwood, the troubled son of one of the wealthiest men in America. The two could not be less suited for love. But when an old legend draws Landon to a hidden river cove, Tilly and he find each other, are lured by growing attraction, and repelled by competing desires to control Tilly's waters. The hidden pool is replete with valuable mussel beds and the source of everything that makes Tilly who she is. Landon sees the illustrious treasure as the path to proving to his parents he is worth their love and worthy of the Lockwood name. Can Tilly trust Landon with her heart, with her beloved mussel beds? Can Landon trust that he has truly changed and doesn't need his parents' approval to live the life he wants?

Heartbreak, triumph, and a very special baby weave a tale sure to please readers who've read the entire Letter Series and those who are just starting the journey.

Also by Kathleen Shoop

Historical Fiction:
The Donora Story Collection
After the Fog—Book One
The Strongman and the Mermaid—Book Two

The Letter Series
The Last Letter—Book One
The Road Home—Book Two
The Kitchen Mistress—Book Three
The Thief's Heart—Book Four
The River Jewel—A Letter Series Novella

Tiny Historical Stories
Melonhead—One
Johnstown—Two

Romance:
Endless Love Series:
Home Again—Book One
Return to Love—Book Two
Tending Her Heart—Book Three

Women's Fiction:
Love and Other Subjects

Bridal Shop Series
Puff of Silk—Book One

Acknowledgments

Thanks, Demi Stevens—your insight and support into publishing A-Z is a true gift. "Year of the Book" just scratches the surface of all you do.

Thanks to Jenny Q for cover and editing work—your perspective into what works and what doesn't is invaluable. You're talented beyond measure.

To Sue McClafferty, author extraordinaire, and gifted editor. Thank you, thank you, thank you for your broad insight early on.

To Marlene Engel—thank you for your eagle eye at the end— Precision Revision says it all.

To Julie Burns—Thanks for proofreading and beyond. You catch it all.

Mom—Thank you for all the reads of early and late revisions and for all the research assistance!

Lisa McShea—your advice and support is embedded in every single book I've ever written.

Manufactured by Amazon.ca
Bolton, ON